FLAME MUSIC

ROCK AND ROLL IS LIFE PART II

By the same author

Fiction

Great Eastern Land
Real Life
English Settlement
After Bathing at Baxter's: Stories
Trespass
The Comedy Man
Kept: A Victorian Mystery
Ask Alice
At the Chime of a City Clock
Derby Day
Secondhand Daylight
The Windsor Faction
From the Heart (Amazon Kindle Single)
Wrote for Luck: Stories
Rock and Roll is Life
Stewkey Blues: Stories

Non-fiction

A Vain Conceit: British Fiction in the 80s.
Other People: Portraits from the Nineties (with Marcus Berkmann)
After the War: The Novel and England Since 1945
Thackeray
Orwell: The Life
On the Corinthian Spirit: The Decline of Amateurism in Sport
Bright Young People: The Rise and Fall of a Generation 1918–1940
What You Didn't Miss: A Book of Literary Parodies
The Prose Factory: Literary Life in England Since 1918
The New Book of Snobs
Lost Girls: Love, War and Literature 1939–1951
On Nineteen Eighty-Four: A Biography
Critic at Large: Essays and Reviews 2010–2022
Orwell: The New Life

FLAME MUSIC

The True Story of Resurgam Records
by One Who Was There

Rock and Roll is Life Part II

D. J. TAYLOR

MENSCH PUBLISHING

Mensch Publishing
51 Northchurch Road, London N1 4EE,
United Kingdom

First published in Great Britain in 2023 by Mensch Publishing

All characters and events in this book are fictitious. References to real people are also fictional – their actions in the book are imagined.

A CIP catalogue record for this book is available from the British Library.

ISBN: 978-1-912914-54-8 (paperback)
ISBN: 978-1-912914-55-5 (eBook)

Typeset in Adobe Caslon by Newgen KnowledgeWorks Pvt. Ltd., Chennai, India
Printed and bound in Great Britain by CPI Group (UK), Croydon CR0 4YY

In memory of Cathal Coughlan 1960–2022

CONTENTS

Part Four: Under the Big Sky

And I'll start thinking about a late summer sun setting over fifteen hundred identical rooftops and my family and bop glasses and Holly Golightly, about being lonesome out there in America and how that swank music connected up with so many things.

DONALD FAGEN – *Eminent Hipsters*

Is it better to endure bad art for the spotless ideology it promotes, or to continue to swoon before sublime art made by bad people?

IAN PENMAN – *It Gets Me Home, This Curving Track*

You know, in the bar Danny and I just bought in New York, there's some graffiti in the men's room – three lines written by three different people. 'Film is king,' 'Television is furniture' and 'Rock and Roll is Life.' I think that pretty much sums it up.

JOHN BELUSHI, quoted in Bob Woodward, *Wired: The Short Life and Fast Times of John Belushi*

You don't need a weatherman to know which way the wind blows.

BOB DYLAN

PREVIOUSLY

And that was how it ended, there in the hotel foyer, in the sparkling Colorado sun, with the stretcher-bearers hoisting Keith's outsize and apparently paralysed form up into the ambulance, and June sniffing into a handkerchief, and the bus boys gawping, and Stefano complaining that there was so much fast white powder to hand that he'd ended up sluicing most of it down the sink. There in that hotel foyer, the Helium Kids, they of the five certified *Billboard* albums, they of the half-dozen No.1 singles and the twenty-seven separate *Top of the Pops* appearances, those stalwart custodians of the *zeitgeist*, this raggle-taggle band of rock-and-roll gypsies, reached the end of the road. The party was over: it was time to go home.

Or so we thought.

From *Rock and Roll is Life: The True Story of the Helium Kids by One Who Was There*

DU PONT, NICHOLAS FRANKLIN McARTHUR. b. 1942, in Norwich, Norfolk, UK. o.s. of Maurice (1913–1971) and Jean (1919–1964) Du Pont. Educ. City of Norwich School, Pembroke College, Oxford (Wharton Exhibitioner in English Literature, Goldsmith's Essay Prize, 1962). Republican Party intern, U.S. Presidential Campaign, 1964. Press Officer, Thames Records, London, 1965–66 (Dwayne Fontane, The Fiery Orbs, Moyra McKechnie etc). Chief Publicist, Shard Enterprises Ltd, 1966–1977, with special responsibility for the Helium Kids. *Nova* magazine 'PR to the Stars' Award, 1968. Publicists' Circle Award for *Low Blows in High Times,* 1971, Managing Director, Resurgam Records, 1978 -. 'Independent Record Label of the Year', *New Musical Express Readers'* Poll, 1979. M. Rosalind Madeleine Duchesne, d. of Allenby Duchesne of Phoenix, Arizona, 1968 (marriage dissolved, 1972). Recreations: English Literature, hanging out, getting down. Contact: Nick Du Pont, Resurgam Records, 26 Newman Street, London W1

The Rock and Roll Who's Who, 1980.

PROLOGUE – AUGUST 1977

Go buddy, go!

Stefano was good in a crisis. It was one of his skills, his default setting. In his eight tumultuous years on the road with the Helium Kids he had signed bail bonds, forged insurance certificates for non-existent equipment, paid off racketeers and rescued stage-hands from howling mobs. Dealing with a comatose drummer undergoing tests in the toxicology department of the Boulder Memorial Hospital was well inside his range of expertise. And so, within 36 hours of the moment at which Keith's unresponsive form had been borne away through the foyer of the Century Canyon Hotel to the waiting ambulance he had had every room occupied by members of the band and their entourage cleared of questionable paraphernalia, settled the extensive tab, appeared personally on the local radio station, issued a wholly misleading statement to the *Boulder Chronicle* and offered Carrie-Ann, his executive assistant, $2,000 plus expenses to stay in Colorado for as long as it took 'to shovel up the shit.' The band dispersed, the gear was put in temporary storage in an aircraft hangar out on the flat, the shit was shovelled up, and on the evening of the following day the pair of us sat in the airport lounge, as the planes crisscrossed like slow-moving darts over the Rockies, nervously awaiting the red-eye back to New York.

'Do you think he'll be all right?'

'Who? Keith? How the fuck should I know?' Somewhere in the innermost recesses of his baggage trunk Stefano had turned up a three-piece charcoal pinstripe suit that, long ago, had been made by a Savile Row tailor. Draped in this sartorial curio, with what looked like an MCC tie dangling from his throat and with the satchel containing $200,000-worth of takings from the tour still wedged under one elbow, he cut an incongruous figure. The departure lounge was full of Eagle Scouts off to summer camp in the Great Lakes. Beyond the orange light of the aerodrome, the long, low ridge of the mountains receded into dusk.

'Is anyone coming out to be with him?'

'I phoned that burglar's dog he went to the NME awards with,' Stefano said, as if this were the greatest favour anyone had ever done anyone else in the otherwise venal world of popular music. 'Trixie or Pixie or whatever her fucking name is. She said she'd fly over if I gave her the cost of the air-ticket. Give him a hand-job or something. Cheer the fucker up a bit....Jesus,' he said, unexpectedly. 'Have you heard from Don?'

The Eagle Scouts were gangling, crop-haired teenagers from the mid-west with extraordinarily bony knees. Hunched over the maps they carried with them at all times, heads bobbing in unison, they looked like flamingos gathered at the water's edge.

'No.'

'Neither have I. I mean, not since we put the original call in...Jesus,' Stefano said again, one red-rimmed eye moving from the thronged hallway of the departure lounge to the shadow-lands beyond. 'Just look at those fucking mountains. Imagine being up there at this time of night with some fucking timber wolf or whatever after your arse.' I saw now that, curiously, all the pent-up passion he had carried around with him for the past three weeks had been released. There was no doubt about it. Keith's putting himself in a coma had done Stefano good. We sat companionably in the big metal chairs for a while, watching the Eagle Scouts and the mysterious old women with nutcracker faces waiting for late-night flights to Oregon and Seattle, as the janitors came round scooping up fallen Coke cans, an irony-primed transistor radio played Fleetwood Mac singing 'Don't Stop Thinking About Tomorrow' and the planes tracked back and forth through the ripening sky.

'Is Keith, ah, *insured* for this?'

'He's insured for the *tour*,' Stefano said, with rather more nonchalance than might ordinarily have been warranted by the situation in which we found ourselves. 'As for what happens afterwards, do you know, Nick, I really couldn't say?'

* * *

At the office on Tenth there was a drift of unopened mail on the carpet together with a pile of fast-food delivery-firm flyers and half-a-dozen prostitutes' cards. It was that kind of joint. As I went through the letters, totting up the record of our obligations and outgoings over the past month, Stefano established himself at the big desk overlooking the smeary window with its patina of snuffed-out insect life and sat musing on his opportunities.

'Christ, the hookers they got in New York these days. Will you listen to this? *New girl in town seeks afternoon play-mates. All major credit cards accepted.*' But there was no solace in the prostitutes' cards. A minute later he said: 'How much do you reckon we owe?'

'Ten, eleven thousand dollars maybe. There's probably some more bills to come in.'

'The *fuck*! I mean, Nick, really, what on earth did we spend all that on?' At times of momentary irritation, Stefano's upbringing leapt back to the surface of his personality. Just now he sounded like a member of White's club querying his bar bill.

'Cab fares. Hospitality. That dinner you gave for the people at *Rolling Stone*. Those chauffeur-driven limos you sent up to Albany you wouldn't even tell me about.'

It was a long and incriminating roster. 'Yeah, well' Stefano said wearily, when I had reached a point about three-quarters of the way through, 'you can take it from me, Nick, that tour took some planning. He threw the invitation to afternoon play-mates high in the air, where it danced beneath the winnowing fan. 'Well, I'm not paying them. You'd better send them to Maddox Street.'

'Don won't like that.'

'Do you know, Nick,' Stefano said, with the same ineffable nonchalance he had brought to the question of Keith's insurance plan, 'I've got beyond caring what Don thinks?'

* * *

For the best part of a week, as the New York smog hung over the roof-line and the sidewalks stank in the sultry mid-August heat, we kept up the pretence that everything in the admittedly bizarre and chaotic world of the Helium Kids would soon be returning to normal. A carefully-crafted press release was couriered to the offices of the principal entertainment weeklies, downplaying the extent of Keith's infirmities – the phrase 'temporary indisposition' may even have been employed – and a story about the 'hundreds' of get-well-soon cards received by the Boulder hospital – in fact, there were precisely three – appeared in the *New York Post.* Meantime, certain notional attempts were made to procure somebody who could temporarily replace what the press release called 'this legendary sticks-wielder' on some even more notionally rescheduled tour-dates. Thus:

'Some promoter up on Forty-Seventh I spoke to this morning reckons that bloke who used to be in Jethro Tull is free. Think he'd do it?'

'No.'

'Why not?' Here in the Tenth Street heat-haze the three-piece suit made Stefano look storm-crossed and unreliable, like a broker in one of those Wall Street soap-operas who, after thirty years of loyal service, is about to go crazy in the dealing room. 'Don't tell me there's previous?'

'It depends if you count the time Garth head-butted him at the Speakeasy.'

'Oh that…' Stefano acknowledged, with the air of a Viking chief whose attention has been drawn to his failure to authorise the sacking of a neighbouring village. 'I'm surprised anyone's still worried about that. Look, John Bonham and I go way back. Zep aren't touring at the moment, are they? Why don't I see if he'll fill in for a couple of weeks?'

'*No*…Anyway, how is Keith?'

'Last I heard he had one tube coming out of his mouth and another one up his backside. Actually, Nick, you're right about Bonzo.' Stefano looked crestfallen, all the bounce suddenly gone from his outsize frame. His heart was not in the business and he knew it. Another cluster of mail fell dramatically through the door, as if a pelican had started regurgitating a pile of flatfish. 'Listen,' he said, urgently. 'Fuck all this. Let's go see an adult movie.'

'A what?'

There was something mad about Stefano's eyes. The long years spent permanently detached from reality, out on the fritz with the Helium Kids, had taken their toll.

'Like I said. An adult movie. Come on, Nick, this is Porn City USA. I mean they're feeling each other up in the kindergartens over here. Society's in fucking crisis and Mayor Beame can't do a thing. Let's go check it out.'

And so we went to a bedraggled movie theatre round the back of Times Square filled with equally bedraggled movie-goers and watched a film called *Swedish Co-Eds Get Mouth Crazy*. Next morning the stack of mail realised further invoices to the value of $4,017. These Stefano ceremoniously incinerated with a cigarette lighter. That afternoon a message came from Don's office in Maddox Street to say that the rest of the tour was cancelled and we should come home forthwith.

* * *

Flaring mid-western dawns; boundless Idaho potato fields; Barry Goldwater's parched white face craning from the elevator door; Ian Hamilton, the Helium Kids' bass player and his wife June drinking English breakfast tea and eating English breakfast muffins on a hotel terrace in the lee of the Adirondacks; harsh white sunlight spilling through my hands; distant fires smouldering in the mountains; drug-addled Keith on his insufficient stretcher: this was the freight I brought back from six weeks in America. Maddox Street, reached late on the following afternoon, was just as it always had been: the same inertia stealthily undercut with menace; the same blonde-haired sugar-babies cheerfully typing away in their hutches; the same bruisers in box-suits lackadaisically on hand to open doors and torch cigarettes; the same overemphatic portrait of Don's daughter Belinda, looking as if she was about to burst out of her school uniform mounted on the wall above her father's big bald head.

'Now let me arsk you sumfink,' Don said, tee-shirted and statuesque and doing his usual trick of seeming to pick up a conversation that had begun the previous afternoon rather than two months ago. 'You heard of a character called McLaren?'

Though shrewd, and on certain occasions far-sighted, Don could not be called *au fait* with the latest developments in popular music. At this stage in the proceedings, he would probably not have heard of punk rock.

'Malcolm? I've met him once or twice.'

'Ave you now? Sounded like a ponce to me. Rung up the other day and offered me that band he manages for – what was it? – fifty grand. Naturally, I haddem checked. Turns out there's a mad kid who sings, couple of geezers off the estate and a bright boy that writes the songs. Only now they've gone and fired the bright boy and got another kid who's even madder than the first one. Sounds like a fucking liability to me, but what do you reckon?'

I had a sudden vision of the Pistols at large in Don's office: leather jackets amid the box-suits; cheap lager spraying over Belinda's chintzy smile; the secretaries in tearful retreat.

'I'd leave well alone if I were you.'

'That's what I thought,' Don said, shifting one fat haunch more comfortably against his chair-back. 'No harm in taking a second opinion though. Or maybe I'm just getting soft in me old age.'

I thought about Don's exploits in the world of popular entertainment over the past fifteen years: the music journalist hung by his heels out of an upstairs window; the star of a rock 'n' roll revival package – Gene Vincent? Chuck Berry? – hurled bodily on stage after lingering too long in his dressing room; the court case that turned on aerial photos of an outdoor concert in Hertfordshire skilfully doctored to support Shard Enterprises's claim to a greater share of the take. You didn't mess with Don in those days, or in any other days that I knew of, and there was no question of his getting soft.

'Anyway,' Don said, returning me to the bright, uncertain present. 'First things first. Where's that fucker Stefano?'

'He said he had to get back to Barnes to see Amanda.'

'Christ! Is he still with her? I mean, she wasn't exactly love's young dream when she used to lick the floors at the Scotch. And that was ten years ago.' The memory of Amanda in her previous calling as cloakroom attendant at the Scotch of St James hung between us for a moment like some blithe and tatterdemalion faery. 'Now, about the tour. Actually, fuck the tour. Between you and me, Nick, I've had it with the Kids. Actually, *everyone*'s had it with the Kids. EMI have passed on the renewal option on account of there's 85,000 copies of the last one still sitting in some fucking warehouse in Staines. I rang Jerry D'Artagnon at East Coast Central Entertainment the other day, *Jerry D'Artagnon*, who'd still be shooting craps out in Hackensack if

I hadn't…if he hadn't…to see about rescheduling the dates and he just…he just *laughed.* So that's it. Finito. Kaboom. There was some geezer in here from one of the indies the other day offering me [*sniff*] ten grand or something to take them off my hands, and I said, 'Nigel [*sniff*], you don't want the fucking bother, son.' That Garth, thinking he's [*sniff*] Abbadon out of the black pit or something…Not to mention the fucking *disrespect.*'

The sunlight streaming through the single plate-glass window was full of dust-motes. The muscles on Don's thick white forearms quivered like live things that might soon take on an existence of their own and go scurrying up the wall.

'His Majesty' – he meant Garth – 'finks he's going to get a solo deal for a hundred and fifty grand or something,' Don droned on. 'Between you and me e can go on thinking that. *I'm* not having anything to do with it. Thing is: what am I going to do about you?'

It was a good question. While I was pondering it, Don played another of his tricks, which was to veer off on one of his free-associative tangents. His biceps had calmed down a bit now.

'What do you think of this reggae nonsense?'

'Not much.'

'Uh huh.' The collective spectre of Bob Marley, Peter Tosh and Haile Selassie hung between us for a moment and then faded gently away. 'Velvet Goldmine have got an album in October. Can work on that if you like.' Velvet Goldmine were one of Don's terrible glam bands, whose moment had passed about three years before. 'Or you can cut loose on your own. *I* shan't mind,' he went on, giving the impression that when one or two other people had cut loose from Shard Enterprises he had minded a great deal.

'Actually, I was thinking of starting a label.'

Don made a vague undulating motion with his badly-shaven chin. Over the years dozens of people had sat in his office and told him things like this: that they intended to found twelve-piece jazz bands; that they wanted a month-long engagement at the London Palladium; that they had too much money; that they had too little money; that they were mad, suicidal or psychologically conflicted. Some of them he had jovially sworn at. Others he had had thrown out into the street. A very few he had actively collaborated with.

'Was you now?'

A fortnight later Don would send me a cheque for £20,000 and a letter requesting – no, demanding – 10 per cent of any subsequent share issue. Now, he simply waved me silently on my way. Outside in Maddox Street everything seemed suddenly more exaggerated than it had done fifteen minutes before. More molten sunshine cascaded over the flagstones. A file of Asian tourists went past exclaiming over the antique house-fronts. Outside the property next door, where builders were at work, on a radio balanced on a plank between two paint-flecked trestles, the Stranglers were playing 'Go Buddy Go' – brutal music, designed to get under your fingernails and ramp up your disquiet. And so, in just the same way as had happened a decade and a half before, when the street-lamps of down-town Phoenix burned through the dusk and Lucille Duchesne, drunk, disorderly and infinitely dangerous, sat waiting in the car beneath my apartment, and with the same faint inkling of all the unshiftable debris, seen and unseen, that lay across my path, I moved hesitantly off from one world into the next.

* * *

In those days I lived in a mansion flat down by the river in Fulham, which overlooked a strip of municipal tennis-courts. All that long autumn, as the tennis players came and went and mist drifted in from across the park and each afternoon the arc-lights went on a little earlier, I sat in the big, airy front room and planned the rise of Resurgam Records. Resurgam in honour of the school Latin master. A record company because I had spent a dozen years as a high-class gopher and wanted to see what I could do myself, secure in the knowledge that there would never be a better time. For this was 1977, the era of buzz-saw guitars and leather jackets, bin-liner tee shirts and punk rock, which might not have sold many records but had left the music business in no end of a tizz. There were bands to be signed, I told myself, late at night as the owls swooped low over the wound-down tennis nets, and money to be made.

With some of the £20,000 I took a two-year lease on a reconditioned maisonette in Shepherd's Bush, with an option to renew for a further year. Hermione, the lieutenant-colonel's daughter, came from the Belgravia Bureau at £100 a week ('Always get some posh bird on reception,' Stefano had counselled. 'Gives the place a bit of tone, and you won't get any trouble. No one ever kicks off with a posh bird on the desk.') It was to Stefano, additionally, that I applied for advice on staff appointments. 'No point in wasting money,' advised the man who had once spent $800 on bottled water during a two-week Helium Kids tour of Scandinavia. 'At this stage you're just feeling your way. I should go down the Speak and hire the first couple of herberts you come across with any kind of a track record.' With this in mind I went to the Speakeasy and engaged the services of a man who had once done the lighting for Pink Floyd and Barclay James Harvest's former tour manager. With these intrepid companions, I established myself in the office at Shepherd's Bush and, not yet oppressed by the reek of the kebab shop next door, sat down to plan the first Resurgam release.

This was less easy than it sounded. The initial idea had been that we should start with one-off singles – you could cut an acetate in a basement for £200 in those days – and use the cash-flow to finance albums by people we thought had some kind of staying power. When this failed, nobody being impressed by the tiny advances on offer, Damian, the man who had worked as Barclay James Harvest's tour manager, said, somewhat shyly, as if he feared giving offence, 'We could always get Wally Bav.' 'Christ! Is he still alive?' 'Saw him at the

Music Machine just the other week,' Damian volunteered. 'His new demo's rather good.' 'Jesus, Dame', said Bruno, the man who had done the lighting for Pink Floyd, 'you're just wasting Nick's fucking *time* here.' 'No, no,' I said pacifically, 'let's hear it.' Unexpectedly, the tape turned out to have merit. If it was not a bona fide New Wave classic, it had a decent guitar sound that almost, but not quite, cancelled out the embarrassment of its being titled 'Street Corner Lady'. The problem lay not in the music but in its creator, Walter 'Wally' Baverstock. It was not that he was in his late thirties and several stone overweight, but that so many iterations of him lay strewn over the popular music of the past fifteen years. Back in the Beat Boom, as a nervous twenty year-old with a Tony Curtis hair-cut, he had masqueraded as 'Wally and the Wal-tones'. I myself could remember him supporting the Helium Kids at the Fairfield Halls, Croydon, as the lead singer of a psychedelic commune called Custer's Last Stand. There had been other outings: the album he had cut with a heavy metal band named Demons and Wizards had turned up in an Oxford Street remainder bin only the other day.

The Wally Baverstock argument lasted a week, during which time we signed a pressing and distribution deal with Virgin. After it was over, Wally and two middle-aged sidekicks were despatched to a basement studio in Harlesden where, in three hours and at a cost of £150 they produced an acetate of 'Street Corner Lady' and a weird rockabilly cover of Chuck Berry's 'Sweet Little Sixteen' that would do as the B-side. On the afternoon it came back from the pressing plant I sat down with Damian – now promoted to Acting Head of A&R – to plot the extensive personal makeover that would be required of Wally before he was let out into public view. It was all rather like the meeting a dozen years before when, with the Managing Director of Thames Records, I had planned the costume in which Moyra McKechnie, the Dundee Dynamo, would sing for the Queen Mother at the Royal Variety Performance. 'We've got three weeks,' I instructed Damian.

'Put him on a crash diet – he could lose a stone in that time – and tell Desmond that if he fucks up we'll halve the royalty rate. It's not going out under his own name. We'll call them the Pimps, and, I don't know' – I was clutching at straws here – 'say they've all just come out of Wandsworth or something. As for the get-up, you'd better put them in leathers, but for God's sake don't let him stand sideways-on to the camera.' I wrote the press release myself. It went: *The Pimps are three ex-cons playing the kind of noise you won't have heard before. This is end-of-the-tether, down in the drain-pipe, mad-as-hell street music from a band who've spent time on the wild side of life. Your mother definitely wouldn't like it, but, hey, what do they care?* There were quarter-page ads in the *New Musical Express, Melody Maker* and *Sounds.*

Meanwhile, there were other things to worry about. From her armchair in Bishop's Mansions, spreadsheets smoothed out across her lap, Holly watched these preparations with tolerant scepticism. She was an accountant at EMI: all this was merely a parody of the seemly usages of her own 9 to 5. 'Nobody's going to buy anything by Wally Baverstock,' she said. 'I saw that picture of him in the silver jacket and he looks like a turkey done up in Bacofoil.' But there was more to it than this, more than shambling Wally Baverstock with his teddy-boy quiff and his hopeful expression. In starting Resurgam I could see that I had lost status in her eyes. She took to staying at work late and making sure that the records she played around the flat were by sun-tanned American five-pieces with £100,000 advances.

'Street Corner Lady' (Baverstock/Kopechnie) by the Pimps [Resurgam 001] – 'more than your average chug-a-lug' – *NME*; 'I wouldn't let these gentlemen babysit my children but they could certainly play at my wedding anniversary' – *Melody Maker* – was released in the spring of 1978. It sold 53 copies in its first week, 17 via the mail-order department now operating from the Shepherd's Bush basement, and 32 in the second. Halfway through the third week I invited the Resurgam plugger, a game twenty-five year-old named

Biff Tregunter, into the office and demanded to know why in the eighteen days since release no Radio One disc-jockey had so much as placed it on a turntable. 'The thing is,' Biff explained – he was good at his job, and both of us knew it – 'the thing is, Nick, there's a problem with old Wally.' 'There is? What's he done now?' 'Too much *history*,' Biff said, as if history ranked alongside murder and grand larceny on the federal statute book. 'Annie Nightingale won't have it on account of he once threw a gin-and-tonic over her at a T. Rex afterparty. I can't even tell you about the beef Kid Jenson has with him. I took one in to Tommy Vance – you never know, might have gone down well with the metal crowd – and he had security called right there on the spot...' There was quite a lot more of this. 'Why won't John Peel play it?' 'It's the fucking *producer* isn't it?' Biff offered, lighting a cigarette off the one he had in his mouth. 'Won't have him on the show. Simple as that. And as for the daytime playlist, you could dress Wally up as Santa Claus, have him sing 'Mary's Boy Child' accompanied by the London Symphony Orchestra and a choir of disabled kids and say the money was going to charity, and the fuckers still wouldn't put him on it.' 'Can't we invite some of them to one of his gigs?' Here on a bright spring day the reek from the kebab shop was worse than ever. 'Slipped a disc two nights ago bending over a snooker table' Biff explained. 'He's not going to be playing live again any time soon. Now, what about that other lot Dame said you were signing? The girls that got expelled from the boarding school in High Wycombe?'

'The Glimmer Chicks? No, we're passing on them.' I was still thinking of John Peel, whose show, tastes and routines I knew well. 'What happened to those skinheads we had in here the other week?' 'The Bash Street Kids?' Biff looked doubtful. The industry grapevine had spread disquieting rumours about the Bash Street Kids all over Soho. 'You don't want to have nothing to do with them, Nick. They had an audition at Chiswick the other day and one of them hit the studio engineer over the head with a pool cue.' 'Never mind that,'

I told him. In the room below I could hear the series of ricocheting thuds which meant that Damian was throwing rejected demo-tapes into one of the metal waste-paper baskets. 'You call their manager and tell him to meet us outside All Souls Langham Place at 8.15 tomorrow evening.' 'Don't think they've got a manager.' 'Well take a cab down to Bermondsey or wherever they come from' – I was getting tired of Biff's stonewalling – 'and walk round the streets yelling their names until you find one of them.' Biff nodded and disappeared, his place behind the desk instantly filled by a man who had once played bass for Uriah Heep and lived in hope of a solo deal. That was the sort of aspirant we got at Resurgam in the early days.

The plot was hatched in a burger bar around the corner from Broadcasting House, between Biff, myself and the three members of the Bash Street Kids who bothered to show. 'Easiest thing in the world,' I explained. 'Peel turns up at reception at about 8.45. When he arrives I want you lads to rush him and pin him up against the wall.' The skinheads listened intently, their pale, bony faces alive with anticipation. They had been promised £20 apiece and the chance to record a demo-tape. 'What do you want done to him?' Toddy, the ringleader, enquired. 'Give him a tap or two?' 'Nothing like that. Just keep him there until the cavalry comes.' Outside, the darkness was stealing over Portland Place: there was no one much about. Peel, walking up from Oxford Circus, cut a lonely and unsuspecting figure. The boys jumped him as he came level with All Souls and bore him off into the shadows. Biff and I, arriving at the scene a few seconds later, made a great show of dispersing them. 'Good job we was here John,' Biff remarked. Peel stood quivering in the twilight, clutching the lapels of his black donkey-jacket, sweat glistening on his balding head. It was clear that in a decade-and-a-half on the pop scene he had endured far worse than this. To judge from the receding football chants, the Bash Street Kids were half-way along Regent Street. As we bade each other farewell, I pressed a copy of

'Street Corner Lady' into his hand. He played it later that evening and the one following. With this favourable wind behind them, the Pimps sold 2,000 copies, covered their costs and left us with £500 to sign a band called Paper Plane, of whose yet unrecorded single I had high hopes.

After that things happened fast, so fast that it seemed as if they would never slow down again. But I remember the day three months later when Holly and I drove down to Tenterden to Sammy Antrobus's summer party, with Paper Plane's first single booming from the stereo and the flyers for a band called The Unclean all over the back seat. Like Don and Stefano and three-quarters of the people I knew in those days, Sammy was a relic of the 1960s, and his parties were intended to commemorate their Dionysiac spirit. Girls in bikinis, or sometimes without them, floated languorously in the pool, Sammy's flock of turtledoves – all dyed in pastel shades – stalked across the lawn and people who got bored amused themselves by setting light to the punch. Holly sat in a deckchair at the end of the garden going through the contents of a box-file. A fortnight later I would come back to the flat at Bishop's Mansions and find her gone. But all this lay ahead, far off in the summer glare. The sun burned on and the music juddered from Sammy's state-of-the-art stereo system. It was the party at which, as I stood a yard from the surface of the pool – oily now and full of cigarette ends and particles of grit – somebody said there was a man called Rory Bayliss-Callingham who wanted to meet me. But I was too far gone for this. The bright, mysterious future had me by the hand. *I know where I am in the world*, I thought. And so, fully clad, I jumped head-first into the water, came up like a cork, righted myself and then lay paddling on my back, until the weight of my clothes started to drag me down, and Sammy's mermaids swam delightedly around me, and Holly, frowning slightly, put down her box-file and came scampering over the grass to see what mischief I had done.

PART ONE

Going to California

'I could lose my way on the shortest of journeys…'

THE FLAME THROWERS

Cris Itol vocals **Joey Valparaiso** gtr/vocals, **Steven DaVinci** bs, **Art Smothers** drms

Blink twice and you could miss the very considerable contribution that this assortment of junkies, desperadoes, one-time juvenile delinquents and all-round irregular guys – which is putting it charitably – made to the Los Angeles scene, and indeed to rock music generally, in the tumult of the early '80s. Sure, their status as a viable musical entity lasted until the decade's end, but even by the time *Breakfast at Ralph's* hit the racks in the fall of 1980 they were shaping up to implode, and practically everything they recorded has an oddly provisional quality, as if singer and sidemen loathed each other so profoundly that another fluffed drum break would see Cris or Stevie – the principal trouble-fomenters – slamming the studio door behind them for the very last time. Which, most eye-witness accounts concur, was pretty much what a Flame Throwers session looked like in their coruscating hey-day. Producers (Bob Ezrin, Jimmy Miller, Steve Lilywhite) came and went; tours concluded – or failed disastrously to conclude – in screaming mayhem; managers crawled off to commit suicide or file for bankruptcy; but somehow the band held it together during Reagan's first term. In that brief time they recorded at least one album that would remain a college radio staple for the next twenty years, played half-a-dozen live shows whose scuffed-up video representation is adjudged to give Hendrix, Zeppelin and the MC5 a run for their money, and, just for good measure, taught Guns 'n' Roses everything they knew. Not bad going for a band of reform school throw-outs over whose ability to cut it those present at the time frankly despaired.

On paper the Flame Throwers represented just about everybody's last chance. Itol and DaVinci were farm boys out of the back end of Wisconsin for whom L.A. represented the kind of topsy-turvey freakster's mothership they'd been reading about all those years in *Rolling Stone* and *Crawdaddy*. Why, when Stevie was taken to Malibu the first time and invited to admire the surf, he is supposed to have goggled in astonishment, never having seen the sea before. Valparaiso and Smothers – Arthur Sidewinder Smotherton III to give him his full title – on the other hand, were classic West Coat roustabouts, leather-jacketed wannabees who'd spent their formative years slam-dancing to the nascent New Wave scene and at one point roadying for Fear, the L.A. punk band patronised by John Belushi. If anything separated them from the hordes of aspiring local scenesters, it was not so much musical proficiency as sheer attitude. As somebody once pointed out, plenty of people in L.A. took drugs and partied. The Flame Throwers *took drugs* and *partied*. Worse than this was their habit of deliberately alienating practically everyone who wished them well, from David Geffen himself, to fascinated booking agents who reckoned that they might be the next big thing, and even their fans, whom they enjoyed abusing from the safety of their stage ('The people who buy our records are retards,' Itol once pithily observed. 'I know 'cos I'm a retard myself.')

None of this augured well. Somehow, though, the boys held it together for long enough to cut a highly-praised demo cassette, *Songs to Forget* – mint copies now sell for north of $3,000 – in the summer of 1980, play a series of legendary New York club dates, sign – finally – for

Geffen and keep on the right side of Ezrin, with whom they enjoyed chronically strained relations for the three weeks it took to record *Breakfast at Ralph's*, of which the *New Musical Express* pronounced that if ever the Stones and the Sex Pistols got together and spawned some bastard musical love child then this, motherfucker, would be it.

It couldn't last. Nothing ever did with the Flame Throwers. Approximately half the record stores in America declined to stock *Breakfast* on account of the scabrous 'Jackie O' (as in Bouverie/Kennedy/Onassis) and a British tour booked to promote its UK release was a disaster. None of this was in any way helped by a series of interviews granted to the local music press in which Itol derided their competitors as 'also-rans', insultedtheir label boss, David Geffen, and predicted – erroneously as it turned out – that two of his band-mates would be dead by Christmas. Still, 'Up in Lisa's Room', *Breakfast's* stand-out track, made the top ten on both sides of the Atlantic in the spring of 1981. The band, which had come within an inch of falling apart, hastily reconvened to start work on 1982's *Straight From Hell*, but by this stage their commercial success was running in inverse proportion to their ability to cope with its material rewards. All four members spent time in rehab and there was a bizarre appearance on *Saturday Night Live* in which the expletive-count grew so high that a studio executive ordered the sound to be turned off half-way through the set.

If drugs, alcohol and narcissism had threatened to undermine the band's shaky foundations, then it was mutual ill-will that sent them crashing to the ground. By the time *Straight From Hell* had stacked up its three-millionth sale the boys hated the sight of each other: Itol and Valparaiso, in particular, are supposed to have spent 18 months communicating only by lawyer. There followed a distinctly below-par covers album – 1985's *Rip-Off Joint* – marked by a ruinous law-suit with Apple, who had specifically refused to license a version of the Beatles' 'Helter Skelter', and the major embarrassment of being thrown off the

U.S. end of Live Aid when some injurious remarks about the event's charitable objectives were inadvertently made public. After a poorly-received final album, the band went their own ways. Itol pursued a sporadically successful solo career. DaVinci was found dead in a Florida motel room. Smothers, possibly the most level-headed of the four – these distinctions are relative – reinvented himself as an abstract expressionist painter, mounting a solo exhibition – *Kooks, Mooks and Spooks* – at L.A.'s Gargosian Gallery in 1998. An attempt to reunite surviving members of the band for an MTV 'Live Acoustic Set' sometime in the early 2000s is supposed to have ended in a fist-fight.

What are we to make of the Flame Throwers two decades after their all-too foreseeable demise? If *Straight From Hell* and *Excess All Areas* are merely your standard '80s glam metal fare, conceived from a template of big hair, pulverising riffs and a lyrical fixation with drugs, hedonism and, er, the *ladeez*, preferably all three combined, then *Breakfast at Ralph's* offers a glimpse of the route they might have traversed had not outsize helpings of Jack Daniel's and prime Bolivian boo worked their melancholy effect: the music terser and leaner; the lyric-sheet filing surprisingly realistic descriptions of the L.A. street scene (Ralph's was the delicatessen-diner where they hung out, the 'Lisa' of 'Up in Lisa's Room' one of the local good-time girls.) Mementoes of this formative phase survive in *Live on the Killing Floor*, a lo-fi but weirdly compelling tape of a New York club gig, and *Needle Hits E*, a 16mm video montage of their early stage-act which give an idea of what a formidable proposition they were, live and dangerous, in front of 200 people in some tiny washroom of a venue, long before the drugs and the debauchery kicked in.

Discography

Breakfast at Ralph's (Geffen, 1980)
Straight From Hell (Geffen, 1982)

Rip-Off Joint (Geffen, 1985)
Excess All Areas (Virgin, 1987)
Burnin' For Ya: The Very Best of the Flame Throwers (Geffen, 1990)
Live on the Killing Floor: CBGBs 13.9.80 (Mutant Records, 1993)

Metal Chronicles Volume III: The L.A. Years (2009)

1. TAMMY GIRL

Tricks of the trade – with Nick Du Pont, MD of Resurgam Records

Don't sign novelty acts
Never work with public schoolboys
Steer clear of the Chelsea Hotel
Don't assume that what you can get on the West Coast will be any better than what you can get on the East Coast
Don't bother with the local girls

New Musical Express, 15 November 1980

'Now look here,' Rory said, in that clipped, high-ironical voice of his, which always brought to mind cavalry charges, Highland Clearances, anguished crofters flushed out at sword-point from the heather. 'I haven't been mucking about. For one thing, I've actually seen them.'

'Where have you seen them?' Rory was a literalist. He could easily have seen them on a street corner or at a dime-store check-out.

'The *Whiskey*,' Rory said, making L.A.'s premier music niterie sound like a run-down gentlemen's club, with unruly servants and a questionable cuisine. 'They're definitely signing to Geffen, Martinez says. There's a contract being faxed over tomorrow.'

There was a pause – one of the many pauses that littered telephone conversations with Rory, when his instinctive good manners got the better of professional brusqueness. Downstairs, a flight or two beneath the top-floor landing, where stoutly-shod yet invisible feet prowled back and forth, a radio was playing what sounded like Freddie Mercury singing 'Another One Bites the Dust.' It was three years since I had seen Freddie. Like many friends made at that time he had moved on into another world where the admission charge was unexpectedly steep.

'What were they like?'

'You know the sort of thing. Like that demo tape we had, only about ten times as loud. And lots of chat. "This one's for the Jew-fags in Beverley Hills." *You* know.'

The telephone had been run to earth in a kind of giant tea-cosy, which in England would have been embroidered with fleur-de-lys or the insignia of the National Trust but here in Los Angeles was covered with a procession of what looked like mutant raccoons. Outside there was warm late-summer air blowing in from the sea, and the pine-trees quivered in the breeze.

'I thought at least two of them were Jewish.'

'They very probably are. A little irony never hurt anyone,' Rory said, who had made quite a career out of this remark. 'Where the hell are you anyway?'

'I'm at Tammy's. What have you got on right now?'

It was 11 o'clock on a Sunday morning here in Pacific Palisades: the hour of back-lawn brunches and outsize Chrysler station wagons ferrying children to peewee league baseball games, of janitorial rakes at work on the leaf-strewn swim-pools; from half-a-dozen of the spacious gardens that adjoined the Pankeys' three-acre spread, little twists of barbecue smoke were rising into the air.

'Actually there's a newsagent's shop on the Strip that sells day-old copies of the *Telegraph*,' Rory said, with the complete absence of self-consciousness that was perhaps his only redeeming feature. 'I was hoping to find out how Middlesex were doing against Warwickshire.'

'Well do that and then come here.' Rory had to be kept up to the mark. 'Where does Martinez hang out when he's in California?'

'Some plague-pit in Encino...How am I supposed to know?'

'See if you can bring him with you.' The radio two floors below had stopped playing 'Another One Bites the Dust' and moved on to Diana Ross performing 'Upside Down.' 'Any idea how much Geffen are offering?'

'A *fuck* of a lot' Rory said. 'Give me an hour or two, all right?'

I gave him an hour or two, put the phone back in its raccoon-covered cradle and stood uncertainly on the landing, where a Brobdingnag-sized linen-cupboard offered glimpses of piled white sheeting and spangled counterpanes and a Puerto Rican maid, conspicuous in her azure pinafore, loitered in a doorway upending a waste-paper basket into a plastic sack. Down below Ms Ross continued to warble about the *boi* who was plaguing her equilibrium. You suspected that, like so many people noisily at large in L.A. here in the summer of 1980, her heart wasn't in it. Everywhere around us, melancholy lurked.

White sheets, melancholy and smoke-stained sky. All of a sudden, as in an avant-garde play where the aim is to bewilder the audience, make them feel that their grasp on reality is way out of kilter, three things happened at once. From the bedroom door ten feet away a woman's voice began to repeat my name, slowly at first, then with increasing desperation. Not to be outdone, the Puerto Rican maid cradled the rubbish sack in her arms, shot me a look of pure inter-racial hatred and then disappeared, gone so quickly that it was if she had vanished on the spot. Finally, from far below, down in the depths of the house, came the sound of raised voices. There was no doubt about it: the Pankeys were having another one of their rows.

'Nick.' The voice had settled into a steady rhythm now. 'Nick... Nicko...*Nick*.'

The English people you met on the West Coast nearly always stressed its placid, undemanding side. Wherever you went there was always some sun-toasted passage migrant to tell you that Californians were regular guys, innocuous even in their dissipations. Here in Pacific Palisades, with the voice from the bedroom turning louder by the minute and the Pankeys sounding as if they were hurling plates at each other, all bets were off.

'Nick,' the voice went on. 'Nicky...*Nick*.'

It was about ten past eleven: not a good time, in California or, experience suggested, anywhere else. Beyond the high windows, in the barber's-pole shadows cast by the slanting pines, lay what could have been the set of a Hollywood teen movie: tall, white-painted houses set back from the road; expensive cars stashed beneath pristine awnings; late-summer lawns quietly a-hiss. Any moment now a high school band would come marching along the tarmac or a punk kid from the wrong side of town on a motorcycle explode into the silence. But there were no marching bands and no punk kids. '*Nick*,' the voice bawled again. Rory would be hitting the paper shop on the Strip to see how Middlesex were doing. The Flame Throwers were signing to Geffen for a fuck of a lot of money. Down in their wide, airy kitchen, with its state-of-the-art technophile hobs and its electronically controlled drape curtains, the Pankeys were busy settling scores. It was time to be moving on.

In the bedroom Tamzin lay on her back on the king-size mattress, one blue-veined breast spilling out of her nightdress like a jellyfish. When she saw me she rolled over onto one side and said in her exasperated mock-hayseed voice:

'Jeez but the folks are actin' up this morning.'

'I expect they have their problems. Just like anyone else.'

Tamzin's attitude to her parents varied between regarding them as a slightly older brother and sister whose quaint conservative ways might profitably be mocked and treating them as a couple of recent additions to the county menagerie, shipped in from the wild and liable to turn nasty.

'Hey Nick,' she said, juggling the breast in the palm of one hand as if she was limbering up to throw a bowling ball, only to squirrel it away beneath starched white calico, 'could you get me a glass of *watter*?'

I fetched her a tumbler from the basin in the room's furthermost corner. This, too, was full of paraphernalia robbed from a Hollywood teen movie: *Star Wars* merchandise: a row of evil-looking trolls with purple hair; an entire wall covered with magazine posters.

'One of these fine summer days,' Tamzin said glumly, 'I'm gonna have to take all of this stuff down.'

Unusually, the collection of posters had a single point of focus. In fact, they were all of Tamzin: Tamzin in Annie Oakley buckskins, perched gamely on a haystack; Tamzin idling at a desk while a severe-looking woman in butterfly spectacles chalked mathematical symbols on a blackboard; Tamzin and a goofy-looking munchkin with a savage crewcut chewing popsicles. Pride of place in this gallery went to a giant picture of her nervously astride a horse beneath the strapline: WELCOME TO THE WORLD OF TAMMY GIRL. A month into my shakedown with the Pankeys, I knew all about the world of Tammy Girl, which had run for three series on NBC back in the early '70s. In Series One, Tammy, newly arrived at Tabernacle High School, was fighting a running battle with the class style-ogress Mary-Lou Madjeski. By Series Two she had acquired a hunky yet unreliable boyfriend named Rob and joined the ice-hockey club. Come Series Three, grown sober and reflective after the death of her grandma and Rob's diagnosis with Lyme Disease, she was part of a cheerleading team that had reached the State Final. There had been guest appearances by Elliott Gould and Karen Carpenter and unrealised plans for a Broadway musical.

The sun caught on the tumbler's edge and sparkled: the half-drunk water could have been tropical foam and the dust-motes oscillating fish swarms. The troll dolls leered from their sill. Above our heads, from math classes, beach parties and prom nights, two dozen teenage Tamzins stared calculatingly down. The real-life Tamzin snatched a bottle of what her friends sincerely hoped was paracetamol and swallowed two or three pills in quick succession.

'Oh. Mah. Gahd' she said, giving equal emphasis to all three words and leaving each of them stranded in an ocean of silence. 'There ain't no hammer like an Alabama Slammer.'

As its heroine cheerfully acknowledged, *Tammy Girl* had seriously messed with her head ('I mean, I was on Bennies all through the second series. Any time I went over 115 pounds my agent gave me stuff to make me throw up.') Mysteriously, it had also acted as a brake on her career. In the five years since the network had pulled the plug she had appeared in half-a-dozen TV commercials and been bludgeoned to death in an episode of *Columbo*.

'Come on, lover boy' she said, with the mixture of resignation and wry amusement which was the main thing I liked about her. 'I can tell you right now, if you haven't already guessed, that this is gonna be the Hell of a Day. Seriously. We'd better get dressed.'

And so I watched her put on her clothes, plucked from a wardrobe commensurate with her status as the daughter of a Hollywood agent whose wealth had been 'conservatively' estimated by *Variety* at between three and five million dollars and in this case consisted of a white pant-suit cut off between waist and torso, a kind of alligator-hide jerkin and enough bangles to imprison a python. As we moved out onto the three hundred square feet of thick white carpeting that was the Pankeys' upper landing, I caught a glimpse of myself in the full-length mirror – collarless white shirt, black jeans, Lobb brogues – knowing that all this amounted to a calling card. I was from England, no question about it. Bright sunshine and sharp flights of descending stairs; pine trees swaying in the distance and the smell of salt. All of California all sorts and conditions of people were cranking themselves up to greet the day. Over in the Valley teenage girls with names like Ondrya and Melody-Anne would be preparing for a morning at the mall. In Malibu the beach boys would be riding the surf. In San Bernardino the furniture dealers would be busy selling antique bedsteads to an assortment of squares, air-heads and – a new expression taught me by Tamzin – space cadets. And me? I was out here in Pacific Palisades, hard by the sea, shoulder to shoulder with Tammy Girl, breakfasting with the Pankeys and hot in pursuit of the Flame Throwers, with all the tact, subterfuge and monumental boredom that these activities naturally entailed.

* * *

By this point in the proceedings – it was the first week in September 1980 – I had been on the Flame Throwers' trail, in America and beyond, for the best part of two months. It had all started back in early July when a freelancer named Gary Le Roux, of all our A&R contacts possibly the only one whose musicological awareness extended beyond a few square miles of central London, waddled jovially into my office and slammed a C-60 cassette into the tape machine with the words 'Believe me, Nick, this is going to be so fucking *huge*.' There was an unwritten rule at Resurgam that anyone who imagined they had discovered the next big thing was entitled to play it to me immediately on pain of treating the entire building to lunch if they proved to be mistaken in this view. Gary was chancing his luck.

'It sounds like the Ramones.'

'No it doesn't.' There was an interval in which Gary fiddled with the machine, got it stuck in reverse and then, by a supreme effort of will, goaded it into fast forward. 'Listen to this.'

'*Jesus*... Has this been played anywhere?'

'Couple of college radio stations in Bumfuck, Indiana or someplace put it out for a bit, until people complained.'

'That figures. What's the situation in the States? I mean, I take it that they're American?'

'Well now...' Gary lowered himself, uninvited, into a chair and sprawled there like a giant maggot. 'They were supposed to be signing to – hold on a minute – Elektra only the president's daughter happened to be in the lift when they were going up to see the head of A&R, and she...well, anyway, then there was a deal with MCA, an actual deal, Nick, just waiting for people to sign it, only then the bass player disappeared or something. Right now the word is that Geffen are after them, only there's some old bollocks about nobody wanting to produce on account of them being fucking animals.'

'So why would I want to work with them?'

'You don't have to work with them, Nick. You can just license them. You don't even have to set eyes on them if you don't want to.'

'Like the Chronics?'

'No, *not* like the Chronics.' The Chronics had been a notional New Wave act whose solitary single had turned out to be a spoof knocked up in an idle moment by a couple of Radio One DJs.

The beauty of the Flame Throwers, aside from their demo tape, was that nobody in England had heard of them. They were the ziggurat in the desert, the iceberg in the Bering Strait, untouched by human eye, ripe for the taking, ready to be brought down. And so the mechanics of the long-distance record deal ground fitfully into gear. Faxes were exchanged with a management company in New York. A sparsely-filled envelope of press cuttings arrived in the mail to confirm the incendiary nature of their live shows. Rory and I, the former protesting that he was missing Royal Ascot, Wimbledon and other key events in the upper-bourgeois calendar, flew into LAX and booked ourselves into the Chateau Marmont. At which point, unexpectedly, the trail grew cold and the wires went crossed. The boys were in Canada. The boys had been thrown out of Canada for drugs offences and were playing some club dates on the north-eastern seaboard. The boys had broken up. Phoenix-like, the boys had reformed and were back in the studio. The boys were stashed away in Topanga Canyon working on a film project with Jean-Luc Godard. The boys were in Manhattan being interviewed by Andy Warhol. Inexplicably, all this burnished up their legend. Having thus far done virtually nothing with their lives, it seemed as if, henceforth, they could accomplish practically anything. So here I was, four weeks later, still with Tammy Girl (met at a party on my first night in LA), still hopefully at large in Pankey-land, still gorging on Pankey breakfasts, treading Pankey carpets, dodging the sprinklers to trespass on shimmering Pankey lawns.

* * *

Down in the tennis court-dimensioned kitchen-diner, life on Planet Pankey was exuberantly renewing itself. Here, in no particular order, could be found Earle and Bobbie Pankey, their tiff now resolved, cooing at each other like a couple of sinister turtle doves across a breakfast bar the size of a snooker table, harassed Latino domestics bringing in coffee-pots and baskets of bread and, in a distant corner, Cody Pankey, Tamzin's UCLA drop-out younger brother, mostly disparaged by his father as 'goddam Code' while spoken of by his admiring sister as 'sort of really out there, y'know', staring suspiciously at a bowl of Golden Grahams as if they were a heap of dog-mess that had turned up out of nowhere on the back step. Here, too, flowed a vast visual chronicle of bygone Pankey World: a long, wall-hung portrait gallery of the TV personalities with whom, back in the day, Earle had populated *Bonanza* and *The Mary Tyler Moore Show*; the Pankeys on their wedding day, magnolia-encircled and gem-enriched, outside a Baptist church in Tallahassee, FLA. Further away on the sparkling terrace could be glimpsed examples of the frail chicken-wire sculptures with which Bobbie beguiled her considerable leisure and which sometimes sold for a few dollars at charity auctions. Flanked by this pageant of achievement and pizzazz, the Pankeys did not, as was sometimes the case in American households of the Carter presidency, seem diminished by it. Somehow they were bigger than the representations of past time that crowded their walls, larger than the lives that glistened around them. Somewhere close by, from a music system built into the kitchen furniture, Gordon Lightfoot was zestlessly intoning that Sundown she'd better take care and he reckoned it was a sin that he felt like he was winning when he was losing again

California, in my admittedly limited experience, was big on sin.

Breakfast with the Pankeys. The double-quart, octagon-shaped flagons of orange juice glinting in the sun. The bespoke pastries brought over every morning from a high-end deli on Sunset. Big Earle Pankey dowsing his Kent cigarettes in a half-empty coffee cup and waving a fat hand the colour and texture of red tyre-rubber across the breakfast bar.

'I cannot tell you, Neckerlass,' he began, with practically fathomless insincerity, 'what a pleasure it is to entertain you this fahn morning, with Bobsie, here, and our daughter Tam, and, uh' – his eye fell on the bowl of Golden Grahams and the charmless vagrant behind it – 'and Code here.'

'Aren't you just darlin'?' Bobbie chirruped, as Tamzin went by. 'Code, will you kindly eat that cereal 'stead of looking at it like it was a fucking rattler.'

The Pankeys' attitude to their children varied between good days, when they regarded them as two of the finest young people ever born in sight of the Golden Gate, and bad days in which they groused about their inability to function without parental subsidy. This looked as if it was one of the bad days. It was a quarter to twelve. By now Rory would have sourced a copy of the *Daily Telegraph* and be up to who knew what mischief. The week's *Pacific Palisadian* lay on the edge of the breakfast bar, bringing news of celebrity clam-bakes and swim-wear fund-raisers on the beach at Malibu, together with an *L.A. Times* from whose cover President Carter stared toothily out of a deputation of black church elders. Earle Pankey caught my gaze.

'Can you believe it?' he said mournfully. 'The guy was a *peanut farmer.*' The italics crackled in the air between us. 'Back in *Jorja.*' The Pankeys had the proper Floridan contempt for anything that came out of the Peach State.

It had taken only a minute or two under Tamzin's roof to divine that the Pankeys were as conservative as the *Variety* estimate of Earle's net worth. Basically they were Southern Dixiecrats who had headed west out of Key Largo in the '50s and, in addition to Earle's televisual activities, got in with Reagan when he was governor and made a small fortune out of beach-side real-estate. Reagan, whom the Pankeys called 'Ron', was everywhere in Pankey-land. He came in with the morning coffee and went out last thing at night with the trash. These prejudices extended to popular art. 'Hell of a book,' Earle had once grudgingly allowed of *The Grapes of Wrath*, 'but don't you think it's kind of *exaggerated*?'

'Hey' he said, no longer outraged by this vision of the Georgia peanut-groves. 'I heard Series Three is up for a re-run on Mexican TV or something.'

Tamzin's right hand went on buttering the outsize bagel she clutched in the palm of her left. She had been here before. 'Do I get paid?'

'How the hell should I know?' Mr Pankey demanded. 'You got an agent, don't you?'

Hardly an hour passed in Tamzin's company without some fraught reminder of the life she had once led. People came up to her in coffee shops to ask for autographs. Even now, one or two of the discount chain-stores were still selling Tammy Girl rucksacks and Tammy Girl starter make-up bags. All this was oddly disconcerting: a world of make-believe and stark reality suddenly colliding in a Tammy Girl cupcake recipe.

Gordon Lightfoot had stopped crooning about Sundown and all the pain she was causing him. Way overhead an intense mechanical clangour suggested that a chopper was coming down on the neighbour's helipad. Nearer at hand, in the kitchen-diner's bleak anteroom, I could hear the maids laughing. There were other worlds out here in California, beyond the margins of Pankey-land: old black men fishing for scrod in tiny creeks while white cranes dipped in and out of the mud; hippy ladies in Laurel Canyon hunched over their Tarot decks. It would be good to explore them sometime. Meanwhile, there were other things to think about: Rory; the West Coast music scene; the overdraft facility; the news from home. The Flame Throwers were clearly maniacs, full-fathom five. Signing them – even if they could be signed – would bring trouble. On the other hand, there was sometimes money to be made out of maniacs. It was all a question of degree.

Back on Pankey Island, Tamzin, having briskly disposed of two bagels, a brace of bananas and a nut-sprinkled bowl of Greek yoghurt – she was one of those American girls who concealed a hearty appetite under the veneer of not eating a thing – prised open the arts section of the *L.A. Times*. This was a mistake, as it brought to view a photo of one of her former co-stars tearfully accepting an Academy Award from Robert Redford. Her deceptively wholesome face went blank and she pushed the paper aside.

'Take the car?' Code suddenly demanded, meaning his father's station wagon rather than the clapped-out Chevrolet in which he pursued his mysterious errands to no one quite knew where.

'Fuck *you*,' said Mr Pankey affably.

By this stage I had established that there was something going on in the Pankeys' kitchen-diner with its ochre and taupe paint scheme, here beneath the portraits of Don Blocker and Lorne Green in their cowboy gear, that went far beyond Earle and Bobbie's semi-customary annoyance with their children. Part of it was to do with the maids, who kept dropping by for little whispered conversations, at the close of which Mrs Pankey would look at her watch and then at Cody or occasionally at the cover of the *L.A. Times*, as if each of them constituted a hindrance to some mighty scheme she had cooking. Another part of it had to do with Earle, who, fifth cigarette of the morning a-smoulder between his saveloy fingers, was clearly in a tremendous stew about some private matter that the nature of the assembled company meant he couldn't quite address head-on.

'Hey, Neckerlass,' he began, having harangued Cody a bit more about the non-availability of the station wagon and given him some extra grief about the smell of dope he had detected out in the *vestabule* the previous night, 'Bobbie and I wanted to tell you how much we appreciate the help you've been givin' Tam with her career. We really do.'

I had sat in enough transatlantic parlours with enough stiff-shirted American patriarchs to know how to deal with this kind of nonsense.

'She's a very talented young woman.'

'Isn't she just *darlin'*?' Bobbie said, without much enthusiasm.

'You got to go where the money is,' Earle Pankey went on.

It occurred to me then that the Pankeys had misunderstood, or had had misrepresented to them, what had brought me to L.A. Well, that was their look-out. Or maybe, in insisting that you went where the money was, Earle had put his finger on it, recognised me as a fellow show-biz entrepreneur, identified a kindred spirit. But where was the money? According to the pundits, the money was all over the place: in the fag-end of Disco; in what was now being called Adult Oriented Rock, performed by men with bubble perms in mid-western amphitheatres; in New Wave bands in shiny leather jackets and skinny ties playing highly sanitised variations on an original noise patented by the Sex Pistols and the Clash. In the past week alone, at least a dozen people had asked me if I liked The Police.

Meanwhile, the air of tension was cranking up by the moment. A semi-distant telephone went off several times, after which another domestic skipped into the room, came in at a safe angle to Ma Pankey's teetering beehive and murmured something in her ear.

'Hey now,' Mrs Pankey proclaimed, like the Snow Queen informed that the temperature is about to drop but all the same not quite delightedly. 'Hey now. Aunt Nance is dropping by.'

'Yeah?' Cody said, supposing himself addressed. '…*Nance*.'

'Hell,' Mr Pankey elaborated. 'Ain't seen Nance in a long time. Not since the '76 Primaries.'

All this – the faint air of secrecy, the cover of the *L.A. Times*, the knowledge of who the Pankeys were, the thought of Pankey-schemes and Pankey-politics ripening to fruition – should have alerted me to what was going on, might even – if I had thought about it – prevented the embarrassment of what came after. All I can say in my defence is that I had other things on my mind. These included Rory, the contract with Geffen, Tamzin, who had said nothing about Aunt Nance, whoever she was, and the overdraft with the bank. Back in Pankey-land the rotor-blades above our heads were lashing the stale, second-hand air back and forth, the plates were being borne off to the dishwasher and Mrs Pankey was fanning herself with a rolled-up copy of the *Ladies' Home Journal*. Breakfast was coming to an end. Cody slunk wearily away, the grit from his sneakers leaving tiny trails on the parquet. 'You kids enjoy yourselves now' Mr Pankey said, assuming the role of benevolent softie dad in a bygone TV series of the kind he had helped to create, and so we drifted off through the endless be-carpeted and ranchero-styled rumpus rooms to a boxed-in plywood square, smelling of Janitor-in-a-drum, that Mr Pankey liked to call his library. Here there was a framed black-and-white photo of Mrs Pankey moistly subsiding into the pained embrace of Paul Newman at some ceremonial dinner, a couple of bubbling fish-tanks, a cine-projector on which her husband watched show reels and a shelf-full of buxom showbiz biographies with titles like *From Boise to Burbank: An Actor's Life*.

'Why does your father think I've been helping you with your career?'

'Daddy?' Detached from the Pankey-party, the flame of Tamzin's personality instantly flared up again. She crossed one white pant-suited calf over another and lit a cigarette, 'He reckons you're some kind of movie guy. I guess mother must have told him. It might have been that time you were talking about seeing John Belushi in a men's room someplace.'

'I thought your parents had other plans for you.'

'Yeah,' Tamzin conceded. 'Yeah, they do. I mean, uh, mother's been on the phone to Larry Dorfman at the brokerage, and she's, like, "This is a very good opportunity, Tamzin, and you ought to be grateful Larry is prepared to do your father a favour." And I'm, like, "Why do I want to go and work in an office at Century City with a creep like Larry Dorfman?"'

The brokerage scheme had been in the air ever since I had started hanging out at Pacific Palisades, accompanied by hints about the non-continuation of Tamzin's allowance.

'What about fuckin' Code?' Tamzin protested, all sibling solidarity gone. 'Why can't he go and work in a brokerage 'stead of sitting in his room all day smoking dope and pretending to write scripts? You know, I read one once and it was all about this space alien who gets to play quarter-back for the Lakers.'

There was a fan of colour photographs spread out over the carpet beneath the cine-projector. In them a collection of teen hunks, major dudes, mainstream studs and borderline twinkies – I was getting the hang of Earle Pankey's professional jargon – and one or two older men in suits and ties piloted speedboats, sat demurely at the wheels of Aston Martins or just stared moodily into the distance.

'Who are these guys?'

However disillusioned Tamzin might have been with showbiz, she was still fantastically absorbed in its procedural ebb and flow.

'That's Lance Mink. He was in *Sourdough Candy*. Well, the second series anyhow.'

'And that one?'

'Gary Dexterside. Now he had a whole lot going for him two years ago, only Daddy decided his teeth weren't sincere. Daddy,' said Tamzin, without irony, 'is really big on sincerity.'

Mr Pankey and his sincerity. Mrs Pankey and her chicken-wire sculptures. Dope fumes hanging over the wisteria-ringed porch...The thing about Earle Pankey and his lissom daughter, I'd decided, was that each of them had missed out on some vital stage in the average human being's development. Tamzin had never had a childhood. It had all been spent starving herself, and hanging out on set, and swallowing tranquilisers, and learning her lines in the car on the way back from part-time attendance at some L.A. high-school exclusively populated by movie brats. Earle, on the other hand, had never made it to adulthood. He'd squandered it juggling percentages and showing the mob round Vegas and working out if people's teeth were sincere. And now here we were in the early fall of 1980, with *Tammy Girl* five years out of commission – there'd been an idea for a new series where a grown-up Tammy would be apartment-sharing in Chicago, but this hadn't got beyond her agent's desk – and the brokerage looming like a shark's fin through the frisky Californian surf.

'Gentleman on the phone for *Mustah* Du Pont,' said a servant, putting her head round the door and smiling at Tamzin, whom all the domestics liked and pitied, and so I padded back along the serpentine corridors to an alcove where, separated from its cradle, a telephone receiver lay glistening on a giant plastic oyster shell.

'Where are you?'

'Some clip joint on Santa Monica. There are rather a lot of black people about. Nothing I can't handle.'

'How did Middlesex get on?'

'Not bad. Radley was 123 not out at the close...Listen, though. I've got one of them,' Rory said, as if he had just enticed a rare parrot out of a tree.

'Which one?'

'The singer. Hang on a moment...No, the bass player. Stevie something.'

'Where did you find him?'

'Honest to God, Nick, I was just driving along somewhere off the Strip thinking how extraordinary all the people looked and he walked past. I recognised him from the photographs. So I got out of the car, introduced myself, explained what I was about, and told him he'd better come with me.'

There was no reason to doubt any of this. Like the Pankeys, in their individual ways, Rory lived by the will. Just as, in a previous life, when he ordered a recruit on the square at Catterick to start sweeping up leaves, and the recruit had started to sweep them, so he had told Stevie to get into his car, and Stevie, sensing a power greater than his own, had obeyed. It was as simple as that. At the same time there were other elements of this transaction that would need going into.

'What sort of...what sort of state in is he in?'

'Come on Nick. He's sitting here eating a – what is that revolting thing? – a cheeseburger. Little Lord Fauntleroy couldn't be more together. You want me to go through his pockets?'

What did I want? I wanted to be light years away from Planet Pankey, whose atmosphere – whatever I thought of Tamzin – was becoming oppressive. I wanted to sign the Flame Throwers, or if not to sign them then to talk to them and see what they looked like. Most important of all, I wanted to be back in London to attend to half-a-dozen things that were going wrong in my absence. All this played a part in what happened next.

'You'd better bring him round here.'

'Roger to that,' Rory said, whose vocabulary came peppered with military slang and sometimes talked about 'sit reps'. 'Be there in twenty.'

Six thousand miles away in London it would be about eight o'clock in the evening. Unless someone had borrowed the spare key and stolen in to pilfer records and spend the night on the board-room couch, the office in Newman Street would be locked up and silent. The white label advance pressings of next month's releases would be stacked up on the Press Officer's desk awaiting despatch. The pile of demo tapes in the wicker basket by the front door would have grown another six inches. The posters advertising Rumble Strips' last album would have been taken down and replaced with flyers for the label-wide 'Red Hot and Rising' autumn tour. Time, which in Los Angeles seemed to have stopped dead, would be moving on.

Back in the study Tamzin had lit another cigarette and was staring at it as if she had never seen one before, wondered what miracles it might perform.

'Can you see me working in a brokerage?'

'Not really.'

'That's what I told mother.'

In fact, it was impossible to imagine her working anywhere. She was Tammy Girl, fixed in time, a creature from history trapped by the glaciers, forever trading gossip with her best friend Lori Kupferberg or wondering whether now was the moment to have her braces off. There was no going forward.

'Maybe I should put in for one of those high-school movies.'

Over the past decade and a half I'd had plenty of time to reflect on the difference between English girls and American girls. The really vital separation, it seemed to me, was that English girls were either sophisticated or naïve, whereas American girls could display both these qualities simultaneously. Tammy, so shrewd about sex, relationships and 'people', alert to the faintest shifts in social protocol, still hadn't noticed that her career was over. Her English equivalent would already have signed up for teacher-training.

'Was that your friend Rory on the phone? He's kind of cute.'

Rory had gone down well in California. He had adopted his most punctilious manner, shaken every hand offered to him and told all and sundry that he was frightfully pleased to meet them. Being called the Honourable Rory Bayliss-Callingham helped, too.

Beyond the window, on the Pankey's virid and astro-turfed lawn, all kinds of things were going on. Two or three of the servants, bossed by an elderly black man in a chef's apron, were trying to put up a kind of gauzy-curtained gazebo. Other domestics – the Pankeys called all their retainers 'the help' – were bringing out trays of sandwiches and chicken wings. Code, dressed in tee shirt and jeans, crouched a little way off next to a beat box whose roar of noise – rumbling, lo-fi bass, sheet-metal guitar and screeched vocals – made it sound suspiciously like the Dead Kennedys' 'Too Drunk to Fuck'. Mr Pankey, now got up in a striped summer blazer, white duck trousers and deck shoes, darted out from the side of the house and, his face contorted with rage, began to gesticulate at the beat box, which Cody picked up and bore off in the direction of a garden shed. Even now the enormity of what was in train hadn't occurred to me. It was just Americans playing at being Americans. They could look after themselves.

'I guess Aunt Nance always did like to see me in a skirt,' Tamzin said, a reek of dissatisfaction and thwarted promise wafting out of the room in her wake.

In her absence there was nothing at all to do in Mr Pankey's sanctum. The fat Hollywood biographies lay on the bookshelf like saints embalmed in their tombs. The look on Paul Newman's face as he reluctantly angled his torso into Mrs Pankey's moist embrace confirmed that he knew her husband was the godawfullest old fraud that ever drew breath. Pankey-land seemed flawed, shriven, ready to blow. And so I wandered back through the warren of inter-connected rooms, some of them furbished up to look spacious and unadorned, others of them toned down to seem cosy and confidential, some of them apparently designed for political caucuses and jamboree nights, others of them intended for sleepy afternoons of drift and slide, but all of them somehow suggesting that no kind of human life had ever really got going in them. Out in the hall the front door was wide open, so that great square parcels of sunlight seemed to have been arranged across the floor. Mrs Pankey emerged like some vestal goddess from an ante-room wearing a long, flowing seasonal dress designed for a woman at least twenty years younger than herself and a pair of open-toed sandals from which her feet bulged like cottage loaves, and the feeling I had brought with me out of the study hardened into certainty. Something was going to go wrong. You could feel it in the swish of Mrs Pankey's trumpery robes, in the faint breath of air stealing through the doorway and the sunlight streaming through the pines.

'*Nick*,' Mrs Pankey said beseechingly, her voice somehow stricken with dread. The Pankeys were not great anglophiles, although Earle had once conceded that Mrs Thatcher was a spunky lady. I never quite knew whether they regarded me as a potential son-in-law or a piece of English shit defiling the fountain of their daughter's unpolluted heart. Here in the Pankeys' airy hallway, it looked as if some secret compact had suddenly bound us together.

'Earle's out back somewhere' Mrs Pankey explained. 'Could ya just...go out there and see what the hell's happenin'?'

Mr Pankey would still be bawling Cody out over the Dead Kennedys. Or maybe by now he had moved on to other things. Outside there was a hum of voices, borne back on the breeze, a car door slamming gently shut, but beyond that a greater stillness, as if all the things that usually went on in Pacific Palisades on a late-summer forenoon here in the last months of the Carter administration had unexpectedly ground to a halt. Twenty yards away, at the farthest extent of the Pankeys' front lawn, disdaining the tarmacked driveway that snaked downhill to the triple car-port, a white convertible was parked up on the verge. One hand resting on the bonnet, the other slapping his knee, Rory was administering what, even at this distance, sounded like a pretty serious talking-to to a tall, gangling figure who, if not absolutely collapsed over the passenger door was clearly having difficulty in making his way out onto the pavement. From the other side of the road, three kids had stalled their dirt-bikes to stare pruriently at the spectacle. Meanwhile, a low-slung black limousine had emerged out of the trees forty yards away where the road bent round and was hastening sharkishly towards us. The effect was oddly mesmerising, otherworldly, picturesque. Rory reluctantly acknowledging that he was but a bystander in this collision of urban styles, straightened up. The three dirt-bikers gaped. There was an electrifying rustle behind us as Mrs Pankey's sandals went flapping by over the concrete. More noise from the space behind her confirmed that Mr Pankey had arrived in the vestibule and was making his presence felt.

There were three people in the limo, which now stole gracefully to a halt a yard or so from the convertible's rear fender. Two of them – a weaselly chauffeur and a dark-suited security guy with a crew-cut who leapt out of the seat next to him to tug open the passenger door – were straight out of central casting. But there was no mistaking the dainty, elfin woman with the jutting jaw and the curiously over-bright eyes who, outsize handbag clasped manfully to her bosom, stepped dauntlessly out of the car. I had seen her on TV just the other night at some GOP rally in Dallas.

'Oh my,' Nancy Reagan said.

I was about ten feet away by this stage – a good three ahead of a faltering Mrs Pankey (big Earle had been left for dead on the patio), close enough to see that the gangling figure – Stevie – had toppled out of the car and, having fallen full-length on the verge, was being violently sick. There were already two or three pools of ochre vomit not a yard from Mrs Reagan's expensively shod feet. Instantly, the scene exploded into drama.

Mrs Pankey, who knew long-hair trash when she saw it, gave a high-pitched shriek. Mrs Reagan bolted smartly to one side, but not before Mrs Pankey had grabbed her in a despairing embrace. The security man loomed over them both, looking as if he was ready to tear Mrs Pankey limb from limb on the spot. Meanwhile fat Earle, more nimble than anyone had given him credit for, was bearing down on us.

Over in the Valley the girls with names like Ondrya and Melody-Anne would be coming back from the mall. In San Bernardino, the furniture salesmen would be closing for lunch. It was time to be moving on., Crimson-faced from the effort of jogging twenty yards up a slight incline, and looking as if he might be about to join Stevie on the tarmac, Earle Pankey laid a plump hand on my shoulder.

'Get this piece of shit off my driveway.'

In those days I was still coming to terms with the innate resourcefulness of celebrity, and the paradox that lay at its core. However frail and unworldly they might appear on the outside, famous people, it always seemed to me, could look after themselves when it mattered. Deep down, they were tough cookies. And so it was with Nancy Reagan, Aunt Nance, who gave a disapproving but not exactly unsympathetic glance at the figure sprawled on the stone, steered her way dextrously around him and within a few seconds was stalking down the driveway, handbag banging against her elbow, as Mrs Pankey hung remorselessly on her arm. Instantly Rory took charge of the situation. 'You can fuck off,' he said to Earle, who still looked as if he were about to drop dead on the grass, and then turning to the security man, 'I'll take care of this.'

The security man nodded, as one thug to another, and moved away. By now the Pankeys and their guest had reached the front door. Together Rory and I contemplated the one serious casualty of the past five minutes. Stevie had stopped being sick, but his face, framed by shoulder-length black curls, was the colour of parchment. Rory bent down and flipped him expertly onto one side.

'Those body guards are the limit. Never like getting involved.'

'I can't say I blame them…What on earth happened?'

'How the hell do I know?' With an unlooked-for delicacy he drew Stevie up into a sitting position, swung both arms about his chest and began to haul him into the car. 'He was all right when we left Santa Monica. Do you want to say goodbye to anyone?'

'Not sure it would serve any useful purpose.'

Rory shrugged. Comatose bass players; domestic upset in Pacific Palisades: it was all the same to him. Five yards away, Mrs Reagan's security man was leaning against the bonnet of the limousine smoking a cigarette. The trio of bicycling children had disappeared. Stevie was fast asleep. Like a pair of morticians lovingly at work in some chapel of rest high in the Hollywood Hills, we arranged his long, lanky body on the back seat of the convertible and drove off into the afternoon sun.

* * *

Back at the Chateau Marmont there was a TV crew filming in the lobby and the janitors' wagons were out on their rounds. With the fat brown envelope pressed on me by the reception desk wedged under my arm, I wandered off along the shabby corridors, where dust particles hung in the air and there was a smell of damp, to the bolt-hole in Bungalow 3 where I had taken up residence, far away from the awe-struck tourists who seemed to be the hotel's stock-in-trade. The envelope was from Newman Street and contained what Maxine, the PA, termed 'the really important stuff.' There were letters from the managers of successful bands who were being courted by the majors and wanted to be released from their contracts; there were letters from the managers of unsuccessful bands who were not being courted by the majors and who did not want to be released from their contracts; and also a note, written on expensive Basildon Bond paper, from the mother of the drummer of a power-pop three-piece who had recently been thrown off *Top of the Pops* for what the letter sent back with them called 'deeply objectionable behaviour', thanking me for helping Christopher with his career. And then, at the very bottom of the stack, an airmail sent from New York and returned across the Atlantic, harbouring a letter in a spidery yet suggestive hand and a tiny, tissue-covered rectangle.

Dear Nick,
Sorry not to have been in touch. Found some stuff you might like to have. Yr pa's.
Think he would have wanted.
Daphne

Daphne had been the woman with whom the old man had spent most of the Sixties: loaf-haired, vague and unreliable. I hadn't seen her in six years. The oblong of tissue-paper turned out to contain a second letter, written in wavery green Biro on a page torn out of a spindle-ring notebook, and a tiny black-and-white photograph.

The House of Peace, Love and Serenity, Echo Beach, Oregon, 27 November 1969

My dear, dearest boy
How stands the name of Du Pont? Is its éclat *unsilenced? Its lustre undimmed? I live a detached life now, as you know. Far away from the clangour of the storm-crossed world. But the feelings of a fond parent should never be repressed, for they are rapt and inalienable. In anticipation of our next meeting I send you the enclosed: the memento of a time that was precious to me, and a mode of life which, to my lasting sorrow, I was unable to sustain.*
Your ever-loving father
Maurice Chesapeake Albuquerque Seattle du Pont

The House of Peace, Love and Serenity had been the hippy commune where the old man had fetched up round about the time of Woodstock. It was here, on a winter's morning in 1971 that I had helped to bury – or rather immolate – him in the depths of the Pacific Ocean. To be reminded of all this nine years later on a late-summer afternoon in the shadow of the Hollywood Hills was a profound shock.

But there was more to come. The photograph, not more than two inches square, showed a girl, obviously pregnant, with a Veronica Lake hair-do standing in front of what looked like a row of beach-huts and a man in USAF uniform with a peaked serviceman's cap jauntily askew on his high, wide forehead. Here, indisputably, were my mother and father on the Front at Southwold in what could only have been the summer of 1942. The Flame Throwers: Tamzin: Nancy Reagan: the news from Newman Street: all the things that had silently, or not so silently, oppressed me for the past four hours faded away, and I was alone, once again, in the great, echoing caverns of the past.

2. SOUTHWOLD

There ain't no going back.
You'll fall beneath the cracks
Of the place you used to call home
THE FLAME THROWERS – *Ain't No Going Back*

All through the 1950s, and out into the decade beyond, we go to Southwold. Sometimes these are day-trips, begun on a whim at dawn and concluding as the twilight wells up over the corn-fields, but more often we stay for a week – a fortnight, even, if the weather is good and the funds hold out. There is something odd about my mother's interest in this Suffolk town, set back from a shingle beach halfway between Lowestoft and Aldeburgh, for Southwold is a world away from our usual beat, 35 miles distant from Norwich and requiring two bus journeys and a stop-over in Bungay to negotiate. Still, there is a look of triumph, almost amounting to exaltation, on my mother's face as the red double-decker ploughs on through the Suffolk verdure, through Beccles and Shadingfield and on into a landscape of tenantless back-lanes and tumbledown pubs where the grass grows six feet high on the verge – the thought of a victory won over an unseen but implacable foe. Next year, my mother says, as the bus slams to a halt behind a stalled tractor or a hay-cart becalmed in a cloud of dust, we will charter a taxi and damn the expense. We never do. Beyond the A12 the road bends round to the sea, the light glints strangely off Reydon Water, the white birds cascade through the thermals and the breeze tumbling in through the open window is suddenly filled with the smell of salt.

It is the same as the bus grinds up the slight incline of Station Road into Southwold High Street, where the salt-smell is soon replaced by the reek of malt from the brewery and the bulk of the town slides into view. There is something proprietorial about the glance my mother gives the side-streets of fishermen's cottages, the Methodist church with its neat gravel frontage and, in the distance, looming above the market square and the ornamental blue and gold clock, the long arm of the sea: she has been here before. No minor change in the landscape – a shop changing hands, a new hotel opening up, an addition to the stock of beach huts – escapes her notice. The Southwold hotels have names like the Swan, the Crown and the Pier Avenue, emit paralysing rays of gentility and are all owned by the brewery. Next year, my mother assures me, we will stay in one of them, occupy twin rooms with a view over the beach and be brought afternoon tea by a parlour maid in a black-and-white pinafore dress and Lisle stockings. We never do. Instead we are quartered on bed-and-breakfast establishments or lodging houses run by sinister old ladies in floral print dresses where there are squalid little arguments over charging for the cruet and my mother is alternately pitied and patronised for being an unattached female in charge of a small boy.

Despite these constraints, my mother enjoys her time in Southwold. It is her kind of place, with her kind of entertainments. She likes the Conservative Club, in whose musty interior hang portraits of Mr Macmillan and Mr R.A. Butler and where sales of work occasionally beguile a dull afternoon. She likes the genteel tea shops, where giant slabs of Dundee cake lie mouldering under glass and respectful waitresses call her 'madam', and she likes the long, plate-glass windows of Dennys, the tailoring shop, where mannequins in morning coats and belted Norfolk jackets nod austerely at the passers by. The Southwold crowds – pink-faced fathers in flannel trousers, with copies of the *Daily Express* under their arms, neatly be-cardiganed mothers in summer frocks from Dorothy Perkins – are like us and yet somehow unlike. The boys, in off-duty uniforms of grey Aertex shirts, belts with snakehead clasps and gym shoes, are not unfriendly, yet somehow they are not my kind of boy, and the scent of their prosperity hangs in the air between us. Sometimes, in one of the boarding houses or the genteel tea-shops, my mother will 'get talking', as she puts it, to a woman keeping a cautious eye on a brood of children or knitting quietly at a table, but nothing ever comes of these conversations. My mother is too separate, too detached from the ebb and flow of life for these casual acquaintanceships to work. And so the pleasures she allows herself are solitary, or material. She likes early suppers in the fish and chip shop at the High Street's farther end, walks across the common, where pony-riding girls in black jackets and hard hats canter back and forth and it sometimes necessary to duck beneath mis-hit shots from the golf course. One day, my mother says, we will walk along the coast to Dunwich, whose original settlement has disappeared into the sea and where the sound of the church bells can be heard rising from the waves. We never do.

All this suggests ulterior knowledge, familiarity, even design. But what my mother knows about Southwold, or whatever she may have done there in the past, she keeps to herself. On the rare occasions she is encouraged to supply personal information, my mother gives out that she is a widow. This seems to me perfectly fair. Ten years have gone by since my father vanished into the transatlantic mist, with only the peaked USAF serviceman's cap on the hat-stand back in North Park to confirm that he ever existed. On the other hand, every so often my mother will buy a representation of a local view – the white-painted lighthouse whose steps we sometimes ascend on Sunday afternoons, Gun Hill, where half-a-dozen miniature cannon retrieved from the Battle of Sole Bay bake in the sun – and hopefully despatch it to one of the several addresses at which my father, Maurice Chesapeake Albuquerque Seattle Du Pont, may or may not reside. In this adventurous spirit, postcards are sent to Boise Idaho, Billings Montana and Providence Rhode Island. No reply is ever vouchsafed. Catching a glimpse of one of these effusions, I am startled by its innocuousness, its telegraphic record of walks taken and sights seen – as if sender and notional receiver last set eyes on each other a week ago rather than the small matter of a decade. *Nicky sends his love*, my mother writes. Perhaps there are other things she hesitates to say. After all, a true account of how she feels about Maurice Chesapeake Albuquerque Seattle might take up many more pages to file. Who can tell?

And all the while time is moving on. 1954. 1955. 1956. There are tough boys with back-combed hair and oil-stained hands preening themselves on street-corners or outside the Lord Nelson and the Sole Bay Inn – all the Southwold pubs have a nautical air – in drape coats and brothel-creeper shoes, and odd, syncopated music rasping out of the transistor radios that sit on the counters of the beach-side cafés. In the summer of 1955 there is a General Election, the balcony of the Conservative Club breaks out into a riot of Union Jacks and pictures of Mr Eden and the Labour candidate, who makes the mistake of canvassing the town, is jeered from one end of the High Street to the other. By this time, like my mother, I am getting the hang of Southwold, tracing its margins, burrowing down into the other kinds of life that run beneath its surface. Inspired by Mr Knowles, the school geography master, I conceive a passion for cartography. A map of the common, at six inches to the mile with the gorse bushes done in blocks of green ink; a map of the town's landmarks (lighthouse, sailors' reading room, church spire, brewery chimney); a map of coastal walks to Walberswick and Covehithe: all these are borne proudly back to North Park Avenue and sellotaped to the parlour wall. There is a bookshop kept by a distracted middle-aged woman who looks as if she would rather be somewhere else and is indulgent of browsers, and, in the summer of 1958, a week-long romance with a girl named Margaret McAllister, which extends to half-a-dozen ice-creams eaten in the shadow of the pier and games of tennis on the public courts, and is summarily concluded at the moment when it is revealed that, while Margaret is the daughter of the Assistant Chief General Manager of the Norwich Union Insurance Society, I am the son of a woman who stitches baby clothes for a mail order firm in a council house on the Earlham estate.

Southwold. The smell of the malt drifting over the brewery and the dray-horses rattling off along the High Street. The bathing belle competition on the pier, with a line of roly-poly girls ready to burst out of their skimpy costumes. Margaret McAllister pausing in her execution of an immaculate forehand stroke to confide that boarding school was really rather super once you got used to it and there were some very nice people. The picture-postcards winging out to Tallahassee, Florida and Cheyenne, Wyoming. At the same time there are other things about Southwold, or rather about my mother and me, that a summer fortnight spent there brings sharply into focus. My mother is more voluble on holiday, or perhaps less silent. She talks about her sister, Aunt Dorothy, who lives in Canada and works as a creative realtor, whatever that may be. One day, my mother says, as we inspect a boarding house teapot whose contents have been stewing for the past half-hour and a sugar-shaker with no sugar in it, we will go to Canada and stay with Aunt Dorothy and her husband Eugene in their clapboard house in Toronto. We never do. Other times she talks about her family, the Mickleburghs, who cast her aside when she married Maurice Chesapeake Albuquerque Seattle, and the existences they are still thought to be pursuing out on the Norfolk flat. Life, my mother says, is about making choices without sometimes possessing the information necessary for choices to be made. Nothing has been heard of my father now for seven years.

But my mother does not repine. She puts on a pair of dark, single-frame sunglasses like a croupier's visor and a calf-length polka-dot skirt and challenges me to play a round of Krazy Golf. She goes to Lowestoft on the bus to inspect the fish market and brings back dabs and rock salmon – the polite name for dogfish – which can be grilled on the boarding-house gas-ring. Here in my mid-teens, my mother likes talking about my future. One day, she confidently proposes, I will work in a bank, or in the Housing Department at Norwich City Council. My mother's concept of the world of middle-class employment is necessarily limited. Banks and building societies, municipal departments and government offices: that is about all there is. It occurs to me at this time that my mother is rather in awe of me, that while proud of my grammar school blazer and the nine 'O' Levels I acquire in the summer of 1958 she is nervous of their implications. Once or twice, over late breakfasts in lodging-house dining-rooms, or partaking of afternoon snacks in dusty tea-shops, catching sight of her face over the Formica table-top, I deduce that there are things she is burning to tell me, but that some inner fear or delicacy stays her tongue. Maybe I will be a solicitor's clerk, my mother suggests. Meanwhile, Cliff Richard is in the charts and, fresh evidence of my father's possible whereabouts having come to light, a postcard of the market square is sent to an address in Utica, New York State. There is no reply.

Southwold, too, is responsible for Mr Matlock, who for two or three years is as much a part of the surrounding scenery as the Homeknit factory or the schooners drawn up in Sole Bay harbour where the river Blyth flows in from the point. Mr Matlock is a tall, thick-set, middle-aged man with a luxuriant moustache that makes him resemble the actor Terry Thomas who turns up at one of the boarding houses where we lodge. Each morning on the south beach the tide recedes to display a collection of objects discarded by the passing ships: plastic containers; strings of onions; sawn-off blocks of wood. It occurs to me that Mr Matlock is another piece of Southwold flotsam: blown in from nowhere; washed up on the strand. Though nattily dressed, affable and scrupulously polite – he calls my mother 'Mrs Du Pont', myself 'old chap'- Mr Matlock is, it seems to me, and even by the standards of provincial England, deadly dull. Sometimes he talks about speedway racing. At breakfast, mouth hanging open like a goldfish, he can be seen leafing impressionably through the *Daily Sketch*.

Our relationship with Mr Matlock hardens by degrees. We take afternoon tea with him at one of the genteel coffee shops. We are invited to accompany him on what he calls a 'saunter' along the High Street, where Mr Matlock stares earnestly into the frontages of the bric-a-brac shops as if he can't imagine how such an extraordinary collection of artefacts could ever have been assembled in one place. Hanging in the window of one of the shops is a painting of a small girl in a tam o'shanter and a gabardine mackintosh bending down to examine a slumbering hedgehog. Mr Matlock is profoundly affected by this scene. 'Isn't that a wonderful thing?' he says several times. 'Quite wonderful in its way.' Nobody dares contest this opinion, and so we wander down the granite steps to the sea front, past the life-guard in his chair and the line of beach-huts, where old ladies are swigging tea out of vacuum flasks and dogs lie exhausted in the shade, three tiny figures under the wide Suffolk sky.

My mother likes Mr Matlock. She likes his deferential manner, his creeping moustache, his prodigious wardrobe of suits and his job as the assistant manager of a paper-manufacturing concern in Rayleigh, Essex, a calling to which Mr Matlock occasionally draws attention by taking a handful of tiny white globules out of the depths of his trouser-pocket and explaining that they are paper samples. Another point in Mr Matlock's favour is that he served in the war, supervising the flight of barrage balloons above Hyde Park. At Christmas there is a card on the mantelpiece next to the regular items sent by my mother's North Park cronies and Aunt Dorothy in Canada, wishing 'Jean and Nicholas all the best for the festive season with every good wish from Vic.' My mother says that it is very kind of Mr Matlock to remember us. A fortnight later, when the Christmas decorations have been taken down, I find Mr Matlock's card carefully preserved between two photograph albums. Whatever may or may not go on between Mr Matlock and my mother in the ensuing months is never revealed, but it is a fact that when we next arrive in Southwold there he is in the boarding house parlour to greet us. Also present, parked up on the kerb outside the boarding house's front door, is a maroon-coloured Morris Minor. This, Mr Matlock proudly informs us, is 'at our disposal.'

It is clear that something has changed in Mr Matlock and my mother's collective outlook. The tectonic plates have shifted. They call each other 'Jean' and 'Vic', and the boarding house table at which we breakfast is invariably set with an extra place. There are little jokes, betraying a private compact that I strain to decipher. Still, the Morris Minor is at our disposal, along with Mr Matlock's wallet, and in it we bowl off through the Suffolk countryside: to Framlingham and its Angevin castle, Aldeburgh with its shingle beach, Orford Ness with its mock-Tudor mansions. My mother likes these excursions. She likes Fram and its dusty market square, and she likes the Aldeburgh antique shops with their Edwardian fire-tongs and trays of brightly burnished horse brasses. Mr Matlock, too, is in his element – earnest and attentive, the morning's *Daily Sketch* folded into a parcel under his arm, with one eye on the uncertain sky and another on the supply of parking spaces. It is as if the great business of his life is conducted here in the streets of Suffolk market towns, handing my mother in and out of cars and astonishing waitresses with sixpenny tips. My mother, he tells me in an unguarded moment, is 'a wonderful lady'. On the day of our departure I am abandoned to the boarding house parlour while he and my mother go for a walk over Southwold Common. On the journey back to Norwich, as the bus cleaves through the avenues of cow parsley, my mother tells me that Mr Matlock thinks I am 'a clever lad.'

But it is nearly all up with Mr Matlock. Like the pleasure cruisers on the Blyth, he is drifting out to sea, sailing headlong into the wild waves. At Christmas the post brings two substantial parcels. My mother receives a hairdryer. For me there is a copy of *The Kon-Tiki Expedition* by Thor Heyerdahl. My mother suggests that it is very kind of Vic to think of me. For some reason Thor Heyerdahl's account of his adventures in the South Seas gets mixed up in my head with their donor. It is Mr Matlock who broods over the tiller of his balsa-wood raft as the din of the surf billows in his ears; Mr Matlock who forages for jetsam on the Polynesian strand. But come the summer, when we arrive in Southwold – my mother is nervous on the journey and fiddles with the buttons of her newly-bought lemon and duck-egg blue cardigan – there is no sign of him at the boarding house and the linoleumed floors of the genteel tea-shops no longer echo to his tread. And then, out walking on the cliff-top one stormy afternoon – my mother has abandoned her cardigan and gone back to a sensible rain-coat – we chance upon Mr Matlock, affable as ever, but accompanied by a woman with a fierce, vulpine face, a shiny white mackintosh and elaborately marcelled hair. 'These are two friends of mine, Jean and Nicky,' Mr Matlock explains, with a terrible, embarrassed jauntiness. 'Charmed I'm sure,' my mother says to the woman, who is called Elsie, as she shakes hands. 'Nice to see Vic again,' my mother remarks, with what is clearly an effort of will, as we wander back along the cliff-top, heads down against the slanting breeze. Nothing more is said, but a week later, back in North Park, my mother takes the hairdryer out of its shiny cardboard box and, having prudently removed the electrical fuses, smashes it to pieces with a hammer.

And that is the end of our time on the Suffolk coast. There will be no more breakfasts in boarding house dining-rooms that smell of fried bacon-fat or walks across the Common. I am in my late teens now and off to Oxford, set against which seaside holidays are the smallest of small beer. My mother now prefers charabanc rides with her friends from the Eaton Park Ladies' Bowls Club. In another few years, in any case, she will be dead, with only a scattering of picture postcards, kept in a drawer, to remind me that she ever went there. The fat Southwold housewives will still march down the High Street to the Homeknit factory; the stately pleasure-cruisers will still be lined up along the banks of the Blyth; out in Sole Bay the yachts will still embark on their endless, criss-crossing dance; but my mother – Jean, Mrs Du Pont, at whose disposal the maroon-coloured Morris Minor was so kindly placed – is no longer there to see them.

3. WHITE PUNKS ON DOPE

> Just got back from 'Frisco to my favourite part of town
> Hanging with the guys again and back on the brown
> THE FLAME THROWERS *Back on the Brown*

'What on earth is this?'

'It's called Porto Flip. Why, don't you like it?' Freddie gave a little gopher's grin so that his buck teeth fell forward onto his lower lip.

'Is it supposed to taste as if someone had mixed an egg up in it?'

'Do you know, dear, I think that's exactly what they do. Somebody told me they used to give it to girls at finishing school as a tonic.'

As ever, Freddie was a mine of obscure information he was anxious to get across. Already, a bare five minutes into this chance encounter, he had filled me in on the little-known facts that one of Rod Stewart's legs was a prosthesis and that Elton John ('Reg') lived on a diet of potted shrimps. In the distance, dense early afternoon sun was burning off the Hollywood Hills and there was a helicopter winding erratically across the skyline. Here in the arbour where we had settled ourselves, twenty feet below the restaurant's terrace, the atmosphere had a freakish, hallucinogenic quality. The gigantic blue butterflies and the brightly-coloured songbirds that swarmed about in the foliage looked faintly unreal, as if they were the winning entry in a competition for the best psychedelic album sleeve of 1968.

'Well, if you're not going to drink it I think I shall,' Freddie volunteered, upending the glass of Porto Flip into his mouth. 'But then you always were so terribly fastidious.'

It was three years since I had last seen Freddie. In that time he had acquired a new look. The raven locks and the Pre-Raphaelite painter's gear (Holman Hunt at the Royal Academy Summer Exhibition? Rossetti at the easel?) had given way to moustache, aviator sunglasses and a white singlet from which heavily muscled arms extended like a couple of glutted anacondas. There was nothing unusual about this transformation. All over the Western Hemisphere music people were busy re-inventing themselves to take account of exacting new dress codes. With the Porto Flip disposed of, a waiter came hurrying along the approach path of shrubs and cacti and, practically abasing himself on the marbled tiles, set down a small flagon of what the memory of several late-night drinking sprees with Tammy Girl assured me was an Alabama Slammer, on which Freddie gamely feasted.

'Well, dear, I don't suppose you came here to sample the night-life. You must be after a *band*. Is it one of those New Wave ones everybody's so excited about? I was talking to that nice young man from the Police only the other day – Buzz, is his name?'

'Sting... They're called the Flame Throwers.'

'Oh, *them*. I've heard about them. You're way out of your league,' Freddie said, not unkindly, but with a sudden, devastating shrewdness. 'Somebody told me Polydor were coming in for a quarter of a million quid. Not to mention underwriting a European tour. Just fancy a record company underwriting a tour of Europe. In my day they wouldn't have paid for a trip round Shepherd's Bush Market. Don't tell me you can afford that with your little office in Newman Street and your Mr Bayliss-Callingham and his *expense account*.'

There was a moment or two's silence, while we contemplated the spectre of the little office in Newman Street and Rory's expense account. All this stirred powerful feelings of regret. I had lingered too long in L.A. with Tammy Girl, the Pankeys and Aunt Nance. Much longer and they would drag me down into the ooze. There, unquestionably, I would drown. The helicopter had all but disappeared into the horizon now but there was a long vapour trail uncoiling in its wake. Nearer at hand, a little puddle of Freddie's drink had spilled onto the marbled tabletop and a pair of wasps were gamely applying themselves to its rim. But the combination of amaretto, sloe gin and Southern Comfort – viscous and unyielding – was too much for them. In the end they unhooked their legs from the swamp into which they had fallen and flew wearily away.

'Talking of your Mr Bayliss-Callingham,' Freddie said languidly, 'I'm sure I've come across him in another life. Would he have been with some merchant bank we were told to put our money in? Did he sell Brian a house? Or Roger one of his ridiculous cars? But I do recall he was the kind of young man who could *hide behind a corkscrew*.'

Whatever reservations I had about Rory wouldn't be helped by getting Freddie to add to them. In any case, I was still annoyed at being told I was out of my league. Meanwhile, the butterflies seemed to have grown larger than ever. They could not possibly be real. As so often in this world of ten-minute sit-downs, exotic drinks and wild-goose chases it was time to be moving on.

'I wish you'd stay and keep me company,' Freddie said peevishly as I got to my feet. 'I've got absolutely nothing to do until this evening. We could have one hell of a time. We could go to the Whiskey and *tear the place apart*.'

'I thought you were supposed to be on tour?'

'Ten days' furlough, dear. We're reconvening in in – oh, I don't know – Cincinnati or somewhere in a week's time. Playing to a lot of *farm boys* and their *dates* I expect. But where is it you're off to?'

'Like I said. I'm after a band. Rory and I are meeting their manager.'

'The managers are so terribly *different* now, aren't they?' Freddie seemed unexpectedly wistful. The past – never something he took much interest in – had suddenly jumped up to claim him. 'Terribly up-to-date. In the old days they were all middle-aged oafs in peculiar trousers. Now they all seem to have gone to international business schools. What will he be like, I wonder?'

'He's called Rudi Martinez. I expect he goes back a bit.'

'Bound to, dear, with a name like that. Probably rescued Sinatra from the mob. But then we all go back a bit now. Do you know' – Freddie looked strangely animated, gripped by a sudden awareness of the world and the place he might be supposed to occupy in it – 'when we started out, in that little rehearsal room in Ealing – would you believe it, they actually sound-proofed the wall with egg-boxes? – I used to think we were so far ahead of the pack that they were barely visible. Just dust along the horizon. Right now, I've got a horrible suspicion that I'm simply running to keep up. In ten years' time I expect I'll be completely *passé*. Just a blighted *husk*, my dear, washed up on the lone, lorne shore for the tourists to stare at.'

It was past three o'clock now, and the Californian sun was rising to its zenith. Too hot to be sitting on a marbled terrace talking about blighted husks.

'The important thing,' Freddie said, aphoristic to the end, 'is to enjoy yourself while you can.'

* * *

The car-hire firm had come up with an ailing Maserati whose gearbox clanked. In this suspect equipage I descended slowly out of the hills and headed south into town. Here the L.A. tribes were in their usual ceaseless flight. Station wagons cruising slowly west along Santa Monica. Boulevard. Open-top convertibles filled with beach bunnies on their way to Malibu. Mysterious vehicles with sealed-up windows and tight-lipped security goons hunched furtively over the wheel. With three months of summer sun behind them, the girls looked honey-coloured, shading to caramel. All this reminded me of the tasks that had to be accomplished by nightfall: the phone call that had to be made to the office; the decision that had to be taken about the thus-far fruitless pursuit of the Flame Throwers; and the accommodation that had to be reached with Tammy Girl. Each of them in their various ways threatened trouble. On the radio Steely Dan had given way to a greengrocer talking about vegetable prices. A big stretch limousine with a woman who could have been Goldie Hawn lolling disdainfully in the back passed me at speed and went bounding off into the gasoline-clouded heat-haze. Santa Monica was turning into Westwood. Hollywood was turning into Holly-weird. Once again, out in the middle distance, the ground was beginning to rise. Set back from the road, beyond long, serpentine driveways, behind piled granite surrounds and three-metre high security palisades, white-painted mansions gleamed fatly in the sun. 'You can't miss it,' Rory had said. 'Just into Holmby Hills. If you get lost, look for the redwoods.' Rory was right. There was no missing it. The wrought-iron gates were wide open. Alongside them milled athletic but unsmiling flunkeys in tweed jackets bearing lofted clipboards ('Mr Nicholas, uh, Doo Pont? Could we have some identification sir?') WARNING declared a sign level with the Maserati's bonnet. YOUR VISIT MAY BE RECORDED OR TELEVISED. There were other cars parked up inside the gates: squat Studebakers and sparkling Cadillacs by whose rear wheels off-duty chauffeurs in striped shirts and sun-visors lounged about smoking stogies. Beyond them reared the statue of Aurora, Goddess of Dawn, and her bevy of attendant nymphs. I had read about this in the guidebooks: close up it had all the novelty of a Coke can or a cream cheese bagel. 'That's OK, sir. Please proceed,' said the meeter-and-greeter, dawdling back from his security fox hole with the Epsom and Ewell Constituency Labour Party membership card I had proffered as ID. And so, like Frodo before the Black Gate of Mordor, or Thorin Oakenshield and his retinue of dwarfs at the portals of Moria, I passed through the sweeping lawns of Playboy Mansion West and headed toward the brooding grey-stone palace whose very own demon king, Mr Hugh M. Hefner, I was assured, stood waiting to greet me.

* * *

'Now, you may think you know all about snobbery,' Rory said with an air of seriousness that sat uneasily with the porphyry grotto and its outsize cactus surround in which he was reclining, 'but let me tell you that your experience of it barely scratches the surface. For example, my father used to call Winston Churchill "the Harrovian."'

'To his face?'

'Don't be silly. And then there was the time he agreed to give a dinner for the local MFH. Absolutely basic affair. Not even the Lord Lieutenant invited. And he spent five minutes arguing over whether some girl who was the grand-daughter of an Earl should be taken in by a man who'd won a pretty decent MC at Anzio.'

Here at the back of the Playboy Mansion, the air of Tudor Gothic gone horribly wrong was a bit less oppressive. In fact, the assortment of mock-medieval towers, fanciful crenellations and bay windows with leaded glass looked like a rather successful joke. Who the joke was being played on was anybody's guess. It could not be the guests, who clearly accepted everything offered to them at face value. Just now there were about forty people in view. Some of them were swimming – noisily – in a meandering pool that wound here and there around the grottos, but there were takers for the tanks of koi carp, the stone bathrooms and an upland lawn, manicured to the last degree, where three or four llamas and a couple of peacocks quietly grazed.

'Someone told me Hefner's latest thing is backgammon,' Rory said. 'I've a jolly good mind to offer to give him a game.'

It occurred to me that Rory was perfectly at home in Hefnerland. He had cracked its codes, mastered its lore. If a naked cheerleader had clambered out of the pool and thrown herself on his lap he would have known exactly what to do.

'How did you manage to get us invited here?'

'Well, it's all rather odd. Apparently, when Hefner was last in London somebody took him to the Flyfishers. You know that little club above Brooks's? Anyway, he liked it so much he set up a reciprocal arrangement on the spot. I simply rang up and had us put on the guest-list.' A faint tremor of unease seemed to pass over Rory's regular, patrician features. 'Do you think I'm wearing the right sort of clothes?'

I inspected the Neapolitan ice-cream-patterned jacket and white canvas trousers which Rory had thought suitable for an afternoon party at Playboy Mansion West and then stole a glance down the hill, where the teeming Hefner-hordes were disporting themselves. Here withered old men in scarlet blazers that suggested Butlin's Redcoats lurked by the rim of the pool exchanging small talk while, over a sagging net, four girls in bikinis moving as if their legs were tied together at the knees with string were ineptly playing badminton. As a spectacle, all this was uncannily like the beginning of an *ensemble* piece in a Broadway musical. Any moment now, you felt, one of the withered old men would open his mouth and start to sing. The badminton players would start performing cartwheels as a file of waiters pranced in counterpoint behind them.

'I don't think anyone could have made a better effort to go native.'

The fact that Rory and I were sitting here sunning ourselves in Holmby Hills – or rather that Rory was wearing his school old boys' blazer and talking airily about the Flyfishers' Club – was another mark of how the music business had changed in the decade-and-a-half since I had first racketed through Dixie with the Helium Kids. There had been plenty of public schoolboys flitting around the

Chelsea boutiques and crowding out the record company boardrooms back in the Summer of Love, but in those days social advantages were something you kept quiet about. Now, obscurely, the tenor of the times – what poor, sea-horse-faced Florian used to call 'the mood of the moment' – had shifted up a notch. For some reason, the people we came across liked Rory, liked the fact that he had been to Charterhouse, that he had served in Ulster with the Blues and Royals and that his father owned so much of Perthshire that a day's hike wouldn't take you from one side of the estate to the other.

Reassured about his get-up, the heir to Inversnicket sat back on his haunches and peered – a bit suspiciously – down the slope. Socially, Rory was a wild card. Sometimes he complained that the people he met on his professional beat were too bohemian. At other times, he complained that they were not bohemian enough. Now, taking in the pool-side loungers, the sorority of the badminton court and a more exclusive group who sat at tables on the mansion's terrace with a sweep of his hand, he said:

'Of course, what we're witnessing here is the absolute last gasp of the nineteen-sixties. The final charred fragments scraped out of the crucible. I mean, fifteen years ago Hefner was hanging out with…' – cultural lodestars weren't Rory's strongpoint – '…Norman Mailer and Stokely Carmichael. Now, if I'm not mistaken, the principal ornament of the buffet bar down there is Robert Culp. It's all gone, all the bright colours and the pastel shades, and chasing the zeitgeist – although I very much doubt that Hef ever knew there was a zeitgeist there to chase in the first place. I mean, can you think of anything more *conservative* than the circumstances in which we find ourselves?'

I liked it when Rory was being oracular. It made other aspects of his character easier to bear. All the same, what he had said about the 1960s hinted at a range of cultural resources I hadn't previously associated him with. The bikini girls had given up even pretending to play badminton and were standing with their hands on their hips, as if they were about to begin on a round of physical jerks. Meanwhile, a small and unmistakeably Italian man in a cream-coloured suit, both hands plunged into his pockets, was labouring up the hill towards us, his keen glances at the groups of party-goers he passed indicating that he was looking for someone.

'Here comes Rudi,' Rory said in the same tones I remembered the Old Etonians at Pembroke College, Oxford using whenever a grammar school product such as me wandered hopefully into view.

'What do we know about him?'

'I ran some lines,' Rory said, as if his brigadier had just asked him about security clearance. 'Comes from Chicago, which is how he knows Hef. Actually, he did some surprisingly counter-cultural stuff back in the day. Used to co-manage Zappa at one time. Not to mention those women who used to take impressions of people's meat and two veg – the Plastercasters, would they have been called?'

I was used to Rory's career-encapsulations: a presentiment of doom would not be long in coming. 'Since then it's all been soul acts from Philadelphia. What my father would call 'n....r jazz'. How he came by the Flame Throwers I can't imagine.'

A memory of the incident on the Pankeys' sunlit verge, three days ago, suddenly broke upon the proceedings.

'What did you do with Stevie once you'd got him back in the car?'

'What anyone would have done,' Rory said stiffly, as if whole handbooks had been written about how to deal with musicians who fell out of convertibles onto the roadside in the mid-day sun. 'Told him to pull himself together and not to piss the seats. Then I took him back to the place where I'd picked him up, found some girl who seemed to know who he was and told her to look after him on pain of my serious displeasure...Why, Mr Martinez, how very good of you to look in.'

'Jesus,' Rudi Martinez said affably. 'I never seen so much skirt in one place.' Closer at hand, he looked more substantial than the figure seen labouring up the hill a few moments before, short, stout and a little out of breath, like one of those toys, weighted at the base, that spring back if pushed over. 'If my wife knew I was here she'd have a seizure. Seriously, fellers, don't go near any of the girls. Hef finds out, he goes fuckin' ballistic.'

Had Rudi ever managed the Plastercasters? It seemed unlikely that he would have been allowed to spend ten unrebuked minutes in their company, but you could never tell. One thing that seemed beyond doubt was that, beneath the bonhomie, lurked a deep-dyed melancholia, all of which boded well for the plans that Rory and I had for him.

'Hey,' Rudi said. The sweat stood out on his corrugated forehead in huge, raisin-sized blobs. 'Hear ya met fuckin' Stevie the other day?' Once again, there was a sense of feigned high spirits flickering up through a miasma of deep unease. A bright blue butterfly settled on his elbow and he goggled at it. 'How did that go?'

'Ah yes, Stevie,' Rory said. 'How's he right now?'

'How the fuck should I know? You think he calls me up every day to tell me how he is?' All trace of Rudi's good humour had disappeared. He seemed terminally out of sorts. 'Jesus, the guy could OD in a motel room and I'd be lucky if the concierge phoned a week later.' There was a silence for a moment, in which we contemplated the thought of fuckin' Stevie overdosed in a motel room somewhere. Then, suspecting that he might have gone too far, Rudi quietened down.

'You gentlemen want to know about the Flame Throwers? OK, I'll tell you. The good thing is, they ain't connected.'

'Connected to whom?'

Rudi threw a despairing glance down the hill to where the badminton players, two of whom had now removed their bikini tops, had started up again. 'There was a guy in New York the other month thought he was buying half of The Deaf Boys. Only, a week after the deal was signed he discovered forty per cent of them was owned by the Genovese and another forty per cent was owned by the Gambino. Figure that one out.'

'Let me get this clear,' Rory said, in a tone that any employee of Resurgam Records beneath the rank of A&R director would have known meant trouble. 'Are they signing to Geffen?'

'Yeah, they're signing to Geffen. Well, to be straight with you, they're signing to Geffen once I can get Joey to apologise to David Geffen.'

'Apologise for what?'

'Aw it ain't nothing,' Rudi said, like some medieval tyrant in whose dungeon the torturer has slightly exceeded his brief. 'Was just some interview where he said David was a f....t and could they take a shower together. It'll blow over.'

In Rudi's expression as he said this could be seen tantalising visions of the quarter-century he had spent in showbiz: suppers with the rat-pack in Atlantic City; ringside seats as Sinatra wowed Vegas; water-ski parties at Lake Tahoe; eyeing the hippy cavalcades at the Filmore West; nine-to-five and safe percentages. Nothing in this catalogue of Wholesome Post-war American Entertainment could have prepared him for the Flame Throwers. The wave had exploded over his head and left him washed up on the beach with the star-fish tangled in his hair. The worst of it was that this sense of isolation was contagious. Rory. Tamzin. Daphne. The old man's lost letter. What did any of them mean to me? In the end, I was on my own.

Back in Hefner-land, Rory the genteel assassin was moving in for the kill.

'Where are the boys right now?'

'Last I yeard they wuz in a studio with Bobbie Ezrin someplace.'

'That's not what his agent told me.' Rory was always conspicuously well-informed about music-biz to-ings and fro-ings. 'Where would they be if I wanted to talk to them?'

'How the fuck should I know? They got this place in Ticonderoga Street, up off the Boulevard, but they ain't always there...Listen,' Rudi volunteered, with the air of one offering futile encouragement to an exceptionally backward child. 'Next week they're playin' some dates in New York.'

'Where exactly?'

'The Mudd Club...CBGBs' Rudi said, who had clearly never set foot in either of these hip and happening places in his life. Later – much later – he would write a celebrated book called *Secret Agent Man*, which revealed him as a catspaw of the FBI hired to investigate racketeering in the entertainment industry. Just now, he was way out of his depth and he knew it.

'As it happens, my partner Mr Du Pont here, intends to be in New York City in a few days' time' Rory said courteously. 'He could quite easily attend one of these performances.'

'Yeah?' Rudi said meekly. 'That'd be swell.'

In the half-hour since we had arrived at the grotto, the sun had grown even hotter. The girls had put their tops back on, picked up their badminton kit and retreated into the shade. In their absence, the space had been filled with groups of sedately strolling middle-aged men in linen suits and semi-glamorous women with forearms the colour of goldenrod in elaborate supper dresses. From a boom-box on the terrace a little saccharine music drifted weakly up the hill.

'Let me tell you,' Rudi said mournfully, 'I once saw Sinatra telling Elvis Presley not to be an asshole. I wuz there in a parking lot in Vegas when the mob came after Sammy D. Audrey Hepburn once made me a cup of coffee and asked after my mother's sciatica. None of this amounts to a row a beans.'

'I think,' I said, 'coming from England, we don't see it in quite the same way.'

A moment or two later a grey-haired man with a cast-iron jaw dressed in what looked like a pair of silk pyjamas came out of the house and stood belligerently on the terrace as if inviting anyone who fancied his chances to come and take him on. A flunkey ran up with a bottle of Pepsi Cola on a tray and held it reverently before him. Catching sight of this apparition, Rudi cheered up a bit.

'You see,' he said, 'people who really know him don't call him Hef. They call him *Ner*.'

('Take my word for it, Martinez is desperate for anything he can get,' Rory had explained a couple of evenings ago. 'He can't wait to have those nasty boys off his hands and go back to seeing whether Gloria Gaynor will do a gospel album. It's even money that if we go in with something derisory he'll accept it out of sheer relief.')

'Now, look here, Mr Martinez,' Rory said, sounding more than ever like a public school master complaining about litter in the playground. 'This isn't at all satisfactory. So far, despite strenuous efforts to touch base, as I believe you Americans call it, our contact with your clients has been limited to a single meeting with one of them in which he passed out cold in the back of my car. There's no guarantee they even exist, much less that they'll ever record anything. We'll give you fifty thousand for anything they manage to put out on Geffen. Fifty thousand dollars, that is. But naturally you'll have to indemnify us.'

The badminton girls had come scampering up to Hefner rather in the manner of Nausicaa and her handmaidens approaching Odysseus on the beach, but he waved them away.

'Indemnify ya for what exactly?'

'That the record's fit for radio play, for one thing. That they tour to support it, for another. I'll be frank, Mr Martinez, we're not used to these...' – he paused for a moment, trying to find some phrase that would do justice to the sheer enormity of the Flame Throwers and the deeply questionable nature of what they proposed to offer the public, and came out with '...*white punks on dope*, and we want to make sure we get our money back.'

The torrent of precise, elegant expostulation flowed on. This was another way in which the world of music had changed: nobody in the Sixties, a decade of brusque demands and mute acceptance, could ever have come up with anything like this. Don Shard would have hospitalised anyone who had talked to him this way. Occasionally, individual phrases gleamed for a moment out of the boiling surf: '...medical certificates probably required...necessity for third-party insurance... death or self-inflicted injury clause...boilerplate contract *definitely* inadvisable...' Rudi, who already looked horror-stricken, could make of this what he would. Twenty yards away, Hef, or Ner, had subsided into a cane-backed chair while one of Nausicaa's handmaidens whispered something in his meaty ear. It was at moments like this that I realised why I could stand to work with Rory, whose father owned an eighth of Perthshire and who had once kept Richard Branson silent for half-an-hour in his chair while he talked about collateralised European subsidiary rights. Meantime, late-afternoon stasis was settling on Hefner-land. The blue butterflies had flown away. Far above our heads, in the cerulean sky, there were great white birds drifting in the currents. If I went to New York to catch the Flame Throwers at the Mudd Club or CBGBs, or wherever they happened to be playing, I would root out Daphne in her lair. It was as simple – or as complicated – as that.

'Have we got fifty thousand dollars to give him?' I asked, ten minutes later, as Rudi's squat and perspiring figure receded down the hill.

'If we haven't, I'm sure Virgin will give it to us,' Rory said. 'You know what suckers they always are for the next big thing. Look, you'd better have this.' He reached into the inner pocket of his multi-coloured jacket and fished out a C-30 cassette that someone had wedged into a slip-case of vermilion cardboard.

'What's that?'

'*Songs to Forget*. There's only a dozen of them in existence, I believe. I doubt even Rudi knows about it. Self-produced on some eight-track out in Topanga Canyon, I believe.'

'Have you listened to it?'

'I'm your financial adviser,' Rory said. 'Not your A&R man. Yours to decide. Are you really going to New York?'

'It'll make a nice change. I wonder if I should tell Tamzin.'

'I'm afraid,' Rory said, with the ghost of a smile, 'that I let that particular cat out of the bag the other night.'

Next big things. Self-produced cassette tapes from Topanga Canyon. Tammy Girl and Daphne in her bunker. Once again, time was moving on.

'What are you going to do now?'

'First of all I think I'm going to exchange a few words with our host here. Then I might go to the Beverley Hills Country Club to see a friend of my father's who has some sort of vineyard in Napa.' It was characteristic of Rory that he didn't ask me what I intended to do.

'Will Hefner know who you are?'

'I don't suppose he knows who anyone is much.'

We set off down the hill, Rory's elaborately-patterned brogues making huge indentations in the over-manicured grass. Any doubts that Rory might fail to reach his objective were instantly dispelled. Within the blink of an eye, the bright buttons of his blazer flashing in the sun, he had displaced a bikini-girl or two, finessed a newly-charged glass of champagne, penetrated Hefner's inner circle and was shaking his hand. Hef, swivelling anxiously in his chair, looked suddenly like some gaunt, seed-eating bird raising its bill in the expectation of a treat. Round at the front of the house, all was quiet. The party could have been taking place several miles away. A couple of refrigerator men were bringing in a block of ice shaped like a giant female torso and there were gardeners picking up what looked like pieces of confetti out of the gravel. All this suggested that the Mansion had a more prosaic side: come midnight the girls would all be in their dormitories, chastely bedded down in pyjamas and white nighties and drinking cocoa, needles poised over their embroidery samplers. Down by the main gate the frowning meeters-and-greeters and their clipboards had all disappeared, but the Maserati, prised from its parking spot, turned out to have a gift-bag dumped on its bonnet. Inside lay two Playboy match-books, a garter belt for the special person in my life, a cerise-coloured triangle that advertised itself as a pair of edible panties and a greetings card bearing the wavery signature of Hugh M. Hefner. Up here in the hills there was still a blaze of sunshine hanging over down-town Hollywood, but the heat was falling out of the day. Over in Malibu – elsewhere too – the beach bunnies would be feeling the chill.

The Chateau Marmont was sunk in early-evening torpor. The staff at the reception desk had all gone away, but in their absence a man who looked uncomfortably like Dan Aykroyd had pulled out one of the telephones and was conducting a conversation that consisted of him saying 'No shit?' at thirty-second intervals. It was no better back in my room, where each footstep seemed to displace little clouds of dust from the carpet and the late-afternoon sunshine, reflected off a glass paperweight, had burned a hole in one of the pillow-cases. It was 7.30 now, too early, experience counselled, to try room service, not late enough to phone the office in Newman Street. And so time passed, in the way it used to do in those days in West Coast hotel rooms, eating pizza, watching retard TV, hearing the buzz of the insects, reading the *New Yorker*, staring at the light as it faded over a landscape of back-lots, neon motel signs and deserted swim-pools, and – sometime in the small hours – waiting for Hermione, of all Resurgam's employees, the one most likely to reach her desk at an early hour to pick up the phone. Finally, after what seemed like an eternity of waiting, a brisk upper-class voice cut through the static like a klaxon.

'Yes? What do you want?'

The Resurgam reception staff were always told not to stand on ceremony.

'It's Nick, Hermione. What's the news?'

'Let's see... "Girl on the Phone" went in at 29 with that single nobody liked, but there's been a row about the pressing plant not being able to keep up. Terry says he thinks he can fix it and you're not to worry. Chloe and the Cupcakes were supposed to be doing the *Whistle Test*, but apparently the drummer's disappeared again. Oh, and Paper Plane's manager was in the office on Friday and he says they've definitely split.'

'Did they finish the album?'

'The man at Good Earth said they cancelled the sessions half-way through. The bill's just come in this morning.'

'*Jesus.*'

'I don't think there's any need for that kind of language.' Hermione was a pious girl, who had been to St Mary's Convent, Ascot and lived modestly with her parents in Cheam.

'I'm sorry. You're quite right. Anything from the bank?'

'Terry says you're not to worry. What on earth have you been up to?'

It was a fair question. I explained about the afternoon at Playboy Mansion West, Rudi Martinez and the Flame Throwers, the trip to New York. Outside on the bungalow's darkling lawn the shadows welled up out of the shrubbery like black ink and there were owls hooting. Hermione perked up a bit.

'We've been reading about them in *NME*. Isn't the bass player in prison?'

'Not when I last saw him. Anything else I should know?'

'Terry says not to worry, but it really would be awfully helpful if you were back next week.'

It was nice that people didn't want me to worry.

'How are your parents?'

'Mummy's very well, thank you. Daddy says he thinks Mrs Thatcher ought to start taking a firm hand.'

'I'm sure he's right.'

Just now the world was full of people who needed to take a firm hand, countless others with whom a firm hand needed to be taken.

Rudi needed to take one with the Flame Throwers. I needed to take one with Tamzin. With Rory, if it came to that. The cassette tape Rory had given me lay on the bedcovers, incongruous against the blue poplin and its crossover stitch. To listen to it would require technological resources I did not yet possess.

Room service answered on the twenty-third ring.

'Hey there. You want any speed?'

'Actually I want to borrow a cassette player. Is there one at the desk?'

As well as maintaining a relaxed attitude to drugs and the law enforcement agencies, the Marmont also specialised in high-end paraphernalia of interest to those involved in the entertainment industry.

'You got it. Leastways, if that fuckpig Dwayne ain't stole it again. Oh yeah, and a Miss – ah – Pankey bin calling you.'

They were always very matter-of-fact at the Marmont. Matter-of-fact and leisurely with it. Twenty minutes later, a Puerto Rican boy knocked at the door, gave me a nod in which all the miseries inflicted on his race in the past century-and-a-half were transparently gathered up and set about further sticking it to Whitey by up-ending a vintage cassette machine about four feet square onto the sofa. I gave him a five-dollar bill, considered asking for change, thought better of it, closed the door behind him and slammed the cassette into the deck.

Two years into running a record company, I was still keen on the freedom to discriminate that the job allowed. As a publicist, naturally, all values were relative. The artefact put before you by a label boss was the greatest single that anyone had ever crammed into three minutes of vinyl and that was that. Now life consisted of a series of micro-judgments. Over the past two years, for example, I had discovered that I disliked, in no particular order, Kate Bush, reggae, power pop, Mod revivalists and what was fast becoming known as the New Wave of British Heavy Metal. Not, of course, that having formed these judgments you possessed the freedom to act on them. This was not how popular music worked, and the Resurgam roster, nicely calibrated to what the young people out there were supposed to be listening to, already harboured pixy-ish girls who sounded like Kate Bush's younger sister and a reggae band from Coventry called the Dub Imposters. What you did possess, on the other hand, was the liberty to put the Dub Imposters' first album, *Pickney Chorus* – sales 30,000 and rising – on the turntable and silently acknowledge that it was garbage.

Songs to Forget began inauspiciously with a couple of cymbal smashes, what sounded like a microphone stand being kicked over and a male voice loudly demanding that those present fuckin' get it together. But soon, as so often happened, the air of amateurishness became a positive virtue. You could just tell that it had been recorded in some dead-end studio out in the desert with the engineer half-asleep at the desk, the repo man hastening up the drive and the view out of the window a matter of pale sky and encroaching cacti, and mixed by someone who barely knew whether to turn the faders up or down. 'Pinball Woman' was a halfway-hysterical banshee's put-down of someone who had not only made the mistake of trifling with the singer's affections but compounded the offence by being, as my mother would have said, no better than she should be ('ricocheting around/fucking every guy in town.') 'Back on the Brown', on the other hand, was a high-octane shuffle through the narcotic end of the pharmacopoeia ('Peyote won't ever ease my frown/No sir, I'm back on the brown') that would certainly not get played on any radio station on either side of the Atlantic.

Then came 'Mole Rothman's Blues' – simply verse-chorus/verse-chorus and two or three smashed down minor guitar chords to finish – which appeared to have something to do with nicotine addiction. Finally there was an unutterably bizarre number, longer and slower than the rest, called 'Nazi Surf Punks Must Die' which ended with the singer dolefully intoning the words 'Nazi surf punks must die/I don't know why/Just let them die.' All over in a bare thirteen minutes, apart from some long squeals of feedback that trailed off into and were ultimately extinguished by what sounded like the beginnings of a prison riot but was doubtless just the boys horsing around while the engineer made sure his wallet was still in his jacket and the succulents encroached a little further. When it was over I played it again, with a little more circumspection, noting that whoever had contributed backing vocals to 'Back on the Brown' was clearly tone-deaf and that whoever had laid down the bass part on 'Pinball Woman' had omitted to tune the instrument before he set out. After that I lay back in my chair experiencing, or so it seemed, the same feeling that had afflicted me when I first heard *Revolver* or *Ogden's Nut-Gone Flake* or, to narrow the aesthetic focus a little, the MC5's *Kick Out the Jams*. Which was to say that one was in the presence of something altogether beyond the usual run of things, out there in a world of its own, edgy, rare and inimitable, out of which – you had to be practical about these things – a great deal of money could be made.

Back at the reception desk, onto whose polished surface I slid the cassette player twenty minutes later, the world seemed to be running at quarter-speed. The man who looked like Dan Aykroyd had gone away, but the Puerto Rican kid – confidential now and authoritative, and apparently on exceptionally familiar terms with the opposite sex – was telling a dull-eyed fellow-worker that he knew this fox called Mindy who'd take it up the ass, no question. Outside, on the brightly illuminated forecourt, where bats flicked back and forth beneath the sodium glare, with infinite slowness, a taxi drew up and began to disgorge expensive-looking suitcases onto the kerb. It was about 2.30 a.m. In Newman Street they would be unpacking the morning's collection of demo tapes and going through the music papers. At the Playboy Mansion the party would be winding down and Hef's night secretary making herself a cup of tea. Back on Santa Monica Boulevard the Flame Throwers would be out of their heads on fast white powders. It was an odd kind of world I had fetched up in. And then, in one of those conceptual twists to which the artificial landscapes I wandered in were so chronically prone, everything suddenly speeded up. The phone on the reception desk began to ring. Fearing that he might have spoken lightly of a woman's name, the Puerto Rican kid conceded that Mindy was a really nice girl when you got to know her. The lobby door swung violently open and, dressed in a white trouser-suit, lavender-dye waistcoat and stack-heeled gold lamé boots, the owner of the suitcases hobbled in. It was Tamzin. All in an instant the bright, primary-coloured world of the Flame Throwers spun away, the human voices woke me and I drowned.

4. NEW YORK JOURNAL, SEPTEMBER 1980

10 September

LAX for the midday flight to New York. Q: Who wants to travel from California to the Eastern Seaboard? A: Movie people (Tamzin gets several nods from Pankey-*convives* as we stroll over the tarmac). Music people. Blazer and sports slacks-clad junior execs from the fledgling technology companies and the real estate combines. And then all those odd, nondescript camp-followers who take up so much space in any transit across modern America: surfer dudes with fishing lure ear-jewellery hunched over skateboards; big, bronzed, bangled ladies in spreading sun-hats who could be any age between thirty and sixty. Deep down in Departures we come across a vast, dropsical woman standing exhaustedly by the elevator, trying to decide between its opening doors and the staircase that winds up alongside it as a diminutive friend offers encouragement. 'C'mon Bets,' coaxes the friend. 'It's only mezzanine.' The fat woman shakes her head in despair. 'I reckon, uh, *not*.' Here at the airport Pankey-magic has been at work, and my own ticket has been mysteriously upgraded to a roost next to Tamzin in Business. At check-in comes a moment – the sixth such encounter in the past three weeks – when the assistant, straightening up from a wrestle with a suitcase tag, widens the focus of her eyes and says, 'Oh my God. You're Tammy-Girl.' Tamzin nods her head, but with a touch less enthusiasm than on the past five occasions, conveying to me, if not to anyone else, that she is a woman with an audition awaiting her at *Saturday Night Live* – this was the reason for her late-night arrival at the Marmont. In a day or so's time she will be hobnobbing with Gilda Radner, Bill Murray and Eddie Murphy. The future is calling, and the past can look after itself.

'Jesus, why don't they get a move on?' Tamzin sighs from the regal comfort of her seat. The movie people and the music people are unfolding copies of the *L.A. Times*, with its pictures of smiling, unflappable Ron and his sinister running-mate, Big George. But there is something wrong here that the vision of Gilda Radner and Bill Murray cannot displace. 'Who exactly called you?' I ask, not having got the precise details of yesterday afternoon's invitation clear in my head. 'Just some junior executive,' Tamzin says, who shares the parental contempt for anyone who doesn't actually kick ass, commission stuff and make $100,000 a year. She has dressed down for the flight: bolero jacket; discreet blouse; designer jeans. The ringlets on the upper slopes of her hair-do make her look like a slightly less away-with-the-fairies version of Stevie Nicks.

Still, though, there is something amiss. Twenty minutes into the flight she gets into a rabid argument with one of the stewardesses. A chunk of ice too many in the vodka-tonic or a chunk too few? Who knows? The Delta stewardesses are flint-eyed super-vixens whose disinclination to take any shit is written into their contracts, but this one is sufficiently abashed by whatever Tamzin mutters to her, in one of those ladylike put-downs that only the ladies involved can hear, to go scuttling back to her serving hutch with everyone else's orders unfulfilled. Finding her there a moment or so later, slamming down Styrofoam lids onto a row of coffee cups as if each one contains some sportive gopher desperate to get out and start leaping around the place, I catch her eye. 'I'm really sorry about my friend. I think she's rather nervous.' 'I appreciate your concern, sir,' the stewardess says, yet more embarrassed by having her original embarrassment drawn attention to, and we stare at each other, an *habituée* of the Land of the Free and a passage migrant, each transfixed and shamed by its incivilities and the jagged behavioural surfaces that no one seems able to sand down.

'Are you OK?' I enquire, returning to my seat to discover that Tamzin has already downed the plastic tumbler of vodka with its insufficient, or over-sufficient ice tally. 'Sure I'm OK.' The row with the stewardess has released some kind of tension within her. 'Jesus,' she says. 'My dad is such an asshole sometimes.' I forbear to tell her that her dad is an asshole *always*. Then I think of Big Earle back in the mansion at Pacific Palisades, bawling out Code or feeding his tanks of tropical fish. There is comfort in the fact that we are not there to see him do it. 'Jesus' she says again. 'Could you get me some peanuts, honey?' I get her a packet of peanuts, which she feeds into her mouth one by one, like some thrifty creature of the field anxious not to be seen splurging on nature's bounty. Far beneath us Middle America is going by: deserts and plains and mountains, motorcities and rubbish dumps, freeways and lakes and long green orchards. Coming into New York four hours later, I stare interestedly at the sprawl of houses, the geometric patterning of the arterial roads, and remember the time, ten years back, when I lived in the timber-frame house in Westchester, Connecticut with Rosalind, and of all the extraordinary things that went down there, and what a very, very long time ago it seems.

11 September

Staying at the Chelsea Hotel on West 23rd. Serious mistake, as the place reeks of self-conscious bohemianism; always the worst kind. Bell-hops, staff on the desk, maids cleaning the room aflame with the vanity of the artist's model. All the usual celebrity guests still proudly in residence – the 100 year-old artist whose name I can't remember – together with some new ones. The old glam star Jobriath supposed to be holed up in the pyramid apartment in the roof, though no one ever sets eyes on him. Still, there is a mild interest in inhabiting Room 207 – two doors down, the porter assures us, from the suite in which Sid Vicious did for Nancy Spungen a couple of years back.

Tamzin, I notice, in two minds about the Chelsea: impressed by the air of counter-cultural legend, while unforgiving of the sleaze. Draws my attention to the track-marks on the breakfast waiter's forearm ('That is so gross') and the stink of marijuana in the stairwell. Coming down to the lobby this morning, we share the elevator with a very old woman in a chinchilla fur-coat – the temperature outside is in the 80s – with a pack of pugs on a leash, and an albino midget half-collapsed beneath a double-bass.

For a girl with a *Saturday Night Live* audition in prospect, Tamzin is curiously subdued. Seems to have no idea what might be expected of her. Spends hours exchanging one set of clothes for another, putting on her make-up etc. The stack of phone messages from Earle is hourly renewed: no idea if she answers them. Mysteriously, she seems to have hardly any money. 'Hey,' she says this morning as the track-marked forearm recedes out of view and a ballet troupe who have omitted to change since last night's engagement are ushered to their table, 'can you lend me $100?' Dutifully, I pay up.

Newspapers full of pictures of Jimmy Carter looking hangdog and wistful. Reagan, on the other hand, full of bounce. No one seems to think that Georgia's finest stands a chance. Seeing one of the Reagan photo-spreads, Tamzin says, 'Do you know, when I was a kid I used to call him 'Uncle Ronnie' and he used to call me 'Tammy-Whammy'?'

12 September

Another scorching day. Over to Rudi's office in the Sixties. Walls full of pictures of Sinatra, Sammy Davis Jr, Dean Martin. Also a colour portrait of Frank Zappa and the Mothers in drag. Rudi ('I'm afraid

Mr Martinez is not presently available') still in L.A. or Vegas. Instead, a hip young associate called Marty McGuire updates me on 'the situation'. The situation is that the boys are booked into CBGBs tomorrow, but there is a chance, probability put at slight to infinitesimal, that they may be taking to the stage of Max's Kansas City tonight to play a few numbers after the head-lining band have finished their set. As for their precise whereabouts, Cris, Joey, Stevie and Art are supposed to be staying at a hotel on East 47th Street. 'But, you know,' Marty says, unzipping a seventh sachet of Sweet 'n' Low and dumping it into his coffee, 'I wouldn't go there unless I absolutely had to.'

All this prompts me to ask him what he thinks of the Flame Throwers, their music and the prospects that lie before them. Here Marty turns unexpectedly enthusiastic. 'Yeah, I heard the tape and it blew me away. I mean, they sound like the early Stooges, or, I don't know, the Groovies back in the day. If it was me, I'd sign them on the spot, but there are, you know, *personal* issues. I guess they ain't too, uh, respectful, and Mr Martinez, he notices things like that.'

It turns out that though the Geffen deal is going through, with Ezrin lined up to produce, Polydor has lost interest and the UK rights are open to offers. For this, however, Rudi will need the band's say-so ('I mean, he OK'd a publishing deal the other day without running the contract past them and the Itol guy went fuckin' crazy.')

Marty, who must be about 30, keenly aware of what he calls the 'new music.' Says he nearly managed to get Martinez & Associates to represent the Ramones, only for Rudi to nix the deal at the last moment ('Mr Martinez don't like these leather boys.') 'Hey,' he says, as I stand taking my leave in the foyer, 'didn't you used to PR the Helium Kids? I saw them once. They were out of sight.'

Later. Tamzin back from NBC. 'How did you get on?' I ask. 'OK I guess,' she says. 'I read some stuff and then improved a sketch with Eddie Murphy.' 'What's he like?' 'OK I guess,' she says listlessly. 'For a black guy.' This is all I can get out of her. Find myself wondering what the other American girls of my acquaintance would have made of her. Rosalind, I think, would have appreciated the show-biz trappings while pitying her as one whose personality had been squashed by the juggernaut of an all-too transient fame. Angie, I am pretty confident, would simply have laid her out in the gutter. Predictably, all this awakens powerful feelings of nostalgia: Angie in the bedroom of the rented house in Mulholland Drive with the tiger tattoo disappearing into the rind of her buttocks; Angie on the phone to her cats, Jimi and Donovan; Angie doing hundred-dollar mid-flight deals with an insufficiently medicated Stefano for vials of Librium. So much so that I look out a New York City telephone directory – it's been eight years since I last set eyes on her – find a Mrs Shirley Pippalow – that would be her mother – still living at the address in Yonkers, only to discover that the line has been disconnected.

After dinner at a restaurant on Eighth Street – Tamzin eats next to nothing – I take a cab to Max's Kansas City on Park Avenue South. Mink Deville headlining, supported by the Bush Tetras. Naturally the boys don't show, but at the bar I bump into Lou Reed, not seen for half-a-dozen years, but about whose last live album – I get this from Marty – everybody is apparently still talking ('I mean, most of the time he ain't even playing the songs, just telling the audience where they can shove it.') Lou, filled in on my mission to sign the Flame Throwers, is unimpressed ('I don't listen to those shitty Californian bands.'). The New York rock cognoscenti, I notice, are always like this about anything not hatched on the Eastern seaboard. Eventually he goes off to 'buy some speed'. 'How's Andy?' I ask as a passing shot. 'Andy who?' Lou wonders sarkily as he staggers off into the night.

13 September

To the Flame Throwers' hotel on East 47th, stuck between two porno cinemas, one of which is the old Lyceum Theatre. Find the band in the foyer, breakfasting or brunching – it is barely 10 a.m. – off a couple of boxes of KFC. Close up they seem smaller, frailer and paler than I expected. The leather jackets and the lacquered pompadour hairdos make them look like a gaggle of jackdaws. Surly, laconic, but, to my relief, pleased to see me. Do they like the hotel? 'It's OK,' one of them says. 'We ain't never stayed in a hotel before,' another one glosses. Are they, as Marty and before him Rudi indicated, signing to Geffen? Heads nod and the corvine quiffs wag up and down. 'Sure. Had some, uh, notary out here yesterday.' Why didn't they play Max's the previous night? 'Cuz we heard Lou Reed was there. And we fucking hate Lou Reed.' By this time, and for all the identikit threads, I am beginning to take the measure of the four individual personalities on display. Cris, it quickly becomes clear, is the bandleader-cum-spokesman, word not exactly law but to be disregarded at your peril. Joey, who has a guitar in his hand and practises chords the whole time, is the closest the outfit has to a muso. Stevie, the bass player, is either Cris's foil or his whipping-boy, or the age-old friend he can't quite discard despite mounting evidence of his unsuitability, or maybe a bizarre combination of all three, and is, in addition, sporting a black eye after the two of them squared up to each other a night or two back ('Yeah, we're always fighting. Do it all the fucking time.') Drummer Art is so taciturn as to suggest mental impairment, a theme on which the others frequently dilate ('He's so quiet, man, it's like he's not fucking there, you know what I mean?') Collectively, they display a talent for sardonic, tag-along humour, as if the Beatles had come from L.A. instead of Liverpool and decided that they all hated each other. The tension bred by having all four of them in the room at the same time occasionally releases itself in bouts of jostling or mock-duels with cigarettes. Stevie gets one of these in the face, courtesy of Joey. It doesn't seem to bother him in the least. Are they happy to sign with Resurgam? 'Man,' Cris returns, 'we'll sign for anyone who'll put our fuckin' records out in England.'

Joey puzzling over a sheet of foolscap which he more than once turns over in a stricken hand. This turns out to be a letter from a fan, delivered by motor-cycle messenger to the hotel earlier that morning. Among other urgent demands it canvasses the necessity of a race war in which, the writer is pretty sure, the Flame Throwers will want to take part. 'Yeah, we get a lotta stuff like this. Some of those kids are total nut-jobs, real sick fucks. Was this guy the cops busted in Orange County or someplace the other month. Hadda Kalashnikov rifle and 17 unlicensed hand guns stashed in his apartment. And he's, like, only our biggest fan, y'know. Got a dozen tickets from our gigs taped to the wall. I'm telling you man, I ain't responsible for any of this. Cris and me, we just write the stuff, y'know, we just write the stuff and we ain't responsible…'

* * *

Conversation at lunch.

SELF :	How did it go this morning?
TAMZIN :	It went fine.
SELF :	What's Bill Murray like?
TAMZIN :	He's a nice guy. He remembered me from *Tammy Girl.*

Apparently there is another audition booked at NBC tomorrow. After the meal she asks for an extra $50. I dutifully hand it over. Outside the plane trees are moulting in the heat. The skateboarding boys in the park have given up and sprawl in the shade swigging cans of Pepsi Phone call from Trevor in Newman Street: when will I be back? 48 hours I tell him. Time enough for the Flame Throwers, for Tammy to finish at Rockefeller Plaza and the other, more personal, business I have on hand.

* * *

Afternoon. To Staten Island on the ferry. Gulls skirmish in the wash. Heat-haze hangs over the city. As ever, struck by the paraphernalia the passengers bring with them: three college students manhandling an upright piano; old lady with a lemur in a cage; black kids shuffling round a beat box. Daphne's apartment is up on Todt Hill, on the top floor of a block overlooking a breaker's yard. 'I knew ya'd come,' she says, when the last of the half-dozen door-bolts have been laboriously shot back. 'Hey,' she says, regarding me critically. 'Ya ain't changed or nuttin'.' Daphne, on the other hand, looks ancient as the hills. Her hair, which once had an incriminating orange tint, is the texture of seaweed. If the old man had lived he would have been 68, so that puts her in early seventies. 'Look at me' she says, catching a hint of this calculation. 'Ain't I a wreck?' The apartment is tiny and stuffed to the gills with junk: years-old copies of the *New York Post* in a teetering pile; a ziggurat of Plastiware boxes ('I wunnem in a competition. Ain't had no use for them yet.') On the mantelpiece there are mysterious postcards: Alaskan snow-scenes; Galapagos tortoises; the Yangtse River in spate. 'It ain't much of a place,' Daphne says. A suspicion that she means the locale, not the apartment is confirmed when she adds: 'Eye-talians is all over.' 'What happened to the house in Ridgewood?' I ask, remembering the snow-bound visit I paid there a decade-and-a-half ago, the same week I first met the Helium Kids. 'Sold it when we went to Oregon,' Daphne says. 'What did ya expect?' She makes coffee in old Democrat convention souvenir mugs: one of them has Bobbie Kennedy on the side; the other Eugene McCarthy. McCarthy looks horribly chastened: he knows he hasn't a chance. A fan, rasping at her elbow, barely disturbs the stale air.

Back in her arm-chair, wedged between a dozen gilt-bound volumes of *A History of the Prairie States* and a miniature grandfather clock with a fractured dial, Daphne grows confidential. 'I got these here for ya' she says, handing over a buff envelope marked with the logo of the New York State Social Security Department. The grandfather clock – one of several substantial timepieces strewn around the room – ticks remorselessly. Inside the envelope are three photographs. In one of them the Old Man, dressed in his USAF uniform, is lounging outside the Adam and Eve pub on the edge of Norwich Cathedral Close. In the second he and my mother are captured in the act of boarding a bus outside Jarrold's department store. In the third, which looks as if it was taken at the House of Peace, Love and Serenity in Oregon, a much older version of him stands in a clearing making a great show of splitting a log with an axe. His face looks puzzled, fallen in on itself, but still game. Death isn't far away. All this – the heat of the room, the tick of the clock, the seaweed hair, the Old Man hewing logs in hippy-land – is a bit too much to be borne.

'What was it like in Oregon?' I ask. From the depths of her armchair, Daphne stirs, still troubled by the memory of log cabins, pine woods, pasta hoards and the blissed-out girls singing 'Puff the Magic Dragon'. 'Now, Maurice, he really liked it' she says judiciously. 'Said it was the best place he ever fetched up. Me, I figured the guy that ran it was a creep, not to mention some of the women they got there being three-quarters crazy. Hey,' she says. 'I'm seventy-five this fall. And the Federal Government don't do nothing. You want another cup of *corfee*?' She pronounces it like Dustin Hoffmann in *Midnight Cowboy*. Maybe Jon Voight is hiding in the closet in his buckskin jacket waiting for the chance to jump out and ask me for directions to the Statue of Liberty. Who can tell? I have another cup of coffee in a saucer bearing traces of cat fur, although there is no sign of any cat. The sun burns off the window-panes, the fan rustles the top-most copy of the *New York Post*, and I am back at the House of Peace, Love and Serenity with the boat carrying the Old Man's corpse bursting into flames as it drifts out to sea and the hippy girls holding their knuckles to their mouths in astonishment.

'Hey,' says Daphne. 'Ya want me to tell ya fortune?' This has happened before, back in the timber-frame house in Ridgewood,

Queens, with the Old Man urging her on and the sound of the rats running through the roof. 'OK,' I say, 'tell my fortune.' I wonder if, over the intervening 16 years, Daphne has refined her technique, moved on to Tarot, or sortilege or haruspication, say, but no, out comes the same pack of greasy playing cards ("There's maybe a few missing. It ain't no big thing') each dealt out with the same paralysing indifference. Fate clearly means nothing to Daphne. She is just there to pronounce on it. Several nondescript items are followed by the Queen of Clubs and the Jack of Diamonds. These Daphne carefully considers. 'Ya been doing well for yaself,' she says. 'Anyone can see that. But ya need to take care.' I promise her I will take care. 'Ya know what ya want but ya don't know how to get it,' Daphne drones on. 'Sometime soon ya gonna meet a woman. She'll have power over ya. Ya might not notice it, but she will. And there's a guy ya need to look out for.' 'What do I need to look out for?' 'How the hell do I know?' Daphne returns. 'This ain't the meteorological forecast. I'm just telling ya what the cards say. Jesus fuck,' – this as a six, seven and eight of clubs flutter down in quick succession – 'No, hey, it's OK. Ya gonna have a lot of opportunities. Some of them ya'll take, others ya won't. But like I said, ya'll need to take care.' Somehow, this time round, without the Old Man there to laugh, comment and elucidate, the prophecies seem much more sinister. 'Ya think too much' Daphne concludes, as the final card – the Ace of Hearts – lands on the pile. 'Ya need to act more. Cut to chase.' 'Did you ever tell my father's fortune?' 'Sure I did. Plenty of times.' Gathering up the cards, Daphne looks exactly what she is: a little old bohemian lady with seaweed hair and a future that doesn't bear going into. 'Did it work out?' Daphne bridles. 'Well, I told him he was gonna die, didn't I?'

The grandfather clock has wound round to 4.45. The Flame Throwers will be hitting the stage at CBGBs in approximately three and three-quarter hours. Plus I have to phone Newman Street and look at some paperwork Trevor is faxing across. At the door, Daphne hands me a beige-coloured exercise book tied up with string with a picture of Dwight Eisenhower sheared out of a magazine taped to the cover. The fingers of her right hand are tawny-brown with cigarette smoke. 'There's this too.' Having no idea of what the package contains (necromancer's spells? Shipping forecasts? Profit and loss accounts?) I stow it away in my jacket pocket. 'Hey,' she says again, 'who d'ya think'll win? Carter or Reagan? I kind of like Reagan.' 'My father wouldn't have.' 'Maybe not,' she allows. 'But he ain't here to advise.' I thread my way back down Todt Hill, past the breaker's yard and the melancholy asphalt basketball pitches where no children play. On the Staten Island ferry the cars are packed bumper to bumper and there is a troop of girl scouts carrying a bell tent. The twine-tied exercise book sinks in my jacket pocket like a stone.

* * *

Tamzin leaves a note saying she is off to the theatre with an actress friend and will be back late. I take a cab down to the East Village. CBGB's unchanged since I was last there five years ago. The same grimy awning hanging over the sidewalk. The same Rayband-toting guys in scuffed jeans and sneakers who are very probably members of Suicide or Handsome Dick Manitoba and the Dictators travelling incognito. The same early '70s promo photos of Big Star and the Flaming Groovies on the mouldering walls. The same doorless elevator, which nearly takes someone's leg off as it swings down. The place is only three-quarters full. On the other hand, there is a definite buzz, which the boys – whose collective psychology I am now beginning to appreciate – do their best to dispel. Arriving on stage 40 minutes late, they spend most of the first two numbers abusing the audience. Cris, in particular, seems to have modelled himself on Garth Dangerfield, who practised the self-same trick in the amphitheatres of the mid-west: 'We're, uh, rilly pleased to be here, [*smirk*] cuz we know you kids are rilly where it's at [*sneer*]...and, like, New York is just so fuckin' *far out* [*yawn*].' Naturally, none of this goes down at all well and there are thrown beer-cans, which the band obligingly throw back. After that, though, they get down to the serious business of breezing through *Songs to Forget* and some extra material which didn't make it onto the cassette.

What do I think? I think that not only can they actually play, but that the hell-for-leather quality of the performance – Cris counts every song in with a strident '1-2-3-4' – compensates for such technical deficiencies as Stevie being able to pick out only the most rudimentary bass lines and Art – eyes fixed on the ceiling throughout – being ever so slightly ahead of, or on occasion ever so slightly behind the other three. By about half-way through any doubts the audience may have about their out-of-town unsuitability are resolved, and there are tough, heavy kids jumping on the stage to slam-dance like rorting hobgoblins and macaw-haired girls throwing paper napkins with their phone numbers scrawled on them in the direction of the drum-risers. Stevie seizes a fistful of these and stuffs them in the pocket of his jeans. Backstage, afterwards, with the condensation dripping off the ceiling and the plastic beer-glasses splintering underfoot, the mayhem continues unabated. Cris, eyes out on stalks, has his arm round a girl whose parents really ought not to have let her out for the night. Stevie is passed out on the floor. Art, chair-bound, with one endless spindly leg crossed over the other, big toe protruding out of a hole in one of his sneakers, is poring over the funnies in the *Post*. 'You want to sign us?' Joey demands. 'You got to fuckin' sign us *You got to*.' I do, and I will.

* * *

The Flame Throwers, CBGBs, 13 September

The crowd at CBGBs just didn't deserve the Flame Throwers. Well, not to begin with. The first thing that this gang of snot-nosed Sunset Boulevard punkoids have against them is that they ain't from New York, and territoriality is *very important* right now to the knots of Ramone-clones and buzz-cut girl/boy/who knows combinations of wrecked humanity here assembled to run the rule over what certain sections of the music press reckon is going to be the next big palooka. In fact, whisper it not, but a certain proportion of the seething – both senses of the word – audience seem ignorant of their provenance ('Are these guys from, uh, *England*?' Dolores, the big-eyed girl in the spangled sorority smock standing next to me earnestly inquires). The second thing – fatal in the presence of these bug-eyed Yankee taste-brokers shipped in from Queens or the Bowery or wherever – is that they ain't got no respect, reckon Uncle Lou Reed is a klutz of the first water and start mouthing off about Talking Heads almost before the house lights have gone down. On the other hand, boy how they play in a kind of strung-out, souped-up R&B-meets-metal amalgam. 'Back on the Brown', which just happens to be about somebody's drug habit, is simply delicious, while 'Janey Spokane' approximates to what Dr Feelgood – who really are English – might sound like if they came from L.A. rather than Canvey Island. Plus, they have a nice line in defying the audience's expectations, as when, about half-way through the set, the singer brings out a big old Gretsch semi-acoustic and announces that he's going to sing 'a power-ballad for all you REO Speedwagon fans', only to embark on an absolutely scabrous recitation of urban trauma in which sirens wail, bricks are thrown through plate-glass windows, the cops are on the killer trail and the lady ain't asking, she's begging. 'What is the drummer *on*?' Dolores – who I hope to be seeing a whole lot more of – wonders of the Throwers' devitalised sticks-wielder, who by the final number has achieved such a state of petrified abstraction that it's a wonder he doesn't levitate off the drum stool and go sailing up into the rafters. Don't know, honey, I tell her, but I wish we had some. The Flame Throwers, ladies and gentlemen. You have been warned.

Village Voice, 20 September 1980

14 September

Thinking – New York always has this effect on me – of all the other Americas that exist beyond it. Flat, limitless landscapes, empty and lonesome under the wide sky. Hawks wheeling away over the Kansas wheat-fields. The rumble of the Phoenix traffic. Smog blanketing Mulholland Drive. Westchester in the fall.

Here, despite the extreme heat, first signs of autumn on the streets. Leaves gently descending from the plane trees and a faint early morning chill. A breeze blows in off the Hudson. The summer visitors are leaving the Chelsea and heading back to Europe. The bohemian ladies in their greasy furs and the freaky-deakies from the upper floors watch them go. The Chelsea notwithstanding, New York is less conspicuously sleazy than I remember it. There's a realtor's parlour down at the end of 42nd Street, where the hookers used to congregate, and the old rooming houses are being turned into office blocks.

Today at breakfast Tamzin says, 'NBC want to see me one last time, then I'll be done.' Me: 'That's great. We'll celebrate.' I put the jumpiness, which has followed her here to NYC, down to nerves, the prospect – daunting even for a Tammy Girl – of trading lines with Bill Murray, Laraine Newman and the others. Then something happens. By chance, I happen to walk into the foyer just as she saunters out in the street. There are three cabs idling along West 23rd, but for some reason she ignores them and ambles off along the sidewalk. Gripped by sudden curiosity, I set off in pursuit. The NBC studios are in Rockefeller Plaza, not far from where Shard Enterprises had their offices a decade back. But if Tamzin is heading to NBC she is taking a highly circuitous, not to say underpowered, route. Several times she halts to look in a store window. Another time she stops at a set of lights, stares at the Walk/Don't Walk sign and then thinks better of it. All this goes on for about 20 minutes, after which she heads for a coffee-shop. Glancing through the window, a moment or two later, I find her head down over a bagel and a copy of the *Washington Post.* Whatever she's up to, it clearly doesn't involve an audition at *Saturday Night Live.*

Meanwhile, there are other things to worry about. Rory, reached by telephone back in London, is working on the loan from Virgin but hasn't yet nailed it. This means we are imminent danger of signing a band with money we don't yet possess. The studio costs racked up by Paper Plane for a record that will never appear are north of £10,000. Anxious to recoup something from a four-album deal abandoned half-way through, I instruct Trevor to schedule a greatest hits album for the spring. There are only two greatest hits, but we can pad it out with 'rare demos' – i.e. old rubbish quarried out of the studio vault – and live tracks. We can also spring the contract clause inserted as a hedge against eventualities of this kind that drops the royalty rate to 2.5 per cent.

Later. Showdown – what my mother would call 'words' – with Tamzin. It begins with me mentioning – not unkindly – that I'd seen her wandering down Eighth Avenue when she was supposed to have been at NBC. It turned out – something I had half-expected – that there was no audition. In fact, she invented the whole thing as an excuse to come to New York with me. When I point out that she could have come to New York with me anyway, she says she couldn't bear to be thought of as some washed-up old actress who was never going to get another job.

SELF : What are you going to do now?
TAMZIN : I don't know. How am I supposed to know? You have no idea how fucked up my life is right now.

I can see where all this is leading. Tamzin wants to come back to England with me. There are several reasons I would prefer this not to happen. One is that, in the course of the past week, her nervousness has shown every sign of developing into serious imbalance. Another is that $200 has just gone missing from my wallet. A third is that, over dinner, when I make a joke about the NBC business – a nasty crack, admittedly, about Bill Murray missing her in the morning, but it's been a stressful couple of days – she very nearly stabs me with a fork. Afterwards, on our way out of the dining-room – tonight it's full of rodeo guys in Stetson hats and fancy-dan rhinestone jackets – she starts an argument that continues all the way back to the third floor. 'You don't like me, do you? You're just out for what you can get.' I resist the urge to tell her that she probably doesn't like me and is out for what she can get. Fortunately the problem of how to get through the next eight hours is resolved by her downing three sleeping tablets in a tumbler of vodka ordered from room service and more or less passing out on the spot. Afterwards I sit for a long time in an armchair making notes in the margin of a copy of the *Hollywood Reporter* which, like two of Tamzin's vanity cases and a book called *Fifty Ways of Rechannelling Your Essential Focus* has accompanied us from L.A., going back into the bedroom every so often to check up on the recumbent figure lying face-down on the coverlet.

15 September

Over to Rudi's office in the Sixties to celebrate the Flame Throwers signing to Resurgam. Only three of the boys deign to show (Stevie has gone AWOL after the gig – 'probably went to sleep in some fuckin' dumpster,' Joey hazards), but Rudi, back from the West Coast, and in high spirits after persuading a couple of once-were Motown acts to join the Martinez & Associates roster, is unabashed. Struck by the incongruity of it all: Rudi pouring vintage champagne into delicately-fluted glasses; Frank, Sammy and Dean staring down from their frames at the three gangling leather boys; biker boots sinking into the high-end shag-pile; middle-aged secretaries whipping their heads round the door-frame every so often to check that their employer isn't getting robbed, beaten up or having a needle jabbed in his arm. Cris: 'We really appreciate this, man.' Joey: 'It's gonna be a fuckin' great record, man.' Art says nothing. A discussion with Rudi – shrewder and less emollient now his catch is landed – over who exactly will underwrite the UK tour that everyone is so anxious they shall undertake is still going on when I take my leave.

Back at the Chelsea there is something odd about our suite. What is odd about it is that Tamzin has thrown a suitcase at the TV, thereby shattering its screen, and over-turned her breakfast tray before swallowing some more sleeping pills – no idea how many were left in the bottle – and going back to bed. Her breath is coming in short, agitated rasps. But there are ways of dealing with the messed-up children of the well-to-do. An address book in the second vanity case gives me the number in Pacific Palisades and within a few moments I am on the line to Earle Pankey, big Earle, agent to the stars, seated no doubt in his big, bookless study, with the outsize puffer-fish in their tank staring at him as they glide, bringing him up to date with the situation.

'Oh yeah?' Earle says, cutting the recitation short. 'The fuck? Figured something like this might happen again.' He seems neither surprised, nor concerned by the news that Tammy Girl has gone on one of her rampages in NYC. 'Just where would you be right now, son?'

Things move fast in Pankey-land. Within half-an-hour a doctor is at the door, shaking his head over the splintered TV screen and the figure on the bed, and half-an-hour after that, once it has been established that a newly-revived Tamzin is capable of standing upright, a couple of nurses are summoned to escort her to a facility where, I am assured, she can receive the care and attention her condition merits. There is an awkward moment in the doorway, with the medics fussing and the advisability of a wheelchair being courteously disputed, when our eyes meet. She looks regretful, embarrassed and faintly sullen. Clearly I am in some measure responsible for this. 'I'll be in touch,' I say. 'Look after yourself.' The door closes, leaving me alone in the smashed-up room, with a plate of eggs-over-easy and an islet of coffee grounds still trodden into the carpet, sitting at a table covered with junk and an envelope containing copies of the Flame Throwers' contract. After that, making a quick inventory of the damage – she turns out to have gone to town in the bathroom as well – and, assuring myself that it's nothing a bohemian joint like the Chelsea can't handle, I head down to reception to settle up.

Throwers Sign to Resurgam

In the wake of their widely-reported top-dollar three-album deal with Geffen, we can divulge that the UK rights to the forthcoming debut waxing from noted West Coast bad boys The Flame Throwers have been picked up by Resurgam. According to svelte label MD Nick Du Pont, who recently flew to L.A. to meet with the band, 'This is a very exciting acquisition for us. Frankly, they make the Stones look like a ladies' knitting circle.' Insiders opine that the band are currently in the studio with Bob Ezrin, and that the fruits of this stake-out will be on the racks before Christmas, with a string of prestige UK dates to follow…

New Musical Express, 21 September 1980

Back on the flight to Heathrow with a loop of faxes lately received from Hermione strewn over the empty seat beside me. These disclose, among other things, that the Girl on the Phone single has risen to 23 and that 58th Variety (real name Simon Duck), a punk poet signed – against my better judgment – earlier in the year was arrested last Saturday for assaulting a policeman outside Millwall FC's ground in Lewisham. The exercise book that Daphne gave me sits close by, daring me to open it. California already a blur, the Pankeys tiny stick-figures on the rim of my imagination.

Postscript 2009

I never set eyes on Tamzin again – at least not in the flesh – although for several years afterwards a Christmas card used regularly to wing in from Pacific Palisades 'with joyful greetings from Earle and Bobbie Pankey and family'. Come the early '90s, according to Wikipedia, she managed to re-ignite her career by way of an NBC show entitled *Bounceback*, in which, with maximal irony, she played a one-time teen-star doing the rounds of the studios, and of which *Rotten Tomatoes* later remarked: 'Pankey maxes out on her patented goofy smile, but can't really get over the reflexiveness of the conceit. Another one of those bouts of industry navel-gazing in which Hollywood is essentially feeding off itself.'

The exercise book with the picture of Eisenhower on the cover – a stylised, caricaturist's version that made him look like something out of a Looney Tunes cartoon – turned out to contain a series of sketches of the American landscape. Each of them came labelled with a place and a date – *Tetons, Wyoming, 2/5/52; outside of Montgomery, Al. 7/9/59*. Sometimes, too, the Old Man had supplied a more or less relevant caption that was very often a line of poetry. Thus, a view of Lake Huron had been underwritten 'By the shores of Gitche-Gumee', while a portrait of three black field-hands dashed off somewhere in Missouri in 1963 rested atop a lightly-drawn plaque that read: 'I will show you fear in a handful of dust.' Judging from the rubric, he had set foot in at least a dozen states in the period covered by the book – east as far as Vermont, south-west as far as Texas – but the treatment was surprisingly one-gear. Basically, the Old Man liked rivers and wheat-fields rising up to distant bluffs. He liked the Rocky Mountains seen from afar, and he liked long, godforsaken country roads with tumbleweeds blowing over them and perhaps an approaching truck or a line-man perched on a telegraph pole to break the monotony. What with the endless cross-hatched trees and – field-hands and line-men excepted – the absence of people, the effect was horribly sinister: brooding, melancholic, turned in on itself. There was one particular sketch of an old, white-walled mansion looming out of a fantastically overgrown tree-canopy *Near Memphis, Tennessee, 4/1/62* that was practically gothic in its intensity. Why had he done them, and what had he hoped to achieve with them?

And then, on the final page, executed in pen-and-ink rather than brittle charcoal pencil, was something that instantly cancelled out the rivers and the spreading wheat, the brooding mountain-sides and the melancholy faces of the field-hands. It was a drawing of a small boy with a solemn expression sitting on a high-backed chair with both hands folded in his lap and a plastic beaker balanced on top of them, and had clearly been done from a photograph. I knew this, because the small boy was me. The original, meanwhile, had sat on the mantelpiece at North Park all through the long 1950s when the old man – the prodigious sketcher of lakeland shorelines and Teton twilights – was no longer there to see it.

Interview with Nick Du Pont, former MD of Resurgam Records

Q: You've said that one of the things that fascinated you about the Flame Throwers was the mythology they constructed around themselves. How soon did this start kicking in?

A: Oh, very early on. Probably the first or second occasion that I met them. Certainly by the time they turned up in England. Perhaps 'mythology' is putting it a bit strongly. On the other hand, most bands that are any good – and quite a few that aren't – are very keen on what might be called the collective myth, by which I mean all the attitudes and prejudices – delusions, too – that sustain them during their career. I flatter myself that long before the music press got on the case I was trying to decipher this sense of who they thought they were and what the world owed them.

Q: Most people would say that the answers are a) that they thought they were a gang of street punks, and b) the world owed them everything that was going.

A: They probably would. I always thought it was more complicated than it seemed. I mean, somebody once said, back in 1964, that whereas the Beatles wanted to hold your hand, the Stones wanted to burn your town. Now, the Flame Throwers didn't so much want to burn your town as turn it into a high-end brothel in which the prime attraction would be your teenage daughter, while sampling as many drugs as they could without actually dying.

Q: Sounds like a straightforward case of West Coast hedonism to me.
A: Certainly hedonism is somewhere there in the mix. But you would have to say that paranoia ran it a very close second. The world was out to get them and they were out to get the world. Everybody was on their case, and they weren't going to take it. You know the kind of thing. They were also – and I think this was a symptom of the world-view – top-grade conspiracy theorists.

Q: What kind of conspiracies would those be?
A: As you ask, they believed that Area 51 contained the corpses of an entire Venusian army who had landed there by space-ship in the fall of 1957 and been narrowly defeated by the Nevada National Guard. I seem to remember Cris telling me once that Jack Kennedy wasn't dead but living on an ice-station north of Baffin Island. They definitely thought that their phones were being tapped and half the journalists who interviewed them were FBI agents. I also seem to remember something about the Federal Government secretly filling defunct army bases in Southern Texas with drug felons 'and doin' experiments on them.'

Q: There's an impressive solidarity about their early pronouncements, a real feeling of 'we're in this together'...
A: A public solidarity, yes, which was then undermined by jealousy, suspicion...oh, and general cussedness. Let's say they were a rebel

army who hated each other as much as the things they were rebelling against. And if their own relationships were problematic in the extreme, then their dealings with the people who bought their records and went to their concerts were even more fraught.

Q: How so?
A: It's the old stand-off between expectation and reality. Theoretically the only people who understood their complex psychological emotional states and their pharmaceutical needs were their fans – 'They're, like, the only people who're on our side.' They could relate to them because, for all practical purposes, 'they're guys like us.' In practice they were always wary of the kids who queued up outside record shops because they knew that a fair percentage of them were half-way crazy. They liked them for liking them, but they worried about the depth of their obsession. They wanted 20,000 people to come and see them at the Austin Thunderdome, or wherever, but they lived in fear of what those 20,000 people might do.

Q: Final judgment? Sum them up for me.
A: There are no final judgments. And you must remember how much I liked their music. OK, here are some abstract nouns. Cynicism. Idealism – well, up to a point. Fear. Loathing. Resentment…I think you get the idea?

The Flame Throwers: An Oral History (1988)

PART TWO
English Music

'And somebody told me in the early '80s you were going to be the next big thing…'

THE FLAME THROWERS – *BREAKFAST AT RALPH'S* [RESURGAM]

Breakfast at Ralph's/Back on the Brown/Pinball Woman/Mole Rothman's Blues/Nazi Surf Punks Must Die/Up in Lisa's Room/ Santa Monica BV Kiss-off/Jackie O/North Clarke/Janey Spokane/ Burnin' For Ya/When She Lets Me Do My Thing/Breakfast at Ralph's (reprise).

Produced by Bob Ezrin. Running time: 42 minutes.

The modern American pop scene? Well draw up a chair or three, ladeez and gentlemen, poke up the fire – while casting onto the flames unsold copies of that Todd Rundgren album we were shooting the breeze about just the other day – and Uncle Charlie here will tell ya all about it. You see, like punk rock (does anyone remember that?) and those bands of earnest young synthesizer players fronted by guys in army surplus fatigues (and does anyone remember them?) the modern American scene has changed out of all recognition since civilised folk started paying attention to it. And for the better, I hasten to add, which as Bruce Springsteen will tell you, ain't always the case. I mean, Jeez, when I was over there five years back the place was just a kind of cosmic dustbin, like that restaurant Arlo Guthrie sang about where you could get anything you wanted, only none of it was worth eating. Sure, the Noo Yawk bands were starting up, and Debbie Harry was sashaying around the Mudd Club like Betty Boop in a wig, but it was early days ya unnerstand, and the first Ramones LP wasn't even on the racks. Meantime, over in L.A. it was like the clocks had all stopped in 1969, the hippy ladies were still tending their bean-curd – or whatever else it is that they do – and a dope like James Taylor was taken *very seriously indeed.*

Well now, half a decade later and from Broadway to the Vegas Strip, and doubtless down to the back-end of Tuscaloosa as well, the US of A is rocking like a muthafucker, and while you might not admire absolutely every last little goddam thing that's currently emanating from the Land of the Free (me, I reckon Talking Heads are just a mite too *innerleckshuall* for their own darn good, you dig?) you hafta admit that about eighty percent of this sonic revolution – and now Uncle Charles is turning all highbrow again – is as hot as it comes. Not to mention as, uh, *socially relevant* as any of the wide-eyed old sociology lecturers who could be found pontificating for *Let it Rock* and other like-minded periodicals back when yours truly was just a kid could desire. The latest hard evidence to support this proposition comes in the shape of *Breakfast at Ralph's*, which in your tenacious word-slinger's opinion is one of the most righteous slabs of heavy-duty rock 'n' roll to start shifting the stale air around since, I dunno, the Stooges cut *Raw Power* back in '73. For your information – and it was news to me until the end of last week – the Flame Throwers are Mr Cris Itol (and yes, Amelia, that is an anagram of 'clitoris'), Mr Joey Valparaiso, Mr Stevie DaVinci and Mr Art Smothers, which just has to be what the kind of scribe who gets paid a whole lot more than your humble correspondent's NUJ minimum would call a *nom de guerre.**

The first point that probably ought to be raised about this gang of desperadoes – whose cover photo, it should be said, brings a whole new dimension to the concept of the collective sneer – is that, as far as can be deduced from their debut's dozen and a half (sort of) tracks, the music they're laying down, seen as a reflection of the, ah, *milieu* in which they operate, would seem to be pretty much authentic. Which is to say that unlike 90 per cent of UK punk bands warbling about the rat-infested tenements they inhabit and the bruising existential despair to which they are chronically subject, the Throwers really do appear to be living the kind of lives they're so avidly chronicling. In this connection, your intrepid critic would particularly like to draw attention to 'North Clarke', a despatch from the *immensely* scuzzy West L.A. thoroughfare where they all hang out, with name-checks for all the regular guys met in the course of a morning's perambulation ('There's Danny the dealer/And Mikey the squealer/Harry's bleeding/Rico's speeding' etc.) As for the field of, er, personal relationships, 'Up in Lisa's Room' is some far-from-discreet reportage from a hooker's boudoir ('I put ten dollars on the shelf/Lay down and helped myself') while 'Janey Spokane' is a thoroughly nasty put-down of some clinging sourpuss who don't like the kind of company her man keeps and can go chuck herself over a cliff *right now*. And all this, mark you, is just the conventional stuff. For some genuine weirdness, the listener is advised to check out 'Santa Monica BV Kiss-off', which is, believe it or not, a rocked-up version of Duke Ellington's 'East St Louis Toodle-oo', not to mention 'Nazi Surf Punks Must Die', which sounds like a '70s glam rock band slowed down to 16 r.p.m. with the lead guitar replaced by a couple of pneumatic drills.

What else do you need to know? Well, 'Back on the Brown' and 'Jackie O' are unlikely to receive air-play in any country where the station jocks speak English on account of a) enough drug references to stuff a sofa, and b) general all-round bad mouthing on the subject of America's former First Lady. Which is as good a place as any to inform all you Cliff Richard fans out there that these ain't 'xactly nice boys, no way no how, and if it's mature statements of opinion you're after, then the new Dire Straits album will be much more your brand of sassafras, yes indeedy. In fact, to be candid, the material here harbours some attitudes about women, violence and racial politics that you probably wouldn't want to spring on your kid sister or indeed anyone else of a half-way sensitive disposition. To which Mr Itol – who appears to have penned about three-quarters of *Ralph's* – would doubtless retort that these are the kind of people he writes about and this is the kind of shit they think. You pays your money and you makes your choice…

It ain't all top-drawer, mind. Bobbie Ezrin (whose credits include Alice Cooper and Lou Reed) has done his level best with Itol and Co., but you'd have to have ears made out of cloth to reckon that they were the finished article. The bass, in particular, is just *all over the place* and some of Art's fills would have the late John Bonham weeping into his carafe of vodka. Plus there are a couple of tracks where they sound like Ultravox (remember Ultravox?) at their most pretentiously irritating, and maybe a couple more where they sound as if they've been taking lessons from some gnarled old rock 'n' roll sludge merchants like Uriah Heep. On the other hand, when they rock out, then boy do they *rock out*, and some of the licks that Mr Valparaiso – no idea what the guy is on, but it sure as hell isn't oatmeal porridge and cocoa – injects into 'Pinball Woman' are downright tasteful. And if all the foregoing sounds a tad equivocal, then your respectful print-meister should say that once he'd finished listening to the white label kindly supplied by the nice people at Resurgam, then he immediately placed said waxing back on the turntable and, like the kid in *Oliver Twist*, reckoned that it might be a smart idea if he straightaway sampled some more.

As to where all this might end, and what kind of future lies in store for North Clarke's finest, let's just say that I'm sure the boys will be devoting some of their precious time to figuring this thorny conundrum out. At the moment, it's clear that they have no ambition *at all* beyond the usual hipster desiderata of getting high/laid/rich, living fast, dying young and leaving a good-looking corpse. Truth to tell, I never heard an album – not even by the New York Dolls – that conveyed such a desperate screw-you-Jack air of living for the moment and letting tomorrow look after itself. To be honest, the whole caboodle reminded me of some words of Antonio Gramsci, that much-venerated Italian philosopher dude whose acquaintance I've been making over the long autumn nights, to the effect that the past is dying, the future has yet to be born and in the meantime some interesting symptoms will start presenting themselves. Take it from me, gentle reader, the Flame Throwers are one of these symptoms. You, of course, are the disease.

CHARLES SHAAR MURRAY – *New Musical Express,* 17 November 1980

**Apparently not – Ed.*

5. DAY IN THE LIFE

Flame Throwers UK Tour 1980
14 November Lyceum, London
15 November Top Rank, Sheffield
16 November Outlook, Doncaster
18 November Town Hall, Torquay
19 November Metro, Plymouth
20 November Colston Hall, Bristol
22 November Friars, Aylesbury [*abandoned*]
23 November Barbarella's, Birmingham [*cancelled*]
24 November Music Machine, London [*cancelled*]

'Has Margaret arrived yet? I can't say I've seen her.'

'You don't seriously expect us to believe that the two of you are on first-name terms?'

'I'll have you know,' Rory said stiffly, 'that when you were skulking around in your hovel in the Fens, or wherever it was, sucking on some ogress's teat, others of us were taking a serious interest in politics. Why, it was my father got Sir Alec his seat back in 1963.'

You could never quite tell whether Rory meant to be ironic. Sometimes – just now for example – this was a good thing. On the other hand, there jangled in his wake a whole series of business meetings and high-end corporate showdowns which had foundered on the inability of those present to establish whether he meant what he said he did. All around us, the hard, powerful faces looked on. Terry Jacomb, who had no idea what any of this implied, giggled nervously.

'If you see her are you going to clasp her warmly by the hand and remind her of all this?'

'Don't be ridiculous. If there's one thing the P.M. can't stand it's ostentation.'

The room in which the three of us stood was too small for the number of people crammed into it. This meant that towards the edges, where the guests had become hemmed in and the drinks trays never penetrated, there was an increasing air of desperation. Weak, late-autumn sunshine, drifting in through the high, plate-glass windows, enhanced this sense of collective terror, as if we were small animals, caught in the paralysing glare of a car's headlights, anxiously awaiting death.

'Rather a seedy crowd,' Rory said – it was always a point in his favour that he could bring out a phrase like 'rather a seedy crowd' with a complete lack of self-consciousness. 'And if the wine waiters were this slack at the Travellers', they'd be sacked *on the spot*.'

Seedy crowds: wine waiters at the Travellers': pale sunshine streaming through the high windows. If Rory had banked on finding the world of his own mysterious private life reflected in the reception room of 10 Downing Street, he was badly mistaken. The worst of it was that the people who flocked around us, who were alternately beaten back against the walls by the press of newcomers or forged wildly through the throng pushing aside whatever resistance they met with outstretched hands, were all horribly familiar. Nondescript men in suits would have been easier to deal with. Here, alternatively, were TV comedians, talk-show hosts, radio presenters, national treasures, all the neatly sculpted statuary of newspaper arts pages, Miss World contests and late-night line-ups. A man who looked like Anthony

Burgess had cornered one of the waiters up against a grandfather clock and was scooping glasses of wine off the tray and up-ending them into his mouth one by one. At the same time, the weak sunshine had somehow diminished them. They looked smaller than they were supposed to be, parched and thin, like ghosts exhausted by too much haunting.

'Tell me again, Rory. Why exactly have we been asked to this reception?'

Burgess-man was being hustled away now, while the waiters closed ranks around him. Somewhere close at hand a clock was striking the hour.

'The Prime Minister,' Rory said, sounding rather like a newscaster delivering a bulletin to camera, 'has decided that she wants to recognise the outstanding contribution made to our national life by the entertainment industry. To that end she has chosen to welcome two hundred of its representatives to her official residence.'

'But why us in particular?'

'I sent a press release to her private secretary pointing out that turnover was getting towards three million and we were making a significant contribution to the current export drive.'

'Is that last bit true?'

'Strictly speaking, no. Although I believe the Maximum Acceleration album might have done a few in France.'

'And has the Prime Minister – has *Margaret* – ever shown any interest in popular music?'

'I think she said once that she liked 'Telstar' by the Tornadoes.'

There were even more people crowding into the room now. A bishop in a purple cassock. The Captain of the Ryder Cup team. Unless you counted Val Doonican and two members of a middle-aged close-harmony quartet called the Doo-Woppers, there did not seem to be anyone other than ourselves from what Rory still liked to refer to as The Wonderful World of Pop.

'Isn't that Dick Emery?' Terry Jacomb wondered. It was the first thing he had said since we stepped out of the taxi in Whitehall half an hour before.

'I really have no interest in these people,' Rory said savagely. 'In any case, don't we have to be in Soho at half one? What time is it?'

It was two years now since Rory and I had come across each other. At this stage I had no idea of the havoc he was going to wreak on my life. He was simply a brisk, upper-class wielder of cheque books and facilitator of loans, a sizzling commercial titan in whose presence timid bank managers with little experience of underwriting the music biz practically swooned with relief. There had been people like him at Oxford and in the record company boardrooms of a dozen years ago, stealthily concealing their individuality beneath Gieves & Hawkes suits and a polished manner. The trouble lay far ahead, so far ahead as not to be glimpsed at this Whitehall shakedown.

'In any case,' Rory said, 'I have to make an urgent call. *Really* urgent.' 'Really urgent' to Rory could mean anything from renewing his Hurlingham Club subscription to renegotiating the Newman Street lease. 'I've got a cousin who works downstairs in the Garden Room. Do you suppose she'd let me use the phone?'

'Wouldn't that be breaking the Official Secrets Act?'

Two years in, I was beginning to understand some of the looks Rory shot me. This one lay halfway along the spectrum between feigned contempt and serious inner disquiet. Once again, watching him steam off through the crowd like a human juggernaut before whose steady progress all resistance was futile, I realised that here was someone who lived by the will.

'Well I voted Conservative last spring,' Trevor Jacomb volunteered, even more ponderously than usual. 'I don't mind who knows. My wife and I talked it over and we agreed it was the only sensible thing to do.' He was a tall, badly-shaped forty year-old, disliked, by Rory, for his uncouth manner, but hired, by Rory, on the grounds that he was supposed, also by Rory, to have turned Chrysalis Records into 'a lean, mean, fighting machine', and was once reckoned to have sent in an invoice for £359 after entertaining three journalists from *Record Mirror* to lunch at the Speakeasy.

The reception room crowd. The cheerless waiters. Rory and his cousin. All this I was prepared to put up with. But I was not going to listen to Trevor telling me why he had voted Conservative.

'Look, Trev. Why don't you remind me of the schedule?'

Trevor brightened. Minor logistical arrangements always brought out the best in him. 'Paula's gorn to Heathrow. The plane should get in just about now. I told Naz – you know he's doing front of owce? – to pull out all the stops. Canapes' – he pronounced it to rhyme with 'jacka-napes' – 'and the fuck knows what else.' As the adenoidal voice droned listlessly on, I wondered – not for the first time – what my mother would have made of Mrs Thatcher and decided she would not have liked her at all. The politicians my mother tended to admire were Tory gentlemen whose existences were stratospherically removed from her own; Mrs Thatcher's upbringing above the grocer's shop in Grantham would have been a little too close for comfort, whereas the vastness of the gulf between her own life and Sir Anthony Eden's encouraged and consoled her. The knot of people next to us surged and broke apart and Rory stepped out of the chaos, the light of battle in his eye.

'Piece of piss,' he explained. 'Apparently it's Camilla's day off, but I told them I was the Under-Secretary for Food and Fisheries and they let me have an outside line.'

Trevor Jacomb goggled. He was still in awe of Rory, and even more afraid of the circumstances in which he found himself. None of this abject humility cut much ice with his sponsor. 'If Trevor describes himself in my hearing as "just a fat boy from Penge" one more time I shall kick his arse for him,' Rory had once threatened. 'I know those fat boys from Penge and they'll sell you down the river as soon as look at you.'

Meanwhile, all the gathering's incidental scenery – Trevor's self-abasement, Rory's delight at having passed himself off as a government minister, the milky sunshine cascading off their shoulders that made them look as if they had just climbed out of a stained-glass window of the late-Victorian era – had begun to fade away. Over in the corner by the door, where a couple of flunkies stood dishing out name-badges, the geometry of the room was briskly reconfiguring itself. First there was a mass displacement of bodies that sent at least a dozen of the guests stationed near the doorway cannoning into the walls. Then there came an odd sense of airborne movement, like a breeze sweeping over a cornfield, as people turned their heads to see what was going on. Finally, at a sudden stroke, like the Red Sea being flung back, the crowd parted, a circle of carpeting rolled into view, and, jerky and abrupt, moving along it at far too quick a pace to greet any of the well-wishers formed up on either side, came our hostess.

'Here comes the lady,' Rory said.

I had spent quite a bit of the past decade and a half in the presence of celebrity: attending to celebrity's little jokes, say, or running celebrity's little errands. I had once stood in the foyer of the Dorchester Hotel holding Bob Dylan's hat while he retied the laces of his sneakers. I had shared a Mars Bar with George Harrison while the two lookalikes paid to impersonate John and Paul ran up and down the concourse of New Street Station chased by yelling fans. But the celebrity had been off-duty, incognito, grinning from the side-lines; not, as its latest incarnation seemed to be doing, bent on perpetuating its own myth. Was Mrs Thatcher, gliding remorselessly through the clumps of guests, nodding as she went, conscious of the impression she made? Or was she so consummate an egotist that the thought of making an impression hardly occurred to her? As for the effect she was having on the people around her, Trevor Jacomb was still goggling. Rory looked as if he was in a race-course paddock inspecting a thoroughbred that had done its owner proud, and, if properly fed and exercised, might go on to even greater triumphs. As the cortege came nearer and its mechanistic routines – the hand extended and withdrawn, the briefly inclined head,the odd little tentative quarter-turn that Mrs Thatcher made on the carpet like a dancer searching for her mark – became intelligible, all this acquired a single point of focus. How was Rory – clearly deeply smitten – going to behave? Was he going to drop to one knee and clasp the Prime Minister's hand to his breast? Would he, as had once or twice happened in the company of the rich and famous, suddenly turn bluff and man-to-man? Or would he – this had happened in the past as well – revert to some baffling private code,that could be deciphered by the people who traded it but not by anyone else?

In the end, Rory went for a combination of the second and the third approach. As I was shaking hands – Mrs Thatcher's palm was vaguely slippery, as if it had just been dipped in oil – I saw him rock back on his feet and give a slight nod. Nothing was said, but Mrs Thatcher's eye, resting on him for a moment, emitted a faint gleam of – it had to be said – not entirely favourable recognition. Then, as she passed on to give a disdainful tug at the paw proffered by base Trevor Jacomb, he murmured, in a tone so soft that I barely heard it, the words 'Saw Carol in Bond Street the other day. Looked well.'

'Do you really know the Thatchers?' I asked, two minutes later as we were jogging through the Downing Street gate.

'One has been to Flood Street now and again…Although it has to be said that Mark's rather an oik.'

The commanding air with which he had shepherded us away from the reception room was still upon him as we came out into Whitehall. For some reason the road was almost empty, but a deferential policeman, button-holed by Rory in his grandest manner ('Look here, officer') assured him that taxis could be found at the farther end, near Horseguards. Five minutes later we were in a cab heading north towards Trafalgar Square.

'Them indie chart returns've come in' Trevor Jacomb said, out of nowhere. 'Cedric's new one's done nuffink, but the Cupcakes' album is in at nine.'

This was encouraging news. It meant that a record which had taken three separate producers, a mislaid bass player and untold hours of studio time, and of which everyone had frankly despaired, had sold upwards of 2,000 copies and might just go on to cover its costs. Turning to see what Rory made of this, I saw that he was sitting with his legs splayed apart, hands balanced on his knee and a look of absolute exaltation on his face. This was another of Rory's oddities. He went through life assuming that he had total control over the environments through which he moved. Taxis – all taxis, but this one in particular – only worked because he had sought them out and ordered them to. Humanity might reap the benefit, but it had all been Rory's idea.

The early '80s were full of taxi rides. Afternoon trips through the summer heat to dingy rehearsal rooms in Barnes and Lots Road, under the shadow of the power station, to witness replacement guitar players being put through their paces. Late-night sprints to the Tally Ho in Camden and the Greyhound in the Fulham Road to catch bands of melancholic teenagers whose self-produced singles had momentarily caught the *NME*'s eye. Woozy autumnal jaunts with visiting American producers who might just be persuaded to fit us into their busy schedules. Nervy set-downs at venture capitalists in Mincing Lane and London Wall, before whose portals even Rory's self-confidence seemed sometimes to fail him. This one took us through familiar territory: along Shaftesbury Avenue, up into Dean Street, past the clip-joints and the adult cinemas and the massage parlours and all the other evidence suggesting that this part of London, like many of the people racketing around in it, was beginning to show its age. In Noel Street there was an Italian funeral going on and the road was blocked by black horses with purple-dyed plumes dragging a vast, flower-strewn hearse, and I thought of the old man's corpse being launched out into the sea and the hippy girls singing hymns and the kerosene can blasting into fragments as the flames took hold.

'Those Eyetie funerals are the limit,' Rory said, confirming a fact I already knew. For Rory would never die. Somehow he would breast the apocalyptic waves and come up smiling on the other side.

The taxi ploughed back along Carlisle Street through the drifting lunch-hour crowds. Trevor Jacomb was telling a long, involved story about a friend of his employed to take aerial photographs of a Led Zeppelin concert in the grounds of a stately home in an attempt to extort more money out of the promoter ('I mean, Harold goes up in this chopper and there weren't more than a hundred thousand people there, but their manager only tells Freddie he's had it analysed by NASA or someone and there's a quarter of a million of the fuckers and some Mafia type he knows is coming round to collect the extra dush.') It seemed a long time now since we had shaken hands with Mrs Thatcher and watched the man who could have been Anthony Burgess take his leave. What was worse was that the day still had a dozen hours to run. 'Couple of shooters (*shootaz*) on the table an' all,' Trevor said as the cab surged into Wardour Street like some live thing that possessed a spirit beyond its tethering in steel and chrome. 'I wouldn't have gone there if you'd paid me.' Rory, the immortal, stared sightlessly in front of him. And it was here – I am sure – that I experienced that first faint tremor of dread, that feeling, so common in the music business, if not beyond it, that I had released forces I could not control, let some genie out of the bottle that was altogether beyond my power to restrain. There would be a price to pay for all this misjudgement, I decided, as the taxi plunged on to the press conference where the Flame Throwers would charm and delight their audience, intelligibly promote their new record, inaugurate their UK tour and begin to repay the very considerable investment I had made in them. Or something like that.

* * *

Press conferences. Press conferences. In the old days, when expense was no object and geography no impediment, the press conferences had taken place on the roof-terraces of five-star Aegean hotels, in private jets ceaselessly circling the New England seaboard, on specially-chartered Pullmans rattling westward under shimmering prairie sky, had been enlivened by marching bands, fair-ground organs and teams of strippers zealously plying their trade. Ten years later, in an era of elegant economy, the press conferences took place in night-clubs, in de-commissioned art galleries hired for a song, on station platforms or, on at least one occasion, in somebody's front room. Here on the dance-floor of the Imperial Club, Noel Street, W1, beneath a Bacofoil-covered ceiling from which half-a-dozen mirror balls were precariously suspended, it was clear that all those involved had done what they could. A black-stencil poster that read LONDON WELCOMES THE FLAME THROWERS had been tacked to the wooden frontage of the DJ's booth and several plates of sandwiches were turning up their edges in the heat of the strip-lights. Twenty or so journalists, in varying states of sobriety, had been corralled into a double row of what looked like garden chairs. The light enhanced the natural pallor of their skins and made them seem livid, not of this world, sprung from some far-off, subterranean lair and ready to return there at the drop of a hat. Hermione, who had them well in order, was going up and down the lines of chairs crossing off names on her clipboard.

'Not a bad turnout,' Trevor Jacomb said. He was more comfortable now, back in a milieu where he could shine. 'Who've [*who-herve*] we got?'

Hermione ran a seasoned eye over the roster. '*New Musical Express. Melody Maker. Sounds. Record Mirror*...' She made it sound as if she were going through the penitentiary roll. '...*Dorking Gazette. Ealing and Hammersmith Sentinel*.'

'Christ! Anyone from the tabs?'

'I did manage to speak to a man from the *Sun*' Hermione said, who disliked Trevor Jacomb and was further antagonised by his use of the word 'Christ', 'and he told me to tell you they were fed up with being asked to press conferences where something outrageous was supposed to be happening, only to find out when they got there that nothing actually did.'

'Stout girl, Hermione,' Rory said, only just out of ear-shot. 'Always a good thing to have somebody like that in charge. Do you know, just now, one of those goblins sparked up a joint and she absolutely went over and made him put it out.'

Just as Rory had made the Downing Street reception seem his natural milieu, now, chameleon-like, he was equally at home on the Imperial's rickety dancefloor. Meanwhile, the life of Soho flowed on around us. An old man in a brown housecoat came out of a side door and began to sweep the dusty stage on which seating for the band had been desultorily set up, and a couple of girls with dyed magenta hair materialised out of nowhere to pick over the sandwiches.

'Hang on,' Trevor Jacomb complained. 'Hang about now. We're paying for all that.'

'Well, no one's fucking eating it are they?' one of the magenta girls said companionably. There was a slight commotion as the old man with the broom tripped over one of the chairs and came down in a heap. Had the press conferences of ten years ago been this incongruous? I thought back to the day in 1971 when the Helium Kids had appeared at the Plaza Hotel, with Don Shard in his mobster's suit, Angie stuffing the packets of Tuinal into her bra and the leather-jacketed feminist hit-squad rushing the stage, and realised that these things were relative. There came a series of noises from above our heads of doors slamming, booted feet grinding on stair-rods, raised voices in sharp descent. The files of journalists stirred like troubled dreamers, someone said, '*Here* they come' in a lilting, sing-song voice from the Welsh valleys and, as in a cowboy film where the double doors of a saloon crash open and a series of objects are flung onto the sidewalk, half-a-dozen figures – giving the impression that they had been blown into the room by a tornado – tumbled out into the light.

It was two months since I had last set eyes on the Flame Throwers. Admittedly, in that time they had moved on from one sort of life into another, stopped being LA street punks and become apprentice rock stars, sloughed off one kind of skin and acquired another. All this was par for the course, nothing to get alarmed about, in fact a natural development of the sort of people they were and the sort of things that they wanted from life. At the same time, the six weeks' worth of grooming, primping and ego-massaging on which Geffen must have insisted prior to their launch in the States had clearly had a terrible effect on such mundane advantages as morale, appearance and, in the case of Stevie, who was hanging wearily on somebody's arm, the ability to walk in a straight line.

'Strewth' Rory whistled. He had stopped looking at the décor as if only politeness was stopping him from tearing down the Bacofoil and the mirror balls and redesigning the club on the spot and was concentrating on matters to hand. 'What the fuck is going on here?' As he said this Paula, the Resurgam press officer, who had had the enviable task of fetching the band from Heathrow, detached herself from their orbit so rapidly that Stevie fell over a chair and came whirling furiously towards me.

'Nick. Nicko. I need to talk to you. I need to talk to you *right now.*'

As usually happened on these occasions, there was a sense of the world slowing down, sitting back on its haunches, taking five. The magenta-haired girls turning over the sandwiches might have been showroom dummies. Trevor Jacomb, patiently conveying a sausage roll into the raw, red abyss of his mouth, could have been swimming through treacle. Something had gone wrong.

'What's the matter, Paula?'

'Nick, Nick darling. I have never been so insulted *in my life.*' Paula, I recollected, could look after herself. In fact, she was famous in industry circles for once having hit a *Sounds* journalist who had importuned her in a lift so hard that he had needed medical treatment. It looked as if something pretty bad had happened.

'The girl's upset,' Rory said, without much interest. Paula, as he had more than once pointed out, was 'not his kind of woman.'

The trick at these times was to locate the authority figure. Usually this was the tour manager. On the other hand, it could sometimes be the bass player's girlfriend, or even the ratty kid who unloaded the amplifiers. Here in the Imperial Club, Soho it looked as if it was Rudi's assistant Marty who, clad in a fringed buckskin jacket and a pair of black leather trousers, was helping Stevie to arrange his oddly uncoordinated frame in one of the garden chairs.

'So what exactly is going on here?'

'Oh yeah.' Marty, plucked from his lair in Martinez & Associates' office in the Sixties and sent three thousand miles across the Atlantic to ride shotgun on the Flame Throwers, was not quite the man he had been. 'The guys got a little boisterous at the airport. That I will allow.'

'Define 'boisterous', Marty.'

'Look man.' The idea that it might be worth trying to tough this one out swam before Marty's eyes and then faded away to nothing. 'OK, I'll be straight with you. The publishing advance came through the other week and I guess they must have been spending it.'

There was no point in asking what the publisher's advance had been spent on. 'What's the matter with Stevie?'

'My fault entirely' Morty conceded. 'We're half an hour out of Heathrow and I'm, like, "Guys, now is the time to get rid of any, uh, *substances* you may have on your person." And fuckin' Stevie now, he just pulls out everything he's got in his pockets and swallows it on the spot.'

'Dear me,' said Rory, interested in spite of himself. 'What exactly did he take?'

'I don't know. Some Librium. Percodan maybe…Couple of Quaaludes.'

'I didn't think you could still get Quaaludes.'

'Listen,' Marty said, with a kind of infinite weariness. He had grown older in the last eight weeks, older and less cocksure. 'I've been working with these guys. I know what they're like. Stevie could take a shot of horse tranquiliser and come up smiling the next morning. Give him a jug of coffee and he'll be fine is what I'm saying.'

Gradually the room calmed down. The boys, all dressed in leather jackets, black jeans and biker boots, lost their baffling identikit sheen and acquired individual personalities, wandered up and down the line of journalists shaking hands and bumming cigarettes. Stevie, temporarily revived by about a quart of coffee, scuttled off to join them. Outside there were police klaxons going by, all the rattle of London on an autumn afternoon kept narrowly in check. Heard in counterpoint, the human voices seemed weak and insubstantial, not built to last. As often happened at press conference, at least one of them was bent on recrimination.

PAULA :	Before we start I'd just like to say that this fucker here (*she indicates Itol*) tried to put his hand up my skirt in the limo.
ITOL (*bemused*) :	What am I supposed to have done?
VALPARAISO :	Lady here reckons you were hitting on her.
ITOL :	Well, let me inform you, sister, it's, uh, a sick fuckin' world if

	you can't tell whether a chick's putting out for you or not.
JOURNALIST :	How are you enjoying England, Cris? How do you rate the drugs?
ITOL :	Who said anything about drugs? We only just got here. I mean (*warming to his subject*) like, every piece I see about us in the music press is implying we're fuckin' junkies, y'hear what I'm sayin'? But we're just, uh…regular guys is all.
JOURNALIST :	Where exactly will you be playing?
	Itol looks helplessly at Valparaiso
VALPARAISO :	Where are we playing? All the usual venues, I guess. Manchester. Liverpool. Nott…Notwich or someplace. Wherever it says in the press release. Yeah, that's where we'll be.'
ITOL (*raises arms theatrically*) :	The album! Time one of these fuckers asked about the album.
JOURNALIST :	Have you been listening to the New York Dolls?
ITOL :	Who?
DA VINCI :	Yeah, we get asked that a lot.
VALPARAISO :	Bunch of prissy fruits.
ITOL :	I mean, where I grew up in Asswipe Wisconsin, the

Dolls were just fuckin' junkie perverts, which was…cool. But it's like, that was the Seventies, and this is, uh, 1980 you hear what I'm saying.

FEMALE JOURNALIST : There's this line in 'Santa Monica BV Kiss-off' that goes "You may not be a n....r but you surely are a whore." Would anyone care to comment?

ITOL : No.

DA VINCI : I mean, it's just a line in a song OK? It's like…We're not putting anyone down or nuthin'. You know, we got f.....s complaining about our songs, but we ain't got nuthin' against f.....s. Live and let fuckin' live…That's our motto. Its just that Cris, when he's writing he's so fuckin' *intense*, you hear what I'm sayin', that sometimes you can't keep up with it, like he was this alien from another planet or something.

ITOL : And it's like, if the songs are on the radio and the kids in the project or wherever are digging them, then you've got to find a way of dealing with it.

JOURNALIST : Dory Previn has said that your songs glorify chauvinism and

	hatred. How do you respond to that?
VALPARAISO :	I hate them fuckin' hippy chicks. Next question.
JOURNALIST :	Have you a message for your British fans?
ITOL (*brightens*) :	Sure. Tell them we love them. Especially their sisters. We're looking forward to kicking some ass. And seein' the sights. Buckingham Paliss. Fuckin' Beefeaters too.
JOURNALIST :	Does your drummer ever say anything?
DA VINCI :	No, he don't ever talk.
ITOL :	Art's in this fuckin' cult y'know? Swore this vow of silence or something, I dunno. Next question.

These were early days for the Flame Throwers as a workable musical street gang. Later they would refine their public appearances into pageants of semi-comic badinage, but already the essential elements were in place. Joey and Stevie alternated between *raissoneur* and foil. Cris was the tortured genius waiting to lose his temper, Art, silent and self-absorbed, an enigma for the world to puzzle over. All this was oddly effective. The journalists, I realised, would be impressed in spite of themselves. Either they would go away and write flattering profiles, or they would let their irritation get the better of them. Both these responses were worth having. For the boys, I deduced, were not as dumb as they looked. They would have controversial articles written about them in broadsheet newspapers. They would get thrown off tours and banned from the *Old Grey Whistle Test*. On the down side, they would take too many drugs, behave erratically and, like almost every act ever signed to Resurgam only more so, need to be watched.

It was barely four o'clock but already the late-autumn afternoon was seeping away. Outside the last of the daylight would be spilling over the Soho streets. The edges of Green Park would be filling up with shadow and the street lamps going on. The band, exhausted now and tetchy, allowed themselves to be borne away by taxi to whichever West End hotel was having the pleasure of receiving them, in preparation for tomorrow's showcase gig at the Lyceum. Down in the Noel Street basement the chairs were being stacked up and the left-over sandwiches tipped into refuse sacks. It was at times like this that the music business lost its charm and you pined for a life lived out in a panelled room overlooking a Mayfair square where nobody took too many Quaaludes or put their hands up the press officers' skirts. Pale-faced under the strip lighting, red-eyed from the clouds of cigarette smoke, clutching the double brandies that Rory had insisted on standing us, we stood around discussing the hours that had passed.

'Jesus,' said Trevor Jacomb, who was supposed to live uxoriously in Petts Wood with his wife and three children, 'did you see those birds who were eating the sandwiches?'

'Don't go there,' Rory counselled. 'You'll be pissing fish-hooks in a week.'

'Where's Paula?'

'She's gone with the band. She said if anyone laid a finger on her she'd break it in half.'

'What about Hermione?'

'I gave her the rest of the afternoon off. She said her parents were taking her to a reception at the Royal Academy.'

'How are we doing' – this was to Trevor Jacomb – 'with the costings for Red Hot and Rising?'

'I've been into it' Trevor said mournfully. He looked more than ever like a walrus for whom life had lost its savour, floating out to sea on some abandoned ice-floe. 'Six bands. Two dozen venues. All of them staying in hotels. Not to mention the train fares. I suppose they'll all want per diems and that. Can't be done for under a hundred grand.'

The chairs had been put away and the stage was awash with newly-inflated balloons. In another four hours it would be full of Japanese tourists drinking watered-down gin.

'What sort of hotels are you booking them into?'

'Oh, you know,' Trevor said. 'Rat-holes, mostly.'

'Couldn't we see if we could get some of them into youth hostels?'

'Now that,' Trevor conceded, 'is definitely a point. That, now, is definitely a point.'

And so, as the light faded in the darkling streets beyond and the DJ minced into his booth and began, for some reason, to play Harry Belafonte's 'Mary's Boy Child, Jesus Christ', we embarked on one of those conversations, so common to the early '80s independent music scene, in which huge amounts of evasiveness, feigned ignorance and reality-softening are brought to bear on a problem which all those caught up in it know can only be solved by borrowing large sums of money from an institution to whom an equally large sum of money is already owed.

* * *

How do the next half-dozen hours pass? Where do they go? Late-afternoon tea (Earl Grey, cucumber sandwiches, bone china) in the shadow of London Wall with a couple of Rory's venture capitalist chums, professional identities unknown, but addressed by Rory – very much at home in the world of office-blocks and sub-fusc suiting – as 'Farq' and 'Quoodle'; a taxi-dash back to Newman Street to see if any cheques have come in (there is one, from the Virgin Accounts Department, for £37.08); a prospectors' sortie to

Dingwall's Dance Hall, Camden Lock, with Doug Stroessner, the A&R guy, to catch a band called the Flowery Pastel Shades who according to *Melody Maker* are in the vanguard of something called 'the new psychedelia' ('"avant-garde retro?"' Doug wonders, as the first, plaintive Mellotron note sounds out above the heads of the twenty or so persons present. 'How about "nostalgic for an age yet to come?"' I lob back); on to an industry watering-hole around the back of King's Cross station, full of friendly girls with bubble-permed hair, where the talk is of Elvis (Costello), Nick (Lowe) and Tony (Wilson) and a wonderful little record shop in Notting Hill that supplies chart returns to the BMRB but couldn't care less about the same customer returning at five minute intervals to buy multiple copies of the same disc. Time runs on here in the early '80s, it steals away and can't be brought back. There is no room for manoeuvre, no spare hour for quiet reflection, no space for late-night reverie, just time rampaging on, so purposefully that you can barely see it pass.

Later – quite a lot later – I take a final cab back to Victoria and board the train for Ewell. London always looks good at this time of night. The light glints off the shopfronts in the deserted high streets, the shadows bounce back off the viaduct archways and the black dustbin sacks go skittering away in the breeze like cowled monks. The train runs on through the southern suburbs, through Clapham and Balham, gathers speed and then rattles to a halt at forgotten platforms where dull-eyed kids lounge by the vending machines and tattered posters advertise trips to Brighton and Selsey Bill, before pitching into Sutton and Cheam, where the rows of mock-Tudor houses on the hills beyond gleam in the moonlight, and I think about Mrs Thatcher, and whether we are pressing far too many copies of the Flame Throwers' album or simply too many, and a band called the Salamanders, whom Stroessner reckons are going to be the next big thing, and whether we can recoup the cost of the Maximum

Acceleration video shoot, and whether I ought to sack Bernie, the truculent ingrate who runs the mail order department.

At Ewell East a few late-night commuters carelessly unload onto the platform and I follow them over the main road and up into Arundel Avenue and walk with them companionably as they peel off, one by one, into their solid, car-strewn driveways, until there is only me toiling on through the naphtha glare past the meticulously set-out rows of dustbins awaiting next morning's collection. Back at Number 182 everything is just as I have left it. Here is the photograph of my mother. There is the Jim Dine drawing in its frame that I'd bought at Bob Fraser's gallery a dozen years ago. And here, too, gleaming from the door-mat in its cream-coloured envelope, with a neat little candle-wax seal that quivers beneath my fingers, is the letter from Don Shard's highly respectable legal man in Lincoln's Inn Fields in which, with a punctilious courtesy that does not disguise its faint undercurrent of menace, Don demands the return of the £20,000 he had lent me three years before, plus compound interest of seventeen per cent per annum, within the next 30 days.

Keeping Tabs on the Post-punk Revolution

The top end of Newman Street, London W1 – not far from the Middlesex Hospital, you'll understand, with the Post Office Tower aggrandising over the dusky autumn skyline – might seem an unlikely venue for a hip young indie record company to ply their precarious trade. Next door on one side is home to some kind of rag-trade procurer called, I kid you not, Tops & Bottoms, while left-hand neighbours are a snooty PR outfit through whose pristine portals sashays an endless file of corn-haired dollies who doubtless answer to names like Fenella and Antigone. Happily your reporter, struggling through the front door after a minute and a half's tussle with a defective intercom, is reassured by the sight of two or three hundred

Maximum Acceleration LPs piled up on a carpet that is not so much threadbare as threadless, next to somebody's front wheel-free bicycle and a leaf-drift of unclaimed mail. Yup, this is the place all right – a deduction soon confirmed by the unhurried arrival of an intrepid young lady named Hermione, who looks (and sounds) as if she should be out in the street daintily applying lip-balm with the Fenellas and the Antigones, but clearly doesn't take any fucking nonsense *at all*, and, as we ascend a leprous stair-flight to a reception area where half the furniture looks as if it been taken apart with an axe and then hastily reassembled by the Seven Dwarfs under Snow White's negligent supervision, a faint air of unease. This, Hermione concedes, is down to the recent enforced departure from the premises of the Bash Street Kids, a much-hyped addition to the Resurgam roster, who have just been paying a morning call. 'They're very nice boys,' Hermione wistfully opines, 'but they do rather get in the way.'

You can see Hermione's point, for this is indie-land, low-rent and cash-strapped, where the whole caboodle could be squeezed into a space the size of EMI's foyer and the marketing director operates out of a broom cupboard. The Newman Street establishment extends to eight or nine rooms spread over four doll's house floors, plus a basement which usually accommodates the mail order business but has on occasion been given over to video shoots ('We filmed the Girl on the Phone promo down there,' Hermione confides. 'It was so cramped I think the drummer ended up sitting under a table.') Here in reception all one has come to expect from that burgeoning independent sector we hear so much about these days is chaotically in evidence. A snaggle-toothed ex-hippy who looks as if he ought to be toting gear for the Grateful Dead but is apparently the Head of A&R is loudly informing a telephone receiver in a faux-Yank accent that, naw, he won't be coming to Dingwalls tonight to see whichever bunch of also-rans is being lined up for his delectation, and a messenger boy in black leathers is delivering what might, at five yards distance, be taken for a picture of a pool of vomit but soon reveals itself as the artwork for Chloe and the Cupcakes' forthcoming album. Alongside the junk-piled mahogany desk-top sits a monstrous wicker basket, in which the infant Moses could happily have sailed off down the Nile, containing the five or six hundred cassette tapes which have arrived on the premises since the company moved in four months ago ('We try to listen to them in the lunch-hour,' Hermione wearily explains, 'but it's like being the little Dutch Boy with your finger in the dyke.') It turns out that Hermione's current task, abetted by a pair of breeze-block-sized rail directories, is to settle the logistical side of next week's 'Red Hot and Rising' tour, in which half-a-dozen of the label's finest will travel by train and charabanc around the British Isles promoting their wares to audiences as far afield as Aberdeen and Merthyr Tydfil, and on which a great deal of next year's liquidity supposedly depends.

'Is Ska still in?' the A&R honcho wonders, with a dreamy eye that suggests he'd much sooner be back at the Filmore West queuing up for a plate of brown rice and waiting for the Quicksilver Messenger Service to start shifting the stale air around. Meanwhile, a shock-haired girl with a seriously thrombosed vein on her left forearm – where do they get these bohemian chicks? Do they come as a free gift with the office stereogram? – has started ripping open a succession of padded bags and morosely upending their contents (more cassettes, natch) into the wicker basket, and Hermione, for all the world like the chatelaine of some stately home lodged snugly amidst the Home Counties verdure, advises tea ('There's Earl Grey or China. I'm afraid the Pekoe Points has run out'), after which, mug in hand, stumbling a little on staircases strewn with rolls of masking tape and promotional buttons with arresting slogans like 'Fuck Art, Let's Dance', I am escorted hither and yon to the office at the very top of the building occupied by Resurgam's MD, Nick Du Pont.

Here, in contrast to the downstairs free-for-all, all is stately decorum: plush carpeting, the Resurgam back catalogue tastefully arranged beneath polythene covers along one wall (and containing the prodigiously rare picture-disc version of The Unclean's 'Radioactive Man' which your reporter would dearly like to smuggle home with him given half a chance), Aubrey Beardsley prints along the other. Mr Du Pont, now in his late '30s, but not outwardly fazed by all these hip young people who now seem to have the biz in their sweaty grasp, is by all accounts an affable and mild-mannered guy. Why, on the famous occasions when Wayne Golightly, The Unclean's raucous bass player threw up over his outstretched leg back-stage at the Vortex a moment or two before his arraignment by the Feds on a charge of behaviour liable to cause a breach of the peace, he is supposed to have muttered something to the effect that boys will be boys. Now Richard Branson, you suspect, would be *quite cross*.

Two and a half years now since Resurgam first launched its brand onto the marketplace via that sadly neglected Unclean single (#73 on the BBC singles chart) and one or two other hottish items. What can be said of its subsequent trajectory? Sure, there have been occasional hits – Girl on the Phone's new 45 is currently reposing at No. 22 – along with a fair few misses, and turnover is supposed to be running at around £2 million. To counter this ability to give such rival outfits as Stiff and Beggar's Banquet a run for their money come rumours of laggardly cash-flow and a deep-seated reluctance to remit royalty payments on time. The soft-spoken Du Pont is happy to admit that mistakes have been made. 'Are we victims of our own success? Not necessarily, but moving beyond one level of achievement to another is incredibly difficult. I mean, in the early days we were running things on a shoestring. The Unclean single was recorded for £200, and John Leckie produced it for free, simply as a favour to me. In those days it was our policy to sign bands on one-off deals, with the aim of making enough money off one release to pay for the next. If a single sold

3,000 copies we'd break even, but even then the profit would come from mail order sales with better margins. Then we had the Paper Plane album [1979's *Mission Aborted*], which sold 100,000, and I can tell you that if you have one big success you actually need two more to pay for the incidental costs you'll incur with the first one. You know: the band want more money; the band's manager wants a promotional video that isn't filmed in our basement; and then somebody has to support the tour.'

And what about the suggestion that the company sometimes lacks even the ready spondulicks necessary to pay for its postage and stationery supplies? 'Well, I'll be perfectly honest with you. There have been occasions on which I have picked up the morning's outgoing mail, taken it round to Virgin [*major league sponsors with whom Resurgam have inked a pressing and distribution deal*] and quietly put it through the franking machine.' Would Mr Du Pont like to elaborate on the Virgin deal, to the extent of possibly letting us know just exactly what percentage of the Resurgam catalogue Virgin owns? No he would not, but he consents to talk about one or two of the label's most cherished acts. 'Cedric?' [*the gum-chewing, thatch-haired teenager with the NHS glasses and the imperfectly tuned acoustic guitar, none of whose records has done a thing.*] 'I've always had a soft spot for Cedric, ever since he came in that first time with his demo tape. I think we even gave him his tube-fare home. Charysse? People are always going on about how she sounds like Kate Bush. Well, I'm her commercial sponsor, and I think Kate Bush sounds like her.'

At intervals the fragrant Hermione wafts in with more tea, phone messages, cheques requiring signature, scrawled faxes, news of fresh crises and embarrassments and the apparently unwelcome information that three-fourths of weedy Mod revivalists The Scooter Boys are waiting in reception. What does our man think of the current state of English Pop, from the perspective of one who cut his teeth in the razzle-dazzle days of the Sixties and accompanied legendary scenesters The Helium Kids around the frenzied amphitheatres of the mid-West? 'I think it's terrifically interesting. I think we're operating at one of those rare moments when the left-field is able to colonise the mainstream in a way that hasn't happened for a dozen years, and the major record labels haven't a clue. Yes, some of the things we do are aimed at making money, but the money is there to subsidize the things we really like.' As we descend the tottering staircase a terrific racket from below suggests that someone has put the Flame Throwers album our reviewer was so excited about the other week on at full volume. A smiling Du Pont checks his watch and says it's about that time when the PR company rings up to complain about the noise anyway. 'There's a post-punk revolution going on out there' he explains, 'and we're keeping tabs on it.'

Sounds, 15 November 1980.

6. HIT THE NORTH

Yeah, we're away somewhere
Don't know why, but we're away somewhere
You and I, got to fly, get away somewhere.
CHLOE AND THE CUPCAKES – *Away Somewhere*

Here on the 11.14 from King's Cross to Leeds, a moment or so before departure, tension crackles in the air. A couple of British Transport policemen have already put their heads around the door to enquire about the luggage trolleys that have been sailing up and down the platform hard by and been repulsed by know-nothing stares. From their vantage-points a few feet away on the asphalt surround, station staff peer anxiously through the unwashed windows, like aquarium visitors approaching the tank where the conga eels glide. Up and down the two carriages reserved for Resurgam artistes, the bands have formed neurotic and self-sustaining huddles. Maximum Acceleration – four storm-wracked twenty-somethings in army surplus greatcoats – are playing pocket chess and reading the morning's *Guardian*. One of them, additionally, is toting a paperback copy of Dostoevsky's *Notes from Underground*. The five members of Chloe and the Cupcakes, nun-like, demure, and accompanied by Flopsy the bass player's mother in the role of chaperone, are gathered over a bag of boiled sweets. Cedric, bespectacled and be-mufflered, his face set in eerie focus by an outsize poster advertising British Railways day-trips ('A cheap holiday/ Do it today') is playing blues scales on an acoustic guitar that badly wants tuning. The exception to this phalanx of fearful introversion are the Bash Street Kids, they of the skidding luggage trolleys and the surly mien – Bermondsey skin-heads with parched, parrot faces who sprawl at the compartment's farther end, yelling and occasionally throwing things and clearly not giving a fuck about British Transport policemen, the disciplinary fiats circulated earlier this morning to each band's manager, or anything else. As the train lurches forward a half-empty Coke can zings forward with such force that it nearly takes off Flopsy the bass player's flaxen head, only for Rory, no doubt remembering his time in the Charterhouse XI, to loft a hand high over his shoulder and pluck it negligently out of the air. One of the Cupcakes gives a tiny shriek of terror. As well as carrying a copy of *Notes From Underground*, the boy in the army greatcoat turns out to be wearing a peaked cap emblazoned with the slogan NIETZSCHE LIVES. The train stumbles forward, hangs suspended in mid-transit for a second or two as if vast, elemental forces are fighting over its destiny and then bounds on.

At the table nearest the door, remote from the Bash Street Kids and Cedric's blues scales, the atmosphere is appreciably less fraught. 'I'd give her one. Absolutely I would,' Trevor Jacomb insists, slapping down a copy of the *Daily Mirror*, where there is a picture of Lady Diana Spencer – who even now the papers are starting to call 'Lady Di' – fresh from her weekend at Balmoral. 'No you wouldn't' Rory chides him. He looks furious, beyond cross. 'If you knocked at the door of that flat of hers in Coleherne Court she'd send you down to the basement to service the boiler, you oik.' There are financial documents on the table-top: columns of figures in red and blue, tantalising yet ineluctable. The train is rumbling on now, through debased suburbs and sprawling municipal car-parks. In the countryside beyond there is early snow on the ground and the land runs away like muscle. 'Hey,' says Paula, who has the week's music papers on her lap and whose fingers are consequently black with printers' ink. 'There's a review of the Maximum Acceleration single in *Melody Maker*.' 'What does it say?' '*Crystalline refulgence from a fresh dimension*.' 'Is that meant to be a compliment?' 'You tell me,' Paula says, a veteran of the days when record reviews confined themselves to adjectives like 'fab' and 'happening'. 'I just send the stuff in to the review editors. I can't be expected to interpret what they write.' The picture of Lady Di lies on the table between us. She looks game but fragile, like some exotic antelope briefly glimpsed on the forest's edge. Does she have any idea of the vast societal forces that are being unleashed over her innocent head? Who can tell. 'How's *Breakfast* doing?' I ask Trevor, still subdued by Rory's put-down, and Trevor brightens, shifts his *Elephant Man* shoulders sharply to one side and says forty, but the radio play has dwindled away to nothing after the women's groups started complaining about 'Jackie O'. 'You're a woman,' I say to Paula, who is half-way through the cavalcade of omniscience and belittlement that is the *NME* letters page, 'what do you think of 'Jackie O'?' 'I'm a record company press officer,' Paula says severely. 'All my values are expedient. Except if some fucking goblin puts his hand on my tits. Then they get a bit less expedient.' The snow-scape has gone now, to be replaced by sodden meadows, files of ash-trees, spiralling black birds and neatly tilled fields. 'Jesus,' Trevor Jacomb says, as a picturesque, shambling figure materialises at the end of the carriage, trips over a leg playfully extended by one of the Bash Street Kids and goes sprawling in a heap. 'Who the fuck is that?' 'That's Desmond the tour manager,' Paula tells him. 'You were there when he was hired. Don't tell me you don't remember. He used to be in Sam Apple Pie back when the world was young. He's famous for not taking any shit.' 'That's good,' I say, watching Desmond climb gingerly to his feet with one hand clutching his elbow. 'If there's one thing we need on this tour it's someone who doesn't take any shit.' Lady Di. Maximum Acceleration in their great-coats. The rows of washed-out faces. Ten years ago I was sitting on the Oblivion Express as it rose into the skies above New York as the Helium Kids joshed and bickered and experimented with the pharmacopoeia. The difference between then and now, I tell myself, is that back in the Sixties the people were larger than life, whereas now they are mysteriously smaller than it, subtly diminished and ground-down.

Meanwhile, there are more pressing concerns to hand. 'What about the per diems?' I ask Trevor Jacomb. Rory is scribbling abstruse marginalia like *Profit def.* and *4% compound* on the columns of figures. 'Five quid a head a day,' Trevor assures me. 'Give 'em much more than that and they'll just spend it on getting rat-arsed. That's £160 for the lot. Anything else and we go into the red on the tour.' 'Aren't we into the red already?' 'You saw the projections,' Trevor says stiffly. 'What are the ticket sales like?' 'They're good,' Trevor says, who clearly has no idea about the ticket sales, going into the red, or anything else. 'Fucking tremendous in fact.' 'Nick,' Paula says, who has now reached the gossip column of the *NME*. 'Nicko. It says here that Girl on the Phone's manager was seen coming out of United Artists the other day and they're about to sign a four-album deal.' 'Fucking ungrateful *cunts*,' Trevor Jacomb says. The letter from Don's solicitor sits in my pocket. Presently I will discuss its contents with Rory. But not yet awhile. Desmond the tour manager, his brow corrugated with pain, sits crumpled up in one of the aisle seats being fussed over by Flopsy's mother. It can never have been like this in Sam Apple Pie. The train is barrelling north now, beneath lowering skies, over the Midland plain where the fields run on like squares in a patchwork quilt. Heads bent low over the table-top, Chloe and the Cupcakes are playing snap, giving ecstatic little squeals of pleasure when the cards coincide. 'Actually,' Trevor says, all thought of aristocratic dalliance behind him, 'I wouldn't mind giving one of Chloe and the Cupcakes one.' 'That's right,' Rory says approvingly. He is in a better temper now. 'Stick to your social level. That's what I always say' and Trevor bridles as at the wildest compliment. All I know of Trevor's wife, back indoors at Petts Wood, is that she dislikes late nights and loud noises and once, when being taught to drive, crashed a Ford Capri through the garage doors. The account of this epic misadventure ('*Fuck's* sake, Michelle, use the fucking *brakes* you clueless bint') is one of Trevor's party pieces.

There is fine rain falling against the carriage windows now, streaking the grey glass and slashing little rivulets through the accumulated dirt. Stirred by its faint yet ominous rattle, the artistes stare out at the passing terrain. Their pale faces are alive with curiosity. They are city kids. All this – the stoical sheep, the traffic clogging the far-away country roads, the bright chips of colour – is entirely alien to them, quite beyond their power to assimilate. Hermione, dressed in a vivid green trouser suit, prowls silently among them, ticking off the names on her roster. 'I think everyone's here,' she says, reaching the table where we sit. Hermione walks with an extraordinary poise, balancing on the balls of her feet, adroit and pantherine, as if only the respect she owes her employer is preventing her from springing up onto the luggage rack and crouching there with the suitcases. 'Apart from the Dub Imposters. Does anyone know where they are?' 'Coming up in the van, I heard,' Trevor says. 'And just as well too.' The multi-racial nature of the tour is possibly not to his taste. 'Nick' Paula says, who has left her seat to pluck a small, green-complexioned man with an upturned button nose like a hedgehog's from his hidey-hole further down the carriage. 'This is…this is…what did you say your name was? The guy from the *NME* who's covering the tour.' 'Howard,' says the guy from the *NME*, whipping out a Dictaphone from the folds of his jacket and holding it in his outstretched palm like a votive offering. 'Pleased to meet you gentlemen. Could I ask you what your aims are for this excursion?' There is a silence, broken in the end by Rory's precisely modulated drawl. 'Frankly, Howard, we see it as the first step towards world domination…And now I suggest you go and talk to some of the bands.' '*Jesus*,' Trevor complains, as Howard retreats out of earshot. 'I thought they were sending Paul Morley.' 'He's in Norway with Orchestral Manoeuvres in the Dark,' somebody volunteers. By this stage I have Howard by his leather-jacketed shoulder. 'Essentially we have three aims,' I tell him. 'Expose the bands to a wider audience, shift some product and make a splash. You're here to help us make the splash.' Howard smiles gratefully. It is clear that this is the first time the MD of any record company, large or small, has so much as given him the time of day.

'You know what?' Trevor says out of nowhere. 'We ought to do a novelty record.' 'What kind of a novelty record?' 'Well,' Trevor says, a bit nonplussed by this automatic request for details. 'Get some old trouper like Dusty Springfield or' – his mind is roving back through distant canyons, antediluvian strata of the pop firmament – 'or Sandie Shaw. And then have – I dunno – the Cupcakes or someone backing them. 'That's a great idea, Trev,' I tell him. 'What about getting the Band of the Coldstream Guards in as well? Think of that on *Top of the Pops*.' Trevor, for whom irony is a hopeful dream, blinks stolidly. There is a sudden commotion from the rear of the carriage as two members of the Bash Street Kids, Sta-Prest jeans lowered to their ankles, leap onto the table and start mooning at the knot of elderly ladies on the station platform at which the train is now gently drawing in. 'Hell's teeth,' Rory says, jumping to his feet. Anxious eyes follow his transit. 'I wouldn't tangle with them lads,' Trevor says. 'And me from Penge and all.' 'I hear they carry knuckle-dusters,' Paula says. 'Had I better pull the communication cord?' Hermione wonders. But Rory, miraculously, has the situation in hand. 'Now look here,' he declares, arriving at the source of the trouble and quelling it in an instant. 'You're wasting your time, the school's time and your parents' money.' There is a second or two's hesitation, a bashful exchange of glances and then, shamefacedly, the tough boys from Bermondsey start pulling up their trousers. 'That's *much* better,' Rory says encouragingly. 'How did you do it, Rory?' I enquire as he returns to his seat. 'Perfectly straightforward' Rory says. 'It's just a question of having certain standards and making sure you enforce them. And all so much easier if you're dealing with the working classes. People always forget that the key alliance in English social life is between the gentry and the proletariat. All based on their hatred of the upstart middle class. Now, if a *petit-bourgeois* had interfered with those hooligans I daresay there'd have been blood all over the floor.'

* * *

At Leeds there is a banner draped over one of the arches that says RED HOT & RISING, a photographer from the *Yorkshire Post* taking snap-shots, and two representatives of a local punk fanzine anxious to interview the Bash Street Kids. There are also three policemen with a couple of Alsatians slavering at their heels and a riot van parked up on the station forecourt. Happily Rory, the survivor of many a Boat Race night riot and Commemoration Ball run-in, is equal to the task. There is solemn talk of horseplay, youthful high spirits and misplaced enthusiasm. It is amazing that anyone believes this stuff, but still they do. The policemen are obsequious. One of them even removes his peaked cap. Meanwhile, a doctor summoned to examine Desmond's lifeless arm diagnoses a broken elbow. Silently we debouch onto grey streets where the newspaper placards read: LATEST WARNING: RIPPER MAY STRIKE AGAIN. Leeds is grim and rain-swept. 'Fucking northern *dump*,' says Trevor, for whom Petts Wood is the pleasure dome of Kublai Khan and anything beyond it a Mordor ash-pit. As in a film, where everything is contingent and each animate object keenly awaits its cue, a coach arrives to ferry the artistes away to their Holiday Inn in Chapeltown. Rory simply disappears – like many upper-class people he has the ability to teleport in and out of life on the spot – and Trevor and I slink off to a department store coffee shop where elderly ladies converse in genteel north country tones and the waitresses are got up like pre-war parlour-maids. Here, to our surprise and faint dissatisfaction, we are joined by Howard from the *NME*, who turns out to have followed us from the station and for whom no other provision has been made. 'Mind if I join you gentlemen?' he enquires, in the tone of one for whom no place has ever been set and for whom no hotel accommodation has ever been booked, and Trevor takes pity on him, heaves up an extra chair and says, 'Take a pew old man' in the parody of Rory's voice that has taken him all of six months to perfect. 'I saw the Flame Throwers the other week,' Howard says, much more at home amid the tea-cakes and buttered toast than in a crowded railway carriage. 'Oh yes, what were they like?' 'Well,' Howard says judiciously, 'I'd have had the bass a bit lower down in the mix and given it a bit of treble if it was me.' 'Jesus,' Trevor says, 'he means: what were they *like*?' 'Not bad,' Howard says guardedly. 'How many copies of *Breakfast* have you done?' 'Sixty,' Trevor tells him. 'Actually, seventy. Why don't you print that in your fucking paper?' With the prospect of a nervous underling to bully, he is a man transformed. 'Do you think I can get any lemon tea here?' Howard wonders, and Trevor stares at him as if the gates of Buckingham Palace have swung open to reveal a Lost World of mastodons and pterodactyls taking flight.

There are posters on the coffee shop wall advertising stand-up comedians, philharmonic orchestras, brass bands, repertory companies doing *An Inspector Calls*: all the shot paraphernalia of northern cultural life. 'Meant to tell you,' Trevor says, well into his third tea-cake, crumbs a-quiver on his undulating upper lip. 'I phoned the office from the station and Maximum Acceleration are in at 41. They want them to do the *Pops* tomorrow.' 'That won't be easy to arrange, surely?' Howard ventures. 'Why don't you fuck off?' Trevor says in a fatherly tone, recalibrating the angle of his big, ungainly body in its chair. 'What we'll do is hire a van, get down there for rehearsal and see if we can't make it back to Sheffield by 10.' 'How are you sorting out the bill?' Howard asks, who clearly imagines himself to be luxuriating in a new-found three-way friendship. 'Theoretically, we're drawing lots,' I explain. 'But in practice Bash Street Kids and Maximum Acceleration will be headlining on alternate nights.' 'Won't the others mind?' 'They can mind all they like,' Trevor says. 'The Cup Cakes are still ten grand in the hole for production costs on their last album. Them girls'll have to take anything they can get.' 'Can I write that down?' Howard wonders. 'Only if you want your neck broke,' Trevor tells him. Howard laughs. It is clear that much worse things have been said to him, whether at provincial tea-tables or over the bar of the Speakeasy, and that this is the merest gossamer banter.

It is half-past four now. The afternoon is drifting away and the Yorkshire sky beyond the department store windows is as dark as pitch. The old ladies are packing up their reticules and heading off to retirement bungalows in Headingley and Chapel Allerton. The wind, blowing in through the half-open door behind them, brings with it a swirl of fallen leaves and also a faint sense of melancholy. Time is passing. Passing it is. Ten years ago I was checking into luxury hotels under the sour Ohio sky, watching the Helium Kids rack up $800 bar bills and the bell-hops leap to attention as they sauntered by. Now I am sitting in a department store tea-shop in the English provinces with a man who looks like an outsize teddy-bear filled with sawdust and a reservation at the local Holiday Inn. There is also the small matter of my indebtedness to Virgin Records, the bank and, dwarfing both these creditors in terms of the damage is he is liable to do me, Mr Donald Aloysius Shard. Something of this unease seems to communicate itself to Trevor, who finishes his final tea-cake, slaps himself on the forehead as if some vexatious parasite were trying to burrow its way out of his skull and stares at the dirty crockery as if it were a symbol of every blighted hope he had ever nurtured. 'Can't stand being out of the smoke' says the tribune of Petts Wood. 'The beer's piss and everyone talks funny.' Howard, too, has lost his air of breezy companionability. 'Do you know,' he says anxiously, 'that Toddy or whatever his name is from the Bash Street Kids said that if I wrote anything about him he didn't like he'd rip my head off?' 'Yeah, he would and all,' Trevor says. 'Proper hard case, that Toddy. Come on son, cheer up. How much do you want?' And to Howard's and my own considerable astonishment he plucks a roll of notes out of his jacket pocket, slips off the elastic band that tethers them and counts half-a-dozen tens and twenties onto the table-top. 'Go on. Take a cab to Chapeltown and buy yourself a fifty-pound tart. Have one on your uncle Trevor.' 'I can't accept this,' Howard says, genuinely aghast. Beneath the leather jacket and the feather-cut hair, he is just a middle-class boy, perilously adrift in a sea of sharks. 'What would my editor say if he found out?' 'Come on son,' Trevor counsels. 'You've got to go with the flow.' Stealthily, the rank scent of collusion rising above our heads, we head out into the darkling streets.

* * *

Twenty minutes later I am safely installed in my room at the Holiday Inn, far away from Trevor, Howard and the promise of fifty-pound tarts. Or maybe not that far, as propped up on the pillow next to the messages asking me to phone the office, the promoter in Sheffield and the Virgin pressing plant, is a terse letter from the hotel management asking me to sign an indemnity against damages. Meanwhile, from a distant corridor comes the rumble of booted feet in rapid transit and a ripple or two of girlish laughter. It is going to be quite a night. In the hotel suites of California, Florida and the American mid-West one found flower-arrangements and dry cleaners' bills of fare. Here at the Holiday Inn there is a Gideon Bible in the bedside cabinet, a Goblin Teasmade and three pieces of shortbread in a cellophane wrapper. Outside, the dense hummocks of the North York moors rise into the twilit sky. Doug, reached at the office in Newman Street and sounding as if a pile of sludge has been poured over his head, agrees that it's great about Maximum Acceleration ('I always told you those little fuckers could cut it') but confides that the cover of the Planet Claire album has come out purple instead of red and that Girl on the Phone's guitarist has been arrested for possession with intent to supply and will appear at Marylebone Magistrates' Court the following morning. 'Will they let him off, do you think?' I enquire. 'It was only a gram and a half,' says Doug, whose knowledge of the pharmacological end of the statute book is worryingly exact. 'They'll be busting you for taking aspirins soon.'

Down in the bar half-an-hour later the atmosphere is calmer but no less charged with menace. Rory and Trevor, class antagonisms forgotten, are drinking brandies together by the fire. Hermione, who has exchanged her trouser-suit for a pair of Lady Di-style culottes and a pussycat bow, is poring over the evening's schedule. 'What happened to the Dub Imposters?' I ask. 'Oh, they're here somewhere,' Hermione says brightly. Her once impassive face is showing signs of wear and tear. 'I hope the Bash Street Kids aren't giving you too much trouble?' 'Oh no,' Hermione returns. 'They're rather sweet. They think I'm a piece of posh totty. Besides, they're rather over-awed. I don't think any of them have ever stayed in a hotel before. They had to ask how you worked the Teasmade.' 'Hermione,' I jovially remonstrate. 'How can you bear to do this job?' 'It was either the Courtauld Institute, being a Norland nanny or marrying Jonty,' Hermione explains. 'Not much of a choice, really.' 'I say, that bird's rather dishy,' Rory exclaims, looking up from his brandy as Chloe from the Cupcakes – a pale, elfin girl with hair so extravagantly bobbed that it hangs down the sides of her face in outsize commas – wanders by. 'Doesn't say much, though.' It is six o'clock now, and a blanket of responsibility has settled on the room. There is still no sign of the Dub Imposters. The Cupcakes sidle out in ones and twos to the lavatory, come back to their seats and then nervously dash out again. Flopsy's mother, imperious in a cable-knit jumper and a skirt like a bell-tent, can be heard instructing her daughter to take a paracetamol if she must but on no account go near the Codeine. Heads are bent over set-lists. The Bash Streets disappear to a corridor behind the fire escape to – it is presumed – snort lines of amphetamine sulphate. 'I talked to the promoter' Hermione says, 'and they've sold 800 tickets.' 'Is that good?' 'Well, he says Siouxsie and the Banshees sold a thousand…I'm sure we'll make it up in sales at the door.' The rain rattles against uncurtained windows, the gas-fire pops like one of the newly fashionable synth drums that are appearing in every studio from Marble Arch to Spitalfields. The Bash Street Kids, fresh from their sulphate binge, look extra-worldly, like the gaunt, bony survivors of cataclysm and famine. Imperceptibly, the proceedings take on an abstract, mechanical air. Soon, without anybody appearing to be in the least responsible for them, things will begin to happen. Somehow, without obvious effort, the geometry of the evening will fall into place. 'How did the soundcheck go?' I ask, and Desmond the tour manager, right arm strapped to his chest, bobs up to opine that the PA is seriously fucked and that Cedric needs to get his act together.

The gig is at the Poly, out in Headingley, to which an ancient coach, like a reconditioned charabanc with curiously high seats two or three feet off the floor, crawls at a snail's pace through the mid-evening traffic. The Dub Imposters lounge at the back beneath clouds of sweet-smelling smoke. Dropping five pieces of paper each bearing the name of one of the bands into an upturned baseball cap borrowed from one of the roadies, and gripping the crown so tightly that only the two marked 'Bash Street Kids' and 'Maximum Acceleration' obtrude, I present it to Chloe and ask her to select this evening's bill-topper. The Bash Street Kids, having made the cut, are warmly congratulated on this lucky chance. Shortly afterwards, the slither and scurry of the roadway yields up to a tableland of playing-fields and meadows veiled in shadow, a view of student hostels and sturdy institutional architecture. Here, as the venue slides into view and the coach drifts neatly into its bay, the novelty of the lot-drawing is forgotten and ritual takes over. The bands drift off to basement dressing rooms. There are scurfy kids lined up by the door and other scurfy kids in the concrete spaces beyond handing out flyers. And here, too, as quick to their cues as anyone, are the pale boy and girl in their trench-coats asking, with an immense, optimistic courtesy, if I am Mr Du Pont and pressing a C60 cassette tape into my hand. Standing half-way up the tier of steps, with the wind in my hair, and the plate-glass portal opening to receive me, I am struck by an extraordinary existential weariness. Like the man in the Velvet Underground song, I could sleep for a thousand years. Meanwhile, a bouncer is telling the first of the scurfy kids that the doors aren't open for another 25 minutes and he can fuck off out of it. From deep within the bowels of the building comes the sound of somebody hitting a snare drum. The pale boy and his companion slip away. The bouncer stamps his feet vigorously up and down as if treading grapes. The wind swoops and eddies. I put the cassette tape in the inside pocket of my jacket, where it nestles next to my heart, and sail on in.

Bash Street Kids/Maximum Acceleration/Chloe and the Cupcakes/ The Dub Imposters/Cedric – *Leeds Polytechnic, 4 December*

The crowd at Leeds Poly are in two minds about the Resurgam package, which debuts here under storm-whacked skies and the rumble of thunder contending with the four (count 'em) drummers who at one time or another take to the stage. Sure, it's no kind of a night to be out in, and, yes, ripper-mania has sent the place into anguished lockdown (there are security patrols outside waiting to escort female members of the audience back to their domiciles) but the smattering of weak applause that greets weedy little Cedric as he wanders on stage with an acoustic guitar slung over his spindly torso sounds like a room-full of three year-olds being taught to play pat-a-cake. It's not much better 20 minutes later when our man shuffles off again, having concluded with a guileless little number about Marvin the Electric Goat or something, but he's a good-humoured lad and waves his hand as if he were guesting with Led Zep at Madison Square Garden. Next come the Dub Imposters, who keep themselves to themselves, lock into a juddering Trenchtown groove that doesn't seem to alter from one song to the next and, being black, don't give a stuff about the mostly white audience. They get, if anything, an even worse reception, leaving it to Chloe and her Cupcakes – mod cuties from Wivenhoe with Cilla Black hair-dos – to liven things up, which would be just fine had not Chloe's voice been so far back in the mix as to render it negligible and the Farfisa organ played by an uber-bobbed babette named Mitzi been dangerously off-key. The PA, by the way, is the worst I've heard since Blue Oyster Cult, playing the Hammersmith Odeon last year, left the first five rows stone deaf.

Maximum Acceleration, who take an age to get their gear into commission – and you can't fault them for that: the stage is strewn with so much clobber that the Cupcakes, who usually like to frisk around a little, are obliged to stand rooted to the spot – look as if they don't overmuch want to be here. Or perhaps sulking goes with their image, which, as it consists of greatcoats, wrap around shades and songs about Russian novels they've been reading, puts this unbiased observer seriously in mind of Joy Division. Still, they play 'Penal Colony', the new single, which has a hook to catch a Bluefin Tuna on, and end up looking cheerier than they did when they arrived. That leaves Bermondsey's finest, the Bash Street Kids, who are what the shaven-headed gentlemen who constitute their audience would call well hard, and – to be fair – knock out a considerable if mostly untutored racket to conclude the proceedings. Ultimately the rama-lama guitar sound gets a mite tedious and Toddy the singer has clearly been indulging in some illegal stimulants, but there is some amusing heckling from the Leeds supporters (the Kids are all Millwall fans) which ends with Toddy announcing that any Leeds cunt who wants to is welcome to come on stage and see what he can do. There are no takers.

'Your Man', Howard Cunningham

Ten hours later, in a grim, high-ceilinged dining-hall under crazed artificial light and with varying degrees of enthusiasm, the company reassembles for breakfast. Trevor champs his way eagerly through three bowls of cornflakes and a rack of toast and then orders the plateful of smoking horror known as the Businessman's Special. One of the Cupcakes checks her face for spots in a hand-mirror. As one who sat innocently by on the occasion when Stefano was presented with a bill for the $10,483.15 worth of damages knocked up the Helium Kids at a hotel in Columbus, Ohio one sultry night in 1971, I sign a cheque for £67.70 to cover the cost of the two fire-extinguishers let off on the second floor sometime in the small hours with an easy conscience. Outside the grey northern sky threatens rain. There is more stuff in the papers about the ripper, vigilante patrols and the roots of male violence. Rory, it turns out, has upped and gone, back down south to talk to the money men. The tour will be moving on to Sheffield, but like Rory, Trevor and I are wanted elsewhere. 'Transport?' I murmur across the seething remains of the Businessman's Special, and Trevor looks up from the line of mini-yoghurts he has picked out for dessert and says 'Got us a transit.' Logistical dilemmas are Trevor's forte. A record company executive stuck in a lift; three bands booked into two studios five miles apart; half a ton of vinyl delayed by strike action – these are the situations in which he excels, deals he can handle. In the lobby, as Trevor buttons himself into an under-sized Gannex mac from which his arms dangle like a cartoon character, the pale boy in the trench-coat glides noiselessly into view and presses another cassette into my hand. 'You'll like this one, Mr Du Pont' he says. 'I'm sure I shall,' I say. The freezing air rolls in through the half-open door, swirls around our ankles and sets the row of pot-plants in anxious motion.

Twenty minutes later we are heading down the motorway into the oncoming rain. Maximum Acceleration sit meekly in the back, wedged against the surprisingly large amount of equipment thought necessary for the trip. Some of this is imperfectly secured: every so often a cymbal or a guitar-lead goes crashing into the tyre-wells. Maximum Acceleration, of whom I haven't previously taken much notice, are one-time Politics students from the University of Newcastle. This fact is revealed when Trevor and I have one of our arguments – so common in the early '80s – about the changing shape of the industry. 'Jesus,' Trevor says, who is thought to have begun his career in a music publisher's office in Denmark Street, 'Give me the old Tin Pan Alley days any time. Kid writes a song. You get a bunch of session guys to cut it at union rates. Then you hire some long-haired wanker on a water-tight contract to mime it on TV. Clear a couple of grand and Bob's your uncle.' On the contrary, I tell him, all the boys in leather jackets in the summer of 1976 that Trevor hates so much struck a blow for self-determination and independent record companies such as ourselves. Whereupon the lead singer notes that we are really taking control of the means of production, only to be corrected by the drummer who wonders whether this isn't merely another manifestation of Adorno's exchange society. 'Something like that,' Trevor says miserably. 'Who are we on with anyway tonight, Mr Jacomb?' asks the drummer, and Trevor consults the cigarette packet on which he recorded this information earlier that morning. 'Some black geezer I never heard of. That Irish lot who did the one about hating Mondays and a fucking kids' choir singing about their grandmas.' Like many a Tin Pan Alley old timer, Trevor remembers repertoire rather than the people who perform it. He gives an angry little flick of his wrist, steers the van cavalierly around a couple of HGVs and surges on.

At Television Centre, where we spend the next five hours, the atmosphere is like a Sixties holiday camp, with men in scarlet blazers ordering droves of docile onlookers from one vantage point to another. The audience – plump girls in sawn-off shorts, pretty boys with frothy, back-combed hair, a punk or two bussed in to give the proceedings an edge – drift listlessly into place at their command. Above our heads, in gantries and camera-towers, technicians scuttle in and out of view. Down in the warren of dressing-rooms, where the bands linger over vending machines and high-heeled production assistants tear back and forth, all is maximally incongruous. The girls from the dance troupe sit around on packing cases smoking cigarettes and dealing with snagged finger-nails. A Radio One DJ goes by eating a piece of toast out of the palm of his hand. The boys are alternately impressed and suspicious: clearly a Politics degree can only take you so far. 'It's a bit *plastic*, isn't it?' one of them wonders. 'Is that Bob Geldof?' someone else asks. When finally summoned to the stage, they are oddly static, motionless beneath the savage light. 'They ought to move around a bit,' Trevor says dejectedly. 'No one ever got anywhere standing still on the *Pops*. Christ, when Freddie and the Dreamers were on here it was like the fuckers were doing the Triple Jump.' As the music, stately and angular, floods out of the speakers and dry ice rises to the gantries, I find myself inspecting the plump girls in the sawn-off shorts. Their movements – shimmying undulations, jerky rhythmic twitches and feints – are curiously half-hearted. Maximum Acceleration are clearly not their kind of thing. Trevor, too, turns out to be watching the plump girls dance. 'You know what?' he says. 'Wouldn't let any kid of mine come down here.' 'No?' 'Fucking knocking shop,' Trevor says. '*Under-age* knocking shop and all.' A jaunty girl from the dance troupe clad in fishnet stockings and a rainbow-coloured tank-top grabs him fondly by the arm. 'Trevor, love! What are you doing here?' 'With this lot aren't I?' Trevor says, jabbing a dismissive thumb over his shoulder as the last strains of 'Penal Colony' steal out upon the dead air. 'What about you?' 'Dancing to Shakatak or someone.' 'Nice gel,' Trevor confides as she disappears back into the crowd. 'Used to go out with Rod Stewart.'

All around us the pale afternoon is waning. The plump girls look sickly and exhausted and are revived with Mars Bars and cans of Coke. From other strategically arranged podia Eddie Grant, the Boomtown Rats and the St Winifred's School Choir do their stuff. Additional guests – faded comedy stars, an Australian metal band, Abba – are glimpsed on video. The Abba girls look thoughtful, as if chastened by the weight of responsibility that settles on their shoulders. Perhaps the pop business isn't turning out how they expected and they would sooner be wandering the fjords and forests of their native land? Who can tell? At six o'clock, just as we are about to down tools, a problem presents itself. There are always problems at *Top of the Pops:* an over-patterned jacket strobing the camera; the presenter (none of the Radio One jocks have a clue) fluffing his lines. This time it takes the form of an assistant producer protesting that Maximum Acceleration have infringed the limits of propriety. 'How's that then?' I demand. 'I should have listened more carefully at the run-through…Isn't he singing "Walk like a bitch" in that last verse? We can't have that.' 'You let Elton John sing "The Bitch is Back"' says Trevor, always invaluable in crises of this sort. 'Just fuck off, will you?' says the assistant producer, without much malice. 'They'll have to change it.' At my suggestion, Hugo the singer takes to one of the demonstration booths to record a fresh vocal containing the line 'Walk like a witch', which is carefully superimposed onto the original. Twenty minutes later, in a haze of cigarette smoke, amid a reek of body odour and the stench of sulphate fumes, we are back in the van.

* * *

The tour continues without incident. Well, more or less. At Sheffield Dorcas the Cupcakes' guitarist trips over her lead, pops a kneecap and is carried screaming from the stage. She returns the following night, leg in plaster, and plays the set propped up in an armchair. At Manchester the Dub Imposters' percussionist Elijah Prince Rastafari simply vanishes, walks out into the street after the concert and is never seen again. His band-mates are unmoved. As Garfield the bass player explains: 'He a natural wanderer. He find his way home in he own time.' From afar comes news of the Flame Throwers' tour, of near-riots and no-shows, and the suggestion – hardening into certainty when the last two gigs are cancelled – that a loss-cutting Marty has already high-tailed it back to New York. At Liverpool we receive the week's *New Musical Express*. Howard has prudently returned to London, but here, spread across three pages, is an account of the tour's first five days under the heading ON THE ROAD WITH THE INDIE RABBLE-ROUSERS. There are photos of Chloe and the Cupcakes hanging out their knickers to dry on motel radiators, the Bash Street Kids jousting with pool cues and Maximum Acceleration furrowing their brows over the *Guardian* crossword. It all looks painfully innocuous to me, but Trevor swears he will have revenge. Meanwhile, here in the winter-bound north, England seems to be falling apart. The grit lies thick on the hotel windows and the weak early-morning sunny looks like the palest of fried eggs dragged across the sky. On a side-street in Hulme, I notice an old man in a serge suit with what seems to be a pair of outsize, hollowed-out bananas on his tottering feet. 'Trevor,' I say, wonderingly. 'Isn't that a pair of clogs?' 'Filthy bloody northern bastards,' Trevor says feelingly. And always, going into the gigs early in the evening, or coming out of them late at night, in hotel lobbies and on badly-lit concert hall steps running away into darkness, there are the pale boy and girl with their cassette tapes – seven of them, now – who won't let up and who won't go away and are as fixed and irrevocable a part of the proceedings as the Pennine stations and the echoing northern sky.

At Carlisle comes the faint intimation of inter-band conflict, when Hermione informs me that latent antagonism between Maximum Acceleration and the Bash Street Kids is about to erupt into outright violence. 'Why do they hate each other? They've been headlining on alternate nights just like we promised.' 'Don't be silly, Nick,' Hermione chides.' She looks more tired than usual and has lost a little of her self-confidence. 'The Kids are from – where is it? – Bermondsey. I don't think they went to school much. Maximum Acceleration have all got degrees in Political Science and they talk about Gramsci over breakfast.' Beyond the window lavender-tinted fog hangs over the Solway Firth. Somewhere beyond the horizon lies the Isle of Man, Hibernia, the Faroes, distant lands gathered up in primeval shadow. 'If they don't like students, Hermione, then what must they think of you?' Hermione thinks about this, head on one side, so that her Titian curls flop onto her shoulder. 'I don't suppose it signifies *in the least*. I mean, the life I lead – well, used to lead – is quite unimaginable to them. It's like that verse in the hymn we're not allowed to sing anymore. *The rich man in his castle/The poor man at his gate/God made them high and lowly/And granted their estate*. But Maximum Acceleration are just far enough removed from their social level to inspire a bit of resentment.' Having delivered this lecture, Hermione goes off to establish whether tonight's hotel runs to an access ramp for Dorcas's wheelchair, leaving me to deal with the urgent messages from London, from Rory, from Doug Stroessner, from *Melody Maker's* gossip columnist, from bank-managers and hangers-on, all wanting to know how the tour is going. How is the tour going? The tour is going fine, except that ticket sales are only 80 per cent of capacity and somebody – evidence points to Trevor Jacomb – seriously underestimated the transport and accommodation costs. It is reckoned – by Trevor – that if we come out of this £40,000 in the red we can think ourselves lucky. As for the record sales supposedly generated by all this publicity, 'Penal Colony', despite its *TOTP* airing, has defied all known precedent by *falling* a dozen places down the Top Forty rather than clambering nimbly up it, and Cedric's new single, issue date fixed to chime with the tour's opening night, has sold all of 177 copies.

And so the days wind on. Frugal breakfasts under bleak, artificial light. Pennine Peaks and Derbyshire Dales. Terraced houses and pale views of hills. Thunder shaking loose rain. Snack joints that smell of cigarette smoke and decomposing tea-leaves. At the gigs, convinced that there are vast demographic lessons to be learned, I study not the bands – they can take care of themselves – but the audiences. It is never any good. The Resurgam crowds are as various as a box of Liquorice Allsorts: Soul Boys drawn out of curiosity; old-style punks in ripped-up tee-shirts and bondage trousers; teenage girls for whom Cedric's wispy demeanour and wide-eyed smile are such a consolation; all sorts of conditions of men and women brought fleetingly together by the promise of drama and spectacle.

Meanwhile, rumours of Don's letter have been gently diffusing through the chill northern air.

'What are we going to do about that twenty thousand quid?' Trevor enquires over coffee one rank December afternoon in a Lite-a-bite a dozen miles south of the Trent.

'I don't know.' At a safe distance, Don may be regarded in more abstract terms: as a pantomime villain, say, or a sea-monster rising from the waves on the margin of some medieval map. 'Try and borrow it from Virgin? Float the company on the Stock Exchange?'

Neither of these suggestions is at all seriously meant.

'Known some right cunts in my time,' Trevor says, apropos the managing director of Shard Enterprises. And so we talk about some of the right cunts we have known in our time: the manager who dangled a disrespectful journalist from a third-floor balcony by his heels; the promoter who offered contracts for signature where half the clauses had yet to be filled in; the agents who sold off merchandising rights to companies controlled by their brothers, their mistresses or their pseudonymous selves. As the file of flash-fisted behemoths marches on, a thought strikes me.

'Trevor. Do you actually like pop music?'

'Fair point,' Trevor concedes. There is a patch of spilled sugar on the forearm of his jacket which, with that characteristic fat man's delicacy, he is removing by finger-tip, grain by grain. 'Very fair point. Didn't mind the Supremes.' There is another pause: the last grains of sugar go skittering away. 'And that black bint, whatever her name was.'

'Aretha Franklin?'

'Martha Reeves.'

Later we go back to the hotel to discover that the Bash Street Kids have stolen the master-key from reception and locked all the other bands in their rooms and that the equipment truck has over-turned in a ditch somewhere near Northallerton.

And finally there comes the morning when, as the rest of us are wearily assembling for breakfast in a vast, unlit cavern where the bowls of cereal and the tiny cartons of orange juice have clearly been set out the night before, Hermione – white-faced and exhausted, yet granted poise and conviction by the enormity of the message she brings – crashes into the room and thumps a table dramatically with her fist.

'I'm afraid some very distressing news has just come over the radio. I really don't know how to tell you all. John Lennon has been shot dead.'

All around us, the faces fall. Flopsy's mother – the oldest person present – gives a disbelieving shriek and puts her hand to her mouth. I am prepared to weep for Lennon, last seen in New York City all of ten years ago. I am prepared to cry uncontrollably over his passing at the hands of some two-bit psycho in an apartment block hallway, only for this comfort to be denied me by the tumult of raised voices that now erupts at the far end of the room. Nobody knows exactly what Toddy from the Bash Street Kids has said to Hugo from Maximum Acceleration, but the result is that Hugo picks up a ketchup bottle and whacks him in the face with it. Happily, the glass doesn't shatter. Undeterred, Toddy kicks over a table and, head down and fists whirling, goes in like a belligerent tortoise. The curious thing is that Hugo is much better at fighting than Toddy. 'Fucking hell' Trevor shouts, as he lands an uppercut on Toddy's chin. 'Go on my son.' The rest of us look on, silent but approving. Nobody likes the Bash Street Kids. In the end, I pull a fire extinguisher off the wall and turn it on them. Eventually, while continuing to yell insults, both sides are pulled apart. 'Don't you think they ought to be made to shake hands?' Hermione guilelessly wonders. The hotel manager, on the point of calling the police, is pacified with a £50 note.

That night Cedric, face gleaming in the angry light, genuine tears streaming down his pixie-ish face, leads the crowd in a rendition of 'All You Need is Love.' Skipping off stage he looks like a tiny hobbit, rapt and thunderstruck, gripped by powers beyond his deserving, out on the road to Mordor.

Some Singles Reviews

Chloe and the Cupcakes – *Riding on the A13* (Resurgam). A gang of Mod girls from Essex, I believe, which means oodles of breathless, close-harmony vocalising, a Rickenbacker guitar-sound that could strip paint off the walls and The Jam's Bruce Foxton at the console. Lyrical fixations include *boys on scooters*, *guys with shooters* and, ahem, *girls with hooters*. Their mothers wouldn't like it, but catching them on the pub jukebox ten minutes before closing time with several pints of Mr Worthington's finest inside you, you very possibly might.
Melody Maker, June 1980

Cedric – *I Like My Dog* (Resurgam). The jury is still out on whether the correct term for Cedric – his real name, apparently – is *faux-naif*, or simply *naif*. My colleague Charles Shaar Murray swears he

was an original member of the Brady Bunch, but your reviewer has his doubts. Song-wise, James Taylor was doing these kind of chord progressions ten years ago, and any self-respecting dog who caught wind of the lyrics would be off to Battersea before you could say 'Heel, Fido!' Doubtless the children of the future will sing this at their school assemblies, but that ain't gonna help him with what's left of his career right now.
New Musical Express, August 1980

The Bash Street Kids – *Down the Boozer* (Resurgam). Yes I *know*, Tallulah, their last London gig ended in a riot and three-fifths of the *ensemble* are fresh out of juvie…Actually, this isn't half bad, given that the Neanderthal drum sound and the heavy metal tendencies observed on their debut album have been prudently culled and someone has explained to lead axeman Billy Hunt how you tune a guitar. For a band of working-class tossers from Bermondsey, they have approximately as much political and social awareness as a piece of lemon peel floating down the Thames, yet, mysteriously, in their cut-throat razor-voiced Artful-Dodger-meets-Noddy-Holder way, the Kids are evidently not quite as dim as they may appear to those of us whose sartorial tastes extend beyond a Crombie overcoat and a pair of Woolworth's braces.
Sounds Single of the Week, September 1980

Charysse – *Ballad of a Sunny Afternoon* (Resurgam). OK all you pop-kids, what is it that distinguishes this auburn-locked *chanteuse* from Kate Bush? Well, Kate has a four-octave range whereas on this evidence Charysse struggles to get beyond two. La Bush's efforts, however tweely conceived and executed, are usually about something, whereas Ms C just squeaks on about nothing in particular. And, save for the fact that image is *rilly important* right now in the world of young lady vocalists with concert halls to fill, I wouldn't dream of

being so ungallant as to suggest that while Kate is a hotsy of the first water, Ms C wears her Laura Ashley frock as if it were an elephant's shroud. Subtract all these deficiencies and what's left is a melody line nicked from Fleetwood Mac's 'Rhiannon'. You'll be pleased to know that said waxing has already been pressed into service as an office ashtray, and that Mick Farren extinguished a cheroot in it only five minutes since.
New Musical Express, October 1980

Planet Claire – *Sea of Glass* (Resurgam). No idea who let this lot into a recording studio, but if it was me I'd be having a *serious think* about my future in the wonderful world of pop. The main riff is – what? – two years old, and all that stuff about faces staring out of dark hallways has already been worked to death by Gary Numan. Meanwhile, the singer sounds as if he's been gargling tin-tacks. All the evidence points to a gang of superannuated public school boys, but they turn out to have come from Ealing so there's really no excuse.
Melody Maker, November 1980.

7. WAITING FOR THE LOVE BOAT

There'll be a space for us
There'll be a place for us
Out among the lost
Deep beneath the frost
Way out in Antarctica
STRAWBERRY SHORTCAKE – *Antarctica*

And all the while, time is moving on. 1979. 1980. 1981. The Seventies are long gone now, and the Sixties only a warm but distant dream. Recording sessions at the Virgin Mobile, parked up in some Oxfordshire back-lane amid forests of cow parsley at £800 a day. Video shoots on blasted East Anglian heaths, under freezing winter sky: the videos are expensive, £3,000 to £5,000 a pop, but Trevor, who has been browsing the American trade magazines, says this is the future. Corporate sit-downs on Richard Branson's Thameside houseboat, with almond-eyed girls, the ghosts of a bygone age, bringing in the tea ('What I could never work out,' Rory says after one of these encounters, 'is whether Rick wanted to be seriously rich or whether he was just mucking about – when he was young, that is.' 'Don't tell me you knew him back then?' 'Wasn't he at Stowe?' Rory says, the pale gleam of reminiscence in his eye. 'I'm not sure we didn't go over there and play Real Tennis once.') Late nights at the Vortex, the Music Machine and the Electric Circus, Camden Town. Early mornings in the Goodge Street coffee shops and the burger bars of the Tottenham Court Road. Once again the music is changing, and the sound welling up out of the London clubs is made by boys in ruffs and picturesque mock-medieval tunics. We miss out on Duran Duran, Spandau Ballet and A Flock of Seagulls but manage to sign Imbroglio, the Conspirators and Strawberry Shortcake, whose debut single 'Antarctica' reaches Number 16. The band appear on *Top of the Pops* dressed as Polar explorers. Newman Street stops being a wayward combination of glory hole, dream factory and countercultural manor house and reverts to an ageing tenement with a leaking roof and not enough parking spaces. It will soon be time to move on.

Meanwhile, the casualties are stacking up. Two members of the Bash Street Kids are arrested on assault charges and sentenced to three months in Pentonville. The band play an incendiary farewell gig at the Bridgehouse, Canning Town, and are never heard of again. Girl on the Phone's bass player has an epileptic fit right there in reception. The Flame Throwers are back in L.A., idling, partying or, according to their new management – Rudi Martinez has given up in disgust – 'working on some really exciting new material.' A rumour that Cris has drowned in the Mississippi River is contradicted by his appearance at a West Coast music awards night where he throws a chair at Blondie's keyboard player. *Breakfast at Ralph's*, by this stage, has sold 80,000 copies. Three tracks from it featured on John Peel's 'Festive Fifty' come to the attention of a Conservative MP and are the subject of a leading article in the *Daily Mail*. The resultant furore is reckoned advantageous. Turnover for the year rises to £1.8 million. The overdraft is north of £70,000.

* * *

22 December 1980

Three days before Christmas and the office is half-asleep. On the floor below, the record deck plays Sleepy John Estes' 'Milk Cow Blues.' Half-frozen snow on the adjoining rooftops the colour of anchovy paste. Hermione sits at her desk at reception surrounded by two or three dozen bottles of whisky, gin and Warnink's Advocaat – gifts from the freelance sleeve-designers, copy-writers and record-pluggers we sporadically employ. Jerked out of my reverie by Doug, the A&R guy, who insists that I join him in his office to inspect 'something you are not going to believe.' Curiously, this is not a tape but a home-made video cassette. 'It's a kind of promo,' Doug explains as he whacks it into our newly-purchased VCR. On the ten minutes or so of footage that follow, a pale boy and a pale girl lurk grimly behind a wall of synthesizers, amble brokenly along cheerless northern pavements or stand peering into what memory suggests is the Manchester Ship Canal as if they intend to drown themselves on the spot. Gradually, recognition dawns. They are the kids from the tour. 'They're called Systems of Romance,' Doug explains. I have rarely seen him so enthused. The music is eerie, angular, full of dramatic octave jumps and humming bass notes. 'We've just got to have them.' 'Who else is after them?' 'No one,' Doug says. 'They've been turned down by everyone in London. We can get them for five.' 'Offer them seven' I instruct. I realise I owe Systems of Romance something for their persistence.

Later. Staff Christmas party at the dark Toby Carvery in Mortimer Street, Asking Hermione where she intends to spend the festive season, I get the answer: 'Berwickshire. And then I might go skiing in Val d'Isère.' Rory unusually animated. 'Is Doug any relation?' he asks over the sherry trifle. 'Any relation to whom?' '*Stroessner*, you idiot. The Paraguayan dictator.' 'Not possible,' I tell him. 'Nonsense,' Rory says. 'When my father was in Munich with the diplomatic he had a friend called Adolf. Turned out to be Hitler's godson.'

23 December 1980

Last crop of Christmas mail brings a letter with an American frank. This turns out to be from Daphne. The frontispiece shows a robin with a scarf round its neck perched on an upturned spade. Inside, in her straggly, other-world hand, Daphne has written: *It was good to see you in the Fall. Hope all is well with you and yours. Guess I was right about Reagan! Found some more stuff of Mo's you ought to have. Will send when I can get round to it. Things are difficult here.* Nine years dead and still the old man is pursuing me. On past form, there isn't the slightest chance that Daphne will send me anything, but on impulse – it is Christmas, after all – I phone the number of the apartment on Staten Island. As I suspect, there is no reply.

24 December 1980

Christmas Eve. Arundel Avenue sleeps under snow. Just an occasional rattle of a train coming out of Ewell East to break the silence. Thinking of the old days in North Park Avenue, my mother making mince pies and listening to the carols from King's on the radio, the old man's photograph in its frame, and beyond them Eaton Park, with its file of elm trees and the giant carp in their pond.

Interrupted by a knock at the door. Opening it, I discover a burly character in a Crombie coat who could be Toddy from the Bash Street Kids' uncle with a brown paper parcel under his arm. At the end of the drive, behind the wheel of a scuffed-up Jaguar, sits a second man, identically dressed. Knowing a Soho frightener when I see one, I try to close the door, but Crombie coat sticks his foot on the lintel and eases his considerable bulk inside. 'It's OK, Nick,' he says. The skin of his big, uneasy face is plum-coloured in the frost. 'Don't want any bleeding trouble. Not at Christmas and that. Don says he'll give you two months, and then he really would like that money back.' We stand looking at each other for a moment, as the Jaguar's exhaust fumes rise vertically in the still air, and then he lumbers off. Expecting to hear the noise of the car moving away, I am startled by an almighty crash as the brown paper parcel – this contains a brick – flies through the mullioned panels of the front window and comes to rest on the hearth-rug.

Standing in the flower-bed a few moments later, the better to inspect the damage, I hear the soft shuffle of carpet-slippers approaching through the snow. This is Mr Pevensey, the retired accountant who lives next door. 'I was wondering, Mr Du Pont' he diffidently proposes, 'if you should like me to call the police. 'Not at all, Mr Pevensey,' I assure him. 'A misunderstanding really. Don't trouble yourself.' Mr Pevensey tosses his head at this explanation, like a horse refusing the water-jump. He is a tiny, spindly man who bid farewell to the firm of Coopers & Lybrand in 1963. For the purposes of paying a morning call, he has dressed himself in a British Warm overcoat, thick woollen mittens and cavalry twill trousers. 'Rather an unpleasant-looking gentleman, I should say.' We laugh in a neighbourly way as the shattered glass gapes between us.

25 December 1980

Not having any other invitation, I take a mini-cab to Petts Wood for Christmas lunch with Trevor and his family. This consists of Mrs Jacomb, red-haired and what my mother would call 'a slip of a thing', and two little girls who look at me as if I were a walrus they had just found swimming in a municipal duck pond. Turkey, devils on horseback and a Christmas pudding onto which Trevor pours so much brandy that it refuses to light. Mrs Jacomb – Michelle – solicitous of her husband in a way I remember from North Park, twenty years ago: 'Have some more sprouts, Trevor, love.' After two glasses of Cinzano, she relaxes a little and tells me that she and Trevor met when she was a secretary at one of the booking agencies. 'Tom Jones came in once. Can you imagine that?' Trevor's Christmas gift to her is *Engelbert Humperdinck's Greatest Hits*. After lunch we decamp to the living room to watch Christmas *Top of the Pops* and the Queen's Speech, for which Trevor insists on climbing to his feet. 'Say goodbye to Uncle Nick,' Trevor urges his daughters as I make my farewells. 'Goodbye, Uncle Nick,' the little girls chorus from the front door as the minicab rolls into view through the late-afternoon slush. They have small, pointed faces, like elf-children.

Later – much later – Rory telephones. Like Doug with the video cassette, he is far more excited than I ever remember him. 'You'll never believe this, Nicholas. It turns out I was right,' he says through a buzz of conversation and disco beats. 'Right about what?' 'Doug. He's Stroessner's great-nephew or something.' In addition to the disco beats, there are upper-class voices whooping and hollering in the background. 'Where are you?' 'I don't know. Some fucking night club or something.' 'Listen, Rory,' I tell him. 'One of Don's goons threw a brick through my window on Christmas Eve. What are we going to do about that?' The back gardens of Arundel Avenue gleam in the moonlight. There are fox-prints running diagonally across the snow. But Rory is too far gone for conversations of this kind. 'We'll get Doug onto it,' he says grandly, as the peacock voices echo around him. 'Tell him his great-uncle's got a cell ready for him in Asunción. And a couple of sergeants with a pair of pliers waiting to rip off his fingernails one by one.'

* * *

Four o'clock on a late January afternoon in Newman Street. Curiously enough, this was the music business's witching hour. It was the time when grudge-nurturing managers, fresh from beery lunches at the Speakeasy, steamed in with the aim of re-negotiating contracts, when bands dropped by to pilfer records, when teenagers in school uniforms breezed up from the suburbs to leave demo-tapes: anything could happen. Just now I was standing in reception inspecting a dozen advance pressings of the new Planet Claire single, on whose picture sleeve someone had mis-spelt the name of the band, the producer and the songwriter, and a piece of paper, left out invitingly on the desk, on which someone else had written: *2.15 p.m. Record Mirror, 3 p.m. Jackie (+ photo!). 4 p.m. Teen Sensation. 4.45 p.m. Boyfriend.* Hermione, coming in from the back office with the week's music papers jammed under her arm, saw the paper and gave a semi-embarrassed nod.

'What's all this?'

'It's Finn Family Moomintroll. I know we're promoting them as a synth band, but all the teen mags have rung up for interviews. Apparently the lead singer's cheek bones have won some sort of award.'

'What does Paula say?'

'She says she doesn't care if the interview's with *Grocers Weekly*.'

The music papers had flaring headlines about the Clash touring and Public Image Limited splitting and the Jam being back in the studio. Twenty feet away at the bottom of the staircase came the sound of the front door opening. A second or two later Rory stepped into the room. Without preamble, but stopping to give Hermione his usual satisfied nod, he said:

'What are you doing tomorrow night?'

'Going with Doug to Dingwalls to see the Gravediggers.'

'Well don't. You know as well as I do they'll be dreadful. Come and have supper at Mark Weatherall's.'

Hermione, I noticed, had perked up and was taking an interest. It was rare for her professional and social lives to coincide.

'Who's Mark Weatherall?'

'He's one of my oldest friends.' When used of Rory's relationships with other men, 'one of my oldest friends' meant absolutely nothing. 'He's an equity partner at Cazenove's.'

'Aren't they the Queen's stockbrokers?'

'The very same. But I don't suppose Mark ever sits Brenda down to discuss her portfolio.'

Like many another upper-class man-about-town, Rory referred to the Royal Family by their *Private Eye* nicknames. The Queen was 'Brenda'. Prince Charles was 'Keith'. The soon-to-be affianced Lady Diana Spencer, already marauding through the public consciousness, was 'Cheryl.'

'Who are you bringing?'

Rory's jaw twitched. 'It's rather embarrassing. She's called Tina. I'm not sure whether we're going out or not.'

Rory's emotional life was unpredictable. Most of the time he tried to stick with the precepts of his upbringing. But then, as he explained, sometimes there were not enough well-bred young women to go round and you ended up sleeping with waitresses.

'Look,' Rory said, back in his role as a captain of industry. 'Mark's got a lot of money and he's looking for something to do with it. We could do worse.'

'All right.'

'He's got rather a nice wife.'

Coming from anyone else, this would have been a statement of intent. With Rory, I knew, it equated to basic social reassurance. Equity partners at Cazenove's had rather nice wives. It was as simple, or as complicated, as that.

'I'll let you have the address,' Rory said, Lobb-shod feet moving blithely into gear up the staircase to his office. In the wake of this visitation from another world – the world of equity partners and their rather nice wives – the atmosphere in reception ticked down a notch. Supposing that the sanctity of the last five minutes' conversation had been sullied by their presence, Hermione scooped up the list of Finn Family Moomintroll's press appointments and hid it in a drawer. The Planet Claire picture sleeve, which had seemed so invigorating on the designer's light box, looked as if it had been mocked up by an orang-utan. What would the people I worked for in the Sixties have made of Rory? They would probably have drawn up a chair and invited him to sit on it. In the back office someone was playing the Clash's 'Spanish Bombs.' The Republican militias would have known what to do with Rory. They would have had him out in the fields with the *peons.*

'My sister used to know Mark Weatherall,' Hermione volunteered. The spell cast on her by Rory was still working its magic.

'Oh yes? What was he like?'

'C.A.U.C.' Hermione said, who was too polite to tell me that one of Rory's oldest friends was a Complete and Utter Cunt.

* * *

The Weatheralls lived in Walpole Street, Chelsea. The house was at the further end, comfortably remote from the tumult of the King's Road. There were expensive cars parked under the plane trees. Through curtainless windows, in basements at the bottom of area steps, sofa-bound children could be glimpsed watching television. The door was opened by a Filipino maid whose face said that of all the terrible jobs she had had in her life, this was easily the worst. In those days people like the Weatheralls hadn't yet moved out of central London into roomier suburbs, but preferred to cram themselves into town houses in sight of Sloane Square. The drawing room, its hubbub of conversation already contending with the creak of the staircase, was on the first floor. Somebody had given the adjoining wall a bohemian touch by framing the photos of cricket elevens and cadet companies against a duck-egg blue background roamed over by shadowy sea-creatures.

Inside the room there was an odd sense of traditional choreographies having been displaced and too many things going on at once. A tall, sleepy-looking man a year or so younger than myself got out of a chair more quickly than he had intended, hung there gasping for a moment as if the effort had been too much for him and then said: 'You must be Nick. I'm Mark Weatherall.' A small boy who was going up and down the double row of sofas saying goodnight to his father's guests stopped in front of Rory. 'Who's this little chap then?' Rory demanded, without much interest, only for the woman sitting next to him – a solidly made blonde girl who looked rather like the actress Elizabeth Moss would look thirty years later – to gather the child up in her arms and practically smother him in her capacious bosom. All this, though, was instantly eclipsed by what happened next. Just as Mark Weatherall was sinking back in his chair and Rory's girl – Tina presumably – had declared, in a pronounced Australian accent, that this little feller was plum tuckered out, the door-handle turned and another woman came noiselessly into the room. It was Alice Danby.

The music business was full of blasts from the past, equinoctial gales that blew in across the decades leaving all manner of flotsam and jetsam in their wake. The last time I had seen Alice was fifteen years ago. On that occasion I had tried to humiliate her by inviting her to an expensive restaurant and then left without paying the bill. How she had responded to this, I had never found out. But it was much too big to be ignored. Was she still seething about this slight a decade and a half later? Or, having half-forgotten it, would she be startled and annoyed to have it dragged back to the forefront of her mind? Did I acknowledge what had passed between us, or simply ignore it? While I was thinking about all this, Mark Weatherall stumbled out of his chair again, rather as if he were about to lead her in some antiquated dance across the drawing-room carpet, and said:

'Nick, this is my wife Alice. Alice, this is Nick…Du Pont isn't it?'

'Oh we've met,' Alice said, conveying instantly to me, if not to anyone else, that she had remembered everything and – this was the implication – forgiven nothing. She turned to her husband. 'The food's ready. Hadn't we better go and eat it? You know how bad Maria is at keeping anything hot.'

'I've only just got myself a drink,' Mark protested. 'And Nick here's barely arrived.'

'Oh for Christ's sake,' Alice said. 'The food's on the table. Let's bloody well go and eat it.' Without waiting to see what her husband might have to say about this, she turned on her heel, stalked a pace or two back to the door and addressed the room at large: 'Come on. We're going downstairs for supper.'

A head count put the number of those present at ten: the Weatheralls; Rory and his Antipodean charmer; two men cut from the same cloth as Mark and their wives; myself and an unattached woman with a Marie-Antoinette hair-do called Marianne. Led by Alice – still emitting paralysing sparks of discontent – we went in Indian file down two flights of stairs to a basement kitchen, where the Filipino au pair, still looking as if she hated the room and everyone in it, was ladling out bowls of soup.

'You can sit where you like,' Alice said. 'I don't care.'

There had been plenty of women back in the days of the Helium Kids who behaved like this: women so gripped by cosmic despair that it was all they could do to stop themselves pulling out a knife and stabbing everyone in sight. With Alice this dissatisfaction was exaggerated beyond any reasonable point. It was as if she was an actress putting on a performance for a group of appreciative friends and could be guaranteed, once the evening ended, to snap her fingers and sink back into her original character. Mark, I saw, took no notice of her whatever. It was just how his wife behaved, here in her Chelsea basement, as the au pair ladled out soup and the world went by.

'I hear you're in the music business,' said Marianne, who had ended up next to me, with a faint air of disapproval. 'I suppose that's quite interesting?'

'Jesus, I just *love* soup,' Tina observed, dropping a shred of parsnip onto her substantial cleavage. 'Is there any more?'

Gradually things settled down. There were cars passing in the street outside and the sweep of their headlights bounced eerily off the window-panes. Darkness welled up over the area steps. All this gave the room the feeling of an aquarium, with monstrous fish floating on its margins who might at any time swoop down to displace the human traffic at its centre. If you excepted the glowering sybil at the table's end, the dinner was like every other one that Rory had invited me to with his City friends. The stockbrokers were polite but non-committal. 'You would have to know us a great deal better than is at all likely before we told you how we truly felt about anything,' they seemed to say. They talked about Mrs Thatcher – 'Margaret' – as if she were an old family servant who, despite bouts of unpredictability, could be relied upon to do her best when the chips were down. Marianne, her interest in the music business disposed of in a couple of sentences, consented to be drawn on her niece's exploits at Bedales. Meanwhile, Tina, who had devoured an extra bowl of soup, smoked one of Rory's cigars and now began to gorge herself on cutlets, was going down a storm. If she had put on airs the other men would have ganged up on her. As it was, her artlessness made her an ally. Rory, on the other hand, seemed to be flagging a bit.

'Just pass that bottle would you, Nick?' It was the first time Alice had spoken to me since she had stormed into the drawing room. I pushed the wine across, aware of being in the middle of one of those moments – more often come across in a film than real life – when a person suddenly declares themselves, stops behaving in one kind of way, throws off their camouflage and becomes the kind of person they were meant to be. It was not that she was any the less discontented – in fact the expression on her face as she picked up the bottle was one of complete and utter fury, as if she might very soon upend the contents over somebody's head. Rather, it was that most of the symptoms of her displeasure – vocal savagery, merciless stare – had an explanation. What she was up to, I deduced, was a kind of clash of wills with Mark. When he said something she disagreed with, she rolled her eyes at the ceiling. When he offered an opinion on Government spending plans, she rapped her fist on the table. When he favoured Rory with an account of the skiing holiday they had enjoyed in Gstaad, she punctuated it with a sigh and a furious rattling of the jewellery coil she wore round her neck.

'Alice is so marvellous, isn't she?' Marianne said wistfully as this charade went on. 'Do you ever go to the opera?'

The party broke up at eleven. 'Jesus, that was a real whurramaloo,' Tina said as she was escorted to the door. Rory had regained some of his mislaid bounce: maybe the evening had gone better than he expected. In the general displacement of persons that followed, I found myself standing next to Alice in a hallway otherwise crowded with Wellington boots and bits of sports equipment.

'It's nice to see you again, Nick,' she said. 'We must have lunch. That's if you're not always seeing your pop people.'

'Most of the pop people aren't up by lunchtime.'

Outside on the pavement, beneath a street lamp that rather exaggerated the state she was in, Rory was trying to steer Tina into a taxi. He gave a little half-salute, finger to forehead. I put the paste-board oblong Alice had given me – a funeral wreath surrounding a phone number and the words *Mrs Mark Weatherall* – in my wallet and walked down to the King's Road where there were fish and chip papers gusting into shop doorways and fat men in Barbour jackets out looking for cabs, and then headed east towards Sloane Square which even now, the style sheets were hastening to assure us, could be regarded as the centre of the known world.

* * *

'What did you think of Alice Weatherall?' Rory asked, eleven hours later.

'Actually I knew her at Oxford.'

'Oh yes?' I was going up in Rory's estimation. 'Oh yes?' was one of his compliments – almost, but not quite, in the same class as 'officer material.' 'What was she like?'

'Pure poison. We're having lunch.' I couldn't resist adding: 'Do you think she'll pay?'

Rory shook his head. 'Rich girls never pay.'

'Is she rich?'

'Her father cut up for half a million the other year. And Mark said they'd put the estate in trust to avoid death duties.'

'How is the lovely Tina?'

'I left her passed out back at the flat,' Rory said gloomily. 'It will be just my luck if she goes and nicks something.'

* * *

Stefano always liked to say – it was one of his most treasured maxims, on a par with 'Ten per cent means fifteen' or 'No exit means exit but we'd rather you didn't' – that when entertaining women, the important thing was not to fuck about. With this exordium in mind, I booked a table at the Ivy. From this vantage point, a week later, having taken the precaution of arriving ten minutes early, I watched her as she walked into the dining hall. She looked smaller and darker than I remembered and more than ever like the girl in the painting by Vuillard who sits reading under the lamplight with one bony hand reaching out into shadow.

'Well, this is nice, Nick,' she said, descending into the chair which the waiter had pulled out for her in a single, sinuous movement. 'But you're wearing some very peculiar clothes.'

'It's what comes of working with bohemians.' I was dressed in a leather jacket, a collarless white shirt and a pair of scarlet corduroys. 'We have a standing order at Oxfam.'

'So I see.' There was a pause in which she dredged a handbag festooned with snaps and clips up from underneath the table and began popping some of them. 'Do you know, I haven't been here in ages? It seems to have changed rather a lot.'

In fact the Ivy was exactly the same as it had been when I had first come here with Don Shard back in the Sixties and he had thrown bread rolls at the barmen: the same showbiz types discreetly – or not so discreetly – drawing attention to their celebrity; the same merchant bankers up from Lothbury and grievously out of their depth; the same absolutely unclassifiable people whose identities could only be guessed at. On the other hand, 'changed rather a lot' in Alice's lexicon clearly meant 'got worse'.

'First things first,' Alice said, who – I now remembered – had the trick of making long-rehearsed speeches sound as if they were absolutely spontaneous. 'Why on earth did you go off and leave me at that restaurant?'

'It was quite simple. I was getting some of my own back for the way you behaved at that ball.'

'What ball? How did I behave? This is very exciting.'

I explained about Midsummer's Eve, 1962, the hours that followed it, the ten-guinea tickets and the time she had preferred to spend with Roley, Gus and the Badger rather than the person who had paid for them.

'Oh *that*? Well, I can tell you that I've known girls who behaved a jolly sight worse than that. And so all this was a *symbolical act of revenge*? Really, Nick, you are extraordinary.'

I nodded my head. I was extraordinary. There was no question about it. 'Don't mind my asking, but what did you do?

'What? After you never came back from the loo? I did what any sensible person would have done. I finished my lunch – after all, a girl's got to eat – and then I telephoned Daddy at his office and he sent one of his clerks over with the money. Then I went back to Lowndes Square and typed some more of Lady Ogilvie-Smith's letters about the Vietnamese orphans.' She hauled a bread roll out of its basket and snapped the end off it, like a shrike let loose on a gamekeeper's gibbet. 'Let me assure you, it was all jolly embarrassing. But tell me, Nick, how did you feel about it? Ashamed? Exultant? Another stunning victory in the class war? Something to tell your middle-class friends about?'

'Let's just say I knew the whole thing was futile from the start.'

'Futile? In what way?'

'I was trying to humiliate you. But I should have known I needed to be far more subtle than that.'

'You are extraordinary,' said Alice, with slightly less interest. 'Now, what sort of thing do they have to eat here?'

They had Beluga caviar, Dover Sole and fresh strawberries. Alice sampled all these delicacies with relish. She was jauntier than she had been when giving dinner to her husband's friends, but every so often the paralysing rays of dissatisfaction that had beamed out over the Walpole Street basement would start making their presence felt again.

'You want to be careful of Rory,' she said at one point.

'Why's that?'

'Oh, he's rather a menace. When he was at Scrimgeour's selling Eurobonds they used to call him the Man Without a Shadow.'

'Not one of us then?'

'I simply have no idea what you're talking about,' Alice said, busy among the dessert menu. A bit later, apropos the morning's *Daily Mail*, which someone had left on an adjoining table, she said:

'Isn't Diana Spencer awful?'

'In what way?'

'Oh just pushy and awful. A friend of mine's daughter was at school with her somewhere, and she said her room was plastered with pictures of Prince Charles, even at the age of fourteen.'

Outside in the Charing Cross Road, flurries of snow were gently descending on the pavement edges, and the taxis plunging down to Trafalgar Square had their headlights on. Back in Newman Street,

Doug would be listening to the demos for Chloe and the Cupcakes' new single and telling Planet Claire's manager that, three records into a not very promising career, their unearned advances now amounted to £37,000. Here at the heart of the Ivy, these things lost their immediacy. One pale hand forking up her strawberries – the nails were bitten down to the quick, I noticed – the other twisting up the tendrils of her glossy black hair, Alice seemed perfectly at home, so finely attuned to her surroundings that you felt she would still be there the following day, like one of the pieces of statuary next to the banquette. To listen to her talk was to become aware of another world rolling on defiantly next to the one that everyone else lived in: a world of yachts tacking across the Solent ('Mark's very keen on sailing'); freshly scrubbed children on antique rocking horses; malign old ladies in country houses telling their parlour-maids how to clean a chandelier; the slam of Volvo doors and the sound of infant footsteps grinding up the gravel.

'What do you do now?' she asked. 'I mean, didn't you used to work for the Rolling Stones or someone?'

'Something like that. I run a small independent record label. It's like being a trout in a tank full of pike.'

'People do terribly odd jobs these days, don't they?' she said. 'I think Cecily's husband – you remember Cecily? – sells photocopiers or something.'

'How is Cecily?'

'Oh she's so boring nowadays. She must have about seven children by this time. There are so many I can't remember all their names, and whenever I write the Christmas cards I have to put "and all your little ones".'

'And what about Mark? Where did you meet him?'

'At a drinks party at the Guards Club. Isn't that a cliché?'

'He seems very nice.' Still not able to work out whether I was being flattered or disdainfully trifled with, I put a certain amount of mockery into this remark.

'Mark isn't nearly as staid as you might think,' Alice said, arranging the fork and spoon that had done for her strawberries crossways on her plate like heraldic insignia. 'Do you know he plays the clarinet in a trad jazz band with some people from work? It's terribly funny. They all think they're Acker Bilk.'

It was nearly half-past two now, and the restaurant was starting to quieten down. Soon the showbiz types would stagger out onto the pavement looking for taxis to take them the few hundred yards to Shaftesbury Avenue theatres or agents' offices in Jermyn Street, and the merchant bankers head back to Lothbury to tell their colleagues all about the famous people they had seen. I thought about Mark in his bowler hat and coloured waistcoat tootling along on his clarinet.

'You made a terrific hit with Marianne.'

'Who is Marianne?'

'You sat next to her at dinner. She was asking about you. I think she wanted your phone number.'

'Would I like her?'

'Oh, she's this dreadful woman we picked up somewhere. Some charity ball committee or something. I think she works at the V&A... I'm so *cross*, aren't I?' Alice said, shifting one of her long, grasshopper legs over the other and lighting a cigarette. 'But you see, it's the life I lead. Waiting for the *au pair* to bring the children back from school. Having to talk to Mark's mother on the telephone. I'm sure your life is an endless stream of pleasure by comparison.'

'Thank you for lunch,' she said in the Charing Cross Road as the taxi idled on the kerb. It had stopped snowing and the sky to the north was turning grey again. 'You know, you could come and see me sometime.'

Another of Stefano's maxims about how to deal with women was that sometimes you have to take the bait.

* * *

Back at the office, Doug reported that the Chloe and the Cupcakes demos were unlistenable and that Planet Claire's manager had signalled his annoyance by smashing up a chair on the way out. Meanwhile, Hermione had been amusing herself by arranging some of the morning's unsoliciteds in a line across my desk.

Dear Nick, You may not remember me but I played bass on several of the tracks on the first Ultravox album…

Dear Nicko, Long time no see! Wasn't the last occasion at the console when the Kinks were laying down 'Waterloo Sunset'? Anyway, I just wanted to update you on the new project that Ashley and I – you'll remember him from Blodwyn Pig – are embarked on…

Dear Mr Du Pont, We are a strictly no-frills rockabilly combo from Penarth whose live appearances have gained us a growing reputation in the Cardiff area…

Dear Mr Ponting, There's no point in false modesty, so I'm telling you now that the enclosed – which I'd be obliged if you'd return when you've finished listening to it – contains some of the greatest music that you or anyone else will ever hear…

Rory put his head round the door.

'Where have you been all afternoon?'

'Having lunch at the Ivy with Alice Weatherall.'

'Well don't try to get that past accounts,' Rory said, altogether failing to disguise the fact that I had gone up another notch in his estimation. 'Last time I looked there was only £1.47 in the petty cash and Hermione was wondering how she was going to get the post out.'

'What's been happening here?'

'Your Mr Shard's lawyers have sent another letter.' The way Rory said 'Your Mr Shard' meant that Don was my problem. 'We're going to have to do something about this.'

I was still flown with three-quarters of a bottle of Merlot. 'Did you know Mark Weatherall plays the clarinet in a trad jazz band?'

'He always was odd. We ought to give them a contract' Rory said. 'They couldn't do any worse than Planet Claire.'

Hermione had let the post pile up on the reception desk. There were about three dozen items: press releases for Charysse's new single; LPs in square cardboard sleeves; cheques for pluggers and designers. Bundling them into a pair of carrier bags, I headed out into Newman Street and made for the Central Line. Virgin's office was in a mews off the Portobello Road. There was no one much about. The receptionist recognised me and smiled. A senior executive came out of a meeting room, nodded, said 'Hello, Nick,' and wandered off somewhere. *Bona fides* established, I made for the post room and spent the next ten minutes feeding the letters through the Virgin Records franking machine.

Oscillating Wildly…

'So, are you two a hot item?' the NME wonders as Magda and Jon, the recently-fledged synth duo known to punters as Systems of Romance, sit demurely before us on the sagging office sofa. It's an innocuous enough question – *much* worse has been asked of artistes visiting the editorial sanctum – but the Systems are currently plagued with enquiries about their emotional life, or lack of same. Magda, elfin, chestnut-haired and looking like the French actress Isabelle Huppert's neurotic younger sister, takes a nervous drag on the fifth Gitane she's ingested since entering the room ten minutes before and stares brokenly out of the window at the grimy Southwark rooftops. Jon, who like his partner appears to have walked straight out of a European art movie and left a whole lot of unfinished business behind him, twists his pale, unshaven features into a grimace and murmurs that, sure, they spend a lot of time together and are, uh, on fairly *intimate* terms, but, er, you know, they're really here to talk about the *music*.

Which is just fine for your attentive scribe here, for whom the music, Systems of Romance's music that is, has been a subject of absorbing interest ever since advance copies of their album *Madames et Messieurs... Welcome to the Hyper-Sound* were delivered to the music mags three weeks ago. Unusually for the instigators of a chart-bound pop noise, many of whom have been known to turn a mite precious about where they want to be interviewed, the Systems have volunteered to show up at King's Reach Tower. Here they have gamely consented to be shown around the office, even putting their tousled heads inside the review room, where some poor bastard who shall be nameless sits listening to the new Uriah Heep album, have approved a case of white-label dub singles new in from JA, and are now attending to polite enquiries about influences, aspirations and urgent desires – all those question that get flung at rock bands in the foothills of their careers. First things first – and a topic on which *Madames et Messieurs* offers little confirmation either way – are they a rock band or, as one or two sceptics have insisted, a kind of musical art project? Magda says she doesn't really know what I mean and goes back to her smouldering Gitane. Jon says they just sit down, write the songs and work out how to orchestrate them, but yes, if push comes to shove, they are a rock band. So what other rock bands inspired them to become a rock band? Magda says she likes the Stylistics, which your reporter takes to be A Joke.

One fact is immediately apparent. Jon does most of the talking. Magda tends to stare out of the window and smoke cigarettes, although she betrays momentary animation when German avant-gardists Can are mentioned ('I like their angles. I like their geometry. I like those white gloves the bass player wears.') Those of you keen on ancestral background will be charmed to know that Magda is half-French but was largely brought up in Surrey. She and Jon met at Leeds University, where they were in a 'kind of' punk band called The Stalactites. NME wonders if it is acceptable to construe 'America

Must Fall' as an attack on U.S. imperialism? Jon looks worried. 'You could say that, I suppose. We always thought it was about, well, historical determinism.' How do they see their position in a pop world they seem to be taking by storm? 'We're oscillating wildly,' Magda says, without the ghost of a smile. 'Soon we may calm down.' Jon looks more uncomfortable still. 'You'll have to excuse Mags' he says, when Mlle Huppert jr. has departed for the ladies, 'she's not very good with people.' 'No?' 'She never knows what to say,' Jon elaborates, 'and it makes her *anxious*.'

All this might make the Systems sound like a couple of prissy fruits. Me, I like them, if only because they clearly have no game-plan, haven't yet worked out how to play the newspapers and are self-evidently astonished to have got where they've got to at such a prodigious rate of knots. 'You know, we were *Top of the Pops* last week,' Magda confides on her return, as if I might somehow be unaware of this fact. 'Jimmy Savile actually shook my hand. Can you imagine that?' All too well, as it happens. Through the mist of her cigarette smoke all the benighted paraphernalia of pop celebrity – tours, fans, foolishness and who knows what else – irresistibly beckons.

New Musical Express, 7 August 1981

8. ARCADY

Party baby, seems so nice
Party baby, cold as ice
Party baby, always lies
See the mischief in her eyes
CHLOE AND THE CUP-CAKES – *Party Baby*

'Where the blazes are we anyhow?'

'Somewhere near Hassocks.'

It was several miles since we had last seen a signpost. I tried to remember the names of the Sussex villages. 'Cuckfield perhaps?'

'If this was a field exercise,' Rory said, who liked recalling his days in the Blues and Royals hauling Bren guns up and down the Falls Road, 'I'd put you on a charge.'

Rory's car, a low-slung Citroën with a rust-speckled bonnet, bowled on through high hedges backed up close to the road. Above our heads, gnarled oaks formed a canopy through which tiny shafts of sunlight glittered and flashed. From the asphalt that stretched before us fresh road-kill gleamed up, red and raw. After a while the tree canopy and the high hedges came to an end and we descended once again into the Sussex back-lanes. On one side neat green fields ran on endlessly to the horizon. From the other, behind wire fencing stretched so tight that it threatened to snap at any moment, varieties of livestock stood and stared. For about half an hour, the oak tunnels and the lack of human habitation had helped the modern world to slide out of sight. Any moment now, you felt, a Roman legion would come tramping into view over the meadows.

'Fourth day of the Headingley Test as well,' Rory complained, as the road showed signs of turning into a farm track. 'I can't think why I said I'd come. What does it say on the invite?'

The invitation card, an album-sized square of pasteboard with gilded rims, announcing that Mr and Mrs Donald Shard and family were at home on the 23rd of July 1981 at Handasyde Manor, Sussex, lay on the back seat next to a golf umbrella, a shooting stick, a box of shotgun cartridges and the various other bits of paraphernalia that Rory thought appropriate for a day in the country. None of the instructions scrawled on the obverse side seemed especially helpful.

'It says something about heading left after you reach the duckpond. I should go down there.'

Rory turned the car abruptly into a tiny lane, winced as the chassis juddered over what might have been a dead badger, plucked the invite from my hand and stared at it.

'Who's Mrs Shard? I don't think I've ever set eyes on her.'

'Gladys? Nobody ever has.'

'And what sort of state will our host be in? The man to whom we owe – what is it? £30,000? Eager to see reason? Anxious to compromise? Out for blood?'

This was a good question, here in the summer of 1981. Although Don's acts continued to make their Dark Lord money, and although Don's legal people in Lincoln's Inn were still beaming out their usual collection of insane writs and threatening letters, the word on the street was that Shard Enterprises was losing its grip. Item one on an extensive charge-sheet was the fact that Don had barely been seen in London since the start of the year, preferring to conduct his business from the country estate to which we were headed. Only the other week a producer called Barry Barrington, famous for his no-frills approach, who had once brought a Girl on the Phone single triumphantly home to port in a solitary late-night session lasting 37 minutes at a cost of £95 had sat in my office and confessed, unprompted, that 'there was something really weird going on with old Donny.' Encouraged to supply details, he went on: 'Just sits there in that place he bought in Sussex – you know it's like a castle? Got a fucking moat and all that – and twiddles his thumbs. Friend of mine went down there the other day about something. Said it was dead strange. Just Donny and a couple of his herberts from Maddox Street sitting and playing three-card brag, freezer full of ice-cream – no birds or nothing – and enough sherbet to keep the Eagles touring till Christmas. Every so often Don would say he was hungry and then one of them would get sent out for a dozen packets of sandwiches. And then the phone rings and it's Peter Grant from Led Zeppelin who Donny's always been as close as close with and the fucker won't even speak to him. Tells one of the blokes to take a message.'

'Sounds like something out of Tolstoy,' Rory said, who sometimes showed unexpected literary leanings. 'The Colonel of Infantry reaches his sixtieth year. Wonders what his life has been for. Retires to his estate to ponder the meaning of existence.'

'I don't think Don's been reading *The Death of Ivan Ilyich*. What are we going to say to him?'

'It depends what he says to us. When dealing with the enemy,' Rory said, as if were still piloting a tank through the streets of Baden-Baden with the British Army of the Rhine, 'you don't prejudge their motives. You take a recce, deploy your forces accordingly, and then hit them where they least expect it.'

The road was widening again now, and there was a cottage or two visible through the tree-line. A deer hastened away into the undergrowth. As if inspired by this vision of bucolic bliss, the car jolted forward and then came to rest at a T-junction made up of two overgrown footpaths and a five-barred gate with a stencilled sign that said, NO ENTRY: TRESPASSERS WILL BE SHOT, and I thought about all the dealings I had had with Don over the years: the press releases I had written at his command; the time I had been sent to Tangier to bring back an absconding Helium Kid and found him lurking there; the time he had sportively thrown the managing director of EMI Records into a swimming pool. But there were other things oppressing me on this hot July morning out on the road from Hassocks. One of them was the imminent release of the BMRB albums chart, on which Systems of Romance might or might not feature.

'Christ,' said Rory, who had got out of his seat and, eyes shaded against the sun, was staring at the top-most rung of the five-barred gate. The Citroën, its engine left running, twitched violently, like a car in a children's cartoon that was about to rear up, paw the ground and go dashing off under its own steam. There was a Royal Ascot parking permit still taped to its windscreen, and the clumps of rust gleamed in the heat like spreading psoriasis. 'Isn't there some sort of tent there?' Rory shouted from five yards away. 'Why don't you go and see if there's anyone who can give us directions?'

Rory was good at telling people to do things. I had once heard him order Richard Branson to shut one of the windows in his office. Beyond the gate a pathway picked out in white chalk led down to a clump of trees and what looked like a makeshift campsite. Here, grouped asymmetrically around a patch of bare earth scarred with the remains of burnt-out fireplaces, were a ridgepole tent, a tumbledown shed with a half-open door revealing piles of agricultural equipment, and a clothes line stretched between two saplings on which three or four shirts flapped in the breeze. A few hens went skirmishing across the grass. It was so like an illustration in an Edwardian children's book that you half-expected Mr Wibley Pig, dressed in a tweed suit and gaiters, to come marching out of the wood with a sack full of turnips. Instead a bald man with red, mutton-chop whiskers stuck his head out of the tent, inspected me for a second or two, and said:

'How are you, Nicko? It's Simon. I don't expect you remember me. I saw you just now opening the gate, so I went to put some clothes on.'

The early Eighties were full of this kind of encounter, when people who had been something in the Sixties re-emerged to offer details of how they were still forging ahead, or getting by, or, in the majority of cases, clinging on for dear life. Sometimes they were playing synthesizers in New Wave groups and trying to disguise how old they were. At other times they were working as studio tape-ops. Occasionally – as now – they were sitting in fields talking about the necessity of having to put on some clothes. This one – his name was Simon Dalrymple – had played keyboards in a band of mod screamers from Birmingham called the Fiery Orbs, famous for sleeping with fifteen-year-old girls and urinating on their audience's heads, who had once featured in an NME expose under the headline 'Must We Fling This Filth at Our Pop Kids?'

'How are you Simon? What have you been doing since I last saw you?'

'What have I been doing?' Simon came out of the tent and sat back wearily on his haunches, so that his lozenge-patterned harlequin's trousers glowed in the sun. The impression his eyes gave of being set slightly too far back in his head suggested that at some stage in his life – possibly quite recently – he had taken far too much acid. 'Oh, you know how it is, Nicko. Things come and they go. I was with Gong in the early Seventies. You remember Gong?'

I remembered Gong. 'That must have been fun.'

'It was in a way. Not like…Not like the stuff we used to play back when I knew you, of course.' As in a film about alternative lifestyles in the English countryside, a bedraggled-looking woman came out from behind the shed and began to unpeg the shirts from their line. 'Anyway…' Simon paused. The past, too remote now to be grasped at, slipped out of his fingers and went skittering away into the trees. 'Now we live here.'

Thirty yards down the track, I could see Rory coming to investigate. When he got here he would probably start telling Simon to do something. Keen to forestall this, I pointed to the wide expanse of grass that ran up the hill beyond us.

'Is this Don Shard's place?'

'Don?' Simon flashed another of his extraordinary glassy-eyed stares. 'Yes, of course. Do you know Don?' He made it sound as if this was a rare privilege, allowed only to a few cognoscenti. 'But of course, you worked for him back when we, when you…Don's really good to us,' Simon said, all in a rush, as if he had decided that he was better off sticking with the present. 'He lets us stay in one of his barns in the winter. Sometimes we go to the house and cook for him.'

Rory had stopped marauding down the path and was standing about ten yards away with his arms folded across his chest.

'Is this the way to the house? We've been asked to a party.'

'Well it is *a* way,' Simon said doubtfully. 'You're approaching from the wrong side. I should leave your car here and carry on up the hill. You can't miss it.'

The bedraggled woman, who looked as if she had strolled off the cover of an album by the Incredible String Band, had finished unpegging the shirts. Now, with an air of bitter disgust, she was arranging them in a wicker basket. 'We're going to the party,' she volunteered, a bit defensively, as if she suspected me of coming down the path with the express intention of warning her off 'Don's really cool about that. Always asks us over when he's got people round. Ringo Starr was there only the other week.'

'This is Migsy,' Simon said.

We shook hands. Migsy's palm was stained purple with what might have been blackcurrant juice, damp and adhesive. All at once, as if someone had flicked a switch, all kinds of things happened. Another woman, with two frail goblin children clinging to the hem of her skirt, materialised from the wood and started making semaphore signals, and an Alsatian dog slunk out of the undergrowth and sent the hens scurrying for shelter. Rory and I set off up the hill.

'What on earth was that?'

'He's called Simon Dalrymple. He used to be in the Fiery Orbs. He seems to be one of Don's tenants.'

'Well, I don't expect Don has much joy when he calls for the rent.'

The grass, calf-high and seething with insect life, went on for about a quarter of a mile. Beyond the hedge that lay at its topmost point, the land fell away again to reveal the towers and pediments of Handasyde Manor. This, too, was as characteristic of the early 1980s as finding Simon in his tent. It was what the people who had plundered the Sixties did with their money. They bought moated granges in the countryside, comfortable and remote, where swans flapped at the water's edge, and they sat in them and took too many drugs and sent their minions out to buy packets of sandwiches when they felt hungry.

'Tennysonian,' said Rory, allowing another glimpse of the phantom library he carried in his head, as we inspected the swans and the hideous gothic turrets which someone had welded onto the roof of the house and looked as if they might fall off at any moment.

'Camelot?

'Locksley Hall.'

The moat turned out to be full of silt and empty bottles. The swans, which had collected threateningly by the footbridge, dispersed the moment Rory began to walk towards them: they knew an Übermensch when they saw one. The back gate hung open. A few half-inflated balloons dangled from the door-post. From the courtyard beyond, where dimly-glimpsed figures stood in groups, came the sound of music.

'What sort of party is this?' Rory asked suspiciously.

It was a good question. Back in the old days, when he had first started staging them, Don's parties had never followed any clear demographic line. There were people you expected to see and people so outlandish that their presence on Don's lawn, eating his canapés and drinking whatever drinks he had bothered to put out, could hardly be guessed at. There were people – not so many of these – to whom he was under some kind of obligation, and there were people – always a great deal more of them – who were under some kind of obligation to him. Fifteen years later the associative nets that Don used to pinion his guests had been cast wider than ever. Record company executives; surly teenagers who could have been in bands Don reckoned on signing or might simply be employed in lowly capacities around the place; seven or eight corn-haired girls in close-fitting tee-shirts and skimpy white shorts; a brace of Don's frighteners, sweating into their thick suits. There was no knowing what Don wanted from them, why they were there, what, as the day wore on, he might try to compel them to do.

A girl in a maid's uniform was going round dispensing glasses of Pimm's. As Rory whipped one of them off the tray, Don, apparently risen out of the courtyard's dusty floor, loomed behind him. Bald, fatter than I had ever seen him, six foot two or three, eyebrows rising off his forehead in savage tufts, he looked more than ever like the heavy father in a silent film, shaping up to throw his daughter's boyfriend down three flights of stairs or menace him with an axe.

'Hello, Nick. Hello, son. Who's this long tall streak of piss?'

'Good of you to invite us, Don. This is Rory Bayliss-Callingham.'

I looked on as Don and Rory sized each other up. 'Charmed,' Rory said.

With Don, especially on home territory, you had to keep things light.

'Nice crowd of people you've got here, Don.'

'That's what I told the missus,' Don said. 'No old dug-outs who want to get pissed at my expense. You see those birds over there? Page

Three girls. You can hire them by the dozen. They're called...What are they called?' There was a faint light of panic in his eyes as he tried to recall the names of the girls he had invited to entertain his guests. 'I can't remember.' Slowly the monologue ground to a halt. 'It don't fucking matter.'

The girls seemed puzzled as to their duties. They wandered round in ones and twos, smiling at anyone who looked their way and begging lights for their cigarettes. Don shifted his bulk uncomfortably from one leg to the other. 'We'll talk later,' he said, as if I had suddenly shot half-a-dozen questions at him, none of which he wanted to answer.

'That's a very nice sunken garden you have over there behind the moat,' Rory offered. 'Is it a Humphrey Repton?'

'Jesus Christ.'

What hung over the party and was already undermining it, I realised as Rory and I wandered further into the courtyard, was an air of self-consciousness. The guests were all awaiting Don's cue and, not receiving one, were wondering how to behave. A tiny, elderly man hobbled out into the middle of the throng and began to operate a hurdy-gurdy with an air of supreme indifference. One of the Page Three girls danced a few steps, stubbed her toe on one of the flagstones and gave up. Honey-coloured light, streaming down from the battlements, bounced off her white shorts and gently diffused into the grey-brick surround.

'What an extraordinary collection of people,' Rory said. He was in one of his sardonic moods. 'Were the parties in the Sixties anything like this?'

I thought about the parties of the Sixties, at which women in kaftans had taken off their clothes and thrown themselves into the Serpentine, in which pagan rites had been re-enacted on sacred stones on West Country moors and troupes of Native American Indians had sung tribal dirges over campfires on rolling suburban lawns.

'Nothing like, as I remember them.'

'Well, you would know' Rory said, with an odd hint of wistfulness. The hurdy gurdy had stopped working and was making an odd whirring noise. 'How are we going to do with this Systems of Romance thing?'

'Trevor says the advance sales are good. Peel played a track the other night.'

'So were the advance sales for the last Maximum Acceleration record. And half the bastards came back to the warehouse six weeks later.'

Rory. Don. The wheezing noise of the hurdy-gurdy as it approached death. The Page Three girl massaging her toe. I was bored by them all. 'I shouldn't be surprised if it got to Number One and made us all millionaires.'

'Well, speaking as one who has his hand on the tiller of our financial affairs, I should tell you that that day can't come soon enough.'

Rory's crossness came and went. Just now the breeze that fanned the flames of his annoyance was blowing fairly hard.

'I need to use the telephone,' he said abruptly. 'Do you suppose our host would mind?'

'From the look of him, I should say our host probably doesn't know which day of the week it is.'

'That can be an advantage in dealing with people,' Rory said. He strode off purposefully, making curious chicken-wing motions with his elbows, towards the courtyard's further side and was lost from view, leaving me to ponder the fate of Systems of Romance, who only last week had been hailed by the most pretentious of the many pretentious young men who wrote for the NME as the purveyors of 'a candy-coated synth-pop bullet headed straight for your heart.' One of Don's heavies waddled past, nodding at me with the respect due to a man through whose front window you have recently lobbed a brick, and I motioned him over.

'What's with Don, Charlie?'

For all the air of menace that their employer carried around with him, Don's retainers could never be got to keep quiet about his activities. The conditions of servitude in which he kept them were so awful that every so often they were forced to let off steam by complaining about him.

'You tell me Nick. Never seen him so weird.' Charlie looked up, saw that Don was a good fifteen yards away and beckoned me conspiratorially to his side. 'For a start there's gear all over the place. That Rodney – you remember him from Maddox Street? – brings it down on a Friday night. But it's not the sherbet so much. I'd say 'e was just losing it. Sometimes 'e'll go and sit on the toilet and you couldn't get him off it if Frank Sinatra knocked on the door. Was some promoter from the States the other day – might have been Harvey Goldstein – and 'e wouldn't even come to the phone. There'll be blokes come down from London for meetings and he won't see them. Just says: "Charlie, tell them to fuck off." Terry – you remember Terry? – couldn't stand it no more and gave in his notice. You take my tip, Nicko, and keep out of his way.' There was a pause. 'Look,' Charlie said, suddenly oppressed by the faint stirring of conscience, 'I was really sorry about that brick.'

There were more guests coming into the courtyard, fanning their faces in the mid-day heat and gawping at the Page Three girls. Simon and Migsy, oblivious to their surroundings, dawdled in the rear. It was a mark of the social basis of Don's party, here in the stone courtyard beneath the high battlements of Handasyde Manor, that neither of them looked at all out of place. Sky-blue cloak brushing against the knees of his lozenge-pattern trousers, face even whiter than it had been back at the campsite, Simon looked desperately out of sorts.

'So there you are again, Nick. Do you know, I wasn't going to come. Not feeling terribly well. But Migsy said I ought to make an effort. Said Don wouldn't like it if we weren't here. He can get dreadfully *cross* sometimes.' He peered vaguely into the middle distance, like a bored child at an Aquapark instructed to look at all the fish. 'I can't say I recognise anyone. But then we don't get out much. Migsy goes down to Brighton sometimes to see her aunt, but…Do you know, Nick, I really shall have to sit down.'

The Page Three girls had given up greeting Don's guests or begging lights for their cigarettes. Instead they sat in a small, resentful huddle looking at their watches. Migsy had gone over to the courtyard wall and was staring at the brickwork as if she expected it to burst into flames at any moment. From the three-legged stool onto which he had now lowered himself, Simon let out a groan.

'Can I get you anything?'

'It's all right, Nick. I'll be right as rain in a moment. Really I shall. In any case, we shan't stay long. The thing is, Don's been talking about you.'

'Has he?'

'Oh yes. Sometimes when we're over here in the evenings – always by invitation, you understand; we wouldn't dream of just turning up – he talks about you. Not nice things, either. I mean, I know Don's got a prickly side. We were playing Monopoly once, and Migsy got a hotel on Mayfair, which you could see Don had set his heart on, and he was *completely furious*. Perhaps you don't know about it, Nick – I mean, it's so easy to offend someone without realising, isn't it? It was always happening to me when I was in the Orbs. It used to upset me a lot. But if I were you I'd ask him what you've done so you can make it up. I always think that's the best way…Oh dear, oh dear.'

The courtyard wall had not burst into flames. I summoned Migsy over from it.

'Is he all right?'

'When you've put as much *stuff* into yourself as he's done over the years, you're never really going to be all right are you?' She looked absolutely at the end of her tether, like one of the Furies out for vengeance. 'Look, have you got twenty quid?'

'Why?'

'So I can go into the village and buy some fucking food with it. We've been living on lentil soup since Saturday.'

As I was in the act of giving her the £20 note, Rory came striding back across the courtyard. His elbows had stopped making chicken movements and he looked faintly bewildered.

'How did you get on?'

'Very queer set-up in there,' Rory said. 'For a start there were loads of children hanging about. Regular little hooligans, too. One of them had the cheek to charge me fifty pence for using the phone. And then nobody seemed to know where anything was. The loo turned out to be in a kind of out-house. Anyway, in the end I managed to get through to Newman Street. They haven't had any word on the album chart yet, but apparently Botham's still making some sort of a stand.' Rory shot me a look that might have been meant to convey prurience, sympathy or half-a-dozen emotions somewhere in between.

'How's Alice Weatherall?'

'Not playing that game.'

'Suit yourself.' All Rory's crossness had vanished. Suddenly he was in the highest of spirits. 'And there was a curious old girl in there, sitting in a chair and reading the *Daily Mail.* Called me 'young man' and asked me to fetch her a glass of water. Can that have been Mrs Shard?'

'If she is, you're the first person I know who's ever set eyes on her.'

Rory nodded. I could see that not only was his mind working hard but that it was stealthily reconfiguring the landscape in which he stood. The stone courtyard was a parade ground. The guests were recruits, awaiting his orders. Soon he would send them out on manoeuvres, charge them to do his bidding, unfurl his ensign and haul it up on the Handasyde ramparts.

Charlie – a new, purposeful Charlie, flushed with the weight of responsibility, came tearing past the clumps of Page Three girls.

'Gentlemen. Mr Shard would like to see you in his office.'

'What sort of state is he in?'

Charlie gave me a reproachful look, all past intimacy gone. 'You'll find Mr Shard over there in the doorway gentlemen.'

Don lurked in the doorway which connected the courtyard to his living quarters. The other guests were giving him a wide berth. Scarcely looking to see if we were behind him, he ploughed on into the house. A kitchen, two long tiled passageways and a dining-room followed in quick succession. Finally we came to what might have been a study, rather like the sanctum in Pacific Palisades where Earle Pankey watched his show-reels. Here a beady-eyed woman sat watching television and there were thee smallish children playing on a sofa.

'Grandkids' Don said bitterly. 'Go on. Fuck off out of it will you?'

'Don' the beady-eyed woman said, raising a hand in rebuke, and then, to us: 'I'm Gladys Shard. I'm very pleased to meet you.'

We shook hands. 'Why do they have to make such a bastard noise?' Don demanded.

'It's very rare that I get to meet any of Donald's friends,' Mrs Shard said. She had a quaint and rather refined voice that recalled old-style BBC announcers. 'Do make yourselves at home.'

To sit even for a moment in Don's study was to appreciate the symbolic value of the artefacts he had surrounded himself with. Two Helium Kids gold discs; a photo of Don shaking hands with a nervous-looking Brian Epstein; another photo of Don at the 1966 NME Poll-winners' Concert at the Empire Pool; a framed poster from the 1950s advertising his celebrated variety hall revue *Young, Free and Shirtless*. There was no doubt about it. Don had been around. Don had paid his way. There were no flies on Don. With the memory of the people who had pronounced these verdicts – most of whom were mysteriously no longer at large in the music business – crowding into my head, I sat on the edge of the sofa and attended to the terrifying figure in the chair opposite.

'Hear you're doing good business with Systems of Romance.' All trace of Don's earlier confusion had gone. If the Page Three girls had been brought in to see him, he would have reeled off their dates of birth, one by one. He looked raring to go. 'Actually, I might be managing them.'

'That's good news, Don' I remarked of this catastrophic piece of intelligence. 'What does Liam say about it?' Liam was Systems of Romance's current manager, a trusting 23 year-old who operated out of a bed-sitting room in the Lower Broughton Road, Manchester.

'Going to buy him out of it, aren't I?' Don said, half-smile indicating what a bountiful old softie he really was at heart. 'You know. Give him five hundred quid and tell him to fuck off.'

Rory, seated next to me on the sofa, was twitching slightly, as if only politeness was stopping him from seizing one of the gold discs – it was for 'Agamemnon's Mighty Sword' – and smashing it over Don's head. Don, the acrid scent of his personality swirling around the room, sat and beamed at us.

'Business is in a funny state isn't it?' he pronounced. 'All them – what is it? – synth bands. Don't understand it myself.' Don was famous for taking no interest at all in the music he made fortunes out of, and preferring the light operas of Gilbert & Sullivan. 'Went to see a lot called the Human League the other night. This geezer with a back-to-front haircut and a couple of birds dancing. You never saw anything like it.' He rattled on for a bit about the various abominations that had caught his eye in a way that indicated to any experienced Don-fancier – I was one – that he was working his way up to some dramatic statement of intent. Mrs Shard, clearly bored by this monologue, picked up a half-knitted sweater from the floor beneath her chair and shuffled off. Finally, when the death of Led Zeppelin's John Bonham ('I still miss the fucker you know?') and the dancers they had on *Top of the Pops* these days ('Regular old boilers. That won't shift many records') had been disposed of, he bounced up out of his chair like a big, evil puppet suddenly tugged by invisible strings.

'Now, you good people. About that £30,000.'

'£20,000' Rory corrected him.

'£30,000 my accountant says, what with inflation and compound interest and no dividend for two-and-a-half years.'

'Who said anything about dividends?'

'Don't get clever with me, son' said Don, all hint of bonhomie gone. I remembered what Ainslie Duncan had said to me back in 1967, shortly before his enforced removal from managing the Helium Kids: 'If I heard Don wanted to see me I'd take Kenny and that Mad Ernie with me and I'd tell someone the exact time I was going in there and to phone the police if I didn't come out within twenty minutes. That's what I'd do.'

'Now I've been doing some thinking,' Don went on, a shade more affably. 'I've got my spies' – it was clear that he meant this gloss to be taken literally – 'and I reckon you're doing OK. Not making any money yet, but doing OK. So what you need is some proper investment. This being the case, and notwithstanding our previous arrangement' – Don liked dropping the odd archaism into his speech to see the effect it produced – 'I'm prepared to write off the £30,000. It's yours. Spend it how you like. Get in some load of coons who can play this ska nonsense – *I* don't mind. Up to you. In return, I get a seat on the board. You get the benefit of my considerable expertise. Plus you get the bands I send your way. Everybody wins. Am I right?'

Needless to say, this was a terrible idea, guaranteed to maximise Don's profits while reducing everyone else involved in the enterprise to penury. It had last been tried in the early Seventies with a label called Titan Records, from whom Don had plundered £50,000-worth of management fees after furnishing them with three or four acts from his roster whom no one else would sign only to ceremoniously detach himself a fortnight before they were declared bankrupt. As Rory and I contemplated the enormity of what was on offer, Don breezed on:

'Just to be friendly like, you can have the Plastic Torpedoes for free. Great little demo they made the other week. You probably heard it.'

The Plastic Torpedoes were a mod band from Thurrock who had, famously, remained unsigned for the two years of their existence. To even listen to their demo tape would be an act of abject folly.

'There you are,' Don said. His eyebrows looked like nests of insects, crazily embroiled. 'Couldn't be better. I'll get the lawyers' letters done and away we go.'

Outside, far away from the space in which we sat, there were other things going on in the world. In a room in Broadcasting House someone was examining the BMRB album chart. At Headingley England were playing Australia. Nearer at hand – we could hear the buzz of conversation through the half-open window – Don's guests were drinking his Pimm's and eating his sandwiches. Here, though, there were nettles waiting to be grasped. It was quite possible that Don was having an elaborate joke at our expense. Or it could be that he was entirely serious. Finding out exactly where we stood would take time. Rory, meanwhile, was drumming his fingers on the toe-caps of the brown-and-cream golfing brogues he had thought suitable for a pop mogul's lunch-party in the country.

'I don't think' he began, 'that you quite know who you're dealing with.'

'I don't quite know fucking what?'

'A child of five wouldn't agree to those terms. An infant in its cradle would think twice about signing the Plastic Torpedoes. You can have your £20,000 back – five per cent, non-compound interest – by the end of the year. If you want anything else, you can whistle for it.'

There was a terrible, agonised silence. On past form Don was quite capable of grinding Rory's head into the carpet or throwing him head-first out of the window. For some reason he did neither of these things.

'As for the threats which have been issued against my partner,' Rory said, a touch more formally. 'Should they be repeated, we shall have no hesitation in taking the necessary legal action. Oh, and another thing, Mr Shard. If you feel like cutting up rough – and you may very well do – I've got a brother-in-law training with Three Para at Aldershot just this moment. I daresay he and one or two of his colleagues would welcome the opportunity of a little trip to the Sussex countryside. Or Maddox Street, if it came to that. Do I make myself clear?'

'This is all bollocks,' Don said, not very convincingly.

'No it isn't,' Rory countered. 'Anything else you want to say?'

Don's eyes gleamed. He seemed half-way between bitter, uncontrollable fury and reluctant admiration for Rory's ability to grasp the reins of a situation and make it work to his advantage.

'You lot are hilarious,' he said. I thought of the moment in Tangier when he had appeared from behind the curtain in Garth Dangerfield's rented kitchen and taken control of both our lives. It seemed a lifetime away now. But the symbolism of what had passed seemed lost on Rory, who climbed lazily out of his chair as if he had just been interviewing the secretary of the Hurlingham Club.

'I'll wish you a very good afternoon,' he said. And then we were gone.

* * *

'Have you really got a brother-in-law in Three Para?' I asked, half-an-hour later as the Citroën sped northward through the Sussex back-lanes.

'Certainly not. In any case they're a parvenu regiment. Not that I don't know one or two chaps wearing the khaki who could do some serious damage if they were called upon. You see' Rory said, as if he were explaining some elemental law, 'I couldn't have Don going on like that.'

When we got back to Newman Street it was to discover that England had unexpectedly won the Test Match, that Systems of Romance had entered the album chart at Number 4 and that Alice had left no fewer than three messages for me at reception.

Days in Europa

Ah, those days in Europa, of which so much of this mid-Eighties carnival seemed to consist. Long weekends at David Geffen's rented villa at Cap Ferrat, with the shades of Elsa Lanchester, Coco Chanel and the Duke of Windsor roaming over the terrace to greet us. Riviera vacations, with the wind blowing through the pines and the blue of the Mediterranean stretching out into the distance. Mornings in the Baltic, where tall ships floated under clear, endless sky. Afternoons in Conny Plank's studio outside Munich with Can's rhythm section laying down some impossibly convoluted groove over which Magda and Jon would be set to warble. Evenings at the Hansa studios in Berlin, with the ghosts of David Bowie and Iggy Pop hanging over the mixing desk and Brian Eno's signature scrawled on the Bakelite table-top in black felt-tip. Industry conventions on the beach at St Tropez, with the swim-suited girls looking on as Mick and Keith stalked off into the glare. The harbour at Toulon and the Gibraltar cable-car with its view out over the great grim mountains of North Africa. Breakfast in Paris, lunch in Pisa, dinner in Stuttgart. Alice's face reflected out of the window of the *wagon-lit*. The pigeons taking flight in St Mark's Square. And all the while, in chance encounters, in long-planned meetings, in casual hook-ups in hotel foyers or crowded piazzas, the people flying by. Bumping into Lou Reed at Orly Airport ('How's Andy?' 'The fuck I should know? I never see Andy these days.') Breezing through the (unlocked) door of the bathroom at Cap Ferrat to find a small, dumpy girl with dyed blonde hair, skirts hoicked above her thighs in what the CNS Latin master would have called *latebra pudendis* and be greeted with a shout of 'Jesus, I'm trying to take a shit in here.' ('I see you've met Maddy,' my host observed. 'She's going to be a *really big star*. As she probably told you.') Glimpsing a man who looked so like Brian Jones – the same Mr Fish jacket, the same snakeskin boots, the same watchful stare – inspecting the bric-à-brac in a Marrakech street market that it was hard to believe that his original had drowned in a Home Counties swimming pool a decade-and-a-half before.

Antibes in the sun. The Bosporus in the rain. Bremen in the snow. Alice's face reflected out of the chrome embellishments of the Pompidou Centre. And always – always – the reminder that what has been was not the same as what was now. Going to see U2 as a guest of the band – a favour from their manager on account of some mild encouragement offered back in 1979 – and finding myself in the back of a limousine with Klaus Voorman, not seen since the mid-Sixties, and sitting in silence as the limousine deposited us at the venue, after which we strode through countless flower-ornamented rooms, up endless concrete steps and past numberless deferential security personnel to our celebrity vantage-point, and then, after the two hours of screaming mayhem that followed, Klaus giving me a glance that incorporated the gig, its preliminaries and the shared history that had brought us here and saying, gravely and giving each word an almost sepulchral emphasis: 'These people are not our people. That music is not our music. This time is not our time. Our time is gone.' After which, naturally, we went to the after-party with Bono and the boys and had ourselves a ball, half of me agreeing fervently with what Voorman had said, in strict musicological terms, the other remembering, in mitigation, that I was 43 years old – 43 years old, you hear? – and had been in this business for A Very Long Time.

Systems of Romance: Mesdames et Messieurs…Welcome to the Hyper-sound [Resurgam]

Welcome to the Hyper-sound/Dead Oceans/America Must Fall/ Ballardian/Ambient Highway Pilgrim/Semaphoring Wildly from the Mountain-top/King Shaker/Mind under Glass/A Wizard, a True-star/Phenomenology. Running time: 37.23

Hero, you come at last. Heroine, too. But first, some thoughts on the sociological terrain this animal known as 'pop music' now inhabits, through which it prowls and slavers, shakes its mighty paw and stares, red-eyed into the approaching night. You see, 'punk rock', that sensational charge detonated beneath the battlements of our 'popular culture' a few years back, was essentially urban music, the sound of crazed kids in tenement rooms negotiating with a brutal and monochrome past while envisioning – and these were Blakean worlds, suffused with wonder – a future that they themselves burned to create. Whereas the 'new sound', which has been trickling into our consciousness since at least 1979, is essentially *suburban*, fashioned in a landscape of pebble-dash houses and privet hedges, silent trauma and cascading entropy. Like many another music, then and now, it always intended to move on from its roots while preserving its sense of rootedness, and two of the people it picked up in the course of this highly desirable journey, this Route 66 into the heart of the modern psyche, are Systems of Romance. Welcome to the hyper-sound, indeed.

And what exactly is the hyper-sound? Well, as modern as the tumbling world should be. This is ferocious but gratifying music, intricate and uncompromising, as if Virginia Woolf and Lucian Freud had decided to record an album together and then got Charlie Chaplin in to produce. Yes, it's *that* good. The wave of synths that distinguished their first EP has opened up a bit to reveal all kinds of crevices and exotic by-ways and the audacity of their original orchestration – its dark entries, its sonic brutalism – has been refined into something that can verge on feyness. 'It goes round and round/Sweeps your feet off the ground/Welcome to the hyper-sound,' Magda Peyrefitte repeats, mantra-like, in the closing bars of the title-track, conjuring the thought of a wild, cosmopolitan rumpus room in which Blake, Rimbaud, Kafka, Burroughs and Iggy Pop are all having one hell of a party. 'America Must Fall' is a tract for our uncertain times: artful yet committed, oblique yet determinist, harsh guitars and edgy keyboard washes receding to leave our Magda declaiming that 'Your flag stands tall/We are in your thrall/But after all/America must fall.' Reagan will hear it and weep into his bowl of Cheerios.

These are smart kids, Jon and Magda, smart kids – check out 'Ballardian', which is essentially a hymn to dear old J.G. – with notions in their heads. Where they come from – the glorious north, naturally – is unimportant. What matters is where they're going. On the strength of 'Semaphoring Wildly from the Mountain-top', which is quite beautiful in the spiritedness of its tension and the minimalism of its pomp, I'd say they're headed for the very top of the tree. This is not soft toffee, but neither is it hard cheese. You could listen to 'Mind under Glass' for hours without realising that it's a paean to paranoia, grounded in 'The Burrow', the greatest short story Uncle Franz ever wrote. The demonic pop soufflé that is 'A Wizard, a True-star' sounds like Seventies prog rock brought up to date in a maelstrom of tribal drumming – a sound so uncompromising that the effect on your cerebral cortex is as if a dinosaur had cracked off the top of your head with an outsize spoon and started feasting on the brains within. I loved it, and you will too. In an instant pop music has changed, and don't let anyone tell you different. Welcome to the hyper-sound!

'PAUL MORLEY' – *New Musical Express*, 20 July 1981

21 September 1981

Saturday afternoon in Walpole Street. Early autumn sun falling on the sprigged Peter Jones duvet and the Laura Ashley pillow slips. In the distance the sound of the Chelsea fans barrelling down the King's Road. No sign of Mark or the children and no indication of where they might be. No point in asking either. At one stage in the proceedings, Alice says:

'How do you feel when we're doing this? I mean, are you Mellors and I'm Lady Chatterley? Is that how you see it?'

'People always misinterpret Mellors' social status. He had a commission in the war. I think that more or less makes him a gentleman.'

'Oh don't be so *pompous*. I'm talking about us. Not the characters in some wretched book.'

'If it comes to that, how exactly do you see it?'

'Well, it makes a nice change I must say. You wouldn't think it, but Mark's not terribly interested in this kind of thing. In fact, I sometimes wonder if he isn't a bit of a sissy.'

Chez Weatherall on a Saturday afternoon. The portraits of the children, Fergus and Amy, in their gilt frames. A picture of Mark's mother as a debutante with ostrich feathers in her hair and an expression that would curdle milk. Bowls of pot-pourri on the occasional tables. Sailing club fixture cards along the mantelpiece. The phone rings several times and goes unanswered. As I soon discovered, this is not the first time that Alice has besmirched the honour of her marital bed ('You'd do it too, if you lived in Chelsea and had a husband who worked at Cazenove's.') Any stirrings of conscience I might have had are swiftly dispelled by the hint that Alice thinks Mark is an idiot.

'Now' she says, one hand busy with a cigarette, the other balancing a diary on her bare knee. 'I'm busy on Monday and Tuesday Mark's got some ghastly office thing at the opera. But you can take me out to supper on Wednesday. I'll say I'm seeing Cecily again.'

Cecily, arriving in London on a fortnight's furlough, has already been pressed into service as an alibi. 'I think it's simply wonderful that you and Al have got together' she told me when the three of us met for a drink.

'Surely Cecily disapproves of all this? Didn't you say she had six children or something?'

'Oh Cecily leads such a boring life that anything remotely wicked absolutely *tantalizes* her. She'd probably run off with the butcher's boy if he made a pass.'

By now I feel qualified to sit an exam on the subject of *Alice Weatherall [née Danby.] Her relationship to the class and culture from which she hails. Candidates will be expected to show a precise understanding of the subject's tastes, opinions and attitudes to prevailing upper-class norms.* Basically it is a relationship in which huge amounts of cake are had and eaten too, in which every last compartment of upper-bourgeois life is ransacked for its entertainment value while being simultaneously held up to mockery, proclaimed as not worth doing even as it is done. 'Poor old Marianne,' she once remarked, of the woman who had been placed next to me at dinner that night. 'As long as she can get half-a-dozen lunches a year at the Hurlingham Club, a night or two at Sadler's Wells and an invitation to Scotland in August, she's perfectly happy.' 'But isn't that how you live your life?' 'Maybe it is' Alice conceded. 'But not by sponging off other people.'

When the phone rings for the fourth time, some sixth sense prompts her to answer it. The conversation mainly consists of vocables that are not in current social usage – 'mmmh', 'unnrh' 'nurrgh' – and is accompanied by frenzied doodling on the telephone message pad.

'That was Mark. He says he'll be back in twenty minutes.'

'Where's he been?'

'Overnight exercise with the Territorials. Golf with the clients. I don't know.'

'What would you have done if he hadn't bothered to phone?'

'I expect I'd have thought of something.'

On the doorstep, where the mellow scents of a Chelsea afternoon are crowding out the shouts of the football fans, and sleek, expensive cars are lined up on the spotless verge, she says, with faint animation:

'Isn't it extraordinary? Us meeting again like this. All this happening.'

I shake my head. This is Alice Danby, the girl who I remember walking down Broad Street, Oxford, and into Final Examination Schools on a June morning in 1964 with no fewer than seven bunches of roses presented to her by young men who wished her well. It is not extraordinary at all. In fact, it is the least extraordinary thing I can think of.

Back in Walpole Street, some impulse I cannot subdue makes me linger for a minute or two at the junction with the King's Road. Sure enough, shortly afterwards a black Saab with Mark at the wheel comes shooting round the corner. As in a film, a little swirl of fallen leaves rises in its wake. The effect is vaguely unsettling, like ghostly knocking heard a long way off.

* * *

23 September 1981

A&R meeting at Newman Street. Present: self, Rory, Doug, Paula, one or two others. Tea for some reason drunk out of Royal Wedding souvenir mugs. Inaugurated and invigorated by the news that *Madames et Messieurs*... has just gone gold. Then to the pressing issues of the day.

DOUG : Are we interested in the New Wave of British Heavy Metal?

SELF : No.

DOUG : Do we want to pick up Dr Feelgood? Somebody said UA were letting them go.

SELF : No.

Silence

RORY : What are Maximum Acceleration up to?

DOUG : It's all very weird. I went down to their rehearsal space the other day and it was full of really old stuff from the Sixties – you know, Vox amplifiers and phasers. And one of those early synths that have thousands of wires sticking out of them and you need a degree in electronic engineering to get it working. Their manager says they want to do a concept album about the vernal equinox and it's going to take them ages.

RORY: Didn't there used to be a sort of *mystique* about letting a band stay in the studio for months on end working on some grand project and the music press all wondering when it would see the light of day?

If Maximum Acceleration had tried this old trick on us a couple of months ago they would have been thrown out into the street. As it is, the success of *Madames et Messieurs*...has made us all cash-happy. Their manager, calling at Newman Street three days later, and uncertain of the reception he will receive, is mystified to be handed a cheque for £10,000 and told that his protégés can take as long as they want. At my instigation, Paula crafts a press release for the music weeklies unveiling the band's quest for 'the new sound...a magic carpet-ride to a whole new auditory dimension.' Here in the age of Mrs Thatcher, strikes and Royal Weddings, the Sixties are making a comeback.

24 September 1981

Thinking of the old days in North Park. My mother sewing in front of the fire. The boys with yellow-and-green rosettes coming back through the gloaming on Saturday nights after the football. The smell of chocolate from the Rowntree Mackintosh factory in Chapel Field. The brass band playing in the park on Sunday afternoons and the rooks scattering from the trees whenever they started up. Trips to the back of Norwich market to hear Alf the Purse King selling his bags: 'Python lady, pure python. How do I know? 'cause I went to Caister and shot the bugger.'

Alice rings. 'Mark thinks there's something going on.'

'How do you know?'

'It's his bloody mother. Apparently she told him I was looking far too well and pleased with myself.

'What will he do?' I have a vision of myself being chased around Newman Street by a gang of Mark's Territorials.

'I don't suppose he'll do anything' Alice says. 'Besides, I've got far more money than he has.'

PART THREE

Time Out of Mind

'And luck is always better than skill at things – we're flying blind…'

9. LITTLE LOCAL DIFFICULTIES

Hegemony has me by the throat
But I'm doing what I can…
SYSTEMS OF ROMANCE – *Collapse of World Civilisation*

Waking up in the early mornings, not long past dawn, with pale light stealing in through imperfectly closed shutters and wildlife scurrying about in the eaves, it always took me a moment to remember that the dense, fluttering chaos overhead was the sound of geese flying in from the Wash. There was nothing predictable about this noise, its decibel level, the amount of time it could go on for. Sometimes the cries were plaintive, as if some great tragedy had occurred in the skies over Lincolnshire from which they yearned desperately to escape. More often they were strident and somehow proprietorial, as if the birds had staked out the territory beneath their flight-path and schemed to take possession of it. In the end, though, the geese were creatures of habit. As the morning wore away they would drift off towards Ely, March, flat fields and enticing reservoirs, leaving nothing behind them but empty air and a vague feeling of unease, that thought of primitive patterns re-imposing themselves on a man-disfigured world. On this particular morning the geese were louder than usual. Jerked out of sleep by a furious, implacable honking, I discovered that the shutters were already open and that Alice was sitting by the open window brooding over a cup of coffee.

'What I shall never understand' she said, briskly inspecting the coffee cup as if she had never seen one before and wondered to what ingenious uses it could be put, 'is why you had to come and live here.'

It had rained for several hours during the night, but this was mild for the standards of the area. Now there was bright sunshine sparkling off the window sills.

'Heritage. *Ancestry*.'

'If it comes to that,' Alice said, 'I thought you told me you were left in a plastic bag on the steps of a foundling hospital. It's not as if there's a family mausoleum out in the park.'

Even at the best of times, which this was not, there was a superhuman formality to the way Alice behaved. She was the kind of woman who when stark naked – her present state, as it happened – still seemed to be wearing a suit of clothes.

'Most people who buy a place in the country like it to be near other people's places. Not in the middle of a bog surrounded by a lot of farmers. There are some very nice houses in Northamptonshire.'

Nice houses in Northamptonshire. Shooting lodges in the Ochil Hills. Kensington High Street. The Monopoly board by which Alice navigated her way around the British Isles could be surprisingly limited.

'Some women' Alice said, meaning one woman, and coiling one of her bare ankles over the other as if she were about to execute some complicated ballet step, 'wouldn't put up with this.'

Looking out of the window, where long, erratically-partitioned fields stretched out towards the Fens, and even here in May the landscape was still dotted with meres and mini-lagoons that only the heat of high summer would sweep away, you could see her point. The rain blew in from the North Sea, the equinoctial gales tore through the wet grass knocking over fence-posts as they went and the corpses of drowned livestock floated belly-up in the drainage ditches until the farmers came and dragged them away. On the other hand, this was Mickleburgh country, where my mother's family had lived before heading further into Norfolk at the time of Queen Victoria's Diamond Jubilee. There were Mickleburgh graves in Emneth churchyard, three miles away, and the ghosts of Mickleburgh children playing on the roadside verges. But this was difficult to explain.

'And another thing,' Alice said, on whom the coffee was working its usual galvanic effect. 'You ought to do something about this house. If you're going to spend so much time here now that you're so rich, you shouldn't be living in a midden.'

On the rare occasions that she bothered to come to Elm, Alice was always canvassing schemes for improvement. A gazebo, a sunken garden and a designer kitchen had all been tried and failed. Oddly it was Rory, caste solidarity thrown to the winds, who had strengthened my resolve. 'If you buy a country pile, then you want it to be a bit decayed,' he had said. 'Only a vulgarian digs up his front lawn.'

Outside there was a loud pop as the first of the day's bird-scarers went off. Alice waggled her backside in a gesture of exasperation and began to put on the kind of clothes that, in the three years this had been going on, she was usually seen wearing: clothes that did not absolutely deny that the rag-trade existed but worked such subtle and expensive variations on it that anyone who shopped at Marks & Spencer was left in a state of huge social disadvantage. This morning it was a pair of culottes and a white cheesecloth shirt tied at the neck with a butterfly bow.

'Remind me what it is that we're doing today.'

Another bird-scarer went off. Like the migrating geese and Alice herself, they were unpredictable. 'We're going to get in the car, drive to Oxburgh Hall and watch them film the new Systems of Romance video.'

'What is Oxburgh Hall?'

'It's a National Trust property over near Downham Market.'

'And why do Systems of Romance need to shoot their video there? Why couldn't they go to the Manor?' Alice asked, revealing – not for the first time – that she knew rather more about the music business than she sometimes liked to let on.

This was 1985, when music videos got filmed in hot-air balloons half-way up Mount Kilimanjaro, on the time-weathered battlements of medieval castles, in the Gobi Desert, on yachts in sight of the Balinese shoreline. The correct answer was: why not?

'We're not getting on terribly well with Branson just at the moment' – no more we were – 'and in any case Oxburgh has a particularly fine moat' – I was quoting the art director – 'where Magda can have a whale of a time flapping about in a punt' – I was still quoting the art director – 'pretending she's Lizzie Siddons as Ophelia or something.'

'Actually, Oxburgh Hall sounds rather nice' Alice said, cheered by the thought of all this patrician splendour. 'I'm not sure Mark didn't use to know the people who owned it.'

'How is Mark?'

'Oh he's got some woman or other…Actually he's very worried about this Big Bang nonsense. Apparently Cazenoves had to take some American banker out to Wilton's the other day and he asked if he could have a pastrami sandwich.'

Three years into our relationship, I was getting the measure of Alice's vocal style, and its complex amalgam of over- and understatement. 'Some woman or other' could mean anyone from Princess Margaret to a prostitute picked up in the Strand. The anxiety-palette that lay behind 'very worried' might range from 'panic-stricken' to 'not worried at all.' It was hard to keep up.'

'Your floors are frightfully hard,' Alice said as she stepped out into the corridor.

'What did you do with the children?'

'They're with Mummy.'

'You should bring them here sometime' I said, the ghosts of the dead Mickleburghs still marauding through my head.

'Mummy would have a *fit* if she thought they were anywhere near you. When I had lunch with her last week she described you as my 'fancy man'.'

'And what does she think of you?'

'What she always thought. Mummy used to say that I had an enquiring mind,' Alice said, with what could only have been absolute seriousness, 'but that I wasn't tractable and was easily led. Which is rather a contradiction, don't you think? She also said that when the alarm sounded on the *Titanic*, I would probably have been found playing Bezique with the purser.'

Downstairs the two suitcases we had not bothered to unpack the previous night sat by the front door, and there was a dead bat lying on the bottom-most step. Alice, notoriously unsqueamish where animals were concerned, picked it up between finger and thumb and threw it out of the window.

'Are you sure we'll get back in time for the flight?'

'Trevor says it should all be wrapped up by mid-afternoon. After all, we're only there to watch.'

'Will Rory be there?'

'I can't see why not.'

With the bat disposed of, Alice wandered gravely around the hallway, inspected the row of prints which had come from an antiquarian bookshop in Wisbech and pronounced the mullioned windows that looked out onto the gravelled driveway 'ersatz'. No doubt about it: the day was shaping up well.

'Did you really buy this house because your great-grandmother was the village barmaid back in 1883?' she asked when we were clearing away the breakfast things.

'More or less.'

'Well, my grandfather came from Leicestershire, but I never had the slightest desire to go and live there.'

And so, half-an-hour later, with the light shining through the file of elm-trees to make patterns on the gravel and Alice hawk-like at my side, I climbed into the newly-bought Range Rover and drove off through the May sun and the clouds of midges – another of Elm's occupational hazards – towards Oxburgh Hall, where Systems of Romance were to shoot the video for their hotly-anticipated single 'Full Fathom Five', here in the early summer of 1985, where a great many things would start to go seriously wrong, and where the implications of a whole heap of stuff previously kept hidden from sight would soon become devastatingly clear.

* * *

What had happened in the past three years? Well, like some gigantic steamroller, time had moved on. At least half the acts signed in the first flush of late Seventies enthusiasm had been thrown off the label. Cedric, whose last single had shifted exactly 143 copies, was thought to have joined a Hare Krishna community in the West Country. When last heard of, Chloe and the Cup Cakes were playing supper-clubs in the Essex coastal resorts. The Dub Imposters, blithely despatched by their American label on a tour of the Eastern seaboard, simply disappeared, leaving an empty transit van and a string of cancelled gigs. In their place came such examples of what Doug called 'the new modern sound' as Emotional Disorder, the Klangs, the Fruity Boys, Exploding Bagpuss and Waters of Lethe, whose name the music journalists always pronounced to rhyme with 'Keith'. The Flame Throwers, meanwhile, having made a small fortune out of *Straight from Hell* (3 million units in the US, a million here) were hunkered down in L.A., supposedly making a covers album but in reality bickering with each other, taking too many drugs and issuing crazed press releases about impending race war or the Big Foot Cris claimed to have seen while on a walking tour of the Oregon Hills. But all this, though lucrative, was the merest bagatelle when set against the meteoric rise of Systems of Romance, on the strength of whose second album – advance sales 200,000 – Rory and I doubled our salaries, disposed of the Newman Street lease and bought a sizeable office in Ladbroke Grove, where visiting record company executives could be entertained without shame and bands were not admitted without an appointment.

When asked by deferential journalists to account for the success of Systems of Romance, based as it was on an array of Roland synthesizers, mini-Moogs, Clavichords and Echoplex guitar stylings, I used to take refuge in generalities: the time was right for this kind of music; Jon and Magda were very talented young people. But the truth was more complicated than this. At an early stage, I realised that the Systems inhabited a niche that I had first become aware of nearly twenty years before. If the music they made was utterly preposterous, then the way they presented it was irresistible. Take, for example, the video for the very first single, which basically consisted of Magda crooning the words 'It goes round and around/Sweeps your feet off the ground/Welcome to the hyper-sound' over an assortment of synthesizer squalls and colliding guitars. It began with a shot of white mice squirming inside an upturned bowler hat. This cut into some footage of farmyard poultry bustling back and forth, but artfully slowed down so the birds appeared to glide through gently receding air, followed by a stencilled caption that asked: WILL YOU EMBRACE THE HYPER-SOUND? Cut to a woodland clearing where Jon and Magda and their various sidekicks, dressed in white boiler suits and sky-blue capes, are hunched over a chessboard. To hand lie works by Schopenhauer, Derrida and Lacan. A second caption looms into view: INTELLECTUAL PURSUITS! A bit later Magda performs a dance that involves pointing your toes at 45 degree angles and sewing an imaginary embroidery sampler. DANCE TO

THE HYPER-SOUND advises the caption. At all times the viewer is drawn back to the expression on Magda's face, which manages to be simultaneously fey, anxious and sorrowing, as if all the misery of the world is somehow gathered up behind her mournful grey eyes, while implying that its owner would be happy to have sex with you right there on the forest floor should opportunity allow. The video ended with a shot of her features in close-up, staring out from behind a tree like some elf-princess in terrified flight from the goblin hordes. THE HYPER-SOUND GOES ON assured the final caption. As artfully contrived rubbish went, all this, it seemed to me, stood in a class of its own. In the slipstream of its three TOTP airings, 'Welcome to the Hyper-sound' sold 250,000 copies, was performed 'live' (i.e. not live) on a BBC arts programme and provoked a *New Statesman* symposium entitled 'Has Pop Music Finally Grown Up?'

And time steamrollers on. Turnover hits £5 million in 1983 with profits of 8 per cent. The overdraft at the bank gives way to a pension fund. The drift of freelance designers and Letraset-wielders gives way to a proper art director with a degree from the Courtauld. The house in Ewell gives way to a place in Powis Square, W11, now swept clean of the hippy rag-tag who had squatted there 20 years ago and full of Harrods delivery vans and keen-eyed traffic wardens. EMI, Polydor and Geffen make lavish offers for our back-catalogue and are summarily turned down. As the staff doubles and then trebles, so the roster contracts, bids farewell to the psychobilly bands and the Mod revivalists and the keening singer songwriters with faux-American accents: our aim, we tell ourselves, is to make more money out of fewer acts. There is talk of 'gearing', 'transatlantic synchronicity', 'collateral' and buying a studio in Maida Vale, and the actual purchase of a boardroom table made of imported mahogany from the Amazon rainforest with silver inlays that costs all of £15,000. Picture me in my Wrangler jeans, deck shoes and Union Jack blazer (a relic from 1966 in which the music papers delight to photograph me) calmly attending industry award ceremonies or being interviewed on LBC or lounging with Rory and his City friends – now grown attentive and deferential – at Langham's Brasserie. Bright mornings in Powis Square, with the sunshine tumbling through the plane trees; dim afternoons in West End drinking-clubs with fish-faced Dilly Boys jamming 50p pieces into the slot machines; dull evenings in sequestered hotel rooms with dense aquarium light sliding up and down the pale walls and MTV flickering in the background. And always there is Alice, who half the time I am obsessed with and the other half can only regard as a bad-tempered upper-class bitch by whom I am simultaneously exalted and downcast, enticed and repelled, the presence of whose bobbed dark head on the pillow beside me I still cannot quite believe, who I cannot understand and also do not want to understand, for fear of what this knowledge might do to me, and who, as she constantly assures me, with that habitual slyness that is part of her charm and simultaneously that charm's undoing, *has not done with me yet*.

* * *

'Whose wedding is that we're going to in the South of France?' asked Alice, who had already been told the answer to this question at least twice.

'Stevie the bass player's.'

In the distance, a hundred yards away down the gravel drive, the towers and crenellations of Oxburgh Hall rose dramatically into a blue-and-white Delft china sky.

'And who exactly is he marrying?'

I could tell a cue when it was offered. 'Some woman or other.'

'Will Rory be coming?' This question, too, had been asked several times before.

'I'm sure he had an invitation.'

'You know I don't think earning all that money has been terribly good for Rory,' Alice said, as if she was some discussing some hitherto loyal domestic who had won a fortune on the pools. 'He was much nicer when he was just a younger son with a living to make. Far more eager to please.'

'I can't say I ever remember Rory being eager to please.'

'I introduced him to Daddy once at a party and he was *absolutely slavish.*'

At the far end of the park, where mighty trees rose out of the rank grass, the gravel drive came to a halt. Half-way along the high, red-brick wall there were a couple of wicker turnstiles, and next to them a badly parked lorry from which pieces of film equipment were being carefully unloaded and a refreshment stall at which two or three people were helping themselves to cups of coffee. Vague at first – just blobs of pink flesh against the greens and browns of the backdrop – the faces came slowly into focus.

'Thought you were never coming,' Trevor Jacomb said mournfully. Dressed in a pair of outsize canvas shorts, black socks and open-toed sandals, he was not exactly looking his best.

'Who else is here?'

'Rory's in the house somewhere,' Trevor said, ignoring Alice out of what she assumed was proletarian rudeness but I knew to be sheer terror. 'Zoe's with the band, setting up near the moat or sumfink. Couple of gels from the office come as well. Wanted to see the sights.'

If Resurgam Records had matured as a business unit in the past three-and-a-half years, it could not be said that Trevor had kept up with these developments. Even now, despite several increases in salary and a relocation from the Petts Wood terrace, he still looked as if he were about to walk onto the set of a 1970s sit-com and have his face slapped by Sid James. But I liked Trevor, always had, and was prepared to put up with the air of damp blankets and smoky sitting rooms that he carried about with him.

'What's the house like?'

'Fucking grim old place,' Trevor said weakly. He was finding the going tough here. Something struck him and he unclasped the fingers of his left hand to reveal the scrap of pastry lying within. 'You want a sausage roll?'

'No thanks.'

'Who on earth is that man?' Alice wondered – she had been introduced to Trevor at least half-a-dozen times – as we continued into the grounds. Here, as might have been predicted, there was not a great deal to see. It was too early in the season for there to be many visitors. Those that had made the trip had disappeared into the house. Over by the moat, one or two white-clad figures were arranging some trestle tables into a square. Magda, dressed in a kind of spangled shift and black pom-pom shoes, was practising arabesques on the lawn. Nearer at hand, beneath a sign directing incomers to the tea room, Rory sat in a deckchair reading the *Financial Times*.

In the old days of four-figure budgets and shambling incompetence, promo films had been shot on the hoof and frequently descended into chaos. The Bash Street Kids were once supposed to have set fire to a primary school in which they were filming the video for a song called 'Teacher's Pet'. Here, in a more professional age, an air of desultoriness seemed to have set in. Nothing seemed to be happening. It would probably stay that way for at least an hour. Alice, catching the hint of drift, went off to poke around the gift shop and examine the second-hand books, professed herself satisfied by the amenities and then made for the tea-room. As I watched her saunter off, a woman in a black tee shirt and jeans came hurtling across the lawn and waved a conspiratorial finger in my face.

'Nick. *Nicko.*'

This was Zoe, the deeply rebarbative American girl who had replaced Paula as Resurgam's press officer on the morning after Waters of Lethe's debut single had been described in *Melody Maker* as 'symbolising just about everybody's last chance' and a barge carrying two dozen music journalists to a shindig on Eel Pie Island had sunk in the Thames a mile west of Shepperton.

'Shoot going OK?'

Zoe swept out a lizard-like hand and raked her thick, corkscrew curls – so repeatedly dyed that they were practically scarlet – back over her scalp. She came from Mainline, Philadelphia, via the Bronx, had once been engaged to a member of the MC5 ('a fucking lame-ass, but kind of cute y'know?') worked in promotions for Bill Graham on the West Coast and made it clear that she regarded her current duties as a stroll through Toytown by comparison.

'Jesus fuck, Nicko. I got a director thinks he's Roman Polanski, there's some mad psycho chick with the band that no one's ever seen before who's making Magda uptight, and the moat's so full of gravel they're having to pull the fucking boat through it on the end of a rope.'

The reason why Zoe kept her job, everyone agreed, was because she was so good at it. Anyone else who had kept up this level of sarcasm, occasionally extending to outright violence, would have been gone within a week. Among other exploits, she was supposed to have thrown a typewriter through the editor of *Record Mirror*'s office window.

'Don't mind my asking, Zoe, but…'

'For Christ's sake, Nick, just a couple of Percodan is all, on account of my fuckin' head.'

In this kind of state – a condition in which, to be fair, she often brought off some of her best work – the important thing was to keep Zoe busy.

'What would you do, Zoe?'

'What do you mean, what would I do?'

'What would you do if I told you to go and manage the shoot?'

'Are you serious?' Zoe rocked back on her heels and stared at the horizon, as if there were mighty armies out there that only she could see. 'OK. I'd tell the director to go and fuck himself, I'd forget about the fuckin' boat, and I'd' – she turned her gaze on the hall, as if seeking inspiration in the brick-work – 'have them mime the track in the woods. You know, light coming through the trees, the sun hangs on the skyline like some fucking fried egg or something, stick the drum-kit in the rhododendrons. Make it look real fucking elegant.'

'Well, why don't you go and do that? Tell the art director I said it was OK.'

For some reason, as Zoe strode off across the lawn, I found myself wondering about tomorrow's events in Riberac. I had been to music biz weddings before, but this one would surely outdo them all. Geffen were supposed to be flying in sixty people on a private jet. I had a sudden vision of the likely consequences: sleek, low-slung limousines gliding through avenues of plane trees; beautiful people thronging the porch of some ancient church; Stevie, flanked by his pulchritudinous bride, in – what? A morning-suit? A frock coat? A designer kaftan? It did not bear thinking about.

A faint breeze had got up, magnifying the sound of the raised voices coming from the lake. Rory came labouring across the lawn dragging a couple of deck-chairs behind him like a travois.

'We need to talk,' he said.

Six or seven years into his career in the music business, Rory had made certain concessions to the milieu in which he was forced to operate. His shiny hair now stopped half-an-inch under his ears rather than half-an-inch above them, and he had stopped wearing pinstripe suits. Just now he was got up in a boating blazer and white duck trousers.

'What do we need to talk about?'

'Just one or two little local difficulties.' Like Alice, who could now be seen pottering about the wide porticos beyond the hall's inner courtyard, Rory was very much at home here. In the hand that had not been dragging the deck-chairs he was holding a see-through plastic bag which contained several pots of chutney and a book about fly-fishing. I could see that he approved of Oxburgh Hall, was soothed by its languor and the scent of bygone decencies that rose above its loosestrife-patterned hedges.

'Well, for a start' Rory said. He ran his fingers along the buttons of his blazer as if they were the keys of a musical instrument that might soon be starting up. 'What am I supposed to do about this wretched wedding?'

'I don't know. Turn up at the church like everyone else. Make sure you sit on the groom's side. Unless, that is, you happen to know the bride as well. Sing the hymns with a brazen voice. Won't that be enough?'

'Don't be silly. You know exactly what I mean. What do I wear? Am I expected to give them anything?'

'I shouldn't think so. And I don't suppose anyone will be at all bothered by what you turn up in. Put on a morning suit if you like. I should think they'd be delighted.'

'But surely they'll expect a present?'

'Just buy a bottle of whisky at the duty-free and tell them it's some rare single malt from Islay or somewhere that they can store in a vault and let their children sample in twenty years time.'

'Do you know?' Rory said, 'I might just do that.' He looked enormously relieved. His gaze shortened and he glanced over towards the moat, where Zoe and the director had detached themselves from the rest of the crew and were having some kind of argument. 'Actually, you wouldn't believe it Nick, but this reminds me of my childhood.'

'I thought you said the Sixties never got as far as Perthshire.'

'No more they did. But my godfather was a chap called Benjy Wellbourne. One of those hippy peers the newspapers used to go on about. Grew his hair long and wore a harlequin jacket like Henry Bath. Well, Wellbourne Grange was a bit like this. I can remember once my father ate some hash-cakes by mistake and started hallucinating on the way home. I say, that girl's getting rather cross.'

Twenty years ago, the video shoot would have attracted an admiring crowd. But the trail of *bona fide* visitors making their way around the edge of the lawn took no interest in the goings on by the moat. The freaks, as Trevor Jacomb had once put it, were ten a penny these days. There were other ways, you suspected, in which the times had changed. In the Sixties the people had all pretended to be sophisticated while in most cases remaining fundamentally naïve. Now they all pretended to be naïve while remaining fundamentally sophisticated. In these circumstances, motive was sometimes difficult to winkle out.

'What else do we need to talk about?'

Rory looked peevish again. There were times when he could not be bothered to conceal the contempt he felt for the people he came across in the course of his professional duties, let alone the circumstances in which he came across them. Just now three or four separate emotions – pleasure in his surroundings, approval of the stream of abuse Zoe was now flinging at the director, outrage at how much all this would cost – uneasily contended.

'It's those free concerts they're planning in the summer.'

'The Live Aid things?'

'That's right. You see, when they started all this my instinct was to leave well alone. All very well raising money for a lot of black people in Africa, but does it shift any records? Anyway, I was wrong about that, badly wrong. Not afraid to admit it, either,' said Rory magnanimously. 'Why we couldn't get anyone on that Christmas single I can't imagine.'

'If it comes to that, nobody asked us.'

'These things can always be managed' Rory said, with the robust cynicism he brought to any area of his professional life into which moral feeling had inadvertently strayed. 'Anyhow, when I heard about the concerts – you know, there's going to be one at Wembley and another in the States? – I realised that we had to have a piece of it. If you ask me, what with the knock-on effect of the TV coverage any band that so much as sets foot on the stage will sell a hundred thou' of whatever they happen to have out at the moment. Back catalogue too. Long and short of it is we fixed up a *quid pro quo*. They can have the Flame Throwers for the Philadelphia concert and in exchange Systems of Romance will be on the bill at Wembley.'

'Just Systems of Romance? Why not go the whole hog and get Waters of Lethe and Exploding Bagpuss on as well? Christ know, we could do with shifting a few more of their back catalogue.'

'Never does to overplay your hand' Rory said, who, like Trevor, was sometimes surprisingly off the pace where irony was concerned. 'One other thing while we're at it. Trevor.'

'Trevor?'

'Now, nobody appreciates loyalty more than I do,' said the man who had once tried to get a long-serving receptionist sacked on the grounds that he disliked her voice. 'But have you seen the state he's in these days? I took him to a meeting at Virgin the other week and he absolutely took a pickled onion out of a Tupperware box and ate it right in front of Richard Branson and Simon Draper.'

'I don't expect they minded.'

'I daresay they didn't. But would you like it if someone from Geffen came into the office and found that fat lump in the foyer stuffing one of his Mars Bars? Which, I may add, is about all he seems to do at the moment.'

The noises from the moat were getting louder. The tubs of chutney in Rory's bag were labelled 'Mrs Clenchwarton's Fine Old Norfolk Relish'. 'What are you proposing?'

'I'm proposing that we pay him off – six months' salary say, for old time's sake, and keep the car – and get in someone a bit more presentable.'

I was about to tell Rory that this could not happen, that Trevor Jacomb could eat as many pickled onions as he liked in front of Richard Branson or anyone else, when one of the white-clad figures detached itself from the throng by the moat and came scampering over the grass, like the harbinger of bad news in a classical play. It was Lily, one of the girls from the office who had come to see the fun, which in strict procedural terms meant being sent off for packets of sandwiches and having to brave the attentions of the lighting crew. Ten yards away, she stumbled a bit, put out a hand to steady herself, regained her balance, and gasped:

'Nick! Zoe says you have to get over there *right now*.'

'Another little local difficulty,' Rory said. He enjoyed moments like this, which tended to reinforce his conviction that no one in the world of music really knew how to behave.

Lily ignored him. The girls in the office were scared of Rory. In any case, it was me she was after. All at once, as quite often happened at times like this, the world around us began to slow down. The smoke from Rory's cigarette dwindled away into nothingness. The breeze-blown wood beyond the great house froze into stasis. The ensemble by the lake could have been a medieval frieze, its figures picked out in twists of gold and silver thread.

'What's the matter?'

'It's that Magda,' Lily said, who while appreciating the gravity of the situation had already, in her short career at Resurgam, had quite enough of rock stars giving themselves airs. 'She's gone and locked herself in a shed.'

'Any particular reason?'

'I think that girl Jon brought with them's been annoying her. On the other hand she just told the director what a cunt he was.'

As we came in sight, the dozen or so people sitting on the grass or standing by the moat's silt-stained edge shifted uncomfortably. They were exactly the kind of flotsam that mid-Eighties video shoots tended to dredge up: tired-looking girls in Paul Smith jeans and Dr Martens bearing clipboards; teenage boys in combat fatigues and baseball boots hired to shift scenery. A man in a Hawaiian shirt and a straw hat who could have been the director was awkwardly rolling a cigarette out of a tobacco tin balanced on his knee. Nearer at hand a sullen-looking girl with over-made-up eyes in what looked like a wedding dress was crying quietly into her outstretched palms. Zoe stood slightly to one side, quivering with fury, as if only professional pride kept her from dashing into the house, seizing one of the antique weapons that hung on the walls and laying waste to everyone in sight.

'What's up with Magda?'

'The bitch has only gone and shut herself up in a hut is all. On account of some mad psycho chick coming on to her boyfriend.'

The girl in the wedding dress, not keen on hearing herself slighted in this way, continued to sob.

'Come with me,' Zoe instructed. We wandered off to the point where the moat wound round the side of the house. Here the silt was even thicker. No quinquireme of Nineveh or stately Spanish galleon would ever pass this way. Over beyond the footpath, in the lee of the woods, there was a tiny white-painted potting shed with a KEEP OUT sign hanging on the door.

'OK' Zoe explained as we drew near. 'It's like this. I'm finally getting the faggot in the shirt to see some sense about the camera angles when I notice Magda's looking at me like I'm the Creature from the Black Lagoon. Which, I may say, is no fuckin' big deal. I mean, I was on a set once with Jerry Garcia and the Dead when someone gives them some… peyote or something and they tried to water-ski down a river standing on their fuckin' heads. Then I realise that I'm – what is it? – just the fuckin' *lightning rod*, and it's the mad psycho chick who's holding hands with Jon who's the problem.'

For at least a year now Systems of Romance's emotional geography had defied even the music press to decipher. Sometimes Jon and Magda were going out with each other and sometimes they were going out with other people. Occasionally they were doing both these things simultaneously. A six-bedroom house on the edge of

Hampstead Heath bought with the proceeds of *Welcome to the Hyper-Sound* had lain empty for eighteen months while they worked out if they liked each other enough to move into it.

'Where's Jon?'

'For Christ's sake, how am I supposed to know? Gone off for a cup of tea and a Valium I should think. Magda, honey' Zoe continued, dropping her jaw to the level of the door-knob and resting one knee on the bare earth. 'You hafta get yourself together and come out of here.' There was a silence. In the distance I could see Rory coming to investigate. 'Magda, honey,' Zoe went on, in what might have passed for a wheedling tone, 'come on, do us all a favour. Do yourself a favour. Isn't anything here that can't be fixed.' One or two visitors, passing along the path, glanced at us and continued resolutely on their way. They knew better than to interrupt. 'Jesus' Zoe said, abandoning all pretence that she liked Magda, sympathised with her predicament, thought that she had the faintest vestige of talent or enjoyed promoting her record to an expectant public, 'will you open that door you stupid bitch? There's a dozen people out here waiting to get paid and this shoot is costing two grand an hour.'

As anyone who knew Magda could have told her, this was the wrong approach. She enjoyed wasting time and record company money that could not be offset against advances and had once kept a camera crew waiting for three quarters of an hour while she and Jon had sex on the back seat of a camper van.

'You'd better let me have a go'.

'Suit yourself motherfucker,' Zoe said. It had clearly been a whole lot easier with the Grateful Dead.

I put my hand to the door-knob. Unexpectedly, it yielded to the pressure. The shed was unlocked. Inside there were shafts of sunlight slanting on to the wooden floor. Magda sat at the far end, next to an ancient lawn-mower, head resting on two pudgy knees. Something small and furry ran out of an upturned flowerpot and skittered away into the shadows. The suspicion that the two of us had walked into a Beatrix Potter story was far too strong for comfort. Any moment now Mr McGregor would appear in the doorway and start sharpening his shears.

'May I come in?'

'Is that you, Nick?'

'Is anything the matter?'

'Yes it is.'

'Can I help?'

'I suppose I'm being a dreadful nuisance.' Although she liked being photographed in grim Manchester underpasses or outside Salford youth clubs, Magda had in fact been educated in Surrey by the Girls' Public Day School Trust.

'I expect the budget will stand it.'

'You see, I just wanted to come in here and be on my own for a while.' Informed judges always said that Magda had three vocal styles. There was the little-girl-lost voice used for interviews, the feigned incomprehension voice, when audio technology was being explained to her, and the not-suffer-fools-gladly voice, assumed in conversation with anyone from the record company. This voice, I realised, was slightly different: more mournful and less calculating.

'We all need some time to ourselves, Mags.'

'You've always been very sweet to me, Nick.' This, at least, was true. I always liked Magda, if only because I thought her fundamentally unsuited for the career she had chosen: not tough enough, not decisive enough and too self-pitying.

'I'm afraid I do this rather a lot, don't I?' she said. This, too, was true. Magda was always doing things like this: going off in a huff; taking exception; throwing equipment round the studio; refusing to come out of the dressing room at gigs.

'Has Jon been annoying you?'

'He *said* he wouldn't bring that bloody girl. You know she did some backing vocals on the single? I know I shouldn't mind but I do. I don't think,' Magda said, tears glistening on her pale cheeks, 'that anyone understands what I have to put up with.'

'It must be very difficult.'

People sometimes asked how the pop stars of the 1980s differed from the pop stars of the 1960s. The answer was that the pop stars of the 1960s had been just as vainglorious, as deluded or as self-obsessed, but there was a part of them that expected to be found out and made to pay for their presumption, Twenty years later, Magda and her kind took it all for granted.

'What would you do, Nick?' Magda asked seriously.

This was a tricky one. Sometimes Magda followed advice to the letter. On other occasions she was capable of performing bizarre 180 degree turns. Counsel had a habit of blowing up in the counsellor's face. It was getting hot inside the shed. The film crew would be smoking cigarettes, while Alice rooted through the trays of second-hand books. 'I think I should do what I was supposed to do. Then I might think about the implications.'

Magda got to her feet and began to slap the dust from her sawn-off blue shorts. 'You see, Nick, I've come to the conclusion that this is pretty much the end. It's all gone on far too long. Do you know, I was studying French Literature at the Polytechnic when all this started? I've a good mind to go back to doing that.'

You got a lot of this in the Eighties too: people who wanted to become market gardeners, compose epic poems or found political parties. It was rare for any of these dreams to come to much.

'Are you feeling OK?' Magda had gone paler than ever.

'Just a couple of...*pills* Zoe gave me. You're right, Nick. I ought to do what I have to do.'

'That's the spirit. Hang on to my arm.'

With Magda clinging to my arm, we stepped uncertainly out of the hut. Here there was a ring of expectant faces: Zoe, Rory, Lily, three or four hangers-on. In the five minutes we had been inside, the temperature seemed to have risen by several degrees. The chimneys of the big house were swaying in the heat haze.

'I'm all right, Nick, honestly I am' Magda said. 'Quite all right. Never felt better.'

Why did people always say this? Florian Shankley-Walker, the Helium Kids keyboard player back in their beat group days, used to say it before he passed out cold in the back of the tour bus. Stefano had used to say it in the wake of some calamitous professional meltdown. Was it because they needed reassurance, harboured frail egos that they needed to massage? Or was it that the words had talismanic properties that by uttering them they hoped to activate the will by which they imagined themselves to live? It was hard to say. Freed from restraint or support, watched by half-a-dozen anxious eyes, the sun shining so hard on the white smock that covered her arms and torso that she looked like some sacrificial victim about to be taken off to a standing stone and slaughtered by druids, Magda tottered off across the lawn. Then, unexpectedly, she gathered pace, picked up her pudgy knees and, with her white-clad arms stretched out on either side, zig-zagged off towards the waiting camera. Meanwhile, the rest of us gathered by the open door of the shed – still swinging on its hinges, as in a cowboy film where the sheriff has just marched out of the saloon – looked on in bafflement, searching for clues. 'What the fuck does she think she's doing?' Zoe said.

All this, clearly, was much too big to be ignored. The same thought had occurred to the director, who could be seen moving towards Magda at an angle, trying to cut off her retreat. As he came nearer, she feinted to one side, skipped over his outstretched leg, thundered off again over the pile of film equipment and the costume trunks, threw a backward glance as if to make sure that everyone knew what she was up to, and then, with a flying leap, pitched herself head-first into the moat.

'Fucking stupid *bitch*,' Zoe yelled after her. The sullen-looking girl in the wedding dress who was supposed to have started all this off began to have hysterics.

'I give up' Rory said. 'I absolutely give up. Trevor, would you mind helping her out?'

Gradually things returned to normal. Investigation revealed the moat to be only three or four feet deep. Trevor, always adept in moments of crisis, waded in up to his waist, threw Magda over his shoulder in a fireman's lift and brought her back to the bank. Set down on the grass, she lay with her face to one side crying quietly. After a certain amount of discussion an ambulance was summoned to take her to King's Lynn hospital.

'Have I missed anything?' Alice asked, coming back from the house just as the ambulance drove up.

'Magda chucked herself in the moat.'

'Good gracious! Why should she want to do that?'

'I'm swearing everyone to secrecy' Rory said. 'If this gets in the music papers it will be an absolute bloody disaster.'

Everyone promised not to say anything to the music papers.

'How much footage did you end up with anyway?' Rory asked the director. 'Enough for us not to have to do this again?'

'There's a good half-hour in the can.'

'You can bill us for seventy-five per cent of what we agreed,' Rory said, who was in one of his hard-headed man of business moods.

Later on, various explanations would be offered for what Magda had done. Some people said that she had deliberately meant to injure herself and that her distress at being fished out of the moat was simply down to her failure to finish a task. Other people maintained that the swan-dive into three feet of silt was simply a gesture, and that anyone bent on self-destruction would have thrown themselves further into the water rather than taking care to resurface two or three feet from the bank. Still more people – long-term observers of Magda's emotional life – said that she had done it as a test of Jon's affection, and if he rather than Trevor had dragged her out of the water the situation would have been instantly resolved. All this, though, lay in the future. For the moment there was only a sense of things having gone badly wrong, of consequences that would work themselves out whether the people involved liked it or not. The equipment was loaded back into truck. A minivan came to take the extras back to Downham Market station. Rory went off to see if Oxburgh Hall ran to a fax machine. The mid-day sun sparkled off the roof-tops and the only sign that we had ever been there was the director's straw hat lying abandoned on the lawn at the place where he had tried to stop Magda throwing herself into the moat.

'Why on earth did she want to do that?' Alice asked again as we got back into the Range Rover.

'I think she thought she'd been crossed in love.'

'Well I've been crossed in love several times' Alice said. 'But I never threw myself in a moat just to show how unhappy I was. Some of these middle-class girls are too highly strung.'

'So, in the end, Magda was just showing off?'

'No, just being silly and ineffectual,' Alice said. 'It's not that I don't sympathise with her. But if she really wanted to complain about being crossed in love she should have pushed the other girl in instead. That's what I should have done.'

And so we drove off back to Elm, through blinding sunshine, along roads gleaming with dead hares and partridges ground into the asphalt, talking about the house in Italy that we might some day buy, with its view over the Tuscan hills, a dream which both of us knew had no prospect of ever being realised and was, in its way, just as much of a gesture as Magda throwing herself into the Oxburgh Hall moat.

10. HONKY CHATEAU

You lost your virtue before you could walk
I guess your momma took the blame
Your daddy's inside on a ten-year stretch
Oh, but I love you just the same.
THE FLAME THROWERS – *Love You Just the Same*

'I didn't know you knew the Charringtons.'

'Oh yes. Absolutely. They lived in the same village along from us. Jill and I were practically brought up together.'

'Wasn't her brother that tall chap one used to see at point-to-points?'

'That would have been Henry, the younger one.'

Alice and Rory had begun this exercise in social range-finding shortly before the plane touched down in Limoges, continued it through their dance around the baggage carousel and carried it into its second triumphant hour as the taxi hurtled on towards the heliport. Only now, as the noise of the rotor blades settled down to a high-pitched, clacking hum did they finally fall silent. To hear them talk was to appreciate just how defiantly a certain kind of English life had hung on through the frets and fractures of the modern age. It was a world in which old ladies in tall Kensington houses picked postcards off the mat from grandchildren in Hong Kong and Saudi, where the photographs of dead Cinque Port wardens winked out of their frames and all social disturbance was temporary. Staring crossly at the space above her head, as if she thought she could make the noise stop through sheer effort of will, Alice fossicked about in her handbag and took out the copy of *Pride and Prejudice* she had been reading for the past three weeks. Rory, sweat already gathering on his bony forehead, applied himself to *Euromoney*. Two seats behind him, Zoe, who had turned up unexpectedly at Stansted three hours before, upended her leather jacket onto her lap, shook it until a pen-knife fell out of one of the pockets, and then began to trim bits of superfluous plastic off the points of her monstrous stiletto heels. Meanwhile, with a microphone held up to his mouth, the pilot was making gallant attempts at conversation.

'*Maintenant mesdames and messieurs*... C'est *une voyage de cinquante minutes*... *Regardez*... *Regardez la majesté de Limousin*...

The helicopter dangled in the air for a moment, as if some unseen hand was shaking it by the tail, and then swung in low over a landscape of rolling fields, grey-stone church towers and clumps of trees. Here in the fuselage, among the crates of bottled water that were also being ferried to the wedding, the air smelt strongly of fertiliser. All this brought back memories of the last time I had been in a helicopter, on the way to the Ogdenville Free Festival in 1971: the crowds boiling beneath us like orcs in the Mordor ash-pits; the FBI men stalking Garth Dangerfield; the Fresno biker gang rushing the stage and the lighting tower going over; mayhem, catastrophe and frenzied retreat. It all seemed a thousand years ago.

The clanking sound had receded a bit and the pilot had stopped going on about the majesty of Limousin. In any case we were now flying over what looked like a sewage farm. Rory, folding the copy of *Euromoney* out over his shirt-front as if it were an exceptionally large napkin, caught my eye.

'We need to remember, above all, that this is not simply a pleasure trip.'

'Is the new management coming?'

'Oh they'll be there,' said Rory grimly, as if a leper bell had just clanged a couple of feet behind his ear. 'Never saw such a pay roll.'

As Rory had hinted, there were serious questions that needed to be asked during our trip to Stevie's wedding. Not all of them could be directly stated and at least half of them could not be answered, but they included: Were the Flame Throwers still a functioning unit? Were they up to playing Live Aid? What kind of drugs were they taking, and had anyone tried to stop them taking them? Was their management exerting any control over the pattern of their days? Was there any chance of new material? If so, would they be touring the UK? And if so, would Resurgam be expected to provide financial support? It was two-and-a-half years now since the runaway success of *Straight From Hell*, a year since they had played their last concert – a disastrous stadium gig in San Francisco followed by a riot in which three people died – and a whole six months since Cris, in the words of an anonymous source on terms of considerable intimacy with the band, had 'gone completely tonto and started thinking he was God or something' and effectively slipped from public view. In that time the boys had, it was calculated, earned nearly $10 million, spent – it was estimated – nearly four-fifths of that sum, signed, or had possibly not signed, a four-album deal with Geffen that would guarantee them twice the former amount, sacked three managers and committed themselves to two U.S tours which they did not, in the end, undertake and the legal ramifications of which continued to haunt them. In addition, they were continuing to hang out with the people they had always hung out with, only exponentially so, had been busted, singly and severally, by the L.A. Police Department, and were currently supporting an entourage of wives, girlfriends, dealers, relatives, administrative staff and PR gophers that was supposed to be costing them $500,000 a month. Meanwhile, they had demo-ed enough new product to fill approximately one side of a C60 cassette tape.

'I took your advice,' Rory said, taking out the bottle of Dancing Pipers whisky he had bought at the Stansted duty-free and balancing it on his thigh.

'He'll love it.'

'What shall I say?'

'Tell him that generations of Scottish lairds have overseen its production in a bothy in the glens beneath Killiecrankie. That the McTavish of McTavish personally supervises the distilling process. And it's so rare you had to steal it and smuggle it out under your kilt.'

The helicopter chugged on, hovered over a path of grass hemmed in by high, dense hedgerows and then started fitfully to descend. The other passengers – L.A. scenesters with tanned faces and carefully-sculpted hair, a stricken homunculus in a Panama hat, a couple of cameramen – stirred uneasily. Alice slid the copy of *Pride and Prejudice* back into her bag.

'I thought this kind of wedding took place in Los Angeles.'

'I believe the bride's grandmother lives this way.'

'How did they meet?'

How had Stevie and his intended come across one another? My informant was a junior publicist at Geffen. 'It's quite sweet. Quite touching in its way. I mean, Lizzie works in porno. So she's upside down on some film set out in the Canyon being fucked up the ass by John Holmes or someone, when who should turn up but Stevie on account of the producer is a big Flame Throwers fan and is showing him round the studio. Anyway, Stevie says hi, John Holmes shoots his load all over the bedclothes and next thing you know they're dating. He's quite a romantic in his way.'

It would be difficult to explain this to Alice. 'How does anybody meet anyone?'

'Well, I met Mark at a drinks party at the Guards Club.'

By now we were disembarking from the helicopter, heads bent beneath the winnowing fan. The pilot was still going on about

Limousin. On the further edge of the field on which we had descended, a dozen or so guests stood awaiting their instructions. Once again, watching Alice as she stood among them, I marvelled at her ability to seem completely at ease wherever in the world fate had set her down. A soup kitchen or the Sovereign's Lawn at Cowes: it was all the same to her. Meanwhile, the people who had staggered off the plane stopped being generic representatives of their kind and acquired individual personalities. One of them – the pale-faced man in the Panama hat – turned out to be Howard Cunningham.

'Good to see you, Howard.' In the three years since I had last set eyes on him, Howard had written many a disagreeable piece about Resurgam and its roster. 'Are you still with the NME?'

'Actually' Howard said, with the pride of a Victorian burglar apprehended on the front step of the great house with the squire's plate concealed in a gunny-sack, 'I'm deputy arts editor of the *Daily Telegraph*.'

This was another thing about the Eighties: respectable newspapers, buffeted by the winds of fashion, had started to take on music journalists. Howard would be busy writing articles about Prince's aesthetic or flying to Amsterdam to watch Sade in concert.

'What are you doing here?'

'Covering the wedding of course,' Howard said, a bit uneasily. He lowered his voice. 'What do you think are my chances of getting an interview?'

'Anyone in particular?'

'The happy couple. If not them, the rest of the band.'

'You know as well I as do, Howard, that you haven't the faintest chance of being allowed to interview anyone north of the wine waiters.'

Journalists always over-reached themselves in the end, misjudged the situation, came up short. Sometimes it was because they wanted to be man-to-man when the person they were dealing with wanted deference. At other times it was because they laid on the deference when the person they were dealing with wanted equal treatment. Admittedly, these protocols were sometimes difficult to grasp,

'Well you could at least give me a steer. No one else will. Their US press officer won't. Their manager told me if I so much as mentioned the bride's previous career we'd get a writ. Is it true Cris has joined a religious cult and is sitting in a hut in the Adirondacks waiting for the end of the world?'

'Not as far as I know. Why don't you talk to Zoe? I'm sure she'll tell you everything she can.'

Zoe would settle Howard's hash. She would be the immovable object that lay across his path, the wasp in his salad. I watched him sidle over to the line of guests receiving directions to the church, angle his head, try a pleasantry or two, only to receive a volley of abuse so morale-sapping that he went scuttling off into the crowd. Rory, still carrying the bottle of whisky he had bought at the duty-free, came and stood alongside.

'Stout girl Zoe. How on earth did she get invited to this?'

'I believe she and Stevie have history.'

'Heaven help us.'

Beyond the hedges that enclosed the helicopter's landing space, amid clumps of giant sunflowers, a path ran away towards the church. Here the ground was unexpectedly soft. Zoe, setting a foot down hard on the spongy turf, gave a little shriek as her heel stuck fast. I went over and hauled her out.

'What did you say to Howie?'

'Jesus,' Zoe said. She took off her stilettos and dumped them in her shoulder bag. 'I told him not to be a jerk. No one's doing any fuckin' interviews.' The criss-crossed curls quivered like a nest of scarlet snakes. 'As for Cris, the fucker's just volunteered for Mother Teresa's orphanage. Well, that's what I'm telling people.'

'Zoe, did you really go out with Stevie da Vinci?'

'Yes I did,' Zoe, with unexpected simplicity. 'And in case you're wondering, Nick, he was the worst person in the world. Not, y'know, violent, or, uh, *malign*. Just shiftless. Dead in the head. In the heart, too. But to me, y'know, at the time, he was just this cute little kid from Asswipe, Wisconsin, or whatever rock the fucker crawled out from underneath, wanting to make it in the business, and I figured that a girl could go further and fare worse.'

We stood for a moment contemplating the spectre of the cute little kid from Wisconsin and the throw of the dice that had led to his present whereabouts, being flown in by private jet and helicopter to marry an adult movie actress in a church in the Dordogne. Meanwhile, there were other human casualties I needed to know about.

'What happened to Magda?'

'Jesus, I don't know. They took her off someplace. Hospital or somewhere. She'll be OK as soon as she calms down.'

The church was in plain sight now, a largeish, grey-walled edifice looming behind a file of yew trees. Here, on a grass verge that flanked the clumps of gravestones, the guests hung around talking in loud West Coast accents. Twenty years ago a shindig like this would have brought out the Beautiful People in King's Road finery and Biba frocks. But the Beautiful People were all dead or quietly decaying. In their place came bearded executive trouble-shooters in linen jackets, leathery crones in biker gear with kamikaze-pilot headbands, pale, wispy girls hung about with scarves and expensive jewellery. Art Smothers detached himself from this ramshackle throng and came jauntily towards us.

'Ain't this a fuckin' steal? How're you doing, *garçon*?'

'How's the groom?'

'Stevie?' Art cocked one of his caterpillar eyebrows, as if nothing could have been more *de trop* than enquiring about the bridegroom's health on the day of his wedding. 'OK I guess. Actually,' – he lowered his voice a notch – 'the guy is fucked. I mean, not seriously or nuthin'. He can stand up and such. But he's gonna have real trouble with the fuckin'...with the *responses.*'

'Where's Lisette?'

'I hear they're spraying the dress on her right now.' He fell in beside me. 'Hey. You see Bracegirdle any place?'

'Not yet.'

'Yeah, well you and him need to talk. I mean, notice anything about this, ah, *assembly*?' Art was better educated than the other Flame Throwers and had a wider vocabulary.

'I don't see Cris anywhere?'

'Yeah, well you wouldn't, seeing as the fucker's holed up in a shack in Malibu living off macrobiotic rice-cakes or something. Not to mention all this stuff he's doing with the Children of the Sun.'

This was a new name. 'Who are the Children of the Sun?'

'Just the usual load of nut-jobs.' Art looked thoroughly bewildered, but also slightly knowing. Like many people who lived happily in a world of low-level weirdness, he was deeply suspicious of its upper rungs. 'I used to think it was just your standard hippy crap, y'know, "Let's take all our clothes off and ride the wild surf." But it's worse than that. *Way* worse. Last time I saw him he was sitting in his cabin with his knees up to his chin with the light off talking about the infinite particle of sanctity...Hey. The fuck. Is this your old lady, Nick?'

I could see that Alice, hastening towards us through the unmown grass, was torn between her two standard responses to anyone connected with the music business to whom I introduced her: paralysing disdain or complete indifference. This time she settled for complete indifference.

'Well, this takes me back,' she said, extending a hand towards the church.

Alice liked reminiscing about her own wedding, which by chance had taken place on the weekend of Woodstock. Half-a-dozen images leapt unbidden into the ether: the squat Northumbrian church in sight of the North Sea; the arch of lofted cavalry swords; the Lord Lieutenant smiling from the steps. Here in south-west France, a decade-and-a-half later, she seemed oddly animated. Meanwhile, all the paraphernalia of the rock star nuptials were shifting unobtrusively into place. Outlandish people with odd, blanched faces and coloured hair were mingling with ordinary people in suits and dresses. The huge banks of white flowers had already begun to wilt in the sun. Security guards were busy staking out the church, its exits and its entrances, and casting bleak Raybanned eyes on the congregation as it began to file through the porch. A priest, in full vestments, emerging round the side of the building, stopped to take in the spectacle, gave a tiny shrug of his cambric-covered shoulders and hurried on. Stevie; Lisette; the tatterdemalion hordes: it was all in a day's work to him. Gradually some kind of pattern was imposed on the crowd. People found their seats, took up their orders of service and looked enquiringly around them. Inside, the church was cool, high-ceilinged and lavishly ornamented. The Stations of the Cross could have been painted by Breughel. Half-way back on the right side of the church, and thought to be supporting the groom, the faces were impossibly various: Alice; Rory; the people from Geffen; Cunningham – who, I noticed, had had serious difficulty finessing his way past security; a white-haired old man, doubtless the emissary from some grim, frost-bitten kingdom bringing news of battles in the north. They looked by turns anxious, indulgent, wary, bewildered, alarmed and bored.

'*Voila le cortège*' somebody said as, attended by a couple of censer-swinging altar boys, Larry Bracegirdle, the Flame Throwers' manager and a bedraggled-looking woman who looked like a smaller feminised version of himself, Stevie da Vinci, 'the most fucked up guy in Bel Air' as *L.A. Music Scene* had recently put it, came meandering down the aisle. Somebody, according to the same publication's gossip column, had been paid $20,000 to style the da Vinci/Brisebois wedding.

Somehow Stevie seemed to have escaped this sanitising net. He was wearing a kind of beribboned frockcoat above a pair of tattered black jeans and pink sneakers. The bride, in a Galliano dress that clung to her like a winding-sheet, joining him in front of the altar a moment later, looked faintly nonplussed – annoyed, perhaps, that Stevie had ignored specific instructions on how to comport himself – and then lapsed into matter-of-factness. The priest gave a sharp little command or two, like a director marshalling his cast, to which Stevie graciously inclined his head.

There were times, here in the mid-Eighties maelstrom, when the world suddenly quickened up, when things happened too fast to be assimilated, when things cracked and shattered and the only judgments that could be made were about the fragments. Now, once again, everything had begun to slow down. A long harangue in French. An interminable prayer. A whispered conversation between the celebrants. By the time they reached the declaration of intent, the priest seemed to have lost his bearings. The questions (*'Et promettez-vous de lui rester fidèle...Dans la santé and dans la maladie...Pour l'aimer tous les jours de votre vie?)* sounded three-quarters sarcastic, posed in the certainty that there wasn't the faintest chance of their ever being put to the test. Lisette looked on grimly. No doubt she knew that any promise Stevie made about fidelity was not worth listening to. But then, drawing herself up, she decided to make an effort:

'Moi, Lisette, je te prend Stevie
Pour être mon mari
Pour avoir et tenir de ce jour vers l'avant
Pour meilleur ou pour le pire
Pour la prospérité et la pauvreté
Dans la maladie et dans la santé
Pour aimer et cherir
Jusqu'à ce que la mort nous sépare.'

Meanwhile, there were other things to worry about. What would happen to Magda? What would happen to the Flame Throwers? Could either of them be persuaded to take to the stage at Live Aid? There were new deals waiting to be negotiated on both sides of the Atlantic. How were Resurgam's chances in those? Once again, time was moving on, moving on for the pale indie boys with their jangling guitars, moving on for the fretful synthesizer players in their bedsits beyond the Trent, moving on for Mick Jagger and Tina Turner and all the other ornaments of my youth so mysteriously recrafted and re-positioned for a less forgiving age, moving on for Alice in her big house in Kensington, and Rory, whom half-a-dozen little hints had convinced me was up to something, moving on for the Flame Throwers and Magda in her hospital bed. Already people were talking – just as they had talked twenty years ago, of a decade mired in stasis, of hedonism, shallow surfaces and hidden depths, and the moral reckoning that lay just around the corner.

'*Voila les jeunes maries exit*' somebody said as Stevie and his bride started on their way back down the aisle. But there would be no moral reckoning. There never was. In the end all the checks and remonstrances were arbitrary. No one would ever know who set or sprang the traps. I thought of Florian, the Helium Kids keyboard player, dead in his swimming pool with his veins full of Mandrax back in the Summer of Love. Was that a moral reckoning? Plenty of people had behaved worse than Florian, then and now. In fact there were several ornaments of the world of rock and roll within a dozen yards compared to whom Florian – innocuous, cheerful and confidential – was a kind of moral exemplar. All things were relative. Every judgment was provisional. There was nothing anyone could do. Back outside, like the dust in the Captain Beefheart song, the guests flowed forward and the guests flowed back. Later – and not that much later – journalists would write magazine articles trying to prove that Stevie's wedding was some kind of symbolic high-point of Eighties counter-culture, like the last

Wild Party of pre-war Hollywood, a high tide that no subsequent storm could ever beat: that the bridal cake had been carried into the banqueting hall by a posse of naked cheerleaders; that the champagne had been laced with mescalin. Here on the ground, everything seemed eerily familiar, chastened and subdued by the stultifying heat of rural France. Bright sunshine and grey-stone walls. Distant vineyards and sailing white birds. It seemed wrong that all this should be disrupted by Stevie's wedding. Meanwhile, other kinds of life were going on just as they always had done. The Queen was at Balmoral. Mrs Thatcher was at Chequers. Several hundred miles away the waves would be crashing on the Southwold shore. Alice had disappeared somewhere, but I could see Rory striding dramatically through the throng. When he saw me he said:

'All this makes you think.'

The presence of large numbers of people sometimes stimulated Rory's half-buried abstract side. Unless prevented, he might very soon start talking about Kant.

'What do you mean?'

'About the philosophy of the average pop song. Well, the average Flame Throwers' song. Have you ever thought about it? I mean, you've heard what these people sing about. It's always a series of minute variations on the same theme.'

Most of the guest were streaming pell-mell up the hill towards the chateau, but Rory, warming to his subject, could not be gainsaid.

'Go on.'

'Well, here's the scenario as far as I can conceive it. You're at some party on Sunset Strip or somewhere, knee-deep in the foxiest babes imaginable. For some inexplicable reason, the foxiest of them all makes a bee-line for you. No idea what kind of reverse Darwinism is kicking in, but she does. You've had far too many drugs, but by some heroic act of will you manage to drag her back to your place in your Mustang or your white Merc with fins, or whatever the approved model is, where you frolic away till dawn. At some point around lunchtime you presumably come to. What I want to know is: what happens next?'

Rory looked genuinely puzzled, as if some time-honoured mathematical formula had suddenly let him down.

'I don't think anything happens. I think that, figuratively, you and the foxy babe are just suspended in mid-air.'

'But actions have consequences, surely?'

It was the most anguished I had ever seen Rory on his professional beat. 'Not in a popular song they don't. The Beatles just wanted to hold your hand. That was enough for them. The future could look after itself.'

'I disagree,' Rory said. 'Those Beatles songs are structured according to a conventional lower-bourgeois view of romance. Holding the girl's hand is a prelude to kissing the girl, which, in its turn, is a prelude to marrying her. It's almost a form of reverse teleology. Forty years of domestic bliss instantly foreseen. You can't tell me that's what the Flame Throwers are singing about.'

'There are degrees of stylisation.'

'There are degrees of half-wittedness' Rory said crossly. Against all expectation, he seemed thoroughly outraged by the moral deficiencies to be found in the Flame Throwers' *oeuvre*. Then, abruptly, his manner changed. 'You might go and talk to Larry Bracegirdle. I know for a fact he wants to see you.'

'How do you know it for a fact?'

A faint gleam of shiftiness, like the last ray of sunlight pulsing out of a darkening sky, passed over Rory's face. 'His office were in touch. And Geffen said they wanted things sorted out too. They're quite happy with our domestic arrangements. They want to go on as before.'

'Nothing will go on anywhere if twenty-five per cent of the band is sitting in a beach hut talking about the infinite particle of sanctity.'

'Actually,' Rory said, 'I think he'd quite like to talk to you about that as well.'

'We're just the UK record label. Larry's the manager. It's up to him to check on the mental health of the band.'

'It's all rather complicated' Rory said. '*Christ!* What on earth is that racket?'

High on the ramparts of the chateau, someone was letting off volley after volley of what sounded like fire-crackers. Either that, or some kind of revolution was in progress. None of the guests labouring up the hill took much interest. They were used to the predictably unpredictable. Record launches where teams of dwarfs staged arm-wrestling bouts; nude cyclists; mass abseiling down the side of apartment blocks – it was all in a day's work. We pressed on to the first in a line of gazebos, set awkwardly beneath the chateau wall. Here, relays of girls in stars-and-stripes bikinis with flowers in their hair were handing out drinks and there was a large cage in which several lions sprawled in uneasy repose.

'I expect Stevie will go in there with a whip and make them do tricks' Rory said.

Something else had occurred to me, beyond the thought of revolutions, circus lions, the Flame Throwers' U.S. management team and where Alice might have gone off to.

'Do me a favour, Rory. Go and find Howard Cunningham and make sure he doesn't get near to anyone connected to the band. Invent some new group we're on the point of signing and offer him an exclusive as a trade-off. If he's got a Dictaphone with him, see if you can't steal it out of his pocket. Anything.'

'Roger to that' Rory said. 'I'll tell the little shit we've signed up all the Rolling Stones to do solo albums. There's your man, by the way.' He stared hard at a knot of people in the corner of the tent who were being served cocktails off a tray by one of the bikini-clad girls, seemed to achieve some kind of odd, telepathic communion with them and then waved away as one of them began to semaphore back.

In the past seven years I had sat through dozens of meetings with the managements of American rock bands. Some of them had been convened in the gleaming foyers of expensive London hotels. Others had been conducted in backstage rumpus-rooms or on the steps of the 100 Club in Oxford Street. One of them had even taken place in a punt on the Cam. The personnel were nearly always called Morty or Marty or Randy. There was talk in the music papers of a 'new breed' of U.S. rock managers, but in fact they were not so very different from the old breed, if slightly better dressed, marginally better educated and occasionally in possession of business degrees from American universities. Of the Flame Throwers' current Svengali, a music biz lawyer from Baltimore met on furlough in Soho three months before had said: 'Sure, Larry ain't lived in Kentucky – and he'd still call it Kaintuck – since he was knee-high to a cormorant, but take it from me he's just a country boy at heart. He probably listens to fiddle music when he's back home with Esmeralda and the girls. Why, I once saw him at a Dolly Parton concert. But Larry now, he always had a mind to get on. There ain't many kids from Shitkicker Creek or wherever it is majored in economics from Duke. You be polite to him, you hear?' The subject of this encomium, soon identified by the prodigious respect being offered by the band of associates clustered around him, was just this moment slipping the waitress a folded twenty dollar bill and nodding with approval when, not having space for it in her cleavage, she eased it into the lining of her bikini pants.

'Mr Bracegirdle? I'm very pleased to meet you.'

The American rock managers liked being told that you were pleased to meet them, that you had heard a great deal about them, that you had been looking forward to making their acquaintance. Their delight in basic civility was so transparent that you wondered whether similar meetings in the States hadn't begun in a hail of bullets.

'Call me Larry, son' Bracegirdle volunteered – he could have been two years older than me, but the alligator tan made it hard to compute – pushing back the cuffs of a mohair suit so expensively styled that it might have been cut from shark's hide. 'A very, ah, *moving* ceremony.' ('Talks a lot of bullshit' the music lawyer had said. 'On the other hand, he don't waste your time.')

'Always good to see two young people joined together in the sight of God' I deadpanned back.

Bracegirdle threw me a look which suggested that now we had perjured ourselves we could safely get down to the business in hand. I remembered something else the music lawyer had told me: 'Yeah, back in the day Larry used to run a label over in Memphis. Duelling banjos and that kind of thing. You never saw anything like it. Used to charge the bands for everything. Studio time. Distribution. Promo. Right down to the toilet paper. And *then* cream 60 to 70 per cent off the top. Why, was a guy died the other year who hadn't made a record since 1973 and he still owed Larry money.'

'Duane,' Bracegirdle instructed a lanky associate with raggedy sideburns who looked as if he had just wandered off the set of *Louisiana Hayride*. 'You go fetch this gentleman some refreshment to sustain him.' Then, as Duane lumbered off, he said: 'I know what you're thinking, son. Last thing in the world a guy like Stevie da Vinci needs, this little Eye-talian kid from L.A. who probably grew up eating his dinner out of a trash can, is to marry a porn actress. But I hadder checked out. She's a hard-headed girl. Won't do him no harm. Might even do him some good. Calm him down. Which is something we could all do with, on account of' – he flung another glance which took in guests, bikini-clad waitresses, tent and associated paraphernalia and convicted them all of conspiring against his interests – 'we got ourselves a situation.'

Most of these sit-downs with the management of American rock bands involved the discreet unveiling of situations: bass-players who had run amok with tyre-irons in parking lots; drug busts around the back of Madison Square Garden; drummers who had packed their kits with flash powder and were now in hospital awaiting reconstructive facial surgery.

'What kind of a situation?'

Bracegirdle rocked back on his boot-heels, looked as if he might be about to fall over backwards and then, by an effort of will, regained his balance. His features were stamped with a look that you saw quite a lot on the Eighties rollercoaster: the look of a man whose management skills have proved altogether inadequate for the human flotsam now quivering beneath his grasp.

'They're good boys,' he said without much conviction. 'But they ain't got the schooling. In fact, some of them can't hardly write their names in the dirt with a stick. Just now, the plan is to do a covers album. Now, I ain't normally a fan of covers albums' – it would have been superfluous to add that he disliked covers albums because of the royalty payments they involved to third parties – 'but the boys are keen. Well, they say they are. Also, isn't one of them written any new material in eighteen months.'

'What about Live Aid?'

'The n.....s in Africa? I'm in favour of it.' He made a casting gesture with his hand, as if untold libations stood waiting to be poured over the heads of starving Ethiopians. 'There's some managers won't do charity gigs. Me, I reckon you always recoup on record sales. We're gonna be talking about it later. Between you and me, the situation is Cris.'

'I did hear there were one or two problems.'

'You heard right. Now, a lot of this stuff is exaggerated. These things always are. The time that guy from Mötley Crüe was supposed to have joined a Hare Krishna commune and given all his money to Farm Aid, he was actually in a suite at the Cincinnati Sheraton with hookers being shipped in in relays. Or having a steel rod put in his septum. I can't rightly remember. But Cris, now, he's got *super-reflective'* – the shrink's lexicon jarred discordantly with Larry's homespun tones. 'Plus, he's bin pursuing his, uh, *religious interests.*'

'The infinite particle of sanctity?'

'Something like that. Between you and me he ain't left that place of his at Malibu for a month. Isn't anything that can winkle him out. I mean, they got – what's the name of that black girl? – Whitney Houston to ask him to a party the other week and he wouldn't go. Ron Wood wanted him to do backing vocals on some…fuckin' track or something and he wouldn't pick up the phone. I went over there the other week with a coupla Louisiana hams and some gumbo – you know, stuff a feller would like to eat – by way of a friendly gesture, and he wouldn't see me. Just had this boss chick slam the door on me and tell me Mr Itol was indisposed. Now, all this has got to stop.'

The tent was beginning to empty. Clearly some rival attraction had opened its doors further up the hill. In the distance there was loud, violent music starting up. The waitresses, supposing their work done, had retreated to a shady spot in the corner where they squatted with their hands on their knees smoking cigarettes. Back in their cage, mighty paws extended like squeegee mops, the lions slumbered on. Once again, I had a presentiment that something was about to go badly wrong, here among the scarlet finger-nails and the sheen of Larry Bracegirdle's mohair suit, that some outsize Gordian Knot was about to wheeled on stage that only I had the power to deal with. And so it proved.

'The thing is, we figured you could go to L.A. and fix this.'

One of the lions opened a yellow eye. He would make short work of Bracegirdle. Or would he? I had a vision of Larry pulling a Swiss army knife out of his pants pocket and expertly ripping his way to safety.

'Fix this thing and do us all a favour' Larry said craftily.

In the past I had been despatched on countless errands of this kind: sent to Moroccan hideaways to fetch back errant guitarists; to abandoned studios in the shadow of the Rocky Mountains, where eagles soared in the blue sky, in search of lost tapes. But all that was years ago, far away on the other side of life.

'I don't suppose he even knows who I am.'

'That's where you're wrong, son. Seems like you made a distinct impression on him last time they was in England.' Larry's accent was turning folksier by the moment. 'Always talking about that nice English feller who was so particular. Or so I'm told. Fine, friendly folks,' Larry said menacingly.

'What makes you think he'll see me?'

'Just think about it, Nick. You and me, we got a lot to lose here. They ain't toured in two years. Ain't made a record in three. Pretty soon all them kids in the 'burbs'll find someone else's picture to stick on their wall. How do you think that's going to look on my profit and loss account? But then you could say that if they don't do this covers album and play for the n.....s in Africa and all the rest of it that you've got more to lose than me. Those new contracts ain't signed yet. You go and talk to Cris and I'll sign them tomorrow. Your Mr Bayliss-Callingham reckoned you'd jump at it.'

Rory was definitely up to something. Whatever it was looked as if it would take several days on the West Coast to uncover. In the meantime, Bracegirdle's sidekicks had all drifted away. So had the waitresses. That left the two of us and the cage full of sleepy lions. Larry shot them a disgusted look.

'All whacked out on tranks,' he diagnosed. 'Couldn't raise a claw if they tried to. You know, back in the Sixties I use ta represent a guy who tamed lions. The Grand Pompadour de Paris. Course he came from Nawlins, but who gives a fuck? Anyways, one time his wife, who was part of the act, forgot to give 'em the pills and they jumped up right there and then and chewed his arm off. Place looked like a fuckin' abbatoir.' There was something annoying him, something profound and elemental, which the pleasant memory of all this bygone carnage could not displace. 'You know, Nick, pretty soon all this is going to change. They's big money coming in to music. Not just big money. Huge money. *Corporate* money. Bill Graham use ta think he was doing well if he made twelve grand out of a long-hair night at the Winterland. Pretty soon there's bands going to be playing in South America to 200,000 people. And the guys who're putting them on ain't going to stand for Cris Itol and his particles of fuckin' sanctity.'

'You say hello to your Mr Bayliss-Callingham, d'ya hear?' Larry Bracegirdle enjoined, sounding more than ever like a character from *The Grapes of Wrath*, as I set off up the hill.

In the middle distance, beyond the chateau's walls, there were rolling fields of wheat and barley, Tennysonian in their grandeur. Lines of teal passed rapidly overhead, like a series of stitches in the sky. My Mr Bayliss-Callingham lurked just inside the courtyard on the edge of a substantial crowd, clustered around a long rectangle of banqueting tables. Two gigantic speakers up on the battlements were belting out 'Cecilia-Ann', the lead single from *Straight From Hell*:

Cecilia-Ann, I'm your man and I'm doing what I can
Cecilia-Ann, I'm your fan, and I love your Long Beach tan
Cecilia-Ann, What's your plan? Hear your daddy's in the Klan
Hey Cecilia, Yeah Cecilia, Go Cecilia-Ann.

'I'm going to California,' I said.

'I'm sure it's for the best,' Rory countered, like a deferential game-keeper hearing his lordship's plans for some depopulated grouse moor. Half-a-dozen basket-carrying girls dressed in the style of a Watteau *fête champêtre* went by strewing armfuls of rose-petals. The questions I wanted to ask Rory would have to wait.

'Have I missed much?'

'The usual sort of thing.' Six years into the job, Rory was getting used to the routines of rock star dissipation. 'The straight people stared at the weird people and the weird people stared back. I gather the cider cup is best avoided. Most of the women, too.'

'Not that lot from the Viper Room who they ran the story about in the *National Probe*?'

'The very same. I believe they're all suffering from some sexually transmitted disease that no antibiotics can shift.'

'Did you find Cunningham?'

'They over-promote those journalists,' Rory said, who had once been the butt of a story in the NME headed 'We Name the New Posh Boys of Rock.' 'I told him it was in everyone's best interests – his own included – that he shouldn't go anywhere near the band, but we could probably get him an exclusive with Magda at St Thomas's once she was out of the woods.'

'Wasn't that rather overplaying your hand?'

'Believe me,' Rory said, with a bit more emphasis than was warranted. 'I have never overplayed a hand in my life.' It was an epitaph in its way. Somewhere above our heads, in the uppermost machicolations of the chateau, a cannonade went off. Several of the female guests shrieked. Clouds of smoke, rapidly descending on the courtyard, turned it instantly into a kind of ghastly underworld, full of bizarrely-costumed figures, spectral creatures letting out moans of pain. Twenty yards away I could see the girls from the Viper Room, grave and disdainful, queuing up to sample the cider-cup.

* * *

'Well that was a lively evening.' It was six hours later, just short of midnight, and the hotel room was sunk in shadow.

'Not to your taste?' 'Lively evening' in Alice-speak meant one rung up from catastrophe.

'I know one is supposed to enjoy this sort of thing once in a while,' Alice said, slamming the drawer of the bedside table shut as if it harboured some live creature she very much wanted not to get out. 'But I always think it's much more interesting to read about it in the newspapers. What in earth was the matter with all those women?'

In the end medical attention had had to be sought for the girls from the Viper Room. 'Sheer over-excitement with scene, I should think.'

'That's not what the man from the American label told me' – she narrowed her eyes slightly as if trying to remember the opening lines of a poem. 'He said they'd been *seriously fucked up by some weird stuff*. And I couldn't find a single person I wanted to talk to.'

Alice's attitude to the social functions I dragged her to was still impressively hard-line. Three years into our relationship, she still wandered through the record company jamborees and the Wardour Street press receptions expecting to find High Court judges and partners from the Big Six accountancy firms.

'Any idea where Rory's staying?'

'Haven't a clue. I barely talked to him. I expect he's gone off somewhere. Isn't it *hot*?' Alice stepped out of her tights, left them on the carpet like a spreading cow-pat, and went and stood by the open window. She had mild exhibitionist tendencies and enjoyed padding around without her clothes on. 'You'd think that a place calling itself the Auberge de Victor Hugo could run to a fan.'

Outside the window the sky was turning blue-black, like the Parker ink of schooldays. I thought about the day that had passed – Larry in his tent corner, the lions in their cage, the cannons going off, all those stealthy intimations of disquiet – and then about the vista before me. With all the other women I had known – Rosalind, to whom I had been married for three years, Angie in the bedroom on Mulholland Drive, Tammy Girl back on Planet Pankey – there had come a moment when the formal mechanisms failed to operate, when all the usual behavioural constraints no longer seemed worth the bother and the real person had stepped out into the light. With Alice, I realised, this moment had never happened. No matter how intimate you got with her, no matter how many times she stalked round a hotel bedroom stark naked while you looked admiringly on, she would still speak to you as if you were one of the High Court judges she expected to meet at the record company receptions. If there was something disillusioning about this freezing hauteur, then there was also something fabulously impressive. With Alice, as Rory had once remarked, 'you knew where you bloody well were.'

'Couldn't you go downstairs and ask at reception?' Alice wondered.

To exist in this immensely stylised world that Alice had created around her was, necessarily, to be ordered about. You were always being sent to make telephone calls, fetch foreign currency from banks and once, while on a skiing trip to Switzerland, to procure *un autobus pour cinquante personnes.* Like the recording costs recovered from bands who lingered too long in the studio, it was all part of the deal. On the other hand, reception might harbour more than a means of shifting the dead air around.

'I'll see what I can do.'

The Auberge de Victor Hugo had a literary theme. Balzac, Zola, Dumas and Eugène Sue all stared out of the panelling. At intervals along the corridor there were trays full of calf-bound novels and Second Empire *bric-a-brac.* Down in the reception area, where all but one of the lights had been switched off, the atmosphere was almost supernatural. Fish swam through the shadows, outsize cats were running around the stairwell and the grandfather clock beneath the portrait of Raymond Radiguet looked as if it were about to sprout wings and take flight. But there was still a clerk at the desk.

'Pardonnez-moi? C'est un autre anglais qui reste ici?'

'Voilà m'sieur.'

Two or three yards away to the left there was a cigarette machine with a luminous Marlboro sign. Pausing for a moment to heighten the dramatic effect, Howard Cunningham stepped out from behind it. But I was used to this kind of thing.

'Hello Howard. What are you up to?'

'Staying here for the night like anyone else' Cunningham said. 'It's a free country.'

'Did you get your interview? I hope not.'

'Not exactly. But I did find something that will interest our readers very much.'

'What sort of thing? The low-down on Lisette's trousseau?'

'You know I can't tell you, Nick. You'll have to wait until you see the paper. Is it right you're off to California?'

'I'm off to all sorts of places all the time.' It was far too late to be playing these games. Cunningham took the hint, went over to the cigarette machine and started feeding franc pieces into it. Asked about the fan, the clerk shook his head, spread his hands in a gesture which implied that in the history of the Auberge de Victor Hugo – probably even in the whole Dordogne region, maybe even in France itself – no guest had ever made such a presumptuous demand. Upstairs all the passage lights had been dimmed and it was difficult to find the way back. In the bedroom Alice had switched off everything but the bedside lamps. It was still unbelievably hot. The girls from the Viper Room would be recovering from whatever had been put in the cider-cup by now. Larry and his cronies would be back on the plane to New York. Stevie would be safe in his beloved's arms. All over the western hemisphere the narratives in which I was caught up were steadily unravelling themselves.

'Somebody told me you were going to America.'

'Somebody was right.' There was no point in asking who that somebody was.

I explained about the fan. Alice was always gracious in these situations. An effort had been made. That was enough. Presently she fell asleep. I lay awake for a long while, as the sounds of the Dordogne night floated through the open window, thinking about Howard Cunningham, and what he was up to, and Rory and Larry Bracegirdle, and what they were up to, the Pacific surf falling on the beach at

Malibu, and, from further away, the old man's burial ship bobbing out into the waves off Oregon all those years ago.

Scuzz TV

Interviews Joey Valparaiso and Stevie da Vinci…

INTERVIEWER :	So how you guys doing?
JOEY :	We're doing OK, y'know. I mean Stevie here can't hardly get his dick out the door these days on account of him being a married man and all…Never saw a guy so pussy-whipped.
INTERVIEWER :	Six million dollar question. Stevie, will your wife be continuing with her career?
STEVIE :	Sure. Chicks do what they want these days…Actually, the answer is No Fucking Way.
INTERVIEWER :	I take it you're recommending the married state?
STEVIE :	I mean, it's a beautiful thing, OK? You wake up in the morning and you think: yeah, I know who I'm having my breakfast with, I know who I'm having my dinner with, I know who I'm climbing in the sack with. You know, one of the first things Lissie did when we got together? Took me to this orthodontist or whatever in Beverley Hills and got my teeth fixed. Had all this scientific shit pumped into my gums so they stop falling out. Hafta thank her for that.
INTERVIEWER :	Tell me about the wedding.

JOEY: Man, it was a fuckin' scene. I mean, totally outrageous. For a start, Stevie's parents are there, who he ain't even fuckin' set eyes on since he was, well...just a little kid, y'know. We're waiting outside the church and there's this little old guy and this little old lady step out of a cab, and Stevie's in tears, Lissie's in tears, *I'm* in tears and I ain't even fuckin' met either of them before.

STEVIE: To this day, I still don't know how they fuckin' got there. Wasn't anything to do with me, y'understand. But, well, I'm like: if they're here, they're here. There's enough shrimp cocktail to go round. Whatever.

INTERVIEWER: Can I ask what everyone out there surely wants to know, seeing that you're so settled in your, uh, private lives just now, when can we expect some new product? I mean, it's three years since *Straight From Hell*, and there's all these new L.A. bands saying you can't cut it anymore.

JOEY: Which of these new L.A. bands are sayin' that?

INTERVIEWER: Well, Mötley Crüe are saying it.

JOEY: You get one of those guys from Mötley Crüe – who, incidentally, to my personal knowledge, are a bunch of f.....s – in this studio and let me tell you that there won't be nuthin' left of them other than a hank of hair and a pile of fillings. Seriously, though, there's some new stuff in the can. But what we're really into, right now, is doin' some cover versions. You know, all the punk stuff we were into when we were kids.

STEVIE : We're thinking of calling it *Rip-off Joint*.

JOEY : Only trouble is, though, that word's kinda got out. I mean, there's all these guys who used to be in, I dunno, all those old English bands that toured with the Pistols calling the office and it's like 'Jesus, man, you gotta cover one of our songs. I'm like a 100K in the hole and the mortgage company is looking to repossess. We're fuckin' desperate, man.'

INTERVIEWER : Any idea of a release date?

STEVIE : Release date? You got to be fuckin' kidding man! For a start you got to get the four of us in a studio, and that ain't easy what with Art being in Europe buying his fuckin' pictures or whatever, and Cris... Well, and then when you get us in the studio you have to make sure we ain't out of our heads or shaping up to kick each other's asses or something. It's a real fuckin' problem. I mean, me and Joey here, sure we look like total retards, but compared to Cris and fuckin' Art – 'Mr Abstract' we're calling him now on account of him buyin' all these Abstract Expressionist paintings – we're like, fuckin' *reliable*. I mean, you tell us there's a studio booked for next week and we're fuckin' paying for it, and the chances are we'll probably be there, y'know what I mean.

INTERVIEWER : Where's Cris these days?
JOEY : In Malibu or someplace, last I heard.
STEVIE : In Malibu with this chick.
INTERVIEWER : Is Cris kind of – how do I put this? – is Cris, ah, *involved*?
JOEY : Sure he's involved.
STEVIE : Why wouldn't he be involved?
INTERVIEWER : It's just that people are saying he's turned into a total recluse, living down on the beach and, uh, not even opening his mail.
JOEY : Which people are saying that?

Pause

JOEY : Which people are saying that?
STEVIE : Jesus, give the guy a break. Thing you hafta understand is that Cris is a very...spiritual guy. Right now he's into this process where he's kind of re-evaluating his life. I mean, last time I was over there I'm like 'You wanna blow?' And he's like 'Let's have some China Tea, dude.' You have to respect the guy for that. But, hey, Cris is getting his shit together, with Polly or whatever her fuckin' name is.
JOEY : Holly.
STEVIE : Yeah, Holly. Heard he played at some blues joint over at Encino just the other night. So I'd just like to say all these rumours are fuckin' exaggerated, OK? I mean, we're the fuckin' Flame Throwers, right? Everything we do is exaggerated. Even the fuckin' rumours.

Scuzz TV 'Meet the Band', July 1985

11. MALIBU AND AFTER

Gonna get myself a little shack
Somewhere off the beaten track
Keep myself right out of reach
Watch hot women on the beach
THE FLAME THROWERS – *Malibu Woman*

Bracegirdle Associates had agreed to underwrite the trip to L.A. With this in mind, I booked a first-class return ticket via New York, reserved a high-end bungalow at the Marmont and, for good measure, enquired about the wine-list and the luxury hot-spring herbal massage. I was about to call Hertz and instruct them to set aside the classiest sedan or stripped-down highway cruiser that the L.A. car-pools could offer (and how would that play in Flintridge, or whichever benighted suburb that Larry and his posse of gophers were holed up in?) when a fax arrived at the office in what could only have been Larry's curiously dogged hand – the hand of a man to whom writing, like one or two other human activities, did not come naturally – to assure me that transport was *all fixed up*. 'Go gettem boy' Larry had added at the foot of the page, implying that if I was a hound on the scent, then Cris was a jack-rabbit just waiting to be dragged out of the Kentucky bluegrass. LAX was just as it had always been: polyglot, multicultural, sprinkled with crazies but otherwise home to sun-fried local types making a tremendous fuss about going nowhere in particular. At the barrier a tall, angular, red-haired girl who looked uncomfortably like Wyndham Lewis's portrait of Edith Sitwell only with all the planes sanded down into flatness eased herself out of the ruck of chauffeurs waiting to ferry movie moguls off to Century City or the Burbank lots, indicated wordlessly that that I was to follow her, and bore me silently away. Twenty minutes later, in a top-of-the-range convertible that left the Studebakers and the shark-finned Chryslers buzzing forlornly in our wake, we were out on the Pacific Coast Highway, the beginnings of the Santa Monica mountains on one side, the long blue arm of the sea to the other, while above our heads shrieking white birds blew picturesquely back and forth.

'How did you know it was me?'

There was a turtle on the road fifty yards ahead of us. The girl wondered whether to swerve, reconfigured her grip on the wheel slightly and then mowed it down.

'Larry said to look out for an Englishman. Dark hair. Medium height. Bit like Peter Fonda.'

This comparison had been made before. 'What makes me look English?'

'Well now, there's that prissy way you carry your bag. Not to mention the way you stroll around the arrivals hall like it was full of retarded people. '*Jesus.*' A station wagon full of longhairs wove erratically past on the other side of the road. 'Will you fuck off, you motherfucker?'

The convertible hastened away past the surfer shacks and the coast-side eateries with their signs made out of shells and their sun-bleached hoardings. Eastwards the view was softening to take in secluded slopes and rising greensward. These were ghostlands, the site of Pankey-parties and Pankey picnics, or, a decade-and-a half before, late-night excursions from Mulholland Drive where the Helium Kids were inconspicuously quartered between West Coast tour-dates. It was here, once, in a borrowed car, intending, as he put it, 'to breeze on up to Napa and hoist a couple of crates of whatever the most expensive hooch is they have there' that Stefano had taken a wrong turning, bought from persons unknown what turned out to be a phial of horse tranquiliser, had most of his clothes stolen and been rescued from a drainage ditch by the L.A. Police Department. Fifteen years later the West Coast highway seemed horribly innocuous. The music videos that came out of L.A. these days were all filmed here. They tended to feature blonde girls in sawn-off jeans and sneakers waving from the backs of jeeps as the boys of summer looked on vainly from the kerb or conducted desperate emotional transactions on gas-station forecourts. But the jeeps had all disappeared and the gas-station forecourts were full of sensible-looking people in chinos and seersucker suits filling their tanks in preparation for sober journeys to San Francisco or Fort Bragg. Meanwhile, there was the news from home to think about. Magda was apparently about to be discharged from hospital. Plus somebody reckoned that a tape of whatever Maximum Acceleration had come up with after their three-year studio lockdown would shortly be available. A call I had put in to Rory had not been returned.

There were container ships out on the ocean, so far away that they looked like lumps of balsa wood. For some reason Stefano had not minded being pulled out of the drainage ditch by two contemptuous policemen. 'You just have to experience these things once in a while' he had said. All this – road, car, scenery, memory – worked its effect. The thought that Cris Itol and whatever fantastic mental baggage he had accumulated around him lay at the journey's end was of no account. Only the past had any meaning. The red-haired girl, one hand grasping the wheel, the other rootling through her tawny locks as if there were creatures in there that needed the same treatment as the straying turtle, had decided that this enforced silence could no longer be borne.

'I'm Rhoda-Joe,' she offered, and then, in case there should be any doubt of the status hinted at by the convertible and her off-hand manner, 'Mr Itol's PA.'

Cris's domestic routine had previously been outlined to me by a local music journalist who had spent a day in his company. 'Basically the dude gets up about three. That's if he's been to bed in the first place. There's a fast-food joint that sends in breakfast. After that he might do some drugs. There's usually a pathetic attempt to write a song or something. After that he'll be down at the pool with a fox or two. Was this girl called Holly but I think she walked out on him. There *was* a time when he'd head into town for the night, but I did hear he was getting too paranoid to go outside these days.' It seemed odd that he should need anyone to help him with these far from exacting non-tasks.

'Why exactly does Cris need a PA?'

Rhoda-Joe looked more than ever like Edith Sitwell, brought news of an unflattering review of one of her poems.

'Mr Itol has a number of, uh, business ventures on which he is presently engaged. Not to mention the administrative arrangements of his community. These demand considerably more time than he is currently able to devote to them.'

Five minutes later she took a sharp turn into the uplands. Here, in white-painted miniature mansions deep in the hollow of the hills, the Hollywood A-listers slept. In between the grand estates and their neatly staked-out perimeters, fields of marram grass stretched hazily on into the distance. Puddleglum the Malibu Marsh-wiggle would probably be hanging out here, fishing for eels and smoking his damp tobacco. Rhoda-Joe talked some more about the ceramics class she had taken at the University of Southern California and the batik-importing concern for which she had previously worked as a PR executive. I couldn't decide if she was a nice, efficient West Coast business girl disguising her charm beneath layers of steely resolve, or what Stefano would have called 'a real tough baby.'

Cris's place lay half a mile or so back from the sea, its entry point advertised by a couple of wooden pillars riddled with buckshot and a high electrified fence.

'You see, the West Coast scene has, uh, *developed* a lot in the past twenty years,' Rhoda-Joe said decisively, rather as if she had a band of Japanese tourists in tow, some of whom might possibly have money to invest. 'It's not like the Sixties when Jefferson Airplane and Joni Mitchell were sitting there in Fulton Street or the Canyon having hippy parties and talking about Vietnam. These days people's interests have expanded.' She was still entirely straight-faced. 'They're kind of opening out.'

'What sort of state is Cris in just at the moment? Is he opening out?'

The approach road ended in a square of sun-dried sand, around which three or four modernist buildings wearily clustered. Rhoda-Joe parked the convertible next to a Harley-Davidson motorcycle with only one wheel and a pile of rusting car-parts.

'I guess you could say that Mr Itol is coming to terms with himself.' There was no doubt about it: she was a real tough baby. Then, out of nowhere, the mask slipped. 'Look, I'll be straight with you – Nick, is it? He's *seriously* fucked. Most of the time he's completely out of it. Other times he just goes and stares at the sea. Frankly, we've been having trouble getting much out of him this last couple of months.'

Drawn by the noise of the car, a dozen or so figures had ambled out into the dusty square. They looked different from the 'alternative communities' of fifteen years ago and the hippy children of the network documentaries: at once better dressed and more resentful, as if they had known from the start that this experiment in communal living had been a dreadful mistake and burned to get back to civilised life. Rhoda-Joe stared at them bleakly.

'What kind of thing does the community do?'

'A little meditation. Mr Itol is big on inner resourcefulness.' The look on Rhoda-Joe's face suggested that meditation and inner resourcefulness weren't high on her own list of priorities. 'There's a plantation out back where we grow spinach and okra. But generally' – she took a deep, despairing breath – 'we're just focusing on making the most of our time together before the tides sweep over the planet and bear us all away.'

'It all sounds rather apocalyptic.'

Rhoda-Joe nodded, halfway gracious for once. 'Yeah, it is. Kind of. Some people are more into it than others. And one more thing. When you see him, could you say "Greetings, Brother Ishmael"? It's how he likes to be addressed right now.'

It was difficult to work out how seriously Rhoda-Joe took all this, whether she reckoned her employer was a half-wit whose whims a sturdy professionalism required her to conciliate, or whether the stuff about Brother Ishmael chimed with some fundamental view she took of the world.'

'Where do I find him?'

'I guess he's in the sanctum right now.' She pointed at a kind of glass-walled hut set apart from the other buildings. 'We could try there.'

There was a tall and faintly dishevelled figure standing in the doorway of the hut. It did not look particularly like Itol. On the other hand, musicians in states of mental disturbance were capable of undergoing radical transformations. One of the girls from Chloe and the Cupcakes had shaved all her hair off and lost three stone in a month. By way of a prompt, Rhoda-Joe dug a long finger into the small of my back.

'Greetings, Brother Ishmael.'

'Hi, Nick.' The shoulder-length black curls had been reined in a bit, but the pale, greenish eyes I remembered from the press conferences and the MTV interviews were still blinking restlessly away.

'This gennel-min has come all the way from England to talk to you,' Rhoda-Joe said proudly, like a high school teacher introducing some visiting dignitary to the remedial class, and staring at him as she did so. It was an odd kind of look, not the usual half-way hungry panoptic you got from rock star PAs, but one in which the deference came mingled with faint exasperation. Clearly supposing that a firm hand was needed, she pushed past him into the hut, beckoned me after her and then, with a kind of sizzling impatience, stood waiting on the steps for Cris to follow. Inside there was a sofa, a cassette player and a handful of tapes strewn over the uneven floor, and a Fender acoustic propped up against a chair. What might have been a chipmunk went tearing away across the lintel.

'Has Grishnakh been in here again?' Rhoda-Joe demanded, addressing herself to Itol.

'I guess.' Here in his fox-hole, tools of the trade to hand, he seemed in a better state. He tapped the bottom E string of the guitar and then listened with intense, crafty interest as it oscillated for a second or two.

'Jesus' Rhoda-Joe said. 'You wouldn't believe the trouble I have keeping that fuckin' animal out of the rooms. He's probably dosed it or something.' Duty and an intent, residual fury fought an inconclusive battle. Then suddenly her manner softened. 'Cris, honey,' she said beseechingly. 'Mr Du Pont has come all the way from England. He needs to talk to you about stuff.'

There was a breeze getting up outside, blowing flecks of grit against the quivering plate-glass frames. The afternoon was wearing on. Grishnakh the chipmunk was well away now, zipping blithely in the direction of the square. Curiously, having beaded Cris and his no-nonsense chatelaine in their lair, I was more at ease. I had done this sort of thing before. Staring down half-crazed music-biz types was a task I could handle. The breeze was blowing in harder now, whirling up the U.S. flag that dangled on a fence-pole next to the motor-bike and holding it taut.

'It's good to see you Cris,' I improvised. 'What have you been up to?'

Cris looked flummoxed. Plainly, accounting for his activities was a step further than he was prepared to go.

'I don't know' he said. He looked at Rhoda-Joe. 'What have I been doing?'

'You've been working on some new music,' Rhoda-Joe said, in a way that suggested Cris had had to be reminded of these creative endeavours several times before. 'Why don't you let Nick hear one of your new songs?'

I had spent the best part of twenty years listening to musicians letting me hear their new songs. The Fiery Orbs had played me their jangly mod anthems. The Helium Kids had thrashed out endless earfuls of their rackety blues metal. Charysse had caterwauled to me over the lilting strains of a Bontempi organ in her parents' front room in Hounslow. Heaven knew what Cris had come up with under the wide California sky with the noise of the surf thrumming in his ears.

'Hey now,' Cris said, as if the preceding conversation had somehow been erased from his mind. 'Why don't I play him one of my new songs?' He picked up the guitar, stared at it hesitantly for a moment, strummed what might, with a fair wind behind it, have been an A chord, went for a minor somewhere in the near vicinity, failed miserably and put the instrument down.

'What Cris really wants to do,' Rhoda-Joe said encouragingly – she pronounced his name with an odd, lisping crackle – 'is an acoustic album.' Then she gave it up as a bad job. 'You know, honey, I think it's time for your rest. Why don't I come and fetch you at supper time?'

Back outside, we stood on the sandy square as the grit from the breeze blew against our calves.

'What exactly is he taking?'

'Some of these new psychotropic drugs are really powerful,' Rhoda-Joe said dispassionately. She had lost her intent look and gone back to regarding Cris as an interesting case. 'He'll probably be better in the morning. There's a kind of a guest annexe. You can stay in it if you like.'

'Couldn't I call a cab?'

'They don't like coming out here,' Rhoda-Joe said, in a tone that suggested all discussion would be futile. It occurred to me that she was either furiously angry or bored stiff. From within the compound, funereally, a bell began to toll.

'Have you been working for Cris – Mr Itol – for long?'

'Three months. Before that I was doing a creative realting course.'

California had always been full of this kind of flotsam: goth children with bass instruments who loitered outside the clubs on the Strip begging lifts to Sacramento or the Valley; fat little maggot-men who looked like congregationalist ministers selling drugs in the delicatessens; Native American Indian jewellery designers taking six-week concessions in the Encino shopping malls. But TV and film – film especially – had licensed their idiosyncrasies, brought them together and given them an environment which encouraged their weirdness to get seriously out of hand.

'I'll help you with your stuff,' Rhoda-Joe said, as if in the circumstances she was doing the greatest favour woman had ever extended to man.

The guest annexe was a short walk eastwards along creeper-strewn pathways. Whoever had last stayed in it had left cigarette butts all over the limestone floor and burnt several large holes in the quilted coverlet of the single bed. A solitary paperback lying slant-wise on the dusty sill turned out to be called *Exploding Your Psychic Love-Bomb.* Coming back from the sink in the lean-to, I discovered that Rhoda-Joe had vanished, gone to slash the heads off half-a-dozen chickens or bully the cook. There was nothing to do except wait here until morning. All across the world the people I knew would be making their accommodations with time and contingency. Over in Flintridge Larry Bracegirdle would be shooting craps or whatever else he did to relax from the bump and grind. In London Alice would be sleeping the sleep of the just as the traffic of Kensington High Street faded into murmur and the stiff white shirts her children wore to attend their fancy prep school in Sloane Square aired in the laundry room. In Ladbroke Grove the office would be shut up and silent with the moonlight falling on the reception desk and the wicker basket full of un-listened to demo tapes. In St Thomas's Hospital Magda would be piecing her consciousness back together. Over in L.A. the other members of the Flame Throwers would be getting laid, or wasted, or examining their collections of Abstract Expressionist art, or wandering around their duplexes while expensive-looking women leafed through catalogues or made reservations at the Edison or the Rooftop. After an hour or so, a girl of about fourteen came moving into view along the path from the compound with a carrier bag, left it by the door and then, like Rhoda-Joe, disappeared into nowhere. Inside there were two small beef-burgers, some French fries in a paper cone and a flagon of what looked Gatorade. Later the light began to fade across the tops of the sand-dunes, the tops of the pine-trees shook crazily in the wind and from afar, somehow mesmerising in its intensity, came the thump and judder of the surf.

Rain fell intermittently through the night. In the intervals between these deluges, wild animals came and skirmished round the door frames. When I woke up just after dawn the sky was a faint salmon-pink colour and there were gulls prising molluscs out of the terrace steps. Down on the beach the wind had got up and the sand was dotted with washed-up onion strings. Thirty or forty yards out to sea a woman in a red bikini was swimming purposefully through choppy, blue-grey water. Out on the horizon the container ships seemed not to have moved since the day before. Gradually, like the pieces of a gigantic jigsaw, the key elements of this unfamiliar landscape began to shift into place. Far away to the north there were clusters of beach-huts and wisps of pale smoke being borne away on the breeze. The woman in the red bikini vanished from sight and then re-appeared, still swimming strongly, even further away. In the distance, south of the beach-huts, two figures, male and female, each gesticulating at the other, were moving rapidly towards me. As they came nearer the woman, now recognisable as Rhoda-Joe, stopped in her tracks, gave the man a terrific box on the ears – so hard that he almost collapsed onto the sand – and then bounded away. After a bit the male half of this Punch and Judy Show righted himself and came staggering on.

'Greetings, Brother Ishmael.'

'Fuck all that stuff,' Cris said. He seemed much less shaky than on the previous afternoon, and in some indefinable way smartened up. 'Hey, you want to help me with this shit?'

A hundred yards away down the beach there were anglers' lines pitched at head height and extending out into the ocean. The first two were fish-free, but the third yielded up a brace of severely malnourished scrod. Cris weighed them up in his hands, looked doubtfully at their flapping tails and then smashed their heads against an upturned rock.

'It's good to see you, Rick.'

'Nick.'

'Yeah, Nick. Nickola. Now I remember. They said you were coming. Jesus.' He massaged his left ear, which looked like a chunk of scorched tyre-rubber. 'That chick packs a fuckin' punch. What you want, man?'

There were people sent to chivvy recalcitrant rock stars who made the fatal mistake of exhorting them or appealing to their better natures. I was not going to fall into that trap. The woman in the red bikini had made land now and was drying her Amazonian thighs with a beach-towel. 'I hear Larry Bracegirdle has been asking about that free concert,' I said, as if Flintridge's finest were an importuning junior secretary with a couple of photographs that needed signing.

'I heard about that,' Cris said. The look on his face, in which inscrutability could not quite keep calculation at bay, was identical to the one

I had once seen him give an open-top Caballero that someone had left outside a restaurant in the Hollywood Hills with the key still in the ignition. 'What's your view?'

'It could be a very, ah, humane and charitable act.'

'I guess. Tell me, Nick' – his ear was returning to its normal colour – 'you ever hear of Ayn Rand?'

You got a lot of this in the Eighties. The quasi-philosophical plague pits in which under-schooled rock gods so blithely hurled themselves were nearly always lined with copies of *The Fountainhead* and *Atlas Shrugged*. There was nothing to do but nod.

'I reckoned you would.' The fish were bleeding down his brawny forearms. 'Well, she says the only person who can really help anyone is that person themself. You hear what I'm sayin'? I mean, there's these starving black kids in fuckin'...Africa, but you ain't gonna fix their problems by giving them a million bucks or whatever.'

'You might stop them from dying.'

'Death, man.' Cris was getting properly into his stride now. In a moment or two he would probably start talking about Darwin. 'I mean, death is just a kind of an abstract thing these days...You're not gonna...*scare* me by talking about death. It's like, y'know, you're in the foxhole and the guy next to you gets his head blown off, but you just... scramble over the parapet and blow the guys that did it into a pile of fragments. I mean, that's what the Flame Throwers are all about, right?'

'Absolutely.' Philanthropy had failed. Happily there were baser instincts waiting to be pressed into service. I looked at my watch. It was still only 6 a.m. The bungalow at the Chateau Marmont beckoned me like the scented chamber of Haroun al-Rashid. 'Listen to me, Cris. You play this concert, you go out there in Philly or wherever and give it up for starving Africa and everyone will love you. You won't only get a heap of free publicity, you'll sell – I don't know – a quarter of a million records. And then you can go into the studio and cut that covers album everyone's been talking about with any producer you want and buy yourself, I don't know, a yacht or something or a holiday house at Biscayne Bay. Wouldn't you like that?'

Cris was giving me his full attention now. Like some beleaguered dinosaur watching the first meteorite to hit the earth's surface rolling ominously towards its feet, he had heard something too big to be ignored. The breeze was blowing hard off the ocean now and I had to strain to catch his words.

'Being English, and all, you ever see the Sex Pistols…I mean, in a kind of *live situation*?'

You got a lot of this, too, in the Eighties. In the end most West Coast rock fantasies could be traced back to a Soho cellar, three chords and a defective P.A.

'I certainly did.'

'What were they…I mean, how the fuck did they…I mean, what were they fuckin' like?'

'Unbelievable.' This was a lie. The Pistols, with the talentless Sid now installed on two-note bass, had been beyond terrible. At the same time, I could see that this was a way forward. 'Actually, I saw them all. The Damned. The Clash. Buzzcocks. You know the gig in Manchester where only fifty people showed but they all went and started bands?' This was a lie, too.

'This is so awesome,' Cris said, with the most sincerity I had ever known him bring to any human transaction. 'I mean, those guys are so far out that…I mean, there was an interview with that guy from the Damned, uh Rot Scabies or whatever, in *Rolling Stone* and he was, like, not giving a fuck, y'know.'

'And another thing, Cris,' I said, playing my trump card. 'You make that covers album and you'll be doing *everyone* a favour. Half those guys are on benefits, you know. Think about it. Why not help them *and* the black kids in Africa?'

Fundamentally, the difference between the people you met in the Sixties and the people you met in the Eighties was one of degree. To particularise, the Helium Kids had been cynical, warped, vain, good-for-nothing but essentially tractable. They had been brought up in a world where it was necessary to do things or be punished for not doing them. The Flame Throwers, found in their natural habitat, were cynical, warped, vain, good-for-nothing but essentially deranged. All this brought problems that could not be foreseen, much less dealt with. Companionably – if that was a word that could ever be used of one of these L.A. mutants when he walked in step beside you – heads down against the drifting spray, the dead fish dangling between us, we wandered back to the compound. Here two men in janitors' uniforms were trying to repair a batten that had come off during the night and Rhoda-Joe, red hair tied up in a bun with twine and features contorted in anger, was heaving a set of suitcases into the convertible's half-open boot. 'You know what?' she said as I went timidly by, 'I fucking *quit.*'

* * *

The Chateau Marmont was even dustier and more flyblown than I remembered it, like a sepia photograph of the bygone mid-west, needing only a couple of Sioux warriors or a Canasta wagon to make it a genuine antique. 'Putting you in Bungalow 2' the reception desk clerk said, one eyebrow half-raised, and there hung in the air between us the spectre of John Belushi, who, three years back, had died there of a speedball overdose. But Belushi's spoor was long gone from Bungalow 2. Now there was only a slight smell of damp and some flyers advertising complimentary mud-baths. It was still only 9 A.M. I tried Bracegirdle Associates only to get an answering service – it was too early for the fleshpots of Flintridge – subdued a sudden, inexplicable urge to ring the Pankeys and see how everything was right now in Pacific Palisades, and then put in a call to the office.

'Yes. What do you want?'

They were a little more emollient in answering the phone at Resurgam these days, but only a little.

'It's me, Steph. Nick.'

'You're jolly lucky. I thought you were the man from the cab-hire firm. I was going to tell you to fuck off and we were changing our account. What's happening out there?'

It was too early to start advertising the Flame Throwers' return to concert arenas and recording studios. 'Is Rory still there?'

'Actually, Nick, he's in America too. He said he had to go and see somebody or something. Have you heard about Magda?'

'Not since I got here.'

'Only they let someone from *Sounds* in to see her and there's a dreadful interview about how she sees serpents crawling out of the walls and she wants to do an album where she recites Christina Rosetti's poetry...Oh, and there's a letter from America about some old lady you're supposed to know.'

'You'd better fax it over.'

While the fax machine whirred I dialled up room service and ordered a pot of Earl Grey tea and some cinnamon toast. Like much else in L.A., the Marmont had its anglophile side. The letter, handwritten in shaky capitals, had been despatched from the Robert E. Lee Senior Citizens Care and Residential Home, Memphis, TS, and read: DEAR SIR, HAVE GOT OLD LADY HERE BEEN ASKING FOR YOU. ONE OF OUR RESIDENTS. NAME OF MRS KATZENJAMMER. ASKED FOR YOU SEVERAL TIMES. WANTED ME TO WRITE TO YOU TELL YOU THE DR SAY SHE IS SICK. HOPING THIS REACHES YOU. PS IS VERY SICK.

God knew how Daphne had fetched up in Memphis, let alone installed herself in the Robert E. Lee Senior Citizens Care and Residential Home, but there, apparently, she was. For twenty years she had been haunting me, in locations as far apart as Queens, Bayswater and Staten Island, and now here she was again, like some indefatigable cork bobbing up once more above the waves. Were she to die, the last link with the Old Man would be gone. What was to be done? The schedule could stand another forty-eight hours in the land of the free, I thought, before I crawled home to deal with Magda, and Maximum Acceleration and whatever it was that Rory was up to, and the memory of Alice, silent and glacial in the West Norfolk dawn. I would heed this summons to Memphis, and tend to Daphne – as the locals would say – in her care home next to the churning Mississippi. It was still only 9.30 and quiet as the grave. All around me the rock stars and the dealers and the movie people and whatever other desperate souls had come to rest at the Marmont slept on. And so, light-headed from my stake-out on the Malibu strand – there were still a couple of scrod-scales attached to the back of my hand – with boiling California sun streaming through the window of the room and making the fixtures seem yet more murky and sepia-tinted, I drank the pot of Earl Grey and ate the slices of cinnamon toast as – finally – the ghost of John Belushi in his Blues Brothers gear flew out of the closet and danced and spun beside me.

* * *

L.A. to Memphis. California and New Mexico, Arizona and Kansas and then south-east through the Panhandle and the Gulf. Blue skies, dense heat, smoke rising from the Texas refineries and then the Mississippi River, of which the palsied rube sitting next to me observed to his indulgent wife as we passed over it that that surely was a whole bunch of water. As the plane came in low over the Chickasaw Bluffs, I cheered up a bit. This was the Peter Taylor country, a world of snow-white mansions and hugger-mugger shacks, of night-riders lynching their victims by moonlit lakes, of white-haired old ladies brooding over the uniforms their grandfathers had worn at Appomattox. The Robert E. Lee Senior Citizens Care and Residential Home was on the South Side, half-way along a street where elderly black men walked scrawny greyhounds and wheel-less cars lay propped up on piles of bricks awaiting attention they were clearly not going to get. At the reception desk there was a middle-aged woman drowsing over a copy of the *Tennessee Pioneer* and a row of potted cacti going yellow in the sun.

'You OK there?' It was the way the gas-station attendants had said it on the Helium Kids tour of the South twenty years before, with the ghost of an aitch stealing behind the 'O'.

'Thank you, ma'am.' Southern courtesies came naturally to me. It was a nice change from the cheery camaraderie of the West Coast. 'You have a Mrs Katzenjammer staying here?'

The woman looked sceptical, as if her days were full of people coming in off the street to enquire about non-existent residents. 'You kin to her?'

'Step-son,' I improvised – as far as I knew the Old Man and Daphne had never made it to the altar. 'I had a message to visit.'

'Uh huh.' Reassured, she put down the paper [*Governor says Tennessee Renaissance at Hand... Six bodies found in Chattanooga*] and fished around in the pockets of her institutional smock for a pen. 'I'm Emmagem. Please ta meet ya. Actually, Daphne ain't too well right now. In fact, between you and me she nearly died last week. Would have moved her out into the hospital only the doc said he don't like to shift her. You come a long way?'

Los Angeles would cut no ice down here below the Mason-Dixon Line. They would be more impressed by a trip from Birmingham, Alabama. 'I'm from England.'

'Lordy.' Emmagem blinked in astonishment. 'Well, why don't you go into the residents' lounge just over that-a-way?' – she pointed at a glass-panelled doorway over which hung an engraving of the Battle of Gettysburg in lurid bas-relief – 'and talk to Miz Longenecker who mostly sits there mornins with the old folks. She'll surely assist ya.'

There was a handful of old people in the residents' lounge playing backgammon and staring out of the window, but no one who was obviously Miz Longenecker. Beyond them, a badly-lit corridor smelling of Janitor-in-a-Drum and pine-freshener led to a row of bedrooms with long, vertical spyholes in their doors, like the archers' embrasures in the walls of Norwich Castle. In one of these a woman with a few scraps of reddish hair piled on the top of her head, blankets pulled up to the level of her chin, lay propped up against a stack of pillows.

'Daphne. It's me. Nick Du Pont.'

It was five years since I had set eyes on Daphne, back in the high-rise apartment on Staten Island, amid the piles of old newspapers and the New York skyline aggrandising over the horizon. Frail and self-absorbed, she did not seem to have changed in any essential regard.

'It's good to see you, Nick.' She slid a hand out from under the covers for me to shake, and then, as if this were a clandestine gesture of which a vigilant authority would certainly disapprove, rapidly pulled it back. 'You been here long?'

'I just arrived. Off a plane from L.A.' There were more pots of cacti on the windowsill behind Daphne's head. They had been better cared for than the ones in reception and one or two of the fronds drooped onto the bed-head. This had the effect of making Daphne resemble a Queen of the Jungle, some exotic chieftainess welcoming her subjects in arboreal splendour.

'Uh huh. Only they had a guy in to see me the other day – a preacher he musta been – and I thought you might be him.'

'How are you?'

'I ain't too good' Daphne conceded. 'Got a pain in my side. And some other stuff too. But hell' – she tossed her head and its sparse curls in a gesture that took in bed, cacti, the Robert E. Lee Senior Citizens Care & Residential Home and everyone in it – 'there's nobody here isn't too well. In fact, most of the folks is dying inch by inch. But how about you? How ya doing? You don't look like your dad so much,' she said, a bit suspiciously.

'No?'

'That was a good-looking feller,' Daphne said, who had holed up with the Old Man in the clapboard house in Queens, gone alpaca farming with him in Wyoming, lived a vagrant and apparently purposeless life with him in at least half the states in America and only abandoned him at the hippy commune on the north-west coast.

'Why did you leave him?' I had never got to the bottom of the Old Man's dealings with Daphne and never would, but there was no harm in asking this.

'Jesus! Why do ya want to know that?' It was difficult to work out if she was exasperated or secretly pleased. 'Wouldn't never have happened if we hadn't gone to that place in Oregon. I mean, we're all bohemian right? But it don't mean ya can't have hot and cold and nothing but beans to eat. Thing is, I don't believe he liked it either. Remember he made 'em a crayfish creel the one time, but he never fit and he knowed it. Me, I just quit.'

The jungle spell had gone. She was just an old woman with dyed hair in a bedroom with a lot of cacti.

'How did you end up here?'

'All on account of my sister-in-law Eulalie. My brother's wife. Not that she ever approved of me,' Daphne said furiously, as if entire congressional committees had sat to consider this vexing topic. 'She reckoned there was some nice places where I could stay around here. Only then, 'stead of keeping me company, the bitch takes herself off to Baton Rouge or someplace, and yours truly is left high and dry...' Out in the corridor there was a jangle of stainless steel as a janitor's cart went noisily by. 'Hell,' Daphne went on. 'Nothing but pasta and beans to eat. And some creepin' Jesus feller lording it over us.' Her mind had gone back to the House of Peace, Love and Serenity on the Oregon coast. 'No wonder I lit out.'

A bit later she fell asleep. I sat breathing in the pine fumes for a moment or two and watching her old, mad eyes opening and closing as she dreamed, and then wandered back into the residents' lounge. Here Emmagem was attending to the hair of what looked like the dead spit of Barbara Bush with long, purposeful strokes of a comb.

When she saw me she said shyly: 'I see you found Daphne, so that's all right. Miz Longenecker, she's not here just now. She had to go away. She said if you was to come back in the morning she could have a proper talk with you. No darlin' – this was to Barbara – 'you hold still, and then I'll fix you up like it was your wedding day.'

Outside in the street the dog-walking old men had been replaced by tough-looking black kids on motorcycles and a plump woman in a too-tight pant suit who brandished a wedge of carmined fingers at me and demanded to know if I needed fixing up. It was not the Peter Taylor country. There was a motel a couple of blocks down, so I engaged a room, signed the reception clerk's dockets ('From Engerland, suh? Is that a fact?'), put in another call to Bracegirdle Associates, which once again went to the messaging service – what were they all doing over there in Flintridge? Detained at the pool? Embarked on some 24-hour clambake? – and inspected the local TV news, which was about the arraignment of a Klan vizier apprehended outside a black evangelical church with an assault rifle and two canisters of napalm who claimed that he was transporting these items to a veterans' memorial museum, and some new kind of pepper steak that was taking the state by storm. All that night the rain rolled up from the Gulf, fell ceaselessly on the sidewalks and drummed on the motel's echoey fibreglass roof, while altogether failing to dampen the spirits of some good ole boys who were whooping it up in a juke joint over the way. They were still pumping out the gutters the next morning when, valise in hand and the memory of something called a Memphis Muffin Breakfast befouling the back of my throat, I stepped back inside the street door of the Robert E. Lee Senior Citizens Care & Residential Home to discover that its previous custodian had been replaced by a tall, discontented woman every bit as parched and etiolated as the line of cacti that ran along the sill behind her.

'Good morning, ma'am' – I was getting acquainted with the local argot – 'May I speak with Emmagem?'

'She ain't here right now. I believe she's givin' Mr Abernethy his blanket bath. Hay. Are you the feller that had a mind to visit with Daphne?' I nodded. The woman – Mrs Longenecker, I divined – gave an odd, expansive twitch that spread over her upper body and made her look like a giant bat that was about to take off into the ether. 'Well you can't see her. She was took bad during the night. I'd be foolin' ya if I didn't say she was like to pass any time now. You'll understand how it is.' I nodded again to show that I understood how it was. The Mississippi River was waiting to bear Daphne away, back to wherever it was she had come from. 'Anyhow' Mrs Longenecker said, with a terrible, freezing smile, taking out a square buff envelope that had been pressed beneath the covers of a book called *Tennessee Days and Tennessee Ways* and confirming with a glint of her eye that all transactions between us were at an end and that I needn't think I could ever pass this way again, 'she asked me to give ya this.'

Back at the motel, where there was no one at reception and no-one breakfasting in the breakfast room and the silence gaped and yawned, I shook the contents of the envelopes out onto the unmade bed. Here there was a black-and-white picture of the Grand Canyon on the back of which had been written in a quaint, faltering hand: *Meant to let you have this. Don't know why I didn't. Been on my conscience. Yours respectfully Daphne J. Katzenjammer*, and a second, smaller envelope bearing the insignia of the Illinois Riverboat Freight Company. Inside there were two photographs, one of the Old Man shading his eyes from the sun as he hovered on the edge of a landing stage awaiting the arrival of a canoe, the other showing a much younger version of himself standing with my mother between the two pillars that supported the frontage of the Samson and Hercules ballroom, Norwich. My mother looked demure and faintly embarrassed. The Old Man, USAF cap sat back on his head, open-collared, eyes gleaming, could have been a film star dropped out of the skies to claim her. *My dear boy*, ran the solitary letter that accompanied these items, addressed but for some reason never sent from somewhere in Montana sometime in 1968:

> *I write to you from the Little Big Horn, on the self-same Greasy Grass where Crazy Horse and Chief Gall saw off the mountebank Custer. Yonder lies the Powder River country and the Yellowstone, gun-metal grey in the autumn sun, where I have been wandering this past month and more, down among the buffalo wallows and the wolf bones, where coyotes stray and cattle graze in fields where once a sea of tepees flourished, catching the moonlight's gleam on rocks that have been there since the dawn of time. Would that you were with me, my boy, here on the edge of the bluegrass world amid the tumult of the spreading prairie, but rest assured that I send you greetings fit for the Indian chiefs who dwelt here in days of yore.*
> *Your ever-loving father*
> *Maurice Chesapeake Albuquerque Seattle Du Pont*

As the Old Man's letters went, this was fairly standard, being both rambling, inconsequential, obsessional – he had always had a thing about Custer's vanity and incompetence – and intermittently preposterous, but there was something in it that affected me in a way that the dozens of others – the ones sent from Alabama cotton plantations, from the apple orchards that he had leased in Monroe County, Washington State, from grocery stores in Kansas behind whose counters he had arbitrarily fetched up – had not. For some reason, here on the Montana hillside, hot on the trail of the Indian Wars, monstrous and inexorable, he was closer to me than he had ever been. And so for a moment I sat on the unmade bed with the letter in my hand and wept: wept for the old man, and for my mother and Daphne, whose valediction this clearly was, and for all the phantom worlds to which they summoned me back: to North Park Avenue, to Eaton Park and its stately trees, and my mother's face at the window and the Old Man's air-force cap still hanging from its hook ten years after its owner had left it there, abandoned it, and us, and everything.

It was still barely 9.30 a.m. in Memphis. Back at Resurgam they would be running the late-afternoon post through the franking machine and sending out white-label promo copies to the music papers on delivery bikes. Professional crises take no account of personal trauma. They creep up on you just the same. As I dialled the number I had one of those presentiments of doom which the past twenty years had so regularly produced. Something was going to go badly wrong. And so it proved.

'Who are you and what do you want?'

'Jesus, Steph.' When I got back to London the reception staff were going to get a crash-course in *politesse*.

'Nick. Oh my God.' There was no mistaking the tremor in Stephanie's voice. 'Listen, Nick. Something awful has happened. Well, two awful things. Do you want the bad news first or the really bad news?'

'Start with the bad news.'

'All right. Where do I start?' There was more rain slanting in against the motel window panes. 'Well, the Flame Throwers certainly won't be playing Live Aid.'

'Why not?'

'Some journalist bugged the room they were in or something when they were talking about it at Stevie's wedding. It's all over the papers.'

Despite the labour of the last three days, I could live with the Flame Throwers not gracing the stage at Philadelphia.

'OK. What's the really bad news?'

'Oh, Nick. I don't know how to tell you.'

There was a pause in which the rain continued to cascade down the emptying streets and a military jet, flying low overhead, rattled the windows. And then Stephanie told me the really bad news, which was like much of the other really bad news I had received from music business people over the past two decades, but somehow worse, more dramatic and storm-crossed, and, it would appear, requiring even more tact, sympathy and brute realism to disentangle.

Live Aid

VALPARAISO : …Jesus, isn't that Warren Beatty strollin' around out there? Stevie, how the fuck do you know Warren Beatty?

DA VINCI : No, that ain't Beatty. Never saw him in my fuckin' life before

VALPARAISO : And that writer fairy. Tom fuckin' Wolfe or whatever his name is. What the fuck's he doing here?

DA VINCI : Yeah. How come there's all these people I never seen in my fuckin' life before at my own fuckin' wedding?

BRACEGIRDLE (*wearily*) : Stevie, we talked about this. You met Warren at the L.A. Music Awards, and Tom's writing a piece for *Vanity Fair*.

DA VINCI : *Warren* and *Tom*? I mean, are you sucking these guys' dicks or something?

BRACEGIRDLE : We need a decision on this free concert.

SMOTHERS : What is this free concert? You never said nuthin' about no free concert.

VALPARAISO : Yeah. No pay, no play. That's always been our motto, right?

BRACEGIRDLE : Joey, we talked about this. This Live Aid thing.

DA VINCI : All those starvin' kids in Africa or wherever?

VALPARAISO : Oh yeah. Fuckin' Africa. What's the deal?

BRACEGIRDLE : Joey, we talked about this. There is no deal. It's a free concert. You just turn up at the John F. Kennedy Stadium in Philly and play. The concert gets shown around the world and brings in big bucks for Famine Relief.

DA VINCI : I'm hearing you, man. But, like, what's the deal?

BRACEGIRDLE : It's a free concert, Stevie. The operative word being *free*.

DA VINCI : I'm hearing you man. But you ain't telling me they expect us to do a live gig that's, like, beamed out to fuckin' hundreds of millions of people around the world, y'know to eskimos in their fuckin' igloos in Greenland or wherever, and there's no fuckin' money at all?

SMOTHERS : I'm just saying, y'know, but you ever figured how *lazy* some of those Africans are? I mean, just laying there in the fuckin' sand with the flies crawling over them and whatever, and not even brushing them off?

VALPARAISO : Yeah, there's hillbillies up in the Ozarks take care of themselves better than that.

DA VINCI : That's right. And you're lookin' at all these poor fucks, starvin' to death all over the TV and that, and you're going: "Ain't they even heard of contraception?" I mean, that way there wouldn't be so fuckin' many of them.

BRACEGIRDLE: I appreciate your concerns, gentlemen. But I've been making some calls, and the word is that people are saying it's going to be bigger than Woodstock.

DA VINCI: People got paid at Woodstock! I mean, The Who got thirty thousand dollars or whatever.

VALPARAISO: Who else is on the bill?

BRACEGIRDLE: Crosby, Stills, Nash and Young. The Beach Boys. Black Sabbath…

SMOTHERS: Sad old fucks. Why should we wanna play with some sad old fucks?

BRACEGIRDLE: …Simple Minds. Madonna.

DA VINCI: I'll play if I get to fuck Madonna. Tell them: '*Stevie Da Vinci will play if he gets to fuck Madonna.*'

VALPARAISO: No shit, motherfucker? Didn't I just see you get married back there?

DA VINCI: Are Kiss playing?

BRACEGIRDLE: Don't think I've seen them on the schedule.

DA VINCI: That's it. If it ain't good enough for Kiss, then it ain't good enough for us.

SMOTHERS: Fuckin' black kids lying in the dirt and can't even be bothered to brush the fuckin' flies out of their face. I mean.

VALPARAISO: Tell them $50,000. And we ain't playing anywhere down the bill neither. Evening slot or nuthin'.

DA VINCI: And Madonna. I definitely have to get to fuck Madonna.

National Probe (and subsequent syndication), July 1985

12. FUGUE STATE

> 'All around me the building's imploding
> All around me the floor's falling in
> All around me the world is exploding
> Waiting for a new kind of life to begin.'
> SYSTEMS OF ROMANCE – *New Kind of Life*

'These funerals aren't what they were,' Trevor Jacomb said.

'Are they not?'

'Not by...' – there were times when Trevor's grasp of figurative language deserted him – '...not by a long chalk.' He angled himself closer so that the lapels of the C&A suit he had thought appropriate for the ceremony brushed against my shoulder. 'Twenty years ago you wouldn't have got away with anything like this.'

It was all too much for Zoe. 'There's somebody actually dead here, you fucker.' She raised her head with a jerk so the light from the panels overhead gleamed off her mirrored sunglasses. 'It's not like you're compiling a top ten for *Melody Maker*.'

'I was at Brian Jones's funeral,' Trevor said solemnly, ignoring Zoe, whom he had never cared for, and concentrating on the matter in hand. 'The whole of fucking Cheltenham turned up. All the kids in the schools were let out into the playground to watch the procession go past. Some of the floral tributes were four feet high. This is just your granny being burnt up in some fucking crem.'

He paused for breath, stuck an unlit cigarette in his mouth, thought better of it and stowed it away in the top pocket of the suit. It was a week or two since I had last seen Trevor. In that time, rather like Cris Itol, he seemed to have smartened himself up. I glanced backwards down the double line of chairs. Arriving early, so early that the ushers had not yet taken control of the seating, the Resurgam team – Trevor, Zoe, Rory and myself – had come to rest three rows from the front. Some of places ahead of us were not yet occupied but behind, the room was filled to the brim. Here in Potters Bar, on a baking afternoon in mid-July, all sorts and conditions of men and women had followed the magnet's call: middle-aged relatives of the deceased in their best clothes; goth girls with pale faces in shiny black top-coats and enormous boots; industry people; music journalists by the score. To their rear, kept out of the chapel of remembrance by security guards, hordes of teenagers pressed forward against the plate-glass windows. It bore no resemblance to anybody's granny being burnt up in some fucking crem. All the same, there was something bracing about Terry's doggedness, his refusal to admit that the present had anything to offer when set against the seemlier usages of the past.

'You don't know that,' Rory said, with unexpected interest. He was wearing a black three-piece affair that looked as if it had been cut for Anthony Eden around the time of the Suez Crisis. 'The service hasn't started. They may yet surprise you.'

'What I mean is,' Trevor said, who I now realised was giving off an aniseed reek of Pernod, waving his arm in a gesture that brought the disconsolate middle-aged men, the goth girls and Tin Pan Alley's finest into a single point of focus, 'who are these people anyway?'

'For your information,' Zoe said, who knew a professional slight when she heard one, 'the guy halfway down in the cream suit is

George Michael. Tears for Fears are somewhere. Elton John sent a fucking *telegram*.'

'That's my point,' Trevor said. He shifted around uncomfortably in his seat for a moment as if what lay beneath him was a succession of sharp spikes rather than faded municipal plush and put his head in his hands. 'Jesus. You would not believe the week I've been having.'

'I went to a funeral at the Guards' Chapel once,' Rory said, 'where the chap who was supposed to be dead came in half-way through and said he'd set it all up as a joke. There was no end of a row.'

It was a week and a half since I had returned from the States. In that time a great deal had happened, some of it narrowly foreseeable, a whole lot more impossible to predict. The message telling me that Daphne was dead was on my desk the day I got back along with a copy of that week's *Sounds* with a headline that read MAGDA DIED FOR YOU. Subsequently all three Systems of Romance albums re-entered the chart; advance orders for 'Full Fathom Five' reached 200,000 and the pressing plant was put on overtime. Meanwhile, back in Flintridge, Bracegirdle Associates had stirred itself into action, issued a libel writ against the *Daily Telegraph*, and declared that whatever the waves of moral opprobrium now crashing around them, and whether invited or not, the Flame Throwers could not play Live Aid owing to the emergence of 'some highly sensitive personal issues'. Meanwhile, the boys had been installed in a residential studio in L.A. under conditions of total sequestration ('No chicks, no pills, they have to call me if they want a hamburger, this is fucking serious' – Larry) and instructed to lay down the covers album in the space of a fortnight while their manager negotiated with Mrs da Vinci ('kiss-off money') who had fled the duplex two days after their return from honeymoon and was scheming to sell her story ('she reckons Stevie hit her and stuff, but the way I see it she's more likely to have whaled on him') to the *National Enquirer*. Rory's opinion was that it would all blow over. I wasn't so sure. Alice, not seen for a week, had disappeared somewhere.

'I wonder how long all this will go on for,' Rory said.

'What do you know?' Zoe countered, all vestige of the deference she usually paid to Rory forgotten, 'We're keeping His Lordship waiting.'

The Resurgam employees had reacted to this tragedy in different ways. Zoe, who had what she called 'sisterly feelings' for Magda, had visited her in hospital and was supposed to be looking after her, was deeply upset. Trevor seemed to have interpreted it as simply another symptom of the all-purpose existential horror that was just now blighting his life. Rory's customary even-handedness had declared itself in plans for a compilation album and a Channel Four documentary. Both of these, it had to be said, would do terrific business. And what had I felt? I had liked Magda, liked her songs, wanted to indulge her fancies, while suspecting that she was so wrapped up in the mythology of the life she led that there was no hope of saving her. People like Magda would always die and there was nothing you could do to stop them. It was as simple, or as complicated, as that.

The clock on the crematorium's lemon-coloured wall had reached twenty-five past three. It would be another five minutes before they brought in the coffin. Zoe had slipped a pin from her complicated hair-do and was rolling it furiously between her fingers, as if only the sanctity of the room in which she sat prevented her from jabbing it between the buttons of Rory's double-breasted Anthony Eden waistcoat.

'Tell me what exactly happened, Zoe. I've only read about it in the papers.'

'That's rilly kind of you, Nick,' Zoe said, sounding less like a record company PR and more like a stricken girl from the Bronx whose life has been irreparably ruined. She put the pin back in her hair: Rory was safe for the moment. 'Between you and me they should never have let that guy in from the NME. I mean, talking to her in the hospital day room like that. And then not editing it or nothing. All that stuff about her dreams. It was like she wanted to tell people she was fuckin' insane,' Zoe said fiercely. 'Just some mad chick they were trying to keep out of sight. But the weird thing was that when they let her out, which they never should have done, she was perfectly OK. Well, not perfectly OK, but, y'know, *functioning*. I mean, she phoned me up from her parents and she practically invited me round to play house. I'll never forget it. Never forget I didn't go, I mean. And then what happens? Her mom and dad go out to fetch the groceries, her brother's got the stereo on and don't hear nothing. She tries calling me, only I'm in a meeting with Finn Family Moomintroll and she goes and hangs herself off the bannisters.'

'How's Jon taking it?'

'He's around here someplace. With that Sophie. The fucker.' Zoe unfastened the lip of her expensive, many-zippered handbag and, holding it up to her pink and curiously jasmine-scented face, began to sob into it. It was always the same with these tough American girls. Angie, who had once punched out a feminist protestor at a Helium Kids tour launch, had wept over her cats. The GTOs, Miss Mercy, Miss Foxy and Miss Clytemnestra, had snivelled at the TV soaps. Sentiment always caught up with them in the end.

'Oh Nick, oh Nick, oh Nick,' Zoe cried inconsolably. On cue, as if celebrant, pall-bearers and congregation had all been waiting for exactly this outpouring of emotion to convince them that the job was worth doing, the funeral kicked into gear. Magda's coffin, borne hesitantly down the aisle and laid cross-ways on its trestles, seemed a paltry thing, mocking the enormity of what had happened to the person inside it. The reading was from Corinthians, faith, hope and love abiding and the greatest of these being love. Had love abided for Magda? The jury was out on that one. I remembered Florian's funeral in the church at Ealing, poor seahorse-faced Florian, that rapt devotee of leapers, bombers, downers, uppers, much else besides, who had drowned in his swimming pool at the height of the Summer of Love, with the Beautiful People swarming like butterflies across the graves and the lines of expensive cars running down the hill, and Ainslie Duncan, who had ended up as a Butlin's Redcoat, pretending that Paul McCartney had sent a telegram. A hymn. A morbid lyric or two from one of Magda's adolescent scrapbooks. 'New Kind of Life' played too loud through the P.A., so that some of the older mourners put their fingers in their ears. Another hymn, as from behind the plate-glass window the mob of teenagers bayed in anguish. 'Guide Me O Thou Great Jehovah', to which Rory alone knew the words, but declined to sing above a whisper, while Zoe, who did not, did her best and Trevor looked wonderingly about him as if this was some exotic new entertainment that had never previously come his way. Trevor was right, I thought. Nothing in the present would ever come up to the exacting standards of the past. Meanwhile, it looked as if Magda's passing would bring in something north of £100,000. In the circumstances, this was worth having. As ever on these occasions, it was difficult to keep cynicism at bay. It was part of the process, like Zoe's tear-concealing sunglasses or Trevor's monkey suit.

Outside, gangs of mourners scurried this way and that over the concrete, dazzled by the sunshine. 'Just fuck off and show some respect,' Trevor could be heard instructing a boy in a Smiths tee-shirt who was trying to hand him a demo-tape. Eventually the crowds parted and we came out into a tree-lined avenue where numberless bunches of flowers lay in sheaves on the verge and a man in a straw hat was encouraging a flock of doves to make their way out of a picnic basket. But the doves had no inkling of what was expected of them. Instead of taking off into the cloudless sky above the tree canopy, they hung around on the asphalt, pecked at each other's feathers and started rooting insects out of the grass.

'Fucking shambles,' Trevor Jacomb said disgustedly. He prodded the rear end of one of the doves with his toe, but failed to shift it. Then something else struck him. 'Bloody weird, wasn't it, about Maximum Acceleration?'

'Bloody weird is about right.'

'You just turned up at the studio and there was nothing doing?'

'Nothing at all.'

Trevor shook his head. Of all the blows that had fallen on Resurgam Records in the past ten days – Magda's death, the enforced retirement from public life of the Flame Throwers – my visit to the studio in which Maximum Accleration had supposedly been recording for the last three years to discover only the unassembled parts of a 1977 Roland drum machine, a broken Minimoog synthesizer and a quarter-inch cassette tape with a couple of minutes' worth of what might have been dolphin noises sounding from the deep, had clearly hit him the hardest.

'Doug reckoned the recording costs were over fifty grand. You reckon we'll ever get any of it back?'

'I've cancelled their contract. But we'll probably do a greatest hits in the autumn. We'll see some of it.' As with the Flame Throwers, currently under lockdown somewhere in West L.A., I wasn't so sure.

The doves had all made their way into the boughs of the trees. The man with the straw hat had given up and disappeared. Rory wandered slowly out of the throng, hands in his pockets, and came to rest between us.

'Do you think there's going to be a do?' Trevor enquired, with his usual hang-dog obsequiousness.

'I shouldn't think so.'

'I'm off home then,' Trevor volunteered. He looked as if he might be about to say something else, thought better of it and then slunk off down the path.

'At least that fat klutz put on a suit on,' Rory said, well before Trevor was out of earshot. 'I shall make something of him yet. Although Jeremy Lascelles said they had a meeting last week and he was practically sick into the wastepaper basket.' The funeral, with its sudden divergence from established norms, had unsettled him. Now he was back in command. 'Didn't you come by cab? Why don't I give you a lift home?' He made the lift sound horribly conditional, as if endless obstacles would have to be negotiated before anyone took to the road. Through the dense avenues of trees, like a pair of elves out in Lothlorien, we strolled back to the crematorium car-park to find the funeral was in its death-throes. The hearse could be seen chugging off along the approach road, and a photographer from one of the nationals was stowing a Rolleiflex into the pannier of his motorbike. Here in the front seat of Rory's Range Rover, everything seemed suddenly particularised: the dust-motes hanging in the air; the Ascot Royal Enclosure parking ticket still gleaming from the windscreen; the reek of the hair lotion from Trumper's in Curzon Street that Rory still smarmed over his dwindling locks. Like the actors in a drawing-room comedy, all of them were simultaneously crying out for attention.

'Resurgam Records,' Rory said as we surged out of the crematorium gates into downtown Potters Bar, past the estate agencies and the fast-food joints. He drove the Range Rover with an impossible finesse, fingers of one hand pressed lightly on the wheel, so that the oncoming traffic seemed to melt away at his approach. 'Resurgam Records. How much would it cost me to buy you out of it?'

So this was what Rory had been up to. 'You can't buy me out of anything, Rory. Not if I don't want to sell it.'

'Fair enough,' Rory said. There was a set of traffic lights fifty yards away that hastily turned green at his approach.

'Two hundred thousand? Three hundred thousand? Would that do it?'

'What's all this about, Rory?'

'It's not about anything,' Rory said, bearing down on a Ford Escort and expertly cutting it up. 'I mean, here we are running an independent record label with a turnover of £4 million a year. Huge opportunities for people like us, what with all this...*disintermediation*. All it needs is a little investment.' We were alongside a set of school gates now, with a lollipop lady edging determinedly into the road, but Rory sailed by regardless. 'Separate the wheat from the chaff. Distinguish the promising candidates from the no-hopers. Which is not, frankly, Nick, something you ever seem to want to do. Finn Family Moomintroll going in at Number 35. That's a major triumph as far as you're concerned.'

'I like Finn Family Moomintroll. They remind me of the Small Faces.'

'Of course they do. And they go in at Number 35 and fall out of the charts in a fortnight, and *nobody* buys the twelve-inch single so we lose any profit we might have made. Who cares whether anyone sounds like the Small Faces? What about four hundred thousand?'

We were passing through debased Hertfordshire suburbs now. Rory stared at the red-brick, three-bedroom newbuilds, the Toby carveries with their timber fronts and the half-shuttered newsagents as if they represented everything he most hated in the world and yearned bitterly to destroy.

'You haven't got four hundred thousand pounds, Rory. You probably haven't even got forty.'

'Point taken... *Whoosh*!' Rory always said 'Whoosh!' when he put his foot on the accelerator. 'But what I do have' – he put both hands firmly on the wheel now – 'is a couple of gentlemen's agreements.'

'Gentlemen's agreements with whom exactly? I don't recall gentlemen's agreements counting for much in this business. In fact, I seem to remember you saying that one of the problems with this business was that there weren't enough gentlemen in it.'

Rory let this pass. 'It may have escaped your notice, but the contracts for our two major recording artists – I refer to the Flame Throwers and Systems of Romance – having expired on the release of their last records, are currently up for renegotiation.'

'The reason I trekked out to Malibu was to get the next Flame Throwers album.'

'Precisely. And a very good job you made of it. A1. Bracegirdle told me he was absolutely delighted with the care you had lavished on a performer who was – how did he put it in that homely way of his? – in a somewhat fragile and delicate state. It's a racing certainty the deal will be renewed. But the signature on the contract will be mine, not yours.'

'You can't do that.'

'I've done it. The other week when you were sunning yourself by the sea with born-again Cris, or whatever he is, I paid a visit to Flintridge CA. Played some poker. Ate some crawdad, which I believe is a kind of crayfish, and agreed with Mr Bracegirdle, and Morty and Zak and Duane and whatever other hayseeds he has hanging round the place that henceforth I should be taking control of operations. I may say that on my return to England I concluded a similar arrangement with the management of Systems of Romance.'

'Do they even exist anymore? Now that Magda's dead?'

'Well, the rest of them seem to think they do. In fact, they thought they might be back in the studio at the end of the summer.'

Outer London was passing slowly by: broadways; clustered shopfronts; evangelical churches with outsize crosses; stucco houses with wheel-less cars jacked up in their driveways. Here in the late-afternoon rush hour, the traffic was concertinaing. Not even Rory could forge a path.

'You mustn't think it's personal, Nick. If it was personal I should be doing you a lot more damage than this. *Lots more.* I've enjoyed working with you these past few years. But there comes a time, there comes a time when a man has to…seize his opportunities.'

'What if I say no?'

'Be my guest. It will cost you a lot of money and legally you haven't a leg to stand on. Much better to let my investors buy you out and gracefully depart into a well-earned retirement. If it comes to that, you can take some of the bands with you. Exploding Bagpuss and

Johnny Tambourine, say. I don't think Resurgam's going to miss them very much.'

'Who are your investors?'

'I couldn't possibly tell you at this stage.'

'Is one of them Larry Bracegirdle?'

'Did you know' Rory said, with real, unfeigned interest, forging on into the late-afternoon sun, 'that he's one of the Lafayette Bracegirdles? Real Kentucky royalty, I gather.'

Every so often in the past quarter-century I had found myself engaged on trials of strength where I wasn't up to my opponent's fighting weight. Sometimes these adversaries had been straightforward hooligans, hierarchy enforcers, moral trash, but mostly they were people like this. The smart boys from Pembroke College, Oxford. Alice on the day I had abandoned her in an expensive restaurant without paying the bill, only to realise that the real humiliation was mine. And now here came Rory with his Range Rover, his investors and his hotline to Kentucky royalty. There was nothing you could do in the face of the *Übermensch*. Resistance was futile.

'How's Alice?' Rory demanded as he sat me down outside the office in Ladbroke Grove.

'I'm about to find out.'

'Pleasures unforeseen,' Rory said, with surprising sincerity. 'The best kind.'

The office was locked up and deserted. Sunlight, spilling down onto the tumbled surfaces of white paint, made it look like a giant wedding cake. Inside the air was unexpectedly cool but overlaid with the scent of cannabis resin. People were wont to relax a bit on Friday afternoons. On my desk lay an intemperate letter from one of Richard Branson's factotums about unauthorised use of the Virgin Mobile, several dozen phone messages and a demo-tape by a band called the Electric Tarantulas, whom Doug – whose grip, it had to be said, was on the slide – reckoned were going to be the next Duran Duran. After several false starts, I ran Alice to earth in Kensington.

'How are you?'

'Absolutely foul. Both the children have got chickenpox. How was your funeral?'

I explained about Rory and the car-ride home. 'I always told you he was like that,' Alice said, without a great deal of interest. 'Will there be much money?'

'I shouldn't wonder. That's if I want to accept it.'

'Well I shouldn't take it to law. If I know Rory the whole thing will be cut and dried.' It was difficult to know quite how much Alice was taking in. 'Shall I see you tonight?'

'I thought you said the children had chicken-pox?'

'I'm going to dose them up with Calpol. In any case my cousin Henrietta's staying. She can babysit. We'll have dinner.'

There was one more phone call to make. The Jacombs had recently removed from Petts Wood to more substantial premises in Muswell Hill. Trevor would probably be home by now. And so it proved.

'I take it you know all about Rory's little scheme?'

'Oh yeah. About that,' Trevor said. He sounded hopelessly out of sorts.

'What's your opinion on it?'

'Jesus, Nick. What do you want me to say? He's taking over the firm and he's got the dosh…the money. Either I go with him or I'm out in the street. What would you do?'

'What's he offered you, Trev?'

'Deputy managing director,' Trevor said, with a certain shame-faced pride.

'Three weeks ago he told me he wanted to have you fired for being lazy and incompetent and generally useless and I talked him out of it. How do you feel about that?'

'I don't feel anything about it,' Trevor said, with what, in the circumstances, was surprising vigour. 'It's all right for you, Nick. It's your firm. *Was* your firm, I mean. I'm sorry and all that, but you've got a load of money and you can fuck off out of it and do what you like. Me, I've got a hundred and fifty grand mortgage and the missus nagging me about the kids going to private schools.'

'What about loyalty?'

'Oh yeah, *loyalty*,' Trevor said and left it at that.

I put down the phone. It was about half-past six now. Occasionally telephones rang elsewhere in the building. I wandered back down to reception and stared at its paraphernalia. The wicker basket of unsolicited tapes on the carpet by the potted plants was three-quarters full and several of the posters on the wall advertised bands whose contracts had been cancelled. Each would have to be dealt with. But the afternoon had one more surprise in store. As I came up to the front door somebody rapped feebly on the knocker and there was a faint scuffling noise, as if some timid animal was trying to get away into the undergrowth before the trouble started. Turning the key in the lock, I came face to face with a couple of pale eye-balls magnified into enormous size by the spectacles behind which they flickered and a shock of flyaway blond hair. After a bit, recognition dawned.

'What can I do for you, Cedric?'

'Oh, hello, Nick.' Cedric showed no surprise at all. It seemed perfectly logical to him that, showing up after hours at the offices of a record company who had stopped returning his phone calls two years before, he should have the door opened to him by the managing director. He put down the guitar case he was carrying and straightened his shoulders. 'I expect you've been wondering what I've been up to all this time.'

'Actually I have been wondering. What have you been up to? Why don't you come in?'

Safely inside the vestibule, Cedric put the guitar case to one side, began to brush the dust off the knees of his faded corduroy trousers and looked inquisitively around him. 'I'm so glad there was somebody here,' he said. 'You see, I had to walk all the way from Battersea and I got rather behind-hand. I don't suppose I could have a glass of water?'

I got him a bottle out of the fridge behind the reception desk. It was three years since Resurgam had released one of Cedric's singles. It had sold 274 copies. Shortly after this his manager had gone off to run a mushroom farm in Wales.

Shy, spindly, a small patch of white in the surrounding chiarascuro, Cedric had always needed jollying along.

'Have you been writing any new stuff, Cedric?'

'Actually Nick, I have. In fact, I wrote a new song just this morning. Shall I play it to you?'

'Be my guest.'

And so Cedric played his new song, which was called 'My Dog Growler', had a jaunty, sea shanty-ish chorus and a fast, finger-picked middle eight and would have been considered unviable by any record company in Western Europe. Afterwards, as he put his guitar back in its case, he said:

'Did you like that, Nick?'

'Very much.'

'You've always been very kind to me, Nick' Cedric said, almost tearfully. All this – the walk up from Battersea, the playing of 'My Dog Growler' – had clearly been a tremendous effort. 'You've always been very kind to me and I appreciate it.'

After he had gone I put the cassette tape he had given me in the wicker basket and then went back to my office. The letter from Richard Branson's understrapper was still lying on the desk. After a moment or two's thought I took out a sheet of headed stationery and wrote:

Dear Sir,
In response to your letter to my associate, Mr Du Pont, could I suggest that you go and fuck yourself?
Yours sincerely
Rory Bayliss-Callingham

As Stefano had said back in the days when we laboured in the tiny office on Tenth Street, winding up the affairs of the Helium Kids and awaiting the summons back to London, always best to go out on a high.

Diary July-August 1985

11 July
Tedious morning at Lincoln's Inn. Rory's lawyer is called Gervase Twistleton-Barnett. Scrupulously polite, while giving the impression that I am acting in a slightly ungentlemanly way by making such a fuss and that his own client is behaving impeccably. Mantelpiece of his chambers lined with cricket-club fixture cards. Elderly factotums bring in tea. Beyond the window secretaries with bubble-perms sprawl on the grass eating ice-creams in the sun. An hour or so into our chat, a faint gleam of recognition dawns. 'Weren't you at Pembroke?' After that we get on better. On the other hand, I still think he's an upper-class idiot. We break off shortly before lunch, mostly I think so that Gervase can catch the afternoon session at Lord's. Curious sensation of everything filling up with water, giant fish swimming around the pathways of Lincoln's Inn, tide rolling in to bear all of us – me and Gervase and the bubble-permed secretaries – away.

13 July
Live Aid. Offered a ticket, but declined, now that there are no Resurgam acts on the bill. Watch the Wembley show on the TV set at

Elm, on my own (Alice is at her mother's). Bright sunshine. Charles and Diana in the VIP box. Status Quo. The Style Council. U2. Queen. The Who. Freddie enjoying himself no end. Press comment almost universally favourable, but occasional complaints that scarcely an African face has ended up anywhere near the stage. Pass on most of the Philadelphia show. Geldof reported to have said that 'we're not missing cunts like the Flame Throwers.' Latest news from L.A. is that, contrary to expectations, and under the exacting supervision of Bob Ezrin, the boys have recorded half-a-dozen numbers by the Clash, Buzzcocks and the Damned, with more to follow, and that Larry is 'very excited.'

15 July

More legal sit-downs. Simon, my own lawyer, quietly confident. Alice, having had the case properly explained to her, is now taking a close interest. Nothing is said, but I can see that Rory has gone up in her estimation by embarking on it, that the piratical, double-dealing side of his nature is something that appeals to her. 'He was exactly like that when he was at Scrimgeours.' 'Exactly like what?' 'Taking risks and that sort of thing.' 'What sort of risks?' 'Well, I think he invested a lot of clients' money in a company that made cluster bombs or something. There was rather a row.' Alice likes these genteel euphemisms. Here we are again, in the midst of another little local difficulty.

16 July

Gervase has gone unexpectedly quiet. Barry thinks he may have uncovered behaviour so heinous that Rory's case has stalled. Meanwhile, the news from West L.A. is that Stevie somehow managed to effect a small-hours breakout from the studio compound but took so much mescalin in the three hour furlough before Bracegirdle's goons dragged him back that a session player had to be shipped in for the remaining tracks.

Reaching the end-time with Alice. How do I know this? Repeated use of the first person singular rather than the first-person plural. Frequent mention of future plans that clearly don't include me, but also an outbreak of solicitousness, deference to my opinions, fussing over me that is more or less unprecedented. No more talk of the house in Italy. Find myself – this, too, is characteristic of end-time – marking down all the things I like about her: pushing strands of dark hair off her face as she frowns over a newspaper; prising the lid of the pot of breakfast tea as it steeps to savour the scent within; retailing the news of old friends beyond the Trent ('Gus has been made Deputy Lord Lieutenant…The Pembertons have had to sell their moor.') You would not think that there are still people like Alice and Gus and the Pembertons here in the England of Mrs Thatcher and Princess Di and Freddie Mercury, but still they endure, like barnacled Old Believers, hunkered down before their grim hearths, rosaries to hand, as outside the Protestant mobs go stamping down the street.

25 July

The Flame Throwers' album, provisionally entitled *Rip-off Joint*, is apparently in the can, and, according to Ezrin, fawningly interviewed by *L.A. Music Scene*, 'a motherfucker.' Emboldened by this news, I instruct Barry to send a fax to Bracegirdle Associates demanding – as is contractually my right – a copy of the master-tapes. This provokes a cross letter from Gervase but also an immensely courteous telephone call from Larry Bracegirdle deeply regretting the inconvenience caused and stirring a suspicion that he fears he may have backed the wrong horse.

With time on my hands – Simon has advised me to keep away from Ladbroke Grove – I go on leisurely day-trips. I drive over to Oxford and inspect the college lawns, shiny in the high-summer glare. I spend time at Elm, where the cornfields bake in the sun and the only sound is the pop of the bird-scarers exploding in the distance and the faraway hum of agricultural machinery. At night the owls swoop over the empty lawns, the Mickleburghs sleep soundly in their graves and Alice's ghost wanders through the corridors, haunts the shadowy stair-wells and stands over me in the kitchen while I eat.

27 July

Letter from a firm of Memphis attorneys in a long blue airmail envelope to say that in view of the long association prevailing between our two families, Daphne has decided to leave me all her worldly goods. These amount to $2,153 in a savings account at the First Bank of Tennessee, a suitcase full of old newspapers discovered in a storeroom at the Robert E. Lee after her death and the contents of a lock-up garage in Harford, Connecticut, items unspecified. I tell them to send the cheque and dispose of anything else as they see fit.

29 July

According to Simon, Gervase has gone off on a fortnight's cricket tour ('He plays for the Captain Scott. They're quite famous.') The case is unlikely to be settled before the autumn. Sales of Systems of Romance records in the past month standing at nearly 300,000.

Telephone call from Michelle Jacomb. 'I don't know what Trevor said to you, Nick. I don't know what's going on at the office. He's never known which side his bread's buttered. He won't get anywhere with that Rory, will he? I'm sure you did your best for him.' All of this I meekly concede.

30 July

Alice at Elm. With her scarf tied over her head, dark glasses and a kind of peacock wrap round her shoulders, she looks a little like Princess Margaret inspecting the banana groves on Mustique. It turns out that Alice has met the Queen's sister ('Frightful woman. Couldn't tell you what trouble she's caused.') Having strolled companionably around the lea of the cornfields, we drive to Wisbech and have lunch at what is reputed to be the only tolerable restaurant for thirty miles. Further evidence that we are in end-time comes in Alice's disinclination to follow HRH's example and cause trouble. In this conciliating spirit she drinks two glasses of lukewarm Chablis and swallows several oysters that even I can tell are not what they should be. The old Alice wouldn't have stood it. 'It's been a very nice bohemian time' she says as we head back to Elm with the dust rising in little jets and eddies over the bonnet of the car and the rooks circling over the beet fields. It takes me a moment or two to realise that this is not a comment on the day that has passed but a summary of our relationship.

7 August

A large packing case wound about with rubber straps arrives from Memphis. Daphne's attorneys have misread my instructions. Inside it are six or seven stuffed animals, including a raccoon and a possum, the multi-volume *History of the Prairie States* that I remember from the apartment on Staten Island, two baseball bats, a dense pamphlet entitled *Navigating the Mississippi River* and several artists' pads filled with sketches of rural scenery signed *MACS Du P.* On this evidence the Old Man liked drawing corn mills, dilapidated landing-stages and lobster creels. On the other hand, I can see him examining them: leaning on a fencepost, say, with the sketching pad balanced on the wire as the long Louisiana twilight lengthens into dusk, lifting his face from the wagon as it lurches downhill through the summer violets into the dried-up bottoms of some rain-starved mid-western creek.

10 August

Alice away on holiday with the children. At Elm the leaves are already turning and no amount of water will keep the lawns green. Letter from Branson asking if I want to discuss 'the situation.' Simon advises not, on the grounds that it might be 'counterproductive.'

Memories of the last seven years: the drift of mail under the door of the office on Tenth Street; the thump of the surf on the beach at Malibu; Mrs Thatcher gliding by; the Newman Street rooftops in the winter light; Hefner; Nancy Reagan; Magda weeping in her hut; the Flame Throwers playing the tiny club in NYC; Earle Pankey, one eye on the limousine, the other on thrice-cursed Stevie D, screaming at me to get this piece of shit off his drive.

* * *

And afterwards? What happened then?

Rory turned out to have overplayed his hand. He had presumed to acquire rights which he could not legally possess. Gervase, too, had failed him. Some fatal seed of misapprehension had been sown in the sun-lined chambers at Lincoln's Inn, down amongst the cricket club fixture cards and the china tea-cups. In the end I emerged from a six-month-long war of legal attrition with the Resurgam name, £250,000 and a dozen or so of the acts that Rory reckoned played out for commercial purposes. Rory escaped with the Flame Throwers and their back-catalogue, Systems of Romance and theirs, and a rockabilly band from the Nottingham council estates called the Bucking Broncos who promptly imploded, having accepted (and spent) a generous publishing advance that could not now be recouped. Worse, there was a suspicion that the rights Rory had acquired were scarcely worth the owning. *Rip-off Joint* did good business for a month or so, only to be withdrawn from sale after a licensing dispute. Systems of Romance, bereft of their animating spirit, never made another record, although a compilation album entered the charts sometime in 1987 and Magda's wry, elfin face could still be seen on tee-shirts well into the next millennium.

Having made one more album, *Excess All Areas* ('A total disaster' – *New Musical Express*), its release date coinciding with an exorbitant IRS demand for back taxes and most of its content augmented by session men, the Flame Throwers staggered on until the end of the decade. By this stage they were a group in all but name, forever being touted for live shows that never took place and recording sessions that were never completed. Nadir was reached in 1989 when the band pulled out of a support slot on a Neil Young tour of Canada 24 hours before the opening date and compounded the insult by sending a telegram insisting that this was 'a positive act', or as Itol put it 'We don't play with fuckin' old men.' They were sued for $4 million, lost and were immediately declared bankrupt. All four members subsequently embarked on solo careers with varying degrees of consistency and success. Cris, who emerged from their twilight years with the reputation of being the least unreliable, assembled a backing band called The Vagabond Lovers, whose somewhat chaotic debut, *Troubadour Swamp*, reached #13 on the Billboard chart in 1991. Joey, by his own admission, 'went hardcore', and recorded an album entitled *Metal Destroyer* (#159.) The most unexpected of these vagrant trajectories was that pursued by Art Smothers, who, after one or two desultory appearances on other people's records, began a career as an avant-garde artist – variously described as a 'neo-primitive' or an abstract expressionist – was awarded a Gulbenkian Fellowship and in 1996 sold a picture entitled 'Crow/Entrails/Roadkill' at the Gagosian Gallery for $340,000. Periodic rumours of a reunion concert or studio reassembly were brought to an end by Stevie's death, in a motel room in Florida, some hours after playing a bar show attended by 23 people.

Of the three autobiographies written by surviving members of the band, the best is probably Joey's *Dance This Mess Around*, an unpunctuated stream-of-consciousness memoir of a failed two-week attempt to cut an album at the Record Plant in the summer of 1989. There were also several books written about them, notably *I Took a Little Poison: On the Road with the Flame Throwers*, a scabrous account of one of their early Eighties tours written by a journalist on *Rolling Stone*, of which *Sounds* remarked that 'this can't possibly be true – can it?' and a scandalised Itol protested 'It didn't happen that way. The guy is just making it up,' and *Burnin' On 1980–1988*, an oral history compiled from music press interviews from the years in question. Among various re-packagings of their back catalogue, *Greatest Greatest Hits* reached #7 in the U.S. and Number 3 in the U.K. in the summer of 1989, but the undisputed highlight is *Live From the Killing Floor*, a scuffed-up lo-fi recording, probably made with a hand-held cassette recorder, of one of their legendary CBGBs gigs.

And what about me? For a year or so I hung in there, reassembled some of the staff who hadn't gone with Rory, relocated the office back to central London on grounds of convenience, sold the house at Elm, and together with Zoe and Doug – two among several colleagues unimpressed by Rory's blandishments – set about galvanising the A&R department. We signed Pop Scene, My Favourite Sock and the Technotronics, all of whom saw some kind of chart action, but the music was changing again: the pallid indie boys with their jangling guitars who had never got over their first sighting of the Smiths were on the way out and the clubs were full of dance music and rabbity black kids improvising over the thump of beat boxes. So, too, were the attitudes that sustained them. In the Sixties people had complained about the hysterical girls who wet themselves at Rolling Stones concerts. In the Seventies they had complained about the eye make-up worn by the glam rock troubadours. Now they complained about intractability. All this was brought home to me by a conversation I had with a *convive* called Cyril Hennis, known to me since those far-off days when he had commanded the Helium Kids' lighting rig on American tours, now found managing a hapless band of teenage girls called the Flopsy Bunnies. 'The trouble with all these kids,' Cyril maintained, as I handed back a demo-tape I had stopped attending to halfway through the second track, and acknowledging by the manner in which he stowed it in the pocket of his overcoat the disdain in which he held it, 'is that you can't manage them anymore.' 'No?' 'I mean, nobody used to mind them having a puff of the old Mary-Johanna and such. These days it's more likely to be fucking sheep tranquiliser. And then they won't listen to what you tell them. You can stick them in a studio with some hot-shit producer on a hundred quid an hour and they'll come in late or tell him to fuck off...How did you do with that Cosmic Alligator single?' 'Annie Nightingale played it a couple of times.' 'I'm too old for this game,' Cyril said, who I remembered sharing a spliff with Keith Richards backstage at some mid-western amphitheatre back in 1971 and looking, as the cigarette passed into his hand, as if no greater share of human bliss could ever have been allowed him.

1985. 1986. Video shoots on Hampstead Heath. Smoke-drenched afternoons in the office at Langley Street nervously awaiting the chart returns; late-night trips to Dingwalls in Camden Town in search of non-existent new talent; early mornings in Powis Square listening to the hum of the building traffic; and throughout it all the sneaking suspicion of a world knocked irrevocably out of kilter. The last rites of my career in music were played out on the day in November 1986 when I took the train up north to file a progress report on our dealings with a band called the Skanks. The Skanks were exactly the kind of group that people were going on about in 1986: four lairy hooligans from the terrifying Mancunian suburb of Burnage with names like Wayne and Termite who, when they weren't drawing the dole or getting arrested, played a kind of awkward but danceable rock and roll which the music papers were immensely keen on. Doug had had the bright idea of pairing them up with a celebrated local producer called Marlon Rushkoff, and it was to the latter's studio, somewhere in Salford, on a grey afternoon with sleet falling across the towpath of the Manchester Ship Canal, that I gingerly repaired.

The studio door was half-open. Inside it, Marlon lay fast asleep on a sofa with his head cradled in his hands. An engineer, bent over the mixing desk, was sticking bits of tape together with the aid of a pair of tweezers. 'What's the matter with Marlon?' I wondered. The engineer sadly shook his head. 'I don't know, He's been like that for a couple of hours.' 'Aye,' one of the Shanks observed, woozily emerging from a side-door. 'Y'know it's top fooking draw when y'producer goes to sleep on y'. 'Where's Gazza?' I asked, discerning that the number of other Shanks on the far side of the Perspex divide only amounted to two. 'Search me, pal. Probably gone out f'some KFC.' Even I knew the meaning of this reality-softener. The Shanks' manager, a peanut-butter-complexioned 19 year-old in a puffa jacket and a beanie hat who slouched into the studio a moment later, was promptly informed that the band's contract was being cancelled forthwith and the cheque for £3,000 I had brought with me from London was torn up on the spot. Two weeks later I sold the company, its back catalogue and the lease on Langley Street to Virgin for just under £2 million. Two weeks after that I left London with the aim, like the man in the Velvet Underground song, of going to sleep for a thousand years.

But the trouble with going to sleep is that, however soft the pillows, however peaceful your slumber and however comforting your dreams, in the end you wake up.

'Good but not Great' – The Daze of Cris Itol

It becomes apparent from the moment that Pixie-Boo, the record company PR lady (at least I think this is her name) and I set out to traverse the fifty or so yards of luxuriant carpeting that is the fifth floor of New York's Plaza Hotel that something is seriously amiss. Item one in this catalogue of disquiet is the substantial number of hotel staff who seem to be in flight from its further end (a Puerto Rican domestic trundling a janitor's wagon might be taking part in the Wacky Races, such is her anxiety to escape the scene of the crime.) Item two is the extraordinary figure lurking sepulchrally in the doorway of Room 503. Now, if I had to reckon up what separates this apparition from the ordinary throng of humanity at large on this bright Big Apple morning in the fall of 1988, I'd say that it's: a) the hair, which as well as practically exploding out of its owner's scalp like some kind of psychedelic furze bush is, additionally, dyed two parts bright blue to one part lamp-black; b) a facial pallor approximating to a sheet of antique vellum that the author of the *Finnsburgh Fragment* might possibly have scrawled on a millennium or so ago; and c) the fact that, sprung from whatever subterranean vault it's been inhabiting for the past hundred years or two, the figure clearly has difficulty in standing up straight. All this, naturally, makes for a certain amount of anticipatory tension, to which even Pixie-Boo – a case-hardened veteran of two REO Speedwagon tours, she has hastened to assure me – is not immune. 'I don't know,' she murmurs doubtfully as we approach, clipboard held high before her like some protective amulet. 'I heard yesterday he was kind of OK. But...' Then, as we get near enough to appraise the outfit that this otherworldly visitant has thought suitable for his day out from the tomb (black frock-coat, combat trousers, snakeskin bootees) two things happen. One is that the figure, disdaining the support of the door-frame that has been keeping him vertical for the past minute and a half, staggers out into the corridor to greet us. The other is that, with blank incomprehension finally replaced with a few fleeting memories of our man in happier days, recognition dawns.

'Cris? Cris...Cris *Itol*?'

And here the figure lets out a kind of croak, a dry, dusty cackle, like a key turning in the rust-hardened lock of some underground prison cell, or dead leaves chafing the forest floor as a foot lands squarely on top of them. 'Yeah.' There is a pause. 'Good to see you, man.'

* * *

It is, I hope and trust, a radically below par Cris Itol who receives me at the vestibule of his Plaza suite. I mean, if he's *always* like this, then just exactly how did the album we're here to ponder get made? Curiously, the room our man inhabits, which in former times might have harboured half-a-dozen long-limbed honeys and heaven knows what top-of-the-range pharmacological provender, is wholly unremarkable, with just an advance copy of this month's *Playboy* and a flagon of sparkling water to confirm that human life exists within its high-end décor. First things first.

'How the devil are you?'

Itol looks puzzled. The thought that anyone might be sufficiently interested in his health to ask him how he is clearly hasn't occurred to him.

'I'm good, y'know...I mean, not great. But, well, y'know, *good*.'

And what about the band? How are they right now?

'They're good. I mean...we don't hang out so much these days y'know, but they're *good*.'

This all-round salubrity is heart-warming. 'But what about Joey? [*Joey Valparaiso, Flame Throwers' guitarist, news of whose exploits has been setting the tabloids aflame for the past three months.*] I mean, the papers have been having a field day, surely?'

Pixie-Boo is nervously massaging the clip-board now, but Cris, as if suddenly reminded of his corporate responsibilities, waves her away.

'No, Joey's good. I mean, sure, him and his old lady have been having some problems. I mean, it's like "Why the fuck's sake you want to get married, dude?" But last I heard he was really getting it more together than he has in, uh, a while.'

'And how's Stevie?'

'Uh, well, *Stevie*.' Even Cris's composure is momentarily ruffled by the thought of the Flame Throwers' orthodontically-challenged bass player, last heard of breaking his pelvis while falling off an on-stage monitor. 'I mean, Stevie's so "out there" there'll be times when it's like "we're not even relating to you, man. I mean, you're not pulling that kind of shit *here*." But no, Stevie's...OK.'

'And what about all these new kids on the block the music papers are so keen on. I mean, what do you think of Guns N' Roses?'

There is another long pause, during which Itol stares hopelessly at the Marlboro Light he is smoking, at the flagon of sparkling water and the distinctively chevron-patterned shagpile keeping up his snakeskin bootees, while Pixie-Boo reminds him that they met at the MTV Awards.

'Uh...yeah. G N' R. That Slush' [*he means Slash, Guns N' Roses' corkscrew-curled, top-hat toting guitarist*] is a cool guy. Now and again, if I'm in L.A, I kind of hang out with Slush. But that Axl is just fucking crazy...I mean, we asked him to do backing vocals on 'Vampire Lover' [*single from the forthcoming album*] and he's like "I gotta consult my astrologer to make sure the planets are properly aligned."'

This seems as good a time as any to broach the subject that has brought me hot-foot to the Plaza this fine morning with Pixie-Boo at my side.

'Tell me about the album?' This, by the way, is shorthand for: *is it true, as the titanic amount of injurious scuttlebutt currently in circulation alleges, that it's full of rambling blues jams and diatribes about impending nuclear war, not to mention a track called 'Swamp N....r' that all three of the producers serially involved on the record flatly refused to have anything to do with?*

Uh...well...the album's cool. I mean Art [*famously laconic Flame Throwers drummer Art Smothers*] was playing with a busted hand, on account of, I dunno, some magnesium flare or something going off, but he's still, y'know, Art. Hey' – and suddenly for a brief moment the faintest tinge of animation drifts across Itol's otherwise blanched and impassive features – 'I'll tell you what fuckin' Art says about it. Y'know how Art never says a fuckin' word? I mean, I was there when the letter came – you know, with the divorce papers and everything, and Art's like, just "the fuck?" Well, Art – and this is a guy who never notices *anything*, right? I mean he wouldn't complain if a dog bit his ass, y'hear what I'm saying? Art says it reminds him of, I dunno, eight, ten years ago. You know, the early days.'

* * *

The early days of the Flame Throwers? Aw, honey, I was *there*. Well, if not exactly living cheek by jowl with them in accommodation so bottom of the range that at one point it is supposed to have involved a month spent in a succession of lock-up garages then attending enough of their early gigs to be able to spin you a fine old yarn about these buckaroos in their fledgling pomp. Believe me, L.A. in 1978 and 1979 hadn't seen anything like the Flame Throwers before. The teen-freaks at Rodney Bingenheimer's English Disco shrieked if they so much as sashayed through the foyer. Mind you, in their turn, at least 50 per cent of the band hadn't seen anything like L.A. You see, Cris and Stevie were just farm boys from the mid-West, regular hayseeds lighting out on the Greyhound bus in search of dope and tail and various other manifestations of the modern American dream that we hear so much about. On the other hand, those formative years in Appleton or Pepin or whichever Wisconsin hell-hole had spawned them had given these beauties a burning drive to succeed – 'success' in Flame Throwers terms being defined as access to plentiful amounts of drugs, women and record company largesse – and pretty soon, in the intervals of hustling on Sunset Strip and Santa Monica Boulevard, they'd fallen in with Joey and Art, who, if not precisely soul-mates, were as Cris puts it 'the kind of guys we could fuckin' relate to.'

The latter, whatever anyone else tells you, were classic *untermensch* Californian hoodlums, who'd been thrown out of every high school in Wilmington and were making a living out of dealing grass or basically just stealing things. Details are vague, but some kind of rudimentary line-up was apparently in existence by the end of 1978 and a friend of mine *swears* he saw them at the Whiskey a Go Go that Christmas supporting an early version of Mötley Crüe. As for what was going down on the stage of whichever scuzzy nightclub was desperate enough to hire them, in front of a goggle-eyed audience who had just begun to accustom themselves to the contorted strains of English punk and the so-called 'New Wave' drifting in from New York City, the Throwers kept it down and dirty. To say that their music lacked refinement would be like saying that Hitler had a problem with anyone called Rothschild. In fact – and I speak as a fan – it was completely devoid of charm, grace, ability or any kind of moral compass, had all the subtlety of a set of knuckledusters and was about as close to the mid-'70s post-hippy dream of collective good will and empathy as a pirate flag. On the other hand, they had one hell of a stage presence and – almost uniquely for a West Coast outfit of this era – the knack of writing half-way realistically about the kind of lives they were actually living. 'North Clarke', for example, off the first album *Breakfast at Ralph's*, is a paean – these are relative terms, you understand – to the fantastically low-rent L.A. thoroughfare where they hung out, with name-checks for the hookers. In much the same way 'Janey Spokane' is about a piece of the local talent who used to have psychotic episodes and ended up stabbing herself on the sidewalk.

I loved them, and so did a whole bunch of scene-swellers and L.A. opinion-formers, not to mention visiting rock press journos from the UK, but that didn't mean the mountain was climbed. *Breakfast*, for which Geffen reputedly paid $200,000, completely tanked, mostly due to its radio-unfriendly subject matter. MTV was just starting up, a medium which, as it concentrated on big hair and surface glitter, might have been made for them, but the videos kept on getting rejected on grounds of nudity, swearing and general offensiveness. They weren't *tractable*, you see, and a producer or a director who argued the toss would like as not get a can of Budweiser up-ended over his head. Plus Cris, who'd taken to the L.A. lifestyle in a big way by this time, was increasingly paranoid, which meant that the long-delayed second album, *Straight From Hell*, was full of breast-beating *sturm und drang* about people who were out to get him and chicks who'd done him wrong.

You see, there comes a moment in the career of any halfway-successful rock band – any halfway-successful creative artist if it comes to that – where the gap between the things that are worth writing about and the material rewards of that success widens into an abyss. With some acts this can take six or seven albums to kick in. With the Flame Throwers it started to happen in about 24 hours. One day they were putting out tracks like 'Back on the Brown' – an account of the band's, ah, recreational activities back in the North Clarke days – and the next they were wasting long hours of incredibly laboured metal-ballads – a genre they have some claims to have invented – about Malibu ladies and getting on down in partytown. *Straight From Hell* sold three million copies in the second half of 1982, but if the Throwers had trouble coping with being hoodlums on the Strip, then they sure as hell had trouble coping with being rock stars. By this time they were in and out of rehab or featuring in the *National Enquirer* for jetting off to Hawaii with adult movie stars, and the dates arranged on the back of the album were a disaster, culminating in a gig in Minneapolis where Itol was arrested on stage having pulled out a .03-06 and discharged several shots over the heads of the crowd. There was a plan for them to co-headline a bunch of concerts in the mid-West with the Rolling Stones, but in the end Jagger had them thrown off the tour, basically for being sloppy and unreliable and bad-mouthing him in interviews. Three days after this Art Smothers was pronounced clinically dead after collapsing in a hotel lobby with enough of Bolivia's principal export crowding out his septum to kill an elephant, only to be revived by an expertly-wielded syringe full of adrenalin which the Throwers' current tour manager had taken to carrying round in the inside pocket of his jacket just in case. Clearly it was time to regroup.

* * *

All that was five years ago – five long, devitalising and incident-crammed years. And now, in the wake of a round of marriages – most recently Joey's to a starlet named Dolores del Pompadour, thought to have lasted all of a month – at least two personal bankruptcies, tours of such licentiousness that tabloid reporters would frequently disguise themselves as janitors or take suites in the same hotel, a terrible covers album whose considerable profits were rendered nugatory by a lawsuit, and the occasion on which Stevie was discovered on a sandbank west of the Rio Grande out of his head on peyote and apparently dying of sunstroke, here I am on the fifth floor of the New York Plaza watching Cris pour himself a glass of sparkling water. He does this with a terrible neurotic fastidiousness, neck of the flagon beating a little tattoo on the rim of the glass, causing Pixie-Boo the PR and yours truly to wonder at his quivering hand.

'So tell me about the personal bankruptcy. I mean, you're supposed to be a multi-millionaire. Must have been something really awful for that to happen?'

Itol nods his head vigorously at this entirely reasonable surmise. 'Yeah, that was some serious financial shit going down. I mean, fuckin' Stevie is buying this chick some Tiffany engagement ring for fifty grand or whatever, and the cheque bounces, and the accountant is like "There's no cashflow" and the record company won't release any more until the fuckin' album is remixed. Plus our last manager, Tod…er, Ted [*Ted Mankiewicz, legendary reality-softener to the stars*] basically screwed us over. I mean, we were getting charged $200k for shooting some video that would be shown once on Norwegian TV or whatever and he'd still be taking his 20 per cent, y'know what I'm saying.'

I know what he's saying. In fact the band and Mr Mankiewicz are currently locked in litigation so labyrinthine that in the end you suspect only the Supreme Court will be able to settle it. 'But what about that dissension within the band we're always hearing about? I mean, Stevie was recently quoted in *Rolling Stone* to the effect that you're a devious, manipulative scumbag who's secretly plotting to fire the rest of the group and sign a solo deal.'

'Uh...Stevie?' The effects of the sparkling water are wearing off: Itol looks even more crestfallen and wrecked. 'Stevie's *always* saying that shit...About how we're going to replace him with Duff [*Guns 'N' Roses bass player Duff McKagan*] or whatever. But we're all cool. I mean, a couple of years ago it would have been "Say that to my face you fuck." But now it's like "That *Stevie*", y'know.'

All this leads us to what might be described as the chief difficulty facing your specimen Eighties rock ensemble, which is – not to mince words, you understand – the considerable task of keeping any kind of hold on observable reality, or indeed of merely functioning at all in our increasingly corporate and fault-finding world. Nick Du Pont, on whose UK label the band reposed earlier in the decade, used to say that the problem in dealing with rock stars these days – as opposed to dealing with them in the Sixties or the Seventies – is that the contemporary crowd just aren't amenable to discipline. The Beat groups and the Mod shouters and the Glam cross-dressers, having served pre-musical apprenticeships in Boy Scout troops or marching bands, were mostly prepared to do what they were told, whereas today's pompadour-coiffeured metal-merchants are just fucking maniacs.

'Do you think – how do I put this? – that you could have made things a whole lot easier for yourselves?'

'Uh, you see the thing with the Flame Throwers, it's always been, like, "Whatever the world wants to throw at us, we're OK with that," y'know what I'm saying. I mean, fuckin' Stevie, even when we were back in Appleton, whatever crazy shit the guy was doing and people were saying "You gotta get rid of this moron", it's like "No, he's still, like, *Stevie*."'

Having delivered himself of this homily, and looking even more ashen-visaged than before, Itol puts his jackdaw's skull up close to Pixie-Boo's much-beringed right ear – the New York PR ladies are clanking with facial jewellery these days – and mutters less than audibly into it. Some fond words of love? The table plan for tonight's orgy? Dear me no. The exact words, as far as I can make out when I play back the tape, are: '*Jesus, can you get me a fuckin' aspirin?*' Whisper it not, ladies and gentlemen, the press conferences, the drug-taking and the post-gig parties when Madonna or whoever is borne ceremonially into the room on an antique litter will have to wait, for Cris Itol, lead singer with the most notorious rock band of the whole of the 1980s, has a headache.

Nick Kent, *Q Magazine*, October 1988

Postscript, 1997

Excess All Areas, as you may have inferred from this calamitous sit-down, was a piece of shit and completely stiffed: the band broke up shortly afterwards. Of their subsequent careers, Itol drifted off into a series of half-assed collaborations with major-band throw-outs as desperate and drug-addled as himself. Stevie, meanwhile, was found dead in a Miami motel room in 1991, having spent the last few hours of his life with a couple of dealers he'd probably only met the previous afternoon. Joey started an intransigently hardcore metal band called the Wetbacks, scored a couple of minor chart hits and then disappeared. Art, at first thought merely to have vanished and to be living under a rock somewhere in the Mojave Desert, confounded all decent expectation by becoming a very serious player in the world of contemporary abstract expressionism, and if you don't believe me check out *Avant Garde Painters Vol. III*, published just last week by Messrs Phaidon for the very reasonable price of £24.99. As for what remains, *Breakfast* and, say, the first half of any of the *Greatest Hits* compilations, still have an extraordinary sparkle and pizzazz. For a brief time, you see, these boys – Cris, Stevie, Joey and Art – were genuine contenders – giant, predatory birds soaring on the thermals while the rest of gazed on enviously from the cramped and crowded crags below.

PART FOUR
Under the Big Sky

'Nothing here but history...'

13. DEBRIS

Here in summer, the Southwold beaches are never truly empty. Even now, an hour since dawn, the stealthy early-morning traffic is picking up. There are sun-cured old men in superfluous windcheaters and Wellington boots from the country-wear catalogues out exercising their dogs. Middle-aged ladies with breeze-blown pepper-and-salt hair are already at work in the beach-huts sweeping up sand and brewing fresh pots of tea on their portable gas-stoves. Every so often one of them emerges onto the concrete esplanade to dispose of the previous day's dregs in a waste bin. The dogs – docile Labradors and wire-haired terriers with bouncing gaits – look cowed and uncertain. This isn't their milieu, and the scurrying crustacean life of the rock pools brings unexpected hazards. The tide, half-way up the thin strip of sand, and in sight of the clumps of pebbles, is running strongly. To the left, in the lee of the pier, the sea is boiling away in a hundred tiny detonations of surf and spume. Beyond the whirlpools, the water is the colour of gravy.

Most days at this hour I set off for the point, half a mile to the south, where the river Blyth flows briskly inland past the caravan parks and the harbour. On this particular morning, with the after-tremors of last night's rain still bringing spray in off the sea, I decide to stick to the immediate shore-line. As ever, the storm has left all manner of flotsam in its wake: coils of rope; strings of onions; what from thirty yards looks horribly like a corpse but turns out to be the upper half of a tailor's dummy. Perhaps there is a shoal of them out there, pink and glassy-eyed, rigid arms extended, floating off the Dutch coast. Who can tell? In the distance the wind is tearing into the sand dunes, whipping the marram grass into knots like stooked wheat and sending clouds of grit into the air; the fishermen's lines are drawn taut. The dog-walkers have given way to gaunt, solitary joggers, heads angled against the buffeting air. Like the dogs, their eyes are alert for trouble. They give the abandoned fence-posts and the protrusions of sea-weed a wide berth. I press on for a bit, half-turned into the quivering wind, not liking the flung gravel stinging my sexagenarian's calves, and then head up the path towards Gun Hill. Here there are ancient cannons, the relic of sea-battles against the Dutch, and a panoptic view of the town, the marshlands on its flank, the bracken-covered common, and the endless sky.

Back at the newsagent's along from the market square, the papers are in and I stop to buy a copy of the *East Anglian Daily Times*. The *East Anglian Daily Times* is a proper local paper, which means that it favours regional news over cataclysm in the wider world. A charity garden fete in Ipswich always takes precedence over a government reshuffle or war in the Gulf. Curiously, amid the regular budget of teenage cancer-sufferers and the sprung water-main that recently inundated Beccles High Street, the front page is dominated by a picture of Gordon Brown. It turns out that this is still local news, as Gordon, a glance at the letterpress confirms, has announced his intention of holidaying in north Suffolk. One rumour has him actually resident here in Southwold, but there are also unconfirmed reports that he may be holed up in Shadingfield, a dozen miles distant on the other side of the A12. Why is Gordon – and presumably his wife and children – taking his vacation here rather than in the Caribbean or Thailand? The idea seems to be that this is a suitable response to the austerity that threatens to overwhelm us. A Prime Minister who jetted off to the Algarve is not, the argument runs, in touch with his electorate. In opting to stay in Suffolk, Gordon is showing his sensitivity, not to mention doing his duty.

Outside in the High Street, where there are men in overalls sluicing down the steps of the Crown Hotel and the market stalls are beginning to set up, I take another look at our glorious leader. Somebody once said that Gordon resembled something left behind when a glacier moved on. You can see why. Tony Blair at least seemed to belong to the world he affected to command. But Gordon looks hopelessly ill-at-ease, way out of his comfort zone. The ice has shifted downhill and left him stranded, fur flying in the arctic gale, pitilessly exposed. You can tell from his face – craggy and put-upon – that it isn't working out, that history, mysteriously, is no longer on his side. Meanwhile, above my head the last vestiges of the storm are punching away inland; the clouds are hastening south. A quarter of a mile distant, beyond the shops and the restaurant frontages, the North Sea booms.

* * *

The houses along Centre Cliff are old Edwardian mansions with the rooms knocked into each other and the servants' quarters turned into home cinemas and TV rumpus-joints. Mine sits in the middle, next to two mostly absent neighbours, one of whom is reckoned to be the proprietor of a Mayfair hedge-fund. My mother, I suspect, would have deplored the gentrification of Southwold, the high-end rentals, the over-priced delicatessens and the corn-haired women piloting Range Rovers along the High Street. She had nothing against the upper classes, but she thought they ought to keep to their own backyards. God knows what she would have made of Centre Cliff, with its laundry room, its white-painted alabaster balcony and its hedged-in oblong of Astroturf keeping out the noise of the trippers on the coast path below.

Slowly the day slides into gear. The gulls move down by degrees from the roof to thc snail-strewn garden. The sky turns from gun-metal grey to duck-egg blue. I skim-read the *East Anglian Daily Times*, with its quaint small-ads ('1 doz. Minorca pullets, offers invited. Buyer to collect...Gravel £30 a ton') and its down-home, dim-wit correspondence column where people with names like Billy McKitteridge complain about the 'so-called experts and boffins' who are wilfully misleading us about climate change, and then, with the heat beginning to descend, step out onto the terrace. Here the two characteristic scents of Southwold in summer – salt from the sea and malt from the brewery – breezily commingle. Out to sea there are mini-hydrofoils surging by and fleets of kayaks negotiating the surf. Nearer at hand, older parts of Southwold – church spires, brewery chimney, the Swan Hotel, where self-conscious local gentry in hacking jackets and plus-fours entertain their wives – are hidden from view. From inside the house I can hear the sound of Mrs Stiff, who has her own key, rattling around the kitchen and noisily embarking on last night's washing-up. Like the church spires and the Sailors' Reading Room, Mrs Stiff belongs to an older Southwold that predates the estate agents' cabins and the four-wheel drives. She can remember the great flood of 1953, when the water came half-way up the wall of the Harbourfront Inn down by the river, and her grandmother – Mrs Stiff herself is about my age – once 'did' for the Blairs, George Orwell's parents, when they lived here in placid inter-war era retirement.

The *East Anglian Daily Times*, I discover, has an editorial about the Prime Minister's visit. This commends his choice of location ('a ringing endorsement of what Suffolk has to offer the tourist'), expresses a pious hope that he will seek out the area's 'hidden gems' as well as its more obvious amenities and urges other holidaymakers to follow the First Lord of the Treasury's example. I have a sudden vision of Gordon eating breakfast in his hotel with the tourist gazetteer at his side as some harassed aide brings messages from the cabinet room and the CBI conference. The Suffolk attitude to incomers is peculiarly double-edged. Nobody minds them spending money. On the other hand, there is a faint suspicion that it would be better for all concerned if they stayed away. I once watched a tourist on the promenade drawing the attention of a gnarled old woman in an Inverness Cape who was exercising her Sealyham to the sign prohibiting dog-walking during the summer months. 'I'm *local*,' the old lady insisted, as the Sealyham blithely defecated on the concrete. Council by-laws were for the fly-by-nights. Is Gordon experiencing difficulties of this kind? It would be nice to know.

'Here's your tea,' Mrs Stiff – Elsie – now says, emerging onto the terrace with a cup and saucer so lavishly filled that the slightest jolt sends drops of liquid spilling over the crazy-paving. The tea is mahogany-coloured and smells of saccharine, but oddly drinkable. I catch sight of her hands as she sets it down: yeasty agglomerations of knotted flesh with the rings almost hidden beneath layers of subcutaneous fat. Mrs Stiff – at least, this is my assumption – approves of me on the grounds that when I had the kitchen refurbished I hired a local firm. Some of the second-homers have been known to bring in contractors from outside. You get what you pay for. There is also the fact that I can remember Southwold when it was a proper place, before the light industry went and the estate agents started crowding out the High Street. I am also attentive to family gossip. How are the grandchildren, I enquire, as Mrs Stiff stamps on a snail and side-foots the fragments into one of the flower-beds, and am rewarded with the news that Bradley is a proper terror and Tamarind fixated on her Peppa Pig DVDs. The Stiff's son Shane is separated from his wife, otherwise known as 'that Charmian', and works for one of the boat-builders at the harbour. Most of his mother's spare time, consequently, is taken up with child-care.

Nearly 10 o'clock now. Mrs Stiff goes off to polish the sitting-room windows and flog a carpet or two into submission. Gordon, by this time, will be in sight of Snape Maltings or Aldeburgh beach or whichever other glistening tourist-trap has been recommended to him by his vacation planner. Out in the High Street, on Gun Hill, or striding across the common, fat men in buttock-hugging shorts will be bellowing into mobile phones, seeing if the newsagent has sold out of the *Financial Times* or arranging to play exhausted games of tennis. I head off to the TV room to begin the next stage of my routine, which is a stake-out in front of *Trash for Cash*. Do you know *Trash for Cash*? It airs three mornings a week on Channel Five, in between a protracted domestic shag-a-thon called *Imbroglio* and *Wisconsin Road Wars*. It really is the most awful piece of shit. Each instalment finds Major-D Sophie – Sophie Simmonds – a brassy blonde in her early forties with huge sea-green eyes – descending on some likely-looking but nondescript venue (a car-boot in sight of the M25, say, or a draughty Midlands church hall crammed with trestle tables) with the aim of persuading 'members of the public' to bring in their heirlooms, or indeed any stray fragment of rubbish they have lying around the house, for appraisal. In pursuing this aim, Sophie is assisted by a couple of sidekicks: chunky Greg, who does the furniture and the bric-a-brac, plus camp, moustachioed Phil who appraises the pictures. Sophie herself, with occasional requests for corroboration ('What do you reckon, Phil?') handles the jewellery and old photos.

As for the show's demographic, *Trash for Cash's* punters are not, alas, the placid bourgeoisie of the BBC antiques shows. No, Sophie's supplicating hordes tend to be bald goblins bearing carrier bags full of old stamp albums and their candy-floss-haired other halves, the latter clutching, as it might be, a handful of ancient flexi-discs or a wad of old cigarette cards. Foul language and disgruntled stormings-off are not unknown. The zing, naturally, lies in the gap between expectation and outcome. Sometimes Sophie and the boys will encourage a modest hope of profit, only to frustrate it at the death. Alternatively, somebody's scuffed coin from a bygone era will be about to be cast aside as worthless only for Greg to give one of his trademarked facial spasms and twitch nervously at the supplicant's sleeve with a gasp of 'Jesus, Soph, it's only a George IV bull-head shilling!' As I say, it is the most dreadful piece of shit. Part of the allure lies in a suspicion – this has been growing on me for weeks – that I have seen Sophie before, that here in early middle age, with what looks like a great deal of surplus avoirdupois distributed around her person – the show often ends in a canteen, by the way, where Sophie and the lads are filmed shovelling down burgers or piling into the lasagne – Sophie, Sophie Simmonds, is someone I used to know.

This particular morning, the *Trash for Cash* team have descended on a Royal British Legion hall in Sleaford, Lincs. It is the usual kind of thing. Paul frowns over an anonymous sea-side scene in smudgy greys and blues, wonders if it's a Wilson Steer and then decides not, whereupon the singlet-clad steroid-abuser in whose Giant Hulk's grasp it resides breaks the frame over his knee in disgust. Greg reckons that a spindly fretwork letter-rack knocked up in somebody's shed at around the time of the General Strike might possibly be worth £5 or so. Sophie, I notice, seems oddly detached from the proceedings. When Phil essays a quip about an outsize pair of calico bloomers slammed down on the display table, she gives a bleak little grimace, clearly appalled by the stroke of fate that has set her down amid these lackwit companions. The show ends in a nearby café with the three of them feasting on doughnuts and cans of Tizer. I still have no idea who she is. Meanwhile, there are other enticements calling. By the half-open front door, I find Mrs Stiff buttoning up her scarlet cagoule, one eye fixed on the cloudless Suffolk sky, keen to volunteer the information that it will like as not rain by lunchtime. This intelligence I receive with the respect it deserves. When it comes to the capricious local micro-climate, Mrs Stiff knows her onions. In a better-run world *Look East*, the local TV news programme, would beam out its meteorological forecasts from the Stiffs' front room in

North Road, and have adroit Mrs Stiff prophesying storms rolling in from the Wash or gale-force winds blowing down from Jutland, rather than relying on corkscrew-curled weather-girl Alexis, with her defective command of isobars, to do the business.

Outside the sun is bouncing up off the car fenders and the white kerb-stones and there is the usual ten-person queue at the cash-point outside the bank. Intent, purposeful, bearded men in shiny tee-shirts go cycling by with baby-carriers bobbing behind them. On the crowded pavements, exasperated teenage girls jink around the knots of palsied oldsters idling in the summer haze. Every so often, fastened with bristling green twine to the lamp-posts, come discreet adverts for the local theatre's summer season and the circus that will shortly be opening in a tent on the common, not to mention the Crabpot Boys, currently appearing nightly at the Lord Nelson pub. Halfway down the High Street, I notice that there is a CD and Record Fair taking place in the hut beyond the Conservative Club, and decide to take a look. Do you know those CD and Record Fairs they have in coastal resorts? This one extends to a single, massively disgruntled proprietor, head down over the *Daily Express*, and half-a-dozen formica tables whose surfaces look as if they have once been strafed with machine-gun fire stocked with piles of over-priced and minutely categorised vinyl from 30 years ago ('Soul', 'Pop classics', 'Eighties', 'Easy Listening.') Still, they have a fair amount of old Resurgam stuff, including some Cupcakes' 12″ singles, the Bash Street Kids' *Live Stompers* and Charysse's *The Diversions of Purley*. It seems impossible that Charysse, with her weedy Kate Bush approximations and her Laura Ashley frocks should ever have had a career in pop. In the end, I escape with an old VHS cassette entitled *Systems of Romance Video Hits*, of whose original release I have no memory whatsoever.

Back at Centre Cliff the landline is ringing. Mrs Stiff, £20 note stuffed into the pocket of her smock, has already left for her next client, or possibly the benign superintendence of Bradley and Kayla-Mae. There are only two people who call with any regularity in Southwold. One of them is Xavier. The other is Zoe. This morning it turns out to be Xavier, Xav, who is only one-fourth French but works in a milieu that inclines increasingly to the polyglot. Among other distinguishing marks, Xav labours at XLB, the label, or rather the entertainment industry conglomerate, to which, after many years of legal manoeuvring, the bulk of the Resurgam catalogue devolved. XLB have numberless irons in the commercial fire. They manage transcontinental tour packages for the West Coast rap acts for 20 per cent of the gross. They recycle old prog artists in multi-CD retrospectives. They may even – the promotional literature is coy about this – fund a range of straight-to-online-download adult movies. But they are also in the business of repackaging desirable product from the 1980s for a newly solvent middle-aged audience anxious to revisit the soundscapes of their youth.

'You are not going to believe what I just heard,' Xav begins, and so I mock-mirthfully attend to some industry scuttlebutt about the EMI meltdown and a complicated anecdote about Ronnie Wood and a mislaid bottle of hair-lacquer. 'I used to know him when he was in The Faces,' I interject, and Xav, who in spite of his tender years has acquired an encyclopaedic knowledge of what is now known as 'Heritage Rock' murmurs that he's been overseeing some re-mixes of the early stuff and young Ron could certainly cut it.

'How are we doing on the reissues?' I inquire. The initial plan was to reassemble more or less the entire Resurgam catalogue, which even I think is a touch ambitious. Just lately the Sales Department has been veering towards a couple of heavy-duty box-sets. Much of this, of course, depends on what is lying in the vault alongside the original master-tapes.

'I had Keith go and root around in the tape-box,' Xav says, with the zeal of an archaeologist winching up some fresh pile of bones from an

Angevin plague-pit. 'He reckoned there was all kinds of weird stuff in there. Those Bash Street Kid out-takes. That Planet Claire jazz fusion album that never got released.'

'Nobody's going to want to listen to that, surely?'

'You'd be surprised, Nick. This is a mature market we're dealing with here, with plenty of scope for inter-generational synergy.' Xavier uses expressions like 'intergenerational synergy' with the same complete lack of self-consciousness that Ainsley Duncan, who managed the Helium Kids in the Sixties, used to talk about someone being an Ace Face. 'But we'll definitely be doing the Cedric box. That's already in the schedule for the autumn...'

Of all the Resurgam acts still twinkling in the firmament of twenty-first century taste, the one whose longevity never ceases to astound me is the composer of 'I Like My Dog.' There is, alas, no Cedric around to enjoy this belated success, our man having tumbled off Sigiriya Rock in darkest Sri Lanka sometime in the early nineties while in the spaced-out company of a group of vacationing Beautiful People called the Children of Zarathustra. Meanwhile, in the decade and a half since his death his limping acoustic guitar and frail vocalising have graced at least five film soundtracks and a couple of BMW ads. His estate, of which I am a joint trustee, is currently turning over £2 million a year.

'...Plus there's going to be a BBC Four documentary' Xav continues. 'I told them you'll probably want to appear.'

Do I want to appear? What would I say? That Cedric, with his plastic-frame Health Service glasses and his shock of blonde hair, was a nice kid but temperamentally debarred from any kind of engagement with real life? That I liked him, and his music, but could never understand – to take only one example of his posthumous sanctification – why the Green Party should want to have 'The Whales that Swim in the Sea' playing over the speakers during their annual conference? We didn't bill them for that, by the way.

'That vinyl reissue of *Live in the Greenhouse* did fifty thousand copies,' Xav assures me, as if to clinch the deal.

We talk a little more about Cedric and his 'legacy' – a tantalising abstraction of which the XLB people are particularly fond of as the breeze blows in across the garden and somewhere in the distance a hydrofoil cranks into gear.

'What are you doing for the rest of the day?' I enquire, as the conversation peters to a close.

'We're in the middle of re-mastering a couple of old Spooky Tooth albums,' Xav eagerly returns. No sooner have I put the phone back into its cradle than it rings again.

'Jesus, Nick. You've been engaged *forever*.' I explain about Xav and the updates on Cedric's boxed set, but Zoe is unimpressed. 'That boy needs to get a proper job. Sitting there in an editing suite like it was paid employment.' Of all the thirty or forty people who passed through Resurgam in its seven-year history, Zoe is the only one with whom I more than perfunctorily keep up. Hermione is currently breeding golden retrievers in Gloucestershire. The last news anyone had of Doug Stroessner was that he worked as a game warden in a Canadian National Park. Terry Jacomb, sacked by Rory a fortnight after the legal settlement, was never heard of again. I took no pleasure in this.

'How are the crazies?'

'Fucked up like you wouldn't believe.' Zoe has a robust attitude to her job, which involves the provision of freelance psychotherapy services to Kent County Council from an office in Whitstable. She must be all of fifty-five, but the photo on her website stirs painful feelings of nostalgia. She specialises, I have since learned, in substance abuse, low self-esteem and anxiety issues – all areas in the treatment of which her former calling must offer valuable practical experience.

'Actually I'm between patients' Zoe says, in that hard-as-nails killer baby from the Bronx tone with which she was wont to address bands whose records had stalled in the lower 40s. 'I've just seen one fucking kid whose problem is that he won't leave his room, and I've got another one arriving whose problem is that he won't go back into it. Did Xav say anything about the Throwers?'

'Not that I recall.' Outside the sky is gently darkening to lilac and the gulls are making even more noise than usual.

'Actually he wouldn't. Now I come to think of it, XLB lost the UK rights a while back.' Fifteen years out of the music business, Zoe is still absurdly cognisant of its whirls and eddies. If Bono has a cold in the head, she will have heard of it somehow. Is she happy practising psychotherapy in Whitstable? Who can tell? 'Anyway, the word is they're being inducted into the Metal Hall of Fame next month.'

'The Metal Hall of Fame certainly took their time.'

'Apparently Alice Cooper likes them or something. And Ozzy's supposed to have put in a word. It's in Chicago,' Zoe adds, divining that the ceremonial aspects of the modern rock and roll circus will probably have escaped me.

I know where this is leading. 'Are you intending to go?'

'Wild fucking horses couldn't keep me away.'

'What about the crazies?'

'They'll just have to up their meds and bolt their doors,' Zoe insists. I haven't heard her so exuberant in years.

'Don't you have to play live when you're inducted? There's only three of them.'

'Jesus, Nick. A retard from the county asylum with two fingers missing could play those bass parts of Stevie's. They'll get someone. Go on, say you'll come.'

'You can fix this?'

'The PR guy is my actual ex-husband. Sure I can fix it.'

And then we fall silent, aware of a dark, phantom presence that has strayed into the margins of the conversation.

'Will Rory be there?'

'Of course Rory will be there,' Zoe briskly intones. 'Rory wouldn't miss a hootenanny like this. It would be like *Crime and Punishment* without Raskolnikov.'

On cue, just as Mrs Stiff foresaw, with the gulls screaming in the garden and the sky bruising to purple, it starts to rain.

14. DUNWICH BELLS

The second week in July now, and Southwold is filling up. The state sector hasn't yet disgorged its quota of tinies, but the London prep schools are out in force. The children, seen roaming in packs down the High Street or clustered around the genteel amusement parlour that abuts the pier, look faintly unreal. They have hay-coloured hair and shiny pink-and-white complexions, like miniature film-stars. Like miniature film-stars, they are shrewdly attuned to what the world owes them. 'I've got Mummy's Mastercard,' I heard a ten-year-old with a Lacroix hand-bag slung over her shoulder assure a posse of *convives* as they cruised into the local Costa. Their mothers, meanwhile, are riffling through the trays of designer flip-flops in Fat Face or White Stuff, sitting exhaustedly in the coffee lounges or stepping into Suffolk Country Cottages to protest that the wifi doesn't work. Every so often the reek of an older world wafts into view when a coach full of Suffolk pensioners labours up the High Street and drops its cargo in the market square. The visitors – white-haired old ladies from Framlingham and Yoxford, tiny old men with faces carved out of teak – wander round the town in a puzzled way. This is not their kind of place now, what with the expensive clothes shops and the cafés selling hummus and ricotta wraps. In some curious way it has fallen out of the world they knew. The tourist coaches are soon gone, in any case, out along the back-lanes to the safety of Reydon and Henstead, disappearing into the heat-haze and the wide Suffolk sky.

But if most of Southwold is idling – apart from the shopkeepers, that is – then I am unexpectedly busy. To begin with, I have managed to identify Sophie Simmonds. I have, though. She turned up towards the end of the Systems of Romance VHS in a promo film for 'My Friend the Unicorn', scampering through an exceptionally badly mocked-up spring shower with a plastic umbrella over her head: twenty years younger, perhaps, but instantly recognisable from her slightly lop-sided smile. Sophie, not to put too fine a point on it, is the girl who broke Magda's heart by running off with her boyfriend and breaking up the band. What is Sophie doing on *Trash for Cash*? No doubt she is impelled by the same motive that took Chloe from the Cupcakes into co-presenting one of those terrible Channel Four Friday night shows where the guests are expected to gorge themselves on bowls of termites and the bands are always being rebuked by the regulator for swearing. If the feathers are available, then you line your nest with them. All this, naturally, gives my thrice-weekly stake-out in front of *Trash for Cash* an added piquancy. It is still the most dreadful piece of shit, but Sophie, in some ineluctable way, gives it resonance. Now, fortuitously, there is a context that goes beyond the scheming OAPs avid to unload grandpa's antique chamber-pot. Last week's highlight, by the way, was a pair of middle-aged zombies who had been using the first hardback edition of *Martin Chuzzlewit* as a doorstopper.

Meanwhile, as Xav predicted, the BBC have been in touch about that documentary. All kinds of people, it turns out, have an opinion about Cedric. Elvis Costello thinks he was a misunderstood genius. Joni Mitchell is thought to admire his work. A professor from the University of Salford specialising in popular culture has, the email maintains, detected a political subtext in some of his lyrics. There is talk of a 'metaphorical dimension.' Knowing me to be Cedric's sponsor, and the man in whose office he sat playing 'I Love to Paint' on an out-of-tune Hofner acoustic guitar, the producer is naturally keen to hear what I have to say. Cedric, I now realise, is being quietly transformed into a creature of myth. Posterity, you infer, is anxious to acclaim him for qualities he may not have possessed and importing contexts to his work of which he could not possibly have been aware. On the other hand, I once read a piece in the NME which maintained that the Beatles embodied a collision between the moral orthodoxies of a pre-war puritanism and the hedonism of the consumer age. Meaning, after all, is not always ours to design. By chance, the email from the BBC arrives on the same day that the *East Anglian Daily Times* reveals that Gordon has been seen strolling on Martlesham Heath. There is a photograph of an uneasy-looking man, with the wrapped-up, stoical expression that goes with being a son of the manse. Perhaps, like Cedric, he is waiting to be reinvented as something else, and suspects that the future will look more kindly on him than the present. Who can tell?

* * *

What do I do here in Southwold as the streets concertina with summer traffic and the tubby bankers roll down the High Street jabbering into their mobile phones? One task on which I am busily engaged is tracking down the places my mother and I knew 50 years ago. This is far from straightforward. Most of the houses we stayed in have been furbished up beyond utility, but here and there – like the tourist coaches filled with disbelieving pensioners – lie fragments of an older world. The bric-a-brac parlour on the common's edge with its selection of ancient stamps at £3 the packet and its Edward VIII Coronation mugs is still going strong, along with the old-fashioned sweetshop and its jars of mint humbugs and hundreds and thousands, and so are more or less unshiftable landmarks like the town museum and the Sailors' Reading Room. On the other hand, the new pier is a warren of fancy tea-shops, and even the red-faced fishermen at the farther end are kitted out in Barbour jackets and spotless waders.

The other task on which I am busily engaged is the cultivation of some local talent. In fact, on this particular evening, in the role of enthusiast and prospective impresario, I am part of a select audience gathered in the back bar of the Lord Nelson to listen to an entity known as Wangford Jim perform his repertoire. The vacationing bourgeoisie from Putney and Canonbury Square are all dining in the Swan or the Crown or enjoying barbecues in their spacious rented gardens, but here in the back bar of the Nelson we pride ourselves on knowing where the action is. Wangford Jim is a few years older than me, or perhaps a few years younger. He may be lurching dramatically into early old age or simply a hard-living 50 year-old whose face has cragged up. It is difficult to tell. Just now, hunched over a charity shop Spanish guitar, which he plays with a curious scooping motion of the lower three fingers of his right hand, like Baloo in the *Jungle Book* clawing honey out of a hive, he is singing a plaintive number entitled 'Southwold Train'.

Southwold' train's a long time gone, running on its track.
Only saw it once before. Shan't be coming back.

They closed the Southwold railway line as long ago as 1929, by the way. There is not the slightest chance that Jim, or anyone else in this room, can have seen it. This done, he embarks on another song – brisker and played in 3/4 time – about a girl from Saxmundham met at a village dance, with a jaunty chorus and some elaborate punning on the word 'miss'. In appearance, Wangford Jim – Wangford is a village about five miles from here – is a tall, cadaverous, sad-seeming character with one of those faces which long exposure to the elements has rendered oddly featureless. It is, indisputably, a local face: the kind you see behind the tills at the Co-op, or doling out change in plastic pots at the amusement arcade on the pier. Genre-wise, Jim – apparently self-taught – plays a kind of country-and-western-derived hayseed's shuffle – he has, for example, clearly been listening to Hank Williams and Jimmie Rodgers, 'the Singing Brakeman' – undercut by an intensely localised folk-poetry:

> *She was a girl from Saxmundham, lived on the village green*
> *Eyes like the sea on a good day, face like you'd never seen.*

Naturally, all the songs are fatalistic. The girl always dies or marries someone else, and the bus booked to take you acourtin' in Ipswich invariably ends up in a ditch. If whimsy can't be kept at bay, then neither, too, can intimations of a bygone rural life lived out in windblown fields a stone's throw from the sea with 'th'electric' faltering every time a breeze gets up and the 'little ol' Queen' smiling up from the ten-shilling note. I've never heard anything like it.

Jim's *oeuvre* is not extensive. Another ten minutes and he is done. The last number is a well-nigh lachrymose tour-de-force about a fisherman who perishes at sea, his fiancée having thrown him over, and whose ghost can be seen at the harbour's mouth hauling in phantom nets, night after storm-crossed night. As the applause dies down, he stands blinking – a bit cluelessly but with a certain amount of gratification – in the muted light. Does the experience of performing in public satisfy some deep-rooted need in him that would otherwise go unfulfilled? Is he simply compelled by some trackless inner urging to head into the Nelson's back bar every other Thursday to sing about the girl from Saxmundham who broke his heart and the long-lost Southwold train? Who can tell? Most of the bands I worked with had no idea where their inspiration came from. They were blank slates on which some unseen intelligence scratched a pattern. As he stands there beaming, massive left hand gripping the Spanish guitar by the fretboard as if it were a piece of firewood ripe to be tossed into a roaring blaze, someone hands him a pint of Adnams Broadside. This goes down in a couple of gulps.

Dealing with Wangford Jim, or so my limited experience counsels, demands an oblique approach. Conventional enquiries about health, domicile and dependents rarely get an answer. 'I liked the one about the girl from Saxmundham' I say, as he draws near enough to send draughts of his Suffolk countryman's scent – a compound of woodsmoke, tobacco and scorched bacon – out to colonise my air-space. 'It might need an extra verse,' Jim attests in his high East Suffolk accent. This comes out as *At moight needa extra vuss*. 'Did she really live on the village green?' I ask, but the traditional life-into-art progressions of the popular song are not a subject on which Jim cares to be drawn. 'What ef she did?' he winks humorously as another pint of Adnams appears mysteriously in his fist. This, too, vanishes in a couple of swallows. In my time I have seen many a Suffolk ancient deedily at work among the local ale shops, but Jim, I can tell you, is in a class of his own. His real name is James Dodsworth. He is thought – my informant is Mrs Stiff, to whom he may, in addition (this being the way of things round here) be distantly related – to have at some point served in the Merchant Marine and to have worked at Lowestoft fish market

The bar is emptying now, and the patrons disappearing into the summer night. Interesting fact: the regulars at the Nelson like Jim's songs but they don't especially want to hang out with him. 'So, what's it all about?' Jim matily enquires, as another paralysing wave of tobacco, woodsmoke and scorched bacon pulses out from his humid, sweater-clad torso. I interpret this as glancing reference to a vague plan, hatched a fortnight back, to escort Jim to a small recording studio I know of outside Lowestoft and lay down a track or two. Notwithstanding his previous employment hauling dogfish out of the bins and pricing up skate, Lowestoft is a bit beyond Jim's range these days. The trip will need careful management. But then quite a lot is beyond Jim's range. According to Mrs Stiff, he has neither been married nor apparently indulged himself in any relationship with a member of the opposite sex. On the other hand, here in Suffolk, this is not unusual. The surrounding villages are full of ancient bachelors out walking their dogs or browsing the convenience stores for jars of Camp Coffee and tins of spaghetti hoops. Monasticism is second nature. I buy Jim his third pint myself. 'Staying fine all night, I daresay' he says, one eye on the evening sky rapidly congealing beyond the window, rim of the dimpled glass bobbing against his chest. Unlike his more talented cousin, Jim has no skill as a weather prophet. Five minutes later, as we stand on the Nelson's gum-flecked kerb, the first drops of rain are already cascading out of a damson sky. The holidaying families, who have fetched up out of the Swan and the Crown, are clustered anxiously in shop doorways or cowering under awnings. This isn't what they bargained for. In a silence broken only by the patter of the rain and the surf exploding in the distance, I watch Jim unhook his bicycle from the railings of an adjacent house and, baseball cap tugged down over his forehead, parcelled up copy of the *Daily Express* jammed into his jacket pocket, sail off magisterially down the empty High Street. Just this once, Southwold has returned to its rightful owner.

* * *

Mrs Stiff approves of my interest in Jim, in the same way that she approved of my getting a local firm in to do the kitchen extension. It makes me less of a blow-in. This, it turns out, is the nativist term for non-indigenous transients for whom the beach is just a pile of sand rather than a thousand years or so of accumulated heritage. There is also the thought that, as she puts it, I might be able 'to do something for him.' All the same, I can't help noticing that her approval is qualified by an awareness of some of the difficulties involved. The implication is that a whole lot of people over the years have tried to do something for Jim. Why should I succeed when so many others have self-evidently failed?

Mrs Stiff, meantime, is an increasingly harassed figure. She drinks more cups of tea than usual and has taken to departing a quarter or even a half-hour before her allotted time. The cause of this inattention, I am given to understand, is Shane, who was recently stopped by the police at 80 m.p.h. on the Harbour Road at three in the morning with a four ounce bag of weed leaking its contents onto his dashboard. Mrs Stiff, though critical of this lapse, is not unsympathetic. Apparently it is all Charmian's fault. One consequence of this upset is that her domestic responsibilities have increased. Only yesterday she turned up at Centre Cliff with a double buggy containing two of her grandchildren: Bradley, aged three, and eighteen-month old Tamarind. They are timid, cautious children, with a tendency to whine whenever their grandmother is out of the room. Walking into the sitting-room, where the buggy is usually parked, I can feel their eyes burning into the back of my skull.

* * *

Meanwhile, *Trash for Cash* has grown yet more outrageous. It has, though. Only the other day a middle-aged butterball who had wheeled in a painting of two sunflowers that looked as if it might have been executed by an averagely talented three-year-old – little Bradley, say, snug in his baby-buggy – reacted to the valuation by smashing the frame over Phil's sharply receding head and was hauled off by the security goons. Sophie, in the weeks since I first started watching, is yet more disaffected. There was a moment only the other day when, just as she was examining an antique cutlass brought in by an elderly lady whose great-great-grandfather had wielded it at Trafalgar, know-nothing Greg dropped one of his otiose remarks and it was all she could do not to carve his head off with it. Even more arresting than Phil's misfortunes or Sophie's inner disquiet is the news that confronted me yesterday morning when I stepped out along the High Street. Believe it or not, an episode of *Trash for Cash* is set to be filmed right here in Southwold in a fortnight's time, venue the Conservative Club, tickets *gratis*, on application, first come first served. I leave a completed form at the bar forthwith.

And then, on the way back from a stroll along the front – packed out with extraordinarily lissom teenage girls in teeny-bikinis – coming past the Sailors' Reading Room, where old gentlemen in Panama hats drowse over the *Southwold Gazette*, memory stirs. It was here, perhaps half-a-century ago, that my mother and I embarked on the only proper conversation we ever had in our lives about the old man. Like many of the conversations I had with my mother, it came from nowhere and went from nought to sixty in the space of a few seconds.

'I came here once with your dad,' she said, having made sure that there was no one in the room and that the empty promenade was likely to keep it that way.

'When would that have been?'

'Sometime during the war. Before…' And here my mother made a flapping gesture with her hand, in which twenty years of desertion, dereliction and solitary child-rearing in a North Park Avenue council house were inextricably bound up. 'I don't think…' my mother said, and then stopped, as if there were so many obstacles to side-step in any account of the Old Man's life, hopes and expectations, so much dark, stagnant water to vault across, that it might not be worth making the attempt in the first place. 'I don't think your dad meant any harm.'

I can see her now, sitting anxiously in the Reading Room's sepia-tinted light, amid the back-numbers of *Punch* and the *Illustrated London News* and the photographs of grizzled Victorian lifeboat crews looking as if they had been sent out to rescue the Ark.

'He might have caused some, all the same.'

My mother acknowledged the justice of this. 'All those postcards he used to send,' she said, referring to the brightly-coloured rectangles that had whisked across the Atlantic from Nashville, South Carolina and New York State, bringing news of experiments in fruit farm husbandry, rodeo-management and gas-station tenancy, each bearing the weight of impossible and frankly unhinged dreams. 'He was the kind of man,' she went on, 'who had schemes in his head.'

'What sort of schemes?'

'Just things he wanted to do,' said my mother, a bit defensively and catching the hint of exasperation. To begin with, she had welcomed the postcards, placed them on the mantelpiece, and – at least for the first few years, when the prospect of the Old Man's return was still being actively canvassed – shown them to her friends. But I could see that my mother was, additionally, embarrassed by them, that she regarded them as evidence of some mental decline, that in transmitting these ludicrous visions of a future life, the Old Man was somehow lowering himself in her estimation.

'What would you have done if he'd come back?'

But that was too much for my mother. She picked up her handbag, shook out her dark hair so that it settled more comfortably onto the shoulders of her pink summer frock and bore me away to an ice-cream joint where, as I now recall, Mr Matlock was waiting for us. Was it the thought of Mr Matlock that prompted this exchange? I have no idea. What I think my mother was trying to convey was her notion of why the Old Man behaved as he did, that – like Cedric – he was a creature of myth, subject to mostly ungovernable impulses, that the image he had of himself, and yearned to perpetuate, was more important to him than the everyday materials of life. Which was all very well, unless you happened to be his wife or his son.

* * *

Back at Centre Cliff there is a cluster of messages on the answerphone. The BBC are anxious to confirm the date of my interview about Cedric. Meanwhile, Zoe has left full details of the Flame Throwers' induction into the Metal Hall of Flame. Apparently the live show is on, a temporary bass player has been recruited, and all three surviving members had dinner last week at Trader Vic's. To what length Zoe has had to go to acquire this information, I cannot imagine. Meanwhile, a dog-eared and Marmite-stained manila envelope sealed up with far more industrial-strength masking-tape than is strictly necessary and addressed to 'Mr Nick Du Pont Esq.' in halting green Biro has appeared on the doormat. Inside are several pages torn out of a lined W.H. Smith notebook on which Jim has inscribed the lyrics of a new song: 'Dunwich Bells.' Dunwich is four miles along the coast in the shadow of the nuclear reactor. The ruins of the original church, long ago over-run by an eroding tide, lie several miles out to sea. According to local legend, on which Jim has alighted, the bells can still sometimes be heard above the clamour of the waves. There is also an entertaining play-on-words about the 'belles' who frolic on the Dunwich shore. All this augurs well for our recording session. Outside the gulls are circling in the endless sky.

15. THE GIRL WHO PLAYED THE TAMBOURINE

Beyond the triple-glazed windows, stained with the entrails of many a passing insect, molten sunshine is streaming in over an edge-of-town landscape of back yards and crowded pebble-dash semis. The thirty or forty rooks lined up on the drooping wire between two telegraph poles look Hitchcockian, as if only the heat is preventing them from wreaking vengeance on puny humankind. Nearer at hand, beside me at the console, Darren, the studio's dishevelled proprietor, is sprawled in a basket chair reading a story in the *Lowestoft Journal* about the Trawler Boys' – that is, Lowestoft Town FC's – prospects in the pre-season, while a plate of egg sandwiches sits quietly congealing in the glare.

'Try playing it in A,' I counsel over the intercom. The rooks look nervous, ill at ease. Maybe they are plotting to sweep down and drive us into the sea. Who can tell? 'Then you can take the chorus up to D7 to finish.'

From his vantage point on the other side of the Perspex, head canted towards the microphone, Jim looks puzzled, as ill at ease as the rooks. The recording studio, I suspect, is not his natural milieu. He would rather be plodding the back lanes or turning over the discount items in the Southwold Co-op. All the same, he is conscious that an effort needs to be made. The same cannot be said of Darren, previously commissioned to engineer this morning's session, who has swapped a succinct appraisal of the Trawler Boys' chances in next week's friendly against Giggleswick Town, for a story about a man whose dog was carried out to sea on a spar of driftwood and rescued a dozen miles off the Dutch coast.

'How's that go then?' (*Howzat goo, then*?) Jim wonders, raising a fat hand to massage the back of his shiny scalp. Despite the air-con and the several-times replenished tumbler of water next to his guitar-stand, he is sweating profusely.

'G minor for the middle-eight and then back to the chorus.'

Jim busks a couplet or two – we are hard at work finessing 'Dunwich Bells' – about the cold grey water and the pebbles on the Suffolk strand, but I get the feeling that his heart isn't in it. The mystical compact that exists between the artist and his art has been breached by third parties. Still, in the three hours we have been here – it is getting on for lunch-time now – we have already laid down passable versions of half-a-dozen numbers. Even Danny, notoriously unmoved by the traffic that flows through his premises, concedes that they may 'have something'.

But what exactly do they have? A plaintiveness? A buried literary sensibility? I doubt Jim has read a dozen books in his life, but some of the language is practically Biblical in its solemnity, its hint of lurking retribution and just desserts. He has another go along the lines suggested, quavers his way mournfully yet tunefully through the middle eight, only to hit the chorus a semi-tone out.

'Not so good?'

'Not so bad.'

In fact, there are two perfectly acceptable takes of 'Dunwich Bells' in the can. But the best sessions, memory insists, are those which factor in an element of surprise. After all, despite their protests ('Who are these fucking old geezers then?') the best single that the Bash

Street Kids ever made was augmented by a string quartet. Back behind the Perspex, Jim asks if he can take a break. I suspect he has trouble with his bladder. There have been three such intermissions already. Meanwhile, Darren, having put the *Lowestoft Journal* reluctantly to one side, has three fingers of his right hand raised and is wagging a fourth. This is his way of signalling that the session is about to run into an extra, unbooked hour.

'It's OK, Jim, We can stop there. Plenty of material to work on.'

Standing to one side, as Jim – looking more than ever like Baloo in flight from monkey hordes around the back of the abandoned temple – crashes past on his way to the lavatory, I note the various sartorial refinements he has thought appropriate for a morning at Suffolk Sounds. The old rat-catcher's jacket and the stinking canvas trousers have gone. Just now Jim is wearing an approximation of a Hawaiian shirt two sizes too small for his capacious midriff and a pair of blue jeans sawn off below the leg to reveal pale, spindly legs from which varicose veins bulge like lengths of tubing. The general effect is to make him look faintly submerged, like some sea-creature hauled up from the depths, a manatee, say, keeping its ear cocked for the sound of the Dunwich bells.

The heat of the sun has receded a bit now. The rooks are leaving their perch in ones and two, spinning off languidly into the dense suburban air. There is nothing for them here. Darren, cheered by the fifteen ten-pound notes I have just handed him in a brown envelope, wonders exactly how I am going to release this stuff once the mixing is complete. Will I be starting my own label? Or is the plan to put it on Spotify and see what happens? I suspect that Darren, who in addition to running Suffolk Sounds has a little distribution and mail-order concern on the go, is keen for some more of the action. Naturally, it is early days but I have an idea that the more archaic the format in which I can package up Wangford Jim for public consumption, the better the results will be. Even a vinyl EP would not be over-doing it.

After a longish interval Jim emerges from the loo, buttoning the flies of his sawn-off jeans and casting wary looks around the studio vestibule. His social awkwardness is, I now realise, countered and to a certain extent neutralised by a bubbling inner confidence, a kind of bedrock self-possession. Some people would be badly flummoxed by the interest I am evincing in him. Jim, though suspicious of Suffolk Sounds' paraphernalia – the table-sized mixing desk, the unreliable coffee machine, the signed portrait of The Searchers, who apparently came this way in 1996 – simply accepts it as his due. He can take it or leave it. There is a pile of business cards on a ledge by the door. Jim picks up the top-most wedge and sweeps it into the back-pocket of his jeans. Something tells me that he will be calling his newly-acquired friend Darren very soon.

Outside Darren's back door, partly obscured by infiltrating clothes-lines, the mini-cab booked to take us back to Southwold stands idling on the kerb. Seeing it, Jim's face falls. Clearly he has anticipated a pleasant half-hour, or even a whole afternoon, on licensed premises. But I need to get back to the Conservative Club by two in order to attend the filming of *Trash for Cash*. 'Nice place,' he says wistfully, as we clamber into the cab. The Spanish guitar, which for some reason smells of oranges, lies across our knees. 'Enjoyed myself.' Even now, I can't work Jim out. *Idiot savant*? The canny repository of several centuries of peasant cunning? A dark horse? No doubt in time all this will be revealed. For the moment there is something disconcerting about his hot, heavy breath and the curious intensity with which his eyes follow the road. The mini-cab bowls off along back lanes infested with cow parsley and summer ramblers, past grey-stone churches and village greens thick with dandelions. Set down, at his request, at Reydon he loiters uncertainly at the side of the road, swinging the Spanish guitar from hand to hand, and then lumbers off in the direction of a field of wheat. As he starts to forge a path through the waist-high grain, a shaft of sunlight briefly irradiates the backs of his calves and the washed-out denim shorts. Then, mysteriously, he is gone.

* * *

I get to the Conservative Club just as the camera crew is setting up. The presenting team are gathered by the bar: Greg and Phil supplied with fancy cocktails, Sophie standing a little to one side with the look of a woman labouring under some rare, implacable grievance. Above their heads, portraits of the Queen, Mrs Thatcher and David Cameron stare more or less benignly down. Oddly enough, Cameron reminds me of Rory. There is the same chronic self-confidence, the thought that however great the odds stacked against him, the instincts of his caste will see him through. Set against this, Gordon Brown looks a shifty, starveling ingrate whom hope has abandoned. That *Trash for Cash* is a no-frills production is made abundantly clear by the speed with which the camera crew lick the premises into shape. Also abundantly clear, once the audience begins to show up, is the feeling of incongruity. Southwold isn't really *Trash for Cash's* kind of locale. The place is too up-market for this kind of low-end roustabout. *Antiques Roadshow* would play well here, but the sight of Greg and Phil parading their Sharm-el-Sheikh tans is a step too far, and the middle-aged ladies in the rows of plush armchairs – significantly, the club is only two-thirds full – look deeply unimpressed. There is an amusing moment at which a tremulous daub of a field of cows alleged to be by Sir Alfred Munnings turns out to be a tremulous daub. Apart from this, Greg and Phil are reduced to making off-colour jokes about catching crabs. Further evidence of what a low-budget production this is comes in the director's haste to conclude it. By three thirty the cameras are being hauled off their tripod and the display tables over which Sophie stands feigning interest when members of the public bring out their trinkets wheeled back to the truck.

I make a point of positioning myself at the end of the second row. There is no way Sophie cannot have seen me. Sure enough, once the proceedings are over and the crowd has trooped disdainfully away, she comes sailing over.

'Hello, Nick. I thought it was you.' It seems perfectly natural to her that the audience for a TV antiques show in a far-flung seaside town should include the boss of her old record company.

'Is there time for a cup of tea? Or do you have to get away?'

Sophie thinks about this. Clearly the possibility of a chance encounter or a blast from the prehistoric showbiz past hasn't been factored into her busy schedule. Close up she looks shorter and plumper than pictorial representations suggest. It is hard to connect her with the girl who steered a punt around the moat at Oxburgh Hall.

'Geoff said we had to get away by four. There's another shoot at Bury St Edmunds this evening. That's if he can drag those two fuckers away from the bar.' Greg and Phil, now stolidly embarked on another round of cocktails, grin broadly at this insinuation. Plainly, they have heard worse. We head out through the Conservative Club's north-eastern portal and fetch up in the New Buckenham Tea Rooms, which is full of the usual corn-haired children and girls in designer beach ware. Here Sophie, who claims not to have eaten since breakfast ('Geoff never stops when we're on the road') rapidly consumes two sugar-heavy cappuccinos and a brace of tea-cakes.

'It's nice to see you again, Nick. After all this time.'

'I've been following your career.' This, by the way, is the truth. Five minutes with Google has left me with more knowledge of Sophie's doings in the past twenty years than I really have space for. To particularise, I know about her sterling work on Channel Four's *The Mistress Files*, not to mention the tabloid exposé of her charity trek across the Sahara, when it was discovered that a celebrity chef and a mobile kitchen were accompanying them in a Land Rover. Sophie's husband is thought to be the chief executive of a time-share property firm. Oddly, there are hardly any details of her life in pop.

'*Career*,' Sophie says, irony just about prevailing over rancour. 'Do you know how much I get paid for this, Nick? Two hundred quid a fucking day...Cheers. Good to see you' – she scratches her signature on the table-napkin that some undersized celebrity-spotter has poked in front of her without breaking stride. 'Not to mention that fucker Greg knocking on the door of your hotel room at two o'clock in the morning.'

'Can't your agent get you something better?'

'Jesus, Nick, I'm forty-four. My weather-girl days are long gone. The best I can hope for is sitting on the sofa on some retard's morning show where they junk all the proper news for stories about people's cats.'

Time, it has to be said, is a great promoter of solidarity. Back in the Eighties I can't have had half-a-dozen conversations with hoity-toity Miss Sophie. Now we are like the Queen and her oldest lady-in-waiting exchanging confidences in a Balmoral back-room as the twilight steals over the heather and the fire burns low. This newfound consanguinity seems to have occurred to Sophie, who scoops up a spoonful or two of cappuccino froth, deposits them in her ample mouth, and then says:

'You know, Nick. I always thought you blamed me. I mean, for what happened to the Systems. And Magda.'

'I don't think I knew the personalities well enough to blame anyone.'

'Well, I must say that's very charitable of you, Nick,' Sophie says, rattling the spoon noisily around the rim of her coffee cup. 'Jesus, that Magda was a fucking lunatic. I mean, have you any idea what it's like being in a band like that when you're nineteen and the singer and his girlfriend are having a moment seventeen times a day? Especially when you're just the girl who plays the tambourine. Jesus, Nick, I had no idea what I was doing. And I don't suppose she did either.'

'I seem to remember it was all very complicated.'

'And now she's this *icon* or whatever. Do you know, Nick, even now I still get letters from people telling me it was all my fault. *Magda would still be alive today making wonderful music if it weren't for you, you conniving bitch.* How do you think I feel about that?'

'What exactly happened afterwards?'

'It was a complete disaster. The drummer was Magda's cousin, so he left. As far as I know, Jon never wrote another song. Then he went off and joined the Plastic Fantastics. Do you remember them?' I nod my head, for I do remember the Plastic Fantastics, and in particular the NME album review opining that if this band made it the reviewer would commit suicide.

It is nearly four o'clock now. The truck – Geoff, Gary, Phil, all of the shoot paraphernalia of an afternoon's filming on the Suffolk coast – will be waiting. There are shards of sunlight falling over the New Buckenham Tea Rooms' tightly-packed tables.

'What about you, Nick?' Sophie wonders. 'What are you up to?'

What am I up to? I have my schemes. I have my settlements to negotiate. I have my showdowns with past time to pursue. Out in the street the summer crowds have dispersed a little and the smell of malt from the brewery is stronger than ever. Alone on the pavement, I watch Sophie make her way back to the Conservative Club. Like Wangford Jim vanishing into his cornfield, she is caught for an instant in the enticing surround – the passing traffic of the High Street, the bucket-and-spade clusters outside the bric-a-brac shops – and then disappears.

* * *

Slowly the Suffolk summer wends on. The circus – animal-free now, and with environmentally-conscious clowns who make jokes about soil erosion – sets up on the common. The Salvation Army mission sets up on the beach. In the early morning there is usually a speed boat or two skidding over the choppy water beyond the point and the pier is already thick with what the newspapers have begun to call 'footfall'. My own feet take me to Walberswick and Westleton, to tiny villages out along the cliff top that are collapsing into the sea. A florid invitation from the Metal Hall of Fame arrives, signed by Alice Cooper himself ('Yours in music, Alice') and bidding me to celebrate the induction into this time-hallowed institution of the Flame Throwers at a conference centre in Chicago in three weeks' time. Naturally, I have been prepping myself – another word that has suddenly entered the lexicon – for this event. In particular, I have discovered a Wikipedia entry for Rory, which offers brief details of his later career. Apparently Rory finally detached himself from the music business in the mid-1990s. He has since migrated to investment banking. There is a Mrs Bayliss-Callingham – formerly Miss Caroline Tradescant – and two children named Peter and Marigold. They live in Chertsey, Surrey. He is also, I am informed, a leading light in a London Livery Company known as the Worshipful Company of Cordwainers. There is every chance, in the fulness of time, of his being elected Lord Mayor of London.

What am I going to say to Rory, should we meet in Chicago, and what is he going to say to me? I haven't a clue. The impossibility of this preparing a face to meet the faces that you meet is brought home to me when, on a brisk Saturday morning, with the wind coming in off the sea, turning into the promenade at the foot of Gun Hill, I come upon Gordon Brown. Strictly speaking, Her Majesty's First Lord of the Treasury has no business being here – the *East Anglian Daily Times* has already reported his return to London – but no, there he indisputably is, bent over a mug of tea at the open-air café, with the wind tearing his hair and a couple of security guys two tables down ready to spring up and disable any terrorist or eco-warrior who might be hastening by. Gordon, it has to be said, looks hangdog, brooding, ground-down to the point of inconsolability. The morning papers are fanned out on the table before him. On this evidence, being Prime Minister is not all it might be. Meanwhile, the adviser who counselled that a seaside holiday would play well with the voters is clearly going to get it in the neck. What do you do in such circumstances? The Old Man – I am pretty sure about this – would have sat down next to him, winked humorously, ordered a cup of tea and entertained him with a volley of droll remarks. I can think of nothing. I leave him with his tea, the two security guys in their sharp suits, the weak sun looming over a pale horizon.

* * *

If *Trash for Cash* represents rough-and-ready low-budget modernity, then the BBC camera crew are an echo from an older world. There are eight of them – director, cameraman, interviewer, sound-man, assistant sound-lady, lighting guy, electrician and a nervous, finger-nail-chewing girl with a clipboard. Meanwhile, the equipment truck is so large that it gets stuck in the Centre Cliff entrance-way. Mrs Stiff, impressed by this kind of activity, and also by the deference paid to her employer, brews several potfuls of her mahogany Bohea and at one point disappears to the High Street to buy a packet of Eccles Cakes. They set up in the sitting room, while the girl with the clip-board inspects the Jim Dine drawing and the Sergeant Pepper cut-outs I bought at the Apple fire sale forty years ago. The questions are mostly straightforward – How did I first meet Cedric? What did I think of him? Why weren't his records more successful? – but not for that reason any easier to answer. Later it becomes clear that the interviewer, who turns out to have written a book called *Kick Over the Statues: Radical Pop in the 1980s*, has an agenda to pursue. Thus:

Q: Can we talk about Cedric's political ideas? I'm thinking of 'The Woman at Number Ten' off the first album.

A: As far as I know it was written about his next-door neigh-bour when he lived in Solihull. I believe his address was 8

Thornbush Road. He used to go round there sometimes and feed her cat.

Q: You're telling me that a song called 'The Woman at Number Ten' recorded in the summer of 1980 isn't about Mrs Thatcher?

A: Not to my knowledge. In any case, the demo was recorded sometime in 1978.

Q: And then there's his well-established connection with CND?

I haven't the heart to tell him that Cedric, though indeed invited to entertain the crowds at an anti-nuclear demo in Sydenham sometime in 1983, caught the wrong bus and arrived at the gathering just as they were dismantling the PA. But then we are all busy re-inventing ourselves. Sophie has turned into an antiques show presenter. Rory is shaping up to be Lord Mayor of London. Cedric, whose political awareness was, so far as I recall it, half-way along a scale between non-existent and minimal, is being transformed into a spokesperson for radical youth. The crew stays a couple of hours. From the double buggy parked just inside the front door, Bradley and Tamarind watch them come and go. Everyone is scrupulously polite. There is talk of an appearance fee. On the other hand, I can't see very much of what I tell them making the cut.

* * *

Meanwhile, someone else has been eagerly re-inventing himself. This becomes evident when, opening the *East Anglian Daily Times* three days before the Chicago trip, I discover a substantial photograph of Jim, dressed in his sub-Hawaiian shirt, guitar in hand, beneath the caption LOCAL SINGER HAS BIG-TIME IN HIS SIGHTS. The letterpress is similarly well-proportioned. In it Jim talks about the recording contract he is poised to sign and the 'national exposure' that is soon to come his way. The lyrics to 'Dunwich Bells' are reproduced alongside. The photo downplays the resemblance to Baloo and makes him look more than ever like some creature of the deep, temporarily washed up on Southwold beach. I am unmentioned, although an admiring Darren is quoted to the effect that 'major industry figures' are interested and that he, personally, has never seen anything like it. There are also plugs for Suffolk Sounds and Jim's next gig at the Lord Nelson. I can see that Mrs Stiff, whom I come across reading the piece in her coffee-break, is in two minds about her cousin's one-man publicity campaign. On the one hand, she is anxious that her own flesh and blood should be allowed his moment in the sun. On the other, I can tell that the enormity of his exposure – the mottled old face looking up from the newspaper, the brandished guitar – has alarmed her, that she suspects no good will come of it.

Zoe calls several times. She is taking a week off from the Whitstable psychotherapy practice and seems in excellent spirits. We shall have fun, she more than once assures me. Of all the truisms brought with me from that older life, the idea that 'fun' is permanently there for the taking seems the most questionable of all.

16. CHICAGO

The plane – three-quarters full – tracks westward into the velvet dark. Into the velvet dark westward tracks the plane. Most of the passengers, it turns out, are expat Americans off on vacation to the motherlode: teenage boys, their knees drawn up to their chins like giant grasshoppers; sleekly coiffeured girls with top-of-the-range skin tones and orthodontists permanently on call, the outlines of their elegantly cantilevered haunches discreetly visible beneath stretch-pants. Their parents sprawl in the row behind, mom bent over a nourishing paperback, dad nervously inspecting the *Economist*, for these are bleak times for investment bankers off on furlough. The sub-prime crisis is still unravelling and the markets are in free fall. Gordon, no longer in East Suffolk but back in his Whitehall bunker, is on the front page of *The Times*, talking about retrenchment and modified growth prospects. He looks more devitalised than ever, a limpet-like survivor clinging desperately to the hull of the old world as it slips beneath the waves. Nearer at hand, in fact a couple of rows in front of me, Zoe – who has already drunk three gins and tonic – sleeps fretfully. Every so often her carmine-curled head slides down onto her leather-jacketed shoulder and she jolts irritably awake. The teenagers on either side look on with interest.

As for myself, I have work to do. Item one is to listen to a remix of the three tracks that Wangford Jim committed to tape at Suffolk Sounds a fortnight ago. On the other hand, 'remix' is probably not the operative word. There is, after all, a limit to what you can do with vocals and a strummed acoustic guitar. But Darren, I note, has done his best, sanded down one or two of the imperfections, spliced a modicum of echo to Jim's upper register and – a nice touch – over-dubbed a tinkling keyboard line to the chorus of 'Dunwich Bells'. The other two numbers chosen for the remix are 'Southwold Train' and a supremely odd and fanciful affair about angling on the upper reaches of the Blyth (*'Take out the fish/Put 'im in the dish/Let's make a wish.'*) How do they sound? To my ears, they sound like nothing on earth. Take it from me, as one who was present at a blues club outside Columbus, Ohio all of forty years ago when John Lee Hooker took to the stage, authenticity has to be worked at. It don't come easy. The aim is to press five hundred vinyl EPs – I am thinking of calling it *Suffolk Boy: The World of Wangford Jim* – mail advance copies to the adult music magazines and BBC6 Music and see what happens. My guess is that the pundits and the alt-folk reputation-brokers won't be able to resist Wangford Jim. The big question is whether Jim will be able to resist them.

Item two is some prepping for the day-after-tomorrow's ceremony. What are the three surviving Flame Throwers – whose collective age I estimate at 156 – up to right now? All three of them turn out to have personal websites and are eager to communicate with their fans. Joey, whom I tracked down first on a platform called *Jukin' with Joey*, is discovered, king-size rifle to hand, standing over the body of a dead lion somewhere in the African bush beneath an excitable description of how he stalked the animal to the water-course where it met its end (*So I'm coming out from behind this tree when I see the dude kind of* lurking *in some undergrowth. We got this dead goat or whatever stuck out in the clearing as bait, but, hey, the fucker's way too smart to be fooled by this, and before I can slip the safety catch he's off into the fuckin' jungle.)* Further photos show Joey and assorted big-muscled chums posing athwart the corpses of a leopard, two hippopotami and what I am pretty confident is an ibex. Appended to this *galère* is a blog entitled *Why conservationists can get the fuck off my back.*

As for the others, Cris at least is still, as he puts it, 'making music'. Indeed there is talk of a collaboration ('some really serious shit been going down') with the New York rapper Muthafucka and a series of acoustic gigs on the Eastern seaboard. Meanwhile Art Smothers, dark horse Art, has been shrewdly furthering his career in abstract expressionism. There are pictures of him at the openings of West Coast galleries, signing copies of *Smothers: A Retrospective*, breakfasting with Don Van Vliet, as the former Captain Beefheart now styles himself, and at work in his spacious Long Island studio. Of the three, I'd say that Art is by far the most successful and – to use a current American neologism – 'centred', if only because of the high degree of sobriety and self-effacement that attends his pronouncements (*'Here I am with my friend Don, a truly great artist and companion. If only I could paint half as well as he does!'*) Significantly, he has very little to say about his previous professional calling. It's all water under the bridge, old news. Joey and Cris, alternatively, offer thousand-shot, braggart photo-recapitulations of their time in the Flame Throwers, who were, Joey assures us, *'the greatest band in the history of rock and roll bar none'* and whose music is still capable of *'blowing your fucking head off'*. Cris, I can't help noticing, is marketing fragments of a 1963 Fender Telecaster guitar used in the making of *Breakfast at Ralph's*, together with autographed certifications of their provenance. Meanwhile, there are at least three tribute sites to Stevie, where conspiracy theorists squabble over whether he was murdered by the mob or gang-probed to death by visiting space-aliens.

Raising my head from this torrent of lies, carnage, dissimulation and special pleading, I discover that most of the teenagers have fallen asleep or are watching movies on the overhead screens. Zoe, on the other hand, is sitting bolt upright and reading a copy of Ian MacDonald's *Revolution in the Head: The Beatles' Music and the Sixties.* She has booked us into the Avalon, she says, on the grounds that it will be 'kind of nostalgic'. Outside the window the sky is pitch-black, as dark as the paint Art lays onto his canvases of crows picking up roadkill in the Mojave Desert. Above our heads the fastenings of the luggage-lockers rattle melancholically. Zoe, who has strong views about the Beatles, and indeed many other aspects of musical history, has taken a felt-tip pen out of her reticule and is making furious emendations. As if propelled by some unseen mechanical force, her crinkle-curled hair bobs crazily up and down.

* * *

The flight gets in at midnight, local time. The lanky teenagers clamber to their feet, blithe and unconcerned. Someone else will be on hand to ferry them off across the dark Illinois plain or hustle them onto connecting flights to Akron or Sioux City, It's not their problem. Arrangements have been made. The touring bands I worked with in the Sixties were like this: always happy to go off for a Coke or a cigarette while despairing road managers wept over lost equipment or mislaid tickets. Outside, the floodlit tarmac of O'Hare stretches away towards a megalopolis of hangars and terminal buildings. Cabin staff hasten disinterestedly back and forth: what happens now is not their problem either. Meantime, other things beyond Zoe's choice of lodgement are proving kind of nostalgic. Memory insists that it was on this very concrete, one bright morning thirty-eight years ago, that Dale Halliwell, the Helium Kids' lead guitarist, fell flat on his face having consumed one Drinamyl tablet too many, only for Stefano to pick him up by the scruff of the neck, slap him back into consciousness and explain his subsequent air of hysterical detachment to passport control as a fear-of-flying-induced panic attack. But this,

I remind myself as we traipse off to the terminal building, was back in the bright hippy dawn. Here in 2009 there are security cops at ten-yard intervals: a modern-day Helium Kid would get his head blown off before he hit the ground.

So here we are in the Windy City, home of Wrigley Fields, the White Sox, John Belushi, Theodore Dreiser, James T. Farrell and, I remind myself, electric blues, and an amiable yet frenetic Puerto Rican taxi-driver named Marlon who, on enquiring the reason for our visit, concedes that he knows the Flame Throwers' oeuvre ('Yeah, I heard 'em. They cool') while shyly admitting that his real love is U2 ('They're outtasight.') 'Why were you so keen to come?' I ask Zoe as the car bumps and judders towards the monstrous overhang of the Loop, and Marlon favours us with his opinion of AC/DC ('They're sort of a Zeppelin kind of a thing. I can dig that'), and Zoe, hands zestfully at work re-arranging the primped scallops of her hair-do, says that she wants to revisit some of the scenes of her mis-spent youth. 'Jesus, Nick, when we hit the Avalon I'm going to smoke a joint, and I tell you it'll be just like Proust or whoever crumbling his madeleine biscuit.' Like Zoe's erratic hair-cut, memory stirs. The Avalon, I now remember, was a rock and roll, or at any rate counter-cultural-to-hipster fun palace, where the Helium Kids stayed back in their 1971 roister-doister around the Mid West, and where Keith Shields, denied his nightly solace of an unmade Airfix kit straight out of the box, once drove a Triumph motorcycle slap-bang into a crowded swim-pool.

As the cab sweeps into up-town Chicago, where the cop cars are out and everything seems very laid back and subdued for a Friday night in August, I catch a glimpse of the pair of us in the mirror. How do we look? I look ancient and fatigued. Zoe, though animated, looks like a middle-aged rock chick out to rekindle the warmth of former glories. Marlon drops us at the Avalon's sumptuous but mostly deserted portal ('You have a good time now. Rock and roll!') to face the realisation that it, like us, is not what it was. A few sober-suited business types are still lingering over night-caps at the bar, but otherwise the place is as quiet as the grave. My suite, looking out over Avenue of the Americas, where a few cars discreetly glide, is positively sepulchral. Last time I stayed here, three-and-a-half decades ago, the first thing I found in the drawer of the bedside cabinet, alongside the Gideon's Bible, was a drug facilitator's flyer signed 'Captain Preemo' and advertising Chihuahua finger ash at $5 the bag. Now there is merely a corporate compendium in black leather wrap-round alerting me to the provision of complimentary Thai massages in the steam parlour and morning services at the Presbyterian church along the way. It would never have done for Keith Shields who, last time I saw him, was in a wheelchair and had temporarily lost the power of speech.

* * *

Morning, eight hours later, finds me – still jet-lagged into stupor – moving warily along vast expanses of lavishly-carpeted corridor in search of the elevator. Even the full-on air-con can't disguise the blinding intensity of conditions outside. And here is another example of the way in which time's tide has barrelled on, leaving the counter-culture washed up in its wake. Thirty-five years ago, venturing out of your quarters at the Avalon, you would like as not have chanced upon one of its super-cool janitoriat smoking a spliff. These days the janitors are all solemnly besuited black kids who are probably studying for MBAs on the quiet and, from the glances they give me as I dawdle past, clearly feel that I'm not the sort of person the management wants here anymore. Down in the breakfast room, where what look like the members of a Baptist convention are conferring over glasses of cranberry juice and muffin baskets, I find Zoe unabashedly tucking into a plate of Virginia ham. 'I ordered you some eggs,' she says, fork half-way to her mouth. 'If you don't want them, I'll eat them myself.' We agree that the day will be devoted to tourism and the modest reconnoitring of locale.

'You see any of these?' Zoe wonders, pushing a stack of expensive stationery across the marbled table-top. Here, I discover, are letters of welcome from corporate sponsors, invites to cocktail parties and record company clambakes, even a keynote lecture in which Kiss's Gene Simmons will dilate on 'Heritage Rock: Marketing Your Product in the Digital Age'. Ten hours into her stay in Chicago, Zoe's antennae are primed to seek out data that will be useful to her. Did I know, for example, that Alice Cooper, previously booked to emcee tomorrow's induction ceremony, has cried off sick and that his place will be filled by Chester Weasel, lead singer with the Texas Cowherds. 'Is he really called Weasel?' 'It's pronounced Wea*zel*' Zoe assures me. I confess to never having heard of the Cowherds. 'What kind of music do they play?' 'It's a sort of Tex-Mex grunge hybrid' says Zoe, who always has this kind of information at her finger-tips and can separate out the various layers of the grind-core end of the death-metal scene without turning a hair. Over at the adjoining table the Baptist delegation – if that is what they are – have paused for prayer. Their pale, pious faces are aflame with silent ecstasy.

And so the long day waxes and wanes. There are tourist coffles everywhere, full of haggard pensioners from the East desperate for a sit-down in the shade. Together Zoe and I visit a Blues Bar, which is pretty much like any other kind of bar except for the highly specialised jukebox and the framed portraits of Muddy Waters, Robert Johnson and Ma Rainey. We saunter by the lakefront, where an occasional zephyr blown down from Canada briefly mingles with the 90 degree heat. Zoe, I notice, is even more interrogative than usual. She is, for example, immensely interested in Wangford Jim and the plans I have for him.

'Don't mind me, Nick, but is this really going to work? Picking up some old guy in a pub who's never left East Suffolk in his life?'

'Come on, Zoe. I'm not fixing up a fifty-date tour. I'm just putting out a record. People will either like it or they won't.'

'And what if they do like it?' Zoe, by the way, having downloaded the three tracks onto her iPod, has pronounced them 'weird but interesting'.

'Well, we'll just have to find a way of dealing with it.'

'Good luck with that, Nick.' Zoe, I now see, is reverting to type. All traces of the Whitstable psychotherapist have vanished. Spiritually she is back in the Resurgam boardroom bending a contemptuous ear to the demo-tapes. 'Jesus. It was bad enough when you signed some twenty-one-year-old from Bolton, lobbed the fucker a £20,000 advance, put him on *Top of the Pops* and then wondered how he was going to cope with his...with his *challenging new lifestyle*. How is it going to work with, what is he called, Wangford Jim?'

'I'm not giving him £20,000 and I very much doubt he'll be going on *Top of the Pops*.'

'Don't get me wrong, Nick.' Zoe curls a finger-tip around an overhanging curl and starts twisting it into a knot. The grim Chicago frontages stare sightlessly down. 'You're doing...What is it you're doing? You're helping some old derelict from the boondocks to realise his dream or something. Hats off to that. But it's not going to end well. Something's going to come along and fuck it up. You'll see.'

Another thing about Zoe. All the relish of practical detail – the Texas Cowherds and what kind of music they play – has been overturned by a determination to philosophise. This had happened a lot in the 1970s when, deep into the small hours of a post-gig hootenanny, ranged crapulously around some bottle-strewn restaurant table, various minor personnel – a tour manager and two of the sound-guys, say – hitherto known only for their inarticulacy, would suddenly begin to pick apart the first principles of their calling. It was good to know that the tradition endured.

'Why did you get involved in all this, Nick?' she enquires, as we eat lunch in Schwab's Delicatessen next to a cantankerous veterans' bus party from Cincinnati.

'Why did I get involved in what?'

Zoe flaps the palm of her hand outwards in a gesture that takes in the delicatessen and its sweating waitresses, the Cincinnati vets in their tourists' finery, Joey, Cris and Art and, by implication, a great deal more.

'I don't get it, Nick. You're an intelligent guy...You went to *Oxford,* or wherever. And then you spent twenty years working with the worst people in the world selling a product which you know and I know and everyone else knows has as much material value as a toilet roll, and even now you've got some weird old folkie fresh out of the sheep dip up your sleeve you're convinced is going to be the next big thing.'

Zoe has asked for this. Now she is going to get it with both barrels.

'Don't you think', I innocently propose, 'that popular music is the last refuge of romanticism?'

'Jesus, Nick!' Such is Zoe's consternation that she chokes on a swig of orange juice. 'I've known people who went into music because they wanted to make money. I've known people who went into music because they wanted to get laid. And I've known *artists'* – the way Zoe pronounces 'artists' makes it abundantly clear what she feels about this race of bottom-feeding delusionaries – 'who wanted to sit in a fucking shack near the Mississippi River and write songs to their lost love, or whatever. But I never met anybody who thought it was the last refuge of *romanticism.*'

'When you first heard *Breakfast at Ralph's*, didn't you think it had a life of its own? I mean, that it existed somewhere out there, way beyond the imaginations of the people who made it?'

'The trouble with you, Nick,' says Zoe, not unkindly, 'is that you're over-educated. You are, though. You're telling me that some scuzzy little record by a bunch of shit-heels who could barely write their names, one of whom was the greatest asshole I ever fell into bed with, is *transcendental*? Nick, you really are a fucking lunatic. What is this stuff to you...What are you going to say to Rory if you come across him tomorrow?'

'I'm sure I shall think of something, Zoe. But let me ask you: why did you go into music?'

'I'll be totally honest with you, Nick. It was the only job I could get.'

One more incident from later on in the day confirms the behavioural gap that might be said to exist between Zoe and myself. We are scurrying back to the Avalon through that less than salubrious neighbourhood of chain-link fences and litter-crazed streets where the downtown meets the uptown, some large black gentlemen are dealing wraps concealed in their coat-pockets and one or two surprisingly old-fashioned pimps – real antediluvian throwbacks from the Tenth Street days with peacock suits and fancy canes – are touting for business, when a scrawny kid in a Method Man tee-shirt lurches out from under an awning, sticks a paw on my shoulder and asks if I can help him out. There is no malice in the solicitation, no pressure in his hand, which quivers like the flipper of an ailing penguin, and no time to check how many dollars are left in my wallet, for in a trice Zoe has detached the hand, spun its owner round against a wall and is shrieking at him that he'd better fuck off back to the dumpster he's clearly been sleeping in, say hi to the rats he's left there and leave civilised folks alone, while the dealers guffaw and the pimps swivel on their canes to inspect us.

'I don't think he meant any harm,' I say as we proceed on our way, leaving the kid sprawled over a fire-hydrant and gasping for breath.

'First they put a hand on your shoulder. Then they stick a knife in your back. This is fucking *Chicago*,' Zoe says.

* * *

This is indeed fucking Chicago, up-to-date, down-to-earth, mired in stasis. Certainly the Plaza Convention Centre has seen better days. The blue-veined porphyry pillars that hold up the sagging vestibule are cracked and fissured and the three-foot-square metal plaque commemorating its opening by Richard J. Daley jr. is flaking into amber rust. Also having seen better days are some of the people swarming through its antiseptic portals, where leather-jacketed ephebes in tuxes are frowning over the invites and grim-looking waitresses in leotard-and-fishnet combinations whose last job was clearly helping Janis Joplin back from the bar after her final gig are handing out three-quarter full glasses of sparkling wine. Who makes a habit of attending induction ceremonies at the Metal Hall of Fame? I don't and Zoe doesn't, so that leaves a submerged-seeming collection of far-from regular guys who look as if they last played on an Allman Brothers session back in 1969 and, when not being dredged up from the ocean floor, have spent the past forty years waiting for their agent to call, and a man who may have filled in on bass for the Grateful Dead the time Phil Lesh was getting his varicose veins done. Zoe, hustling us through the security detail, exchanging high-fives with a series of record company execs and hailing rheumy-eyed acquaintances glimpsed through the throng, is clearly in her element.

Five minutes later, seated at a table sideways on to the main stage and affording passable views of overhead video screens, a drum-kit, several microphone stands and a wall of Marshall amplifiers, we inspect our place-cards – mine says *Nicky Dee P.* – and attend to the stream of fellow-guests filling the seats at our side. As ever, Zoe has done her homework. The old lady with the Zimmer frame turns out to be Art's doting mother, Mrs Smothers, flown in specially from Terre Haute, Indiana, while the two listless teenage hoods are Joey's sons from his second, or maybe his third marriage. Also present are an assortment of ex-wives, significant others, proud beneficiaries of child-custody deals, accountants, some people from Sony, who maintain and further exploit the band's back catalogue, and a venerable old gentleman in a linen suit and a bootlace tie who turns out to be Larry Bracegirdle and informs me, jovially, that while he hasn't managed any of the guys for over twenty years and hasn't spoken to Cris since the morning he went tonto in the offices of Bracegirdle & Associates with a fire extinguisher, he is still, as a result of some devious legal manoeuvring executed a quarter of a century ago, taking his three per cent from the current series of re-releases.

By this time a single place card – the one belonging to *The Honourable R. Bayliss-Callingham* – is unclaimed. Meanwhile, all the anguished preliminaries that customarily attend events of this nature are kicking into gear. Somebody unzips a wedge of balloons which bounce and lollop across the wide stage and go skidding off across the heads of the crowds. Embarrassed grey-haired men in tasselled buckskin jackets, variously introduced as 'Mr Rock and Roll' and 'the Original Bluegrass Boy', drift reluctantly into view. '*Ladeez and gennelmin*' bellows a glum emcee, '*the Spirit of the Blues*', and a little old black guy with a seriously ricked back in a purple three-piece wanders stiffly into sight to general bewilderment ('Little Jimmy Culpepper,' Zoe whispers. 'Cut a coupla albums for Elektra back in the seventies) takes a harmonica out of his trouser-pocket, has his offer of playing it firmly declined and is shooed off into the wings without further ado. 'Jesus, I wish they'd get a fucking move on' one of the ex-wives complains. 'I got my aromatherapist to see and a flight to catch.' 'Who got the UK rights for them fellas jest now?' Larry wonders sleepily. 'Not me,' I tell him. Now the smaller fry are being propelled on and off the stage with increasing urgency. Clearly, weightier matters are at hand, and in the end, albeit after an interval so prolonged that another of the ex-wives is able to order, pay for and consume no fewer than three vodka-tonics, a drum roll strikes up and Chester Weasel, dressed in a button-down shirt, Stetson hat and elaborately embellished cowboy boots, arrives on stage, tells us that, no, people, he never got his dick out (a reference to some trifling scandal of the previous week in which the news channels have been taking an interest), pauses for the scattering of weak laughter to wash away and then stares hopelessly at an autocue primed to release a few choice facts about the Flame Throwers' career. Rory's seat is still unfilled. High above the stage, the giant video screen has begun pumping out images: the band loitering on some L.A. street-corner; limbering up to entertain the crazies at some open-air festival; signing with a clearly horrified David Geffen,

Ladeez 'n' gennilmin Chester's down-home, back-end-of-Texas country cousin's voice breezily intones. *We are here today to honour the legacy of one of the greatest rawk bands evvuh to hit this earth. Why, when I was a little bitty boy back in El Paso, this wuz the kind of heavy shit ah'd be listening to. It's a story that begins far away from the, uh, glittering lights of Los Angeles...*

Cue a picture of Cris and Stevie in their Wisconsin days, surly and morose, fists clamped on the handlebars of their kerb-hugging dirt-bikes.

It's a story of, ah, magisterial creativity and, uh, mind-numbing excess.

The Wisconsin snaps are followed, in quick succession, by a photo of Joey puzzling over the uppermost frets of a Rickenbacker guitar and a close-up depiction of Stevie, surrounded by empty bottles, fast asleep in the back of a tour bus.

Let's remind ourselves, ladeez 'n' gennilmin, no one ever kicked ass like the Flame Throwers.

There follows some dramatic footage from what looks like the *Straight From Hell* tour, possibly even the Battersea Park shambles, in which Cris assures a seething, bug-eyed crowd that if he ever comes across the devil while he's out amusing himself he'll just tell the dude to fuck right off outta it, Art's flash-powder-packed drums detonate at five-second intervals and the girls at the front are actually tearing their clothes off and hurling them on the stage, so that a pair of panties hangs from the neck of Stevie's guitar.

Ah cain't tell you, Chester tells us tearfully, *jest how proud ah am to be here with these fuckin' legends, these metal Gods...*

More pictures from the early years: the boys resentfully assembled outside Ralph's with weird back-combed pompadour hair-cuts; the boys on impossibly low-slung Harley-Davidsons outside a porno cinema on the strip; the boys with, of all people, myself in Rudi Martinez's office in the Sixties. The New York photo is an astonishing thing, a bullet winging back across time. 'Oh *my*,' Zoe breathes as it swings into view.

It's a story of, uh, controversy, Chester gamely continues. *A story of defiance, of championing the unorthodox, of fighting for the things you believe in.*

Or a story of drugs, duplicity and selfishness. Or venality, cupidity and plain bad temper. Next batch of photos includes a thronged, torch-lit evangelical protest outside a gig in one of the Southern states, Joey proudly displaying an album sleeve with a *Warning: Contains Explicit Content* sticker on it and Cris arrayed in the flowing robes of a deacon of the Satanist Church of Long Beach CA. By this time, to a modicum of respectful applause, the band – shepherded by a posse of Medusa-haired attendants – have arrived on stage. Keen to see what time's ravages have done to them, I lean forward in my seat. Zoe, meantime, is coming on like a teenager, hammering her plump fists on the table-top and yelling blandishments like 'Oh *wow*!' and 'You *got* it.' It is, I realise, spectacle that she wants, any kind of spectacle, even here in a beat-up old corporate barn in the Windy City in the shambling presence of an equally beat-up trio of ageing degenerates. How do the boys look? There is, it has to be said, no unanimity of style. Cris, squeezed into an expensive suit, rats-tail hair teased and sculpted into odd, perpendicular turrets and waterfalls, is going on fourteen stone. Joey, leather-clad and paint-speckled, seems to have acquired an entirely new skin, on whose sleek patina the light settles in a continuous dazzle. Art, on the other hand, has gone all sobersides, had his hair trimmed and processed like a Republican senator on the campaign trail, and looks a little disdainful, as if he knows that the real action is going on elsewhere and he intends to be off in search of it just as soon as this minor diversion is thankfully concluded. Chester, meanwhile, has recovered himself sufficiently to shake hands, weep on shoulders, tread on a balloon or two, mop the corrugations of his face with an outsize bandana handkerchief and refocus on the autocue. It is at precisely this moment that, to the accompaniment of a large-scale spatial disturbance, shifting chairs and compulsorily rearranged limbs, the vacant space at our table is filled. For once, Zoe's intelligence network has failed her. Rory, though dressed in a Savile Row suit and gleaming black Oxfords, is sitting in a wheelchair, propelled by a tall woman with swept-back blonde hair. Clearly the woman is new to the work, for the minor adjustments required to bring Rory in to harbour are beyond her. The wheelchair ends up at a 45 degree angle to the seat. Rory, thoroughly displeased but silent, twitches a hank of paper tissue out of his top pocket and dabs it at the corner of his mouth.

Back on stage the action is hotting up. The peeled and cadaverous face of Alice Cooper appears on the video screen to remark that, while he's sorry he can't be here, he's sure the boys, troopers that they are will be capable of getting thoroughly wasted without him. Amidst the round of whoops and hollers that greets this announcement, Cris snatches the microphone, grapples with it as if it were a live thing that needed beating into submission and yells that there's one major dude who ought to be here and it's one helluva shame he ain't, you all know what I'm talking about and it's Stevie fucking Da Vinci, God rest his soul ('Yeah,' Zoe murmurs, knuckles to her jaw, 'fuckin' Stevie.') Chester, in whose eyes more tears have welled up at the mention of Stevie, recovers himself, tramples another clutch of balloons, declares that the band are ready to *shake some action* and wonders if there is anyone present who *wants to rock*? Rory, ten feet away, looks puzzled, lost in some private world of dread and anxiety, as if he can't quite work out what all this portends, what he's doing here, how all this fits into the complex system of contingency of which his life now consists. Unregarded by the ex-wives and the delinquent children and Larry Bracegirdle, who is looking tolerantly on, as if to say that nobody checked the schedule with him but he's OK about it, the blonde woman hands him a glass of water. With a shaking hand, Rory spills most of it down the front of his suit and the equally expensive shirt from Gieves & Hawkes that gleams beneath it.

Thirty feet away some action is being shook. An anonymous bass player, two female backing singers who look as if they've been recruited from a Forty Second Street cinema queue and a diffident keyboard operative have appeared on stage. A guitar tech hands Joey a spanking new Fender Stratocaster with a burnished scratch-plate that catches the light and sends it flashing around the ceiling. Art, seated behind his kit, gives a desultory little thump or two at his hi-hat and taps a cymbal. 'Jesus *fuck*!' Zoe shouts, in the depths of whose soul some primal touch-paper has now been ignited. By now there is music playing, but of what kind? After maybe half a minute I identify what sounds to the untutored ear like the death-rattle of half-a-dozen dinosaurs struck down by a meteor-shower as 'Up in Lisa's Room', but the bass is a sidewalk out, Cris's vocals are way too low in the mix and Art, for reasons best known to himself, keeps coming in on the offbeat. Rory, face wholly impassive, has put his fingers in his ears. Zoe, mesmerised and exalted, is carolling along ('*Dontcha think there's a space for you honey, up in Lisa's room?*') It is at this point, half-way into the middle eight, with the blankets of dry ice rising from the back of the stage so dense that the backing singers seem curiously disembodied, that it all starts to go wrong. The culprit, naturally, is Cris, who, microphone in hand, gestures at the languid percussionist to his rear and yells, 'Ladies and gentlemen, on drums, Mr Etch-a-Sketch.' Art greets this with a wave, only to discover, after a second or two's reflection, that he is seriously discountenanced by this slight.

As the route-march 4/4 putters to a halt he decides to kick over the snare drums and wing a drumstick (these are heavy-duty items a foot long). The missile, having narrowly eluded Cris, hits Chester, who has been recuperating at the side of the stage, smack between the eyes. Security are on hand by this point, burly meatheads in dinner-jackets who pretty soon have Cris in a headlock, disarm Art of his remaining drumstick and subdue Joey, who is conducting some private vendetta with the bass player. Some more security men descend on our table to separate a former Mrs Itol and a protemporaneous Mrs Smothers, who have taken their ex- and prospective husbands' sides and are slugging it out with vanity bags.

As peace is restored, and the chatter renews itself – a titanic fuck-up everyone agrees, but there have been worse – I find myself a foot or two away from the wheelchair. Rory has taken his fingers out of his ears, but looks bewildered by the confusion. One of his black Oxfords is quivering slightly, as if an electrical current were passing through it. The blonde woman places herself squarely between us.

'I'm Caroline Bayliss-Callingham.' Her accent is as familiar in its way as the lyrics to 'Up in Lisa's Room'. We could be having lunch at the Ivy. Not far away I can hear Zoe telling an acquaintance that the ill-will on display can be tracked back to a preliminary meeting at which Art jocularly informed Cris that he made more money than you do, *boy*.

'It's very good to meet you.'

Mrs Bayliss-Callingham – Caroline – looks a bit nonplussed at this. Then she says:

'Rory says he's been looking forward to seeing you again.' The figure in the wheelchair gives a tiny, self-abasing nod. 'He says they were great days you had together. He hopes you don't bear him any grudge.'

There are no points to be scored off people in wheelchairs with polite and uncomprehending wives.

'None at all.'

'He was determined to be here,' Mrs Bayliss-Callingham says, all in a rush. 'But I think it's all been a bit much for him.'

'I think it's been a bit much for all us.'

Of the three things I have said to her this one at least, is true.

17. ON THE SHORE

Come October Southwold lapses into silence. The occupying armies have returned to Putney and Wimbledon; the four-wheel drives are back cruising the South Circular. In their wake follow builders, hard at work refurbishing the vacant properties. The house next to mine, for example, is currently having its conservatory extended and its roof re-done. The builders are Poles, imported from London, who sleep on the premises. They are devout men and on Sunday mornings can be seen attending Mass at the Catholic church near the common. Early in the morning mist descends on the shoreline, hanging over the beach-huts and giving the dog-walkers a peculiar wraith-like quality. Perhaps the dogs feel more at home, here amid the fog and the empty streets. Who can tell?

Not, of course, that contingency has failed to work its effects. Life runs on here on the Suffolk coast, just as it does anywhere else. One person on whom contingency has definitely worked its effect is Wangford Jim. Exact details are unclear, but it seems that on several occasions during my brief absence, Jim was found outside the gates of the local primary school, attempting to engage unaccompanied children in conversation. No charges have been brought, but Jim is, as they say, under a cloud. There have been no more Thursday-night appearances at the Nelson, and Jim has been keeping himself to himself in his cottage, through whose window, it is alleged, a brick has been thrown. Plans to release the EP are on hold. Although nothing has been said, I suspect that Mrs Stiff holds me partly responsible for her kinsman's fall from grace. There is a feeling that in enticing him into a recording studio I have disrupted the placid equilibrium of his existence, provoked some inward disturbance that would not otherwise have manifested itself. Other aspects of Mrs Stiff's domestic life have mysteriously improved. Shane, in particular, is off the weed, reconciled with Charmian and returned to the family home. Bradley, Kayla-Mae and their double buggy have not been seen for nearly a month.

Meanwhile, there are regular glimpses of the older world. The Resurgam box set arrived a week ago. If not quite a comprehensive survey of the label's output, its seven CDs and nigh-on ninety tracks ought to be enough to satisfy all but the doughtiest completist. Listening to it, I discover that most of the material I thought significant at the time seems flat and of the moment. Chloe and the Cupcakes, on the other hand, sound jauntier and more substantial than I recalled. Xav, who purports to be 'pleased' by the advance sales – figures unspecified – reports that Chloe is now a fitness coach somewhere on the south coast and that Flopsy the bass player has published three romantic novels. Neither of these destinies surprises me. Neither, too, does the BBC Four documentary about Cedric. By coincidence, this exploration of a 'lost, radical pop voice' is broadcast on the day of the box set's release. There are tributes from Lord Kinnock and Billy Bragg and footage of Cedric playing one of his songs at a Rock Against Racism benefit concert. My own role is limited to a few comments about his early life and the making of his first album.

Resurgam: Ever on the Up contains a half-CD's worth of material from Systems of Romance. Regrettably, *Trash for Cash* has been pulled from the schedules after what the *Daily Mail* describes as a 'back-stage contretemps'. As with Wangford Jim's appearance at the primary school gates, precise details are unclear, but it seems that Greg was taken to hospital with a broken rib. There is talk of Sophie returning to present a Channel Four consumer affairs programme, but no further information has been vouchsafed. For myself, I have every confidence in Sophie's ability. There seems every chance that in television, as in pop, she will find her niche.

The Flame Throwers' aborted induction into the Rock and Roll Hall of Fame – there is some doubt as to whether the ceremony was formally concluded – was of sufficient magnitude to make the English music papers. In an interview granted to *Mojo*, Cris complained that 'there are kids in kindergarten can throw paint on a fuckin' canvas as good as Art Smothers, so how come he gets a hundred thousand dollars and they don't?' In its aftermath, a letter with a Surrey postmark was forwarded to me c/o XLB.

Dear Nick – if I may,
We met very briefly at that dreadful event in Chicago. Rory has asked me to say how sorry he was that we had no time for further conversation, and that there was a great deal he wished to say to you. Or rather, have communicated to you. I am afraid that his speech is not yet fully recovered, but he is making excellent progress and the doctors hold out every hope. He is sure that, like him, you retain many happy memories of the time in which you worked together. Do please get in touch should you be passing this way.
Yours very sincerely
Caroline Bayliss-Callingham

This, it seems to me, is absolutely typical not only of Rory, but of everyone else I ever knew from that world, Alice included: not necessarily insincere, but deluded in their assumption that past transgressions can be anaesthetised in a fog of spurious good-feeling. Nonetheless,

I write a cheery letter back, professing satisfaction in Rory's continued improvement and wishing his family well.

And so the autumn winds on. The Poles next door have nearly finished now: the cacophony of drills and smashed brickwork has dwindled to occasional knocking noises. The delicatessens and the up-market boutiques are reducing their opening hours, and the *Southwold Gazette* reveals that a popular thriller writer who is supposed to live in the town six months of the year has been invited to switch on the Christmas lights. Zoe has called several times. There is talk of her coming to stay. I get the feeling that here in the aftermath of our Chicago trip, psychotherapy has begun to lose its allure.

For some time now I have been thinking of my mother, about the old days in Norwich and the time we spent here half-a-century ago, of the boarding houses that have been turned into flats, and even Mr Matlock and the balmy avenues down which, had things been a little different, my mother might have wandered. In the end I spend £20 on an engraved brass plaque to be placed on a convenient point on the pier-rail, which reads *Jean Alexandra Du Pont 1919–1964, who loved all that Southwold had to offer*. I think my mother would have appreciated the sentiment. For a while the symbolism of this gesture alarms me. But perhaps somewhere in Montana, on some neglected Oregon shoreline or the porch of some rackety clapboard house in Connecticut, someone has put up a plaque to the Old Man. Who knows? We make our accommodations with the lives we live for the people who come after us to judge.

Resurgam: Ever on the Up is respectfully reviewed. *Uncut* attests to 'the sonic encapsulation of a certain kind of English pop sensibility: demure, sometimes naively constructed, but capable of extraordinary detonations of teen and post-teen spirit.' *Mojo* notes the presence of 'many a dark horse galloping the margins of the Eighties *zeitgeist*.' *Record Collector* praises the production values – 'rough and ready but somehow in keeping with the rapt, improvisational spirit of the time.'

Outside, above and beyond Centre Cliff, the sky is the colour of steel wool. The gulls for some reason are far out to sea, hanging in the air like scraps of paper. Just now I saw one of the Polish builders emerge onto next door's front step, glance upwards and raise a moistened finger in the air to check the direction of the wind. Mrs Stiff says it will be a hard winter and very probably snow. I am sure she is right about this. I have a vision of the rock-pools frozen to glass, icicles hanging off the frontages of the beach-huts, sand-dunes blanketed into white oblivion, and beyond them, above the deep north sea, the mermaids out combing the hair of the waves held back, a whole new world, stark and inviolable, ready and waiting for me to explore.

Give thanks.

How to Buy... Resurgam Records

10. The Unclean – *Radioactive Man*

You say: 'Tribal drumming, no-frills production and a guitar noise that would strip paint off the walls. The authentic soundtrack to 1978.'

There was a brief moment around the spring of '78 when Salford's The Unclean looked destined for great things. Instead, come year-end, in the wake of band bust-ups and endless personnel changes, those still present voted to call it a day, leaving behind them a solitary LP. *Carve Her Name With Pride*, of which this 2 minutes 16 seconds of leering anomie is the undisputed highlight.

9. Bash Street Kids – *Live Stompers*

You say: 'Lavishly featured on a recent Channel Four documentary about Rock Against Racism, with a strong inference that they were part of the racism. Classic live album, though.'

Shaven-haired quartet from Bermondsey, known for their support of West Ham United and a fan-base that led to their being banned from half the venues in London. *Live Stompers* (1980) is exactly what it says on the tin. Oh, and the sound of police sirens half-way through side two is absolutely authentic.

8. Chloe and the Cupcakes – *Saturday Night/Sunday Morning*

You say: 'Mod girls! Essex! Uber-bobbed hair! Why on earth weren't they as big as the Supremes?'

There were other all-girl groups in the late '70s mod revival, but none burned so brightly as Chloe Pargeter and her demon accomplices from Shoeburyness. This epic single from 1980 tells the story of 12 hours in the life of 'Suzanne Strange' and her throwing over by Barry the 'Ace Face.' Available on *Rocking With the Cupcakes* (1980)

7. Maximum Acceleration – *Parallax View*

You say: 'The band that sold a thousand army surplus greatcoats. Gloomier than Joy Division. Where are they now?'

The Maxes were one of '80s indie-rocks weirder stories. Having scored a bona-fide chart-hit with 1980's 'Penal Colony', they trousered fat wads of cash from amiable label head Nick Du Pont and retired to a succession of studios to work on what was described as 'the most ambitious concept album in history.' No record ever emerged. Two members of the band were subsequently institutionalised; a third teaches Philosophy at the Open University. This dates from 1980, contains 'Penal Colony' and was described by *Melody Maker* as 'the aural equivalent of a forced march up Everest.'

6. Finn Family Moomintroll – *She's Got Me in Spasms*

You say: 'Some astounding cheekbones, and songs to die for.'

To begin with FFM were the spikiest indie-combo on the block (check out the particularly fearsome racket of their second single 'Coming Apart at the Seams.') Then some bright spark declared that they were really a boy band in disguise, after which the cover of *Smash*

Hits was theirs for approximately the next three years. 'She's Got Me in Spasms', a single from 1981, comes from the transition period before most of the sharp edges got sanded down. Available on the LP *Crying into Other People's Beer.*

5. Exploding Bagpuss – *But Emily Loved Me.*

You say: 'Classic mid-'80s sugar-coated whimsy pop.'

Exploding Bagpuss rode the surf of Resurgam's not always entirely consistent second wave. The albums sound a tad dated now, what with their synth-washes, chiming guitars and twee-ly undulating vocals, courtesy of statuesque chanteuse Gwendolyn Makepeace, but this single from 1985 was a game-changer.

4. Paper Plane – *Turn Up the Dial, You Suckers!*

You say: 'Re-invigorated late '70s rock and roll with a mind of its own.'

Nick Du Pont always maintained that he'd had three serious strokes of luck: discovering Systems of Romance; acquiring the UK rights to the first three Flame Throwers albums; and chancing upon this oddball quartet from Dagenham. Elton John and Keith Richards were among their fans. A kind of outer-London version of the Ramones, but with curious funk shadings, the Papers got to Number Three with this frenzied ramalamadingdong from 1978. Available *on Mission Aborted* (1979).

3. The Dub Imposters – ***Windrush Rasta***

You say: 'Second generation West Midlands reggae by way of Trenchtown. Bob Marley would have been proud.'

Nobody quite knows what happened to the Imposters, who literally vanished off the face of the earth halfway through an American tour, but this album was a revelation in 1980 – thundering bass-lines, percussion clearly recorded in a blacksmith's forge, and some mordant reportage from early-era Thatcher-land.

2. Systems of Romance – *Mesdames et Messieurs… Welcome to the Hypersound*

You say: 'Oh Magda, you left the party far too soon. The soundtrack to a million anguished adolescences.'

The Systems' platinum-selling debut exploded into the world of 1980s Anglo-pop like a depth-charge, by turns fey, pulverising, self-absorbed and wildly expansive, their sound seldom got any better than this. In a better-ordered world the late Magda Peyrefitte could have been the Dusty Springfield of her day, but it was not to be…

1. Cedric – *London Lives*

You say: 'A still small voice amid the surrounding chaos. Never forgotten.'

How Cedric (full name Cedric Aloysius Wickham-Jones) would have rubbed his eyes at the cult that has coalesced around his memory since the day he stepped off a mountain in Sri Lanka. This is one of his oddities – no, let's be honest, they were all oddities – more of an urban prose-poem than the customary ditties about cats, dogs and paint-brushes, but well-nigh Larkinesque in its eye for detail. Available on *Cedric Sings* (1993).

London Lives

In Balham a widow cooks poached eggs
Walthamstow skinheads are on the prowl
A Panton Street comedy's on its last legs
At the Bethnal lads' club, Lonnie's trainer throws in the towel.

Pimlico squares resound to this year's hits
Played by punk bands in the Vauxhall Bridge Road
In a Catford pub lounge a stripper shows off her tits
Near Lewisham High Street an HGV sheds its load.

On the Tottenham estates black kids are looking hard
The homeless girl at Oxford Circus manages a grin
At Warren Street station Jimmy swaps a business card
In Wimbledon pensioners have a quiet night in.

Vacancies in a Shepherd's Bush boarding house mean rooms are to let
Fox cubs run over the tracks at Clapham Junction
On a Green Park deck-chair Maisie rolls a cigarette
In a Putney mid-terrace the electricity ceases to function.

Trunk calls in Ealing villas are disconnected
Vince in Shaftesbury Avenue asks for a light
Tourists in Chinatown are unaffected
By Leytonstone's urban blight.

Haredim on Stamford Hill put on their black coats
At the Boleyn Ground West Ham are 2-0 up
In Hounslow milkmen load up next morning's floats
A nanny in Belgrave Square offers an extra cup.

From *Cedric Sings* (1993)

ACKNOWLEDGMENTS

This project would never have been realised without the enthusiasm of Richard Charkin, for which I am deeply grateful. Warm thanks are also extended to the late Cathal Coughlan, Howard Devoto and Bob Stanley for much-needed situational and technical advice, and to my agent Gordon Wise. Love and gratitude, as ever, to Rachel, Felix, Benjy and Leo and to Steve and Pauline Mobbs for providing a situational backdrop.

AFTERWORD

This is a novel. None of the characters – Nick, Alice, Rory, the staff of Resurgam Records and the countless musicians signed to it – have a grounding in 'what really went on' as Mark E. Smith might have said; any resemblance to a real person is entirely accidental. That said, these unreal people are busily and sometimes controversially at large in a very real world: the landscape of the late Seventies and early Eighties music scene on both sides of the Atlantic. And so they can be found moving in the orbit of such ornaments of the music industry as Richard Branson, grand eminence of Virgin Records, David Geffen, founder of the label that bears his name, the hot-shot producer Bob Ezrin (Alice Cooper, Lou Reed, Pink Floyd etc) and many more besides. However, it should straightaway be said that the references are to fictional versions of these people and that the actions ascribed to them in this book are wholly imaginary. At the same time, all this raises interesting questions for the novelist and the music fan who, in the case of a book like this, follows suspiciously in his wake.

The most obvious point to make about a piece of fiction dealing with certain aspects of (comparatively) recent cultural history is that authenticity has to be worked at. If you are writing a novel about the British music scene of forty years ago, then it has to look and sound like that scene and its characters have to look and sound as if they could have operated in its real-life equivalent. Consequently, although the bands signed to Resurgam – Maximum Acceleration, Bash Street Kids, Chloe and the Cupcakes *et al* – never existed, there are, inevitably, one or two real-life ensembles to whom they bear certain generic resemblances. It could hardly be otherwise. Cedric, the wispy singer-songwriter on whom Nick wastes so much of the label's money until he comes good long years after his death, is a figment of my imagination. On the other hand, there was a well-attested early Eighties vogue for performers like him and it would be wrong to pretend that he has no grounding in real life *at all.* Fiction doesn't work like that, otherwise, how could you write it? Similarly, if there is no direct model for Resurgam, then I am happy to doff my hat to Richard Balls' wonderful history of Stiff Records, whose products I loved so much back in the days of Mrs Thatcher's first administration.

It is the same with the veteran music biz titans whose younger incarnations are featured here. Time has sanctified the Bransons and the Geffens of this world and given them a well-nigh impenetrable aura. To suggest, as one or two of their advocates might possibly want to, that forty years ago the impresarios of major-league labels would have disdained to do business with a bunch of hooligans such as the Flame Throwers is to ignore the fact that such outfits were happy enough to fund the post-John Lydon iteration of the Sex Pistols who recorded material with the former Great Train Robber Ronnie Biggs, and had few qualms in allowing the famously provocative Guns N' Roses to enter the lists a few years later. This is not a moral point, by the way, just an acknowledgment that if the demo tape for *Breakfast at Ralph's* had been doing the rounds of the A&R departments back in 1980, then every self-respecting music biz mogul would have been falling over himself to get hold of it.

And what about me? Where do I figure in all of this? Well, I never played in a band, wrote for a music paper or worked for a record company, but heavens, I sure did listen to the product. I was the kind of late-teenage boy who bought the Jam's singles on the day they came out, played squash in a Dead Kennedys tee-shirt and wore an army surplus greatcoat that I hoped made me look like Joy Division in those celebrated shots taken by Kevin Cummings in snowy Manchester underpasses. John Peel's 10–12 p.m. stint on Radio One had me transfixed and the *New Musical Express's* Charles Shaar Murray and Nick Kent seemed to me the greatest music journalists on the planet. From my angle, the period 1978–1982 is when 'English music' came of age, moved on from the punk roar to an era of tantalising experimentalism pioneered by Magazine, the Fall, Siouxsie and the Banshees, Wire, the Associates, Simple Minds…I could go on, and of course the Associates and Simple Minds were Scottish. They were great days, and this is an attempt to reanimate them, with all the devious manipulations of past time that such exercises habitually imply.

D.J.T.